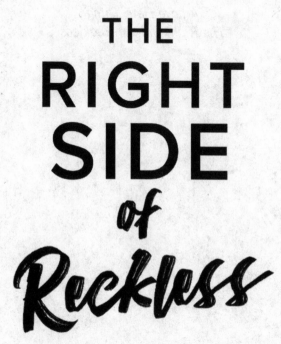

THE
RIGHT
SIDE
of
Reckless

**Books by Whitney D. Grandison
available from Inkyard Press**

A Love Hate Thing
The Right Side of Reckless

WHITNEY D. GRANDISON

THE RIGHT SIDE OF RECKLESS

inkyard
PRESS

Recycling programs
for this product may
not exist in your area.

ISBN-13: 978-1-335-40248-6

The Right Side of Reckless

Copyright © 2021 by Whitney Grandison

1985 (Intro To "The Fall Off")

Words and Music by Jermaine L. Cole

Copyright (c) 2018 SONGS OF UNIVERSAL, INC.

All Rights Reserved Used by Permission

Reprinted by Permission of Hal Leonard LLC

This edition published by arrangement with Harlequin Books S.A.

For questions and comments about the quality of this book, please contact us
at CustomerService@Harlequin.com.

Inkyard Press
22 Adelaide St. West, 40th Floor
Toronto, Ontario M5H 4E3, Canada
www.InkyardPress.com

Printed in U.S.A.

Simone Elkeles,
thanks for telling seventeen-year-old me
to keep her head high and keep forging forward.
I made it!

You gotta give a boy a chance to grow some.
—J. Cole, "1985 (Intro to 'The Fall Off')"

Guillermo

Fresh off the plane and I was already making trouble.

The security guard was staring at me like I was some type of criminal. He stood across from us as we came out of the gate into the terminal at the Akron-Canton Airport, and as soon as he caught eye contact with me, his brows pushed down and knitted together. His hand breezed over the Taser gun on his utility belt, while he stuck out his broad chest.

Sizing him up, I knew I could take him. He wasn't *that* big. But with the way my mother was looking at me, I knew it was better to ignore him.

He probably thought I was trouble. I *was* trouble...at least, I was before.

"Keep walking, Memo," my father said, shoving his carry-on bag into my spine.

I stole a final glance at the security guard. He was still glaring at me.

Pendejo.

Like the diligent son I was now trying to be, I obeyed my

father and kept moving, catching my younger sister, Yesenia, shrinking beside me.

Jostling through the airport, we made our way to the baggage claim, gathered our bags, and prepared to leave. Upon heading toward the exit, I was surprised to see Mr. Security Guard by the door. The glare was still on his face, but this time, he was shooting his dark steely gaze at some other guy.

Guess it isn't just me. For once.

I was used to this type of judgment.

The car service my father had arranged was waiting outside. Our driver was standing in front of a Honda Pilot, holding up a sign with our last name stamped on it.

My father quickly introduced our family before helping the man stow our luggage in the vehicle. At my attempt to help, my father shooed me away.

Having no choice, I handed him my bag, and then I got in the middle row beside my mother and sister.

"It's going to be okay, Memo, don't worry." Yesenia reached out and squeezed my hand gently.

I averted my gaze out the window, not seeing things her way.

"You should listen to your sister, she's right," my mother said.

Once the driver and my father finished packing the trunk, the driver took the wheel while my father sat in the passenger seat.

As soon as we were on the road, my father faced me with a serious look. "We're back now, Guillermo, and things aren't going to be like before. Understand?"

"It won't happen again," I said.

My father grimaced, as if he doubted me. With my mass of screwups, I didn't blame him. "Don't forget to call your probation officer first thing in the morning." He spoke with bitter disappointment laced in every word. "Remember, if you mess this up, it's back to jail for you."

I gritted my teeth. Back to juvie? Fuck that. "I know."

Two weeks in Mexico and nothing had changed.

They still hadn't forgiven me for what happened back in March. Hadn't even mentioned it to the relatives we'd just visited. I couldn't blame them. Unlike the times before, I had fucked up royally.

I stared outside for the remainder of the drive. Summer had slipped away while I was locked up. Now fall was here, a new season, a new beginning. It was seven fifteen at night, the sky above us a reddish orange as the sun sank lower on the horizon. Soon, the leaves on the trees would match.

We got off the highway and began to pass closing businesses as streetlights flickered on. I watched all this, trying to feel a sense of rebirth. A piece of optimism.

It didn't come.

While I was…away, my parents had packed up our house and sold it. They had purchased a new place on the east side of Akron and made it clear we were moving on from the past up north.

Less than thirty minutes later, the driver pulled in to a subdivision called Briar Pointe. A subdivision, as in row upon row of houses that looked exactly alike, as in too bland and boring, unlike the neighborhood we'd lived in before.

A late-night jogger breezed by, her blond ponytail swishing behind her, and I raised a brow. Where we'd come from wasn't exactly dangerous, but nobody ran, especially at night.

The driver came to a stop in front of a medium-size two-story house complete with an attached two-car garage. I gazed at my new home. It was my clean slate, my second chance—or more like my last.

We all vacated the car and grabbed our bags from the trunk.

My mother gathered the house keys and took the lead to the front door with Yesenia and me behind her. My father tipped the driver, and the man drove off.

After I got home from juvie, and before our sudden trip to Mexico, my family and I had only begun unpacking here. Now it was almost the second week of September, and Yesenia and I had missed the first week of school.

After spending spring in and out of court and a lovely ninety-day stay at a detention center, where I'd caught up on all the schoolwork I'd missed, I would be serving my probation in a new part of the city with a fresh start. However, it was beginning to appear as though there was no moving forward as far as my parents were concerned.

They no longer looked at me as their son, but as a petty criminal and a burden.

And given that in the morning I would meet with my parole officer, I couldn't blame them. I was newly seventeen and already the Patron Saint of Fuckups who couldn't be trusted, as far as they knew.

"Guillermo." My father spoke softly behind me as we entered the house and Yesenia and my mother disappeared down the foyer around a corner.

I didn't face him. There were only so many times I could see that look in his eyes. "Yes?"

"In the garage, now."

I turned and found him already making his way to the door that led into the garage. Each step I took after him felt heavier than the first, my anxiety causing sweat to bead down my back.

Inside the garage, my father stood back, waiting for me.

I barely glanced at him before my gaze landed on the two vehicles. One, my mother's silver Acura, and the other, a dark blue Charger. The shiny, vibrant paint made its beauty stand out.

My father cleared his throat. "Matt knew a guy who could restore it, and it took some bargainin', but it's yours."

Another glance from him to the car, and I realized what this was and what this meant. Back in the day, when my father's brother, my tío Mateo, still lived in Akron, he used to keep this beat-up old Charger in his driveway. Tía Jacki used to complain about it, but Mateo wouldn't part with it, swore it was a project in the making. Whenever I was bored, I'd climb in behind the wheel and pretend to drive it, pretend I owned the road, pretend to be as cool as Tío Matt.

Fast forward to today, and gone were those rust-stained doors, replaced with a solid body and fresh paint. Even the inside was new. I leaned over to gape through the passenger window. The black seating and updated system had me grinning like a fool.

Tío Mateo lived in Columbus now, but the gesture wasn't missed. I faced my father, my smile instantly slipping away at the sight of his stoic face. "Thank you, *both* of you."

My father gave me a stiff nod. "I just don't want to be responsible for driving you around. Keys are on the hook by the door."

During the whole ordeal, my mother had attempted sympathy, but not once had my father offered any. The moment I was released from juvie, they shielded Yesenia from me and started keepin' a close eye on us, as if my bad seed would catch on.

"I shouldn't have to reiterate that this is a new start. You will not be in contact with any of your old friends. Especially that girl," my father ordered. "You will go to school, complete your required community service, meet with your probation officer, and stay out of trouble. Do you hear me?"

My fists balled at my sides. "Yes, sir."

"And…" He paused, as if thinking of more things to add to his list of demands. "Get a haircut."

To this I didn't reply. He'd been after the length of my hair since freshman year. Now that I was a junior, you'd think he'd let it go. I would admit, my wavy hair combined with my facial hair did make me look rough around the edges. The judge had taken one look at me and scowled. No wonder that security guard at the airport had kept his eye on me.

"Your mother's going to order some food. Go put away your bag and come down," my father said.

Dinner with my family was often eaten in loud silence.

I would pass.

"I'm not hungry," I told him.

He didn't fight me on it as he went to join my mother and sister.

Home sweet home.

With a heavy sigh, I raked a hand through my chin-length hair and headed up to my room. I was out, I was somewhere new, and I had a car. I couldn't fuck up, not again. Hearing my mom up one night crying—that had hung heavy on my heart for weeks.

This move was my chance to prove that I could evolve.

There were no ifs, ands, or maybes. I was going to do better.

Regan

Troy Jordan slowly eased his hand up the back of my shirt. He thought he was being slick, but he was kissing me too urgently to play it off. I knew what he was after, and like the many times before, he wasn't getting it.

I was supposed to be doing my AP geography homework, but with Troy's advances, that wasn't happening. As his lips and hands roamed my body, I stared up at the Beyoncé poster on my cream-painted bedroom wall.

"Troy," I said, pushing him away and sitting up on my bed, "my parents are right downstairs. Besides, I've got notes to read over."

Troy groaned, rolling his eyes and sitting up beside me. "Come on, Rey, you're never in the mood."

The mood, a topic of conversation Troy had been bringing up a lot lately. What he kept failing to realize was that one does not simply get in "the mood" to lose their virginity. It was an important decision to me, one I wanted to be completely sure of beforehand. While he was all hot and ready day and night, I wasn't so sure.

We had been together since the start of my sophomore year and his junior. One year later, we were constantly talking about my inability to go all the way. It made me feel guilty.

I lay down on my stomach and turned on the TV. Maybe some harmless reality show would lull me. Getting lost in other people's wild lives would be a good distraction from my own.

"Is something wrong, Regan?" Troy asked, starting in on the usual question after I put a stop to things.

It was Friday night and we could've been doing something romantic, or just chilling, but instead I was trying to do homework and study while also contemplating buying a chastity belt made of barbed wire. He'd come by to hang out, but as always, more was on his mind.

I didn't even want to study, but of course I *had* to. I had to get good grades all around, especially in my accounting course.

Between Troy and accounting, I just couldn't deal.

"No, Troy," I breathed out in response to the tantrum he was about to throw.

I was attracted to Troy, sure, but when I thought about having sex with him, I felt weird and unsure. Maybe I just wasn't ready. I *was* sixteen.

"Well then, what's up? You do this *all* the time. I'm not a mind reader, Rey, why can't you just say what you're thinking?"

"I…" *Want you to go.* It always got awkward once we reached this point.

I missed how we'd been at the beginning—the movie nights, the TV binges, the realization of who he was and who he was going to be during that first football game as his girlfriend among all his adoring fans, and mostly, the respected boundary line.

Six months in and our messy tango of kissing had begun not being enough. Cuddling wasn't enough, waiting wasn't enough.

"You what, Rey?" Troy stood in front of the TV, blocking my escape.

I swallowed, fiddling with the heart-embedded infinity symbol pendant on the necklace he'd gotten me last November. How was I to explain myself when *I* didn't even get it?

"I just…need more time." It was all I could muster, and it left me feeling exhausted.

"How much more time?"

His whining was getting annoying. I wouldn't sleep with him just to shut him up—my parents were downstairs, as well as my younger brother, Avery.

I couldn't look at him. My gaze moved to the mahogany shelf on my vintage mirror-dresser combo and stopped on an old figurine my grandmother had given me. I focused on the dancing woman, seeking an excuse.

"I don't know, Troy. Maybe after we're married?" Internally I cringed. It was a poor argument. Hardly anyone waited for marriage anymore. Troy himself was far from a virgin. He was our school's star running back, and he'd hooked up a lot before we got together.

Troy's face fell in utter disbelief. "*Married?* I'm seventeen, you're sixteen. What makes you think I wanna—marriage is on my mind right now?"

It stung when he almost said he wasn't thinking about marrying me. But maybe I was being naive; we were only teenagers. It wasn't *that* deep.

However, having found my way out of the situation, I took

it. "So you don't want to marry me?" I lifted an eyebrow, crossing my arms and appearing hurt.

"Marriage is just a piece of paper."

"A paper of value." I feigned cluelessness as I tapped my chin. "How does that one Beyoncé song go? Something about putting a ring on it?"

Troy waved me off while he shook his head. "Please, that's what you females' problem is, sitting there listening to Beyoncé and letting her fill your heads up with that 'girls run the world' nonsense."

"Excuse me?" Personally, I was more for unity than the idea of one gender on top, but Troy's tone irritated me.

He quickly tried to backtrack. "Rey, I just... Of course I want to be with you." He came closer and pulled me into his arms. "You know when I make it big I'm taking you with me. Big house. Nice cars. All that."

"Troy." I sighed. "I'm not with you because of your ability to play football. If something happens when you're in college and you can't play—"

"God forbid," he quickly interjected.

"Like I said, if something ever happened and you couldn't play pro, I wouldn't leave you. I love you for you, not some sport you play. I don't think about us in a big house, I think about us in a normal house, married at least, living happily ever after."

Troy planted a kiss on my forehead. "That's why I love you, Rey. You're not with me because I'm next."

We were an unmatched pair. Troy was the most popular guy in school and the star football player. I wasn't *that* popular, nor was I a cheerleader. Some people didn't get it, since I was just Regan London, but Troy liked me. Enough that he'd pursued me despite my early rejections.

When we'd gotten together my sophomore year, I hadn't cared about his status at our school. He was just some football player everyone wanted to be with or wanted to be; it hadn't impressed me. But then he started chasing me, ignoring his usual options, showing up around me more often. At first, I told him it was going to take a lot more than him hanging around to wow me, which made him laugh, and he kept at it, little love notes carefully stuffed into my locker, popping up with a single rose or carnation before school or after—the shower of affection wasn't lost on me. Slowly, I fell for him once and for all.

My gaze drifted across my room to my white marble desk, where vase after vase of flowers from him used to sit. Now, there was only the photo of us from last year's homecoming.

When he let his ego go, Troy was amazing—sweet when he wanted to be, and just as stubborn and persistent as well. He was my first boyfriend and my first kiss. It would only make sense if he were my first...*first* as well. A part of me wanted him to be, but another part just didn't know.

Troy caressed my cheek. "I want to show you how much I love you. Don't you want to do the same?"

"I'll try." I nodded, noncommittal. Thinking about it wasn't as hard as actually going through with it.

Troy sniffed the air. "What'd your mom cook?"

"Beans, I think. Probably some corn bread, too."

Troy sucked his teeth, clearly not liking what was on the menu. "Yeah, I better go home. I hate beans."

"They taste good."

"I'll take your word for it." He made his way toward my bedroom door. "I'ma dip out and see what my mom made back at the crib."

Relieved, I led him downstairs, stopping in the TV area so he could say goodbye to my parents.

"Night, Mr. and Mrs. London." Troy politely kissed my mother's cheek and shook my father's hand.

"Another game tomorrow, eh, Troy?" my father said. He was such a huge fan of our school's team. If Troy hadn't been Troy Jordan, the next big thing, I was positive my father wouldn't have allowed me to date him, as strict as he was. I often wondered if he would approve of our relationship if he knew how much Troy wanted to sleep with me.

Troy grinned. He was a star athlete destined to go the distance, aka the NFL. High school football wasn't a challenge for him anymore. "Oh definitely, sir, can't wait to beat Ellet." He turned to Avery, who was sitting on the opposite couch, playing his handheld video game. "A'ight man, see you later?"

Avery nodded, briefly looking up from his screen.

I showed Troy to the front porch and gave him a hug good-night.

"Enjoy your *homework*, Rey," he teased.

It was an excuse, a pitiful one, but it had worked.

"Yeah, you prepare for your game tomorrow, okay?"

"You coming to that party afterward?"

I always ended up going to a party after one of Troy's games. It was tradition to celebrate the Panthers' win and another step closer to Troy's greatness. I couldn't stay out too late, though; I spent a lot of my time on weekends volunteering at the Briar Park Community Center, where my mother worked. Juggling that on top of school left very little energy for partying.

But I didn't tell Troy that.

"Yeah, of course," I agreed.

He kissed me, then pulled back and held me at arm's length. "I love you, you know that, right?"

"Of course, Troy. I love you, too."

But taking in his dark brown face and dark brown eyes, my gut churned with unease, and something I'd started to feel whenever he was with me.

He wasn't the problem.

I was.

Guillermo

My probation officer didn't play. From the moment we met, I knew he wasn't to be messed with.

Harvey Hudson was his name. He was built like a line-backer and could probably break me in half if he wanted.

Harvey was fair, though. He gave respect where respect was given. He didn't judge the rehabilitated for our crimes and pasts—hell, he told me he might've done the same had he been in my shoes. But of course, with Harvey being a smart guy, I was positive he would've never put himself in the position I had.

The judge had been lenient considering the circumstances. I had six months' community service, and the rest of my two-year stint on probation would be spent meeting with a thera-pist to work on my anger.

I guessed it was better than juvie.

I could imagine my record and what it potentially said about me.

Name: Guillermo Javier Lozano

Age: 17

Crime: Simple Assault

Punishment: Keep away from society. Do NOT feed the monster

Maybe it wouldn't be that extreme, but with the way my parents hadn't eased up, I wasn't holding out on a brighter day anytime soon.

Meeting Harvey meant meeting him at his office, which was in the juvenile courthouse—the last place I wanted to be again.

After spending my summer in the detention center, caged like some animal, I could honestly say juvie was a place I didn't like being. I'd deserved it, yes, and it was the reality check I didn't mind cashing. Some guys were in there for some real deal shit, drugs, larceny, grand theft auto—you name the crime, there were kids in there for it. Kids who had no guidance and were planning on getting out to start the cycle all over again.

Why I had turned to the streets could be tied to stupidity and taking my life for granted. Even at my lowest, my parents had been in my corner, including in that courtroom, where they'd made sure that my case wasn't an open-and-shut sentence on my future.

When I arrived at the courthouse, Harvey was still meeting with another probationer. The small waiting area was empty, so I grabbed a seat near the front doors, itching to be outside again. As soon as my butt hit the cushioned chair, I heard it.

Soft rock music was playing. Old-school. Or so I assumed from the singer's voice and the tone of the upbeat song. Rock wasn't my vibe. At all.

The receptionist didn't seem to mind. She was bobbing her head along as she scribbled something down, all while the male singer was going on about being a hero, just for one day. Whatever that meant.

I felt my fist ball up and hoped Harvey wouldn't be much longer.

It was just my luck that he came down the hall escorting a boy about my age.

The kid was scowling, his buzzed head hanging low as he listened to whatever it was that Harvey was saying. In his plain white tee and jeans, he looked kinda scrawny next to Harvey—but who didn't look scrawny next to that guy?

Harvey patted the boy's shoulder. "I'ma keep my eye on you, Zach. We will do better!"

Zach nodded and walked out the exit, his head slowly lifting with each step.

Harvey set eyes on me and cocked his head. "So he made it back?" He held his hand out for me. "Come on, let's catch up."

I stood and went to him, that rock song still playing from the radio on the receptionist's desk.

I wrinkled my nose. "What the hell are you listenin' to?"

Harvey tossed me a look. "First of all, it ain't me. Second of all, watch your tone and step inside, tough guy." His heavy hand fell on my shoulder, with enough force to sting. We both knew he'd done it on purpose. "What you got against David Bowie anyway?"

I followed him down the corridor to his private office. "Is that who that is?"

"The one and only. It's called 'Heroes.' Not a bad song,

even if I wasn't a major fan." Harvey claimed his seat in the plush chair behind the large metallic black desk. I took my seat in front of it expectantly.

I wouldn't admit it out loud, but the song wasn't so bad. *Tough guys don't listen to Bowie.*

Harvey tapped a few keys on his laptop before facing me and settling back in his chair. "So, how was Mexico?"

My grandfather had had a serious bout of pneumonia, causing my parents and uncle and aunt to panic. We'd rushed there as soon as we could to help. My grandparents ran a cocina económico, and while my parents and grandmother attended my grandfather, I had bussed tables and washed dishes at the diner.

Seeing my grandfather like that, so weak and sick, it ate at me, kept me worried even while I worked. Even now with the worst over, I still found myself shaken up about it.

"Thank you for letting me go and do that. I don't know what I would've done if he didn't make it and I didn't get to see him," I said.

Harvey nodded, sympathy in his eyes. "Missing school isn't a good look fresh out, but given the crisis, I understood. If it were anybody else, I would've denied the request."

Harvey liked me, and I guess it could be worse, because at least he believed I'd come out of this probation a changed individual.

"I gotta be honest with you, Mo," he began, "I got some faith in you. You're angry as shit, I will admit, but from what I read about your stay at the detention center, and the fact that you're back from your trip in one piece, I see a good turnout. I won't say I'm holding my breath with you, but for the most part, I'm hopeful you're someone that will change."

I hadn't expected that from him. "Thank you, Harvey."

He nodded and took a breath, seeming to get back to business. "How's your family?"

"Bien," I said sarcastically.

Harvey narrowed his eyes. "Lozano."

"I don't think my pops will ever stop resenting me, my ma pities me, and I feel like a lousy brother to Yesenia. It's shit."

"So, let me run all this back, just so I'm clear on what I know." Harvey gestured widely around us. "You spend a good portion of your youth doin' stupid shit, this last incident resulting in your being locked up. Your parents had to pay legal fees and now probation fees, and not only that, they decided to go through the grueling process that is moving and transferring their jobs just to give you another shot, and—" he was really layin' it on thick "—on top of that, your grandfather gets real sick, so sick you had to drop everything and leave the country to go and see him. All that stress, most of which could've been avoided had you made smarter decisions, and you're sittin' here talkin' about *you* feel like shit? Huh. I wonder why."

The sarcasm wasn't needed. "Harvey. I get it."

"Yeah, well, you *were* shit, for a long time, and if it takes a long time for them to forgive you, you brought it on yourself. Ain't nobody gon' hold your hand and baby you on that, Lozano."

No matter what, Harvey always gave it to you straight, no filter—raw.

"You ready for Briar Park?" he asked.

Now that I was back in the States, I had to start my community service. I'd be working at a place called Briar Park Community Center. Chances were it was going to be hell no matter what, so I told myself to just get it done. "Looking forward to it."

"You are very, very lucky to be free, Guillermo, and I can only hope this experience makes a responsible man out of you. Gloria London and I will be best friends, she will be my eyes and ears, and don't think she's going to be the nurturing kind, 'cause she ain't."

Wouldn't expect anything less.

Harvey handed me a pamphlet for the community center, which thankfully wasn't too far from where I lived.

As I reached out to grasp it, he held it back, meeting my eyes, looking serious. "I know what it's like to just do shit because there's nothing else to do, but I also know what it's like to watch the effects poor decisions have on those not involved. Your family's going to take a minute to come around, but that's on you. Take this time to reflect and grow. No more lousy friends, no more anger, and please, to God, no more girls."

That last one was a particularly brutal reminder of my recklessness.

I accepted the pamphlet and lifted my chin at Harvey. "Yes, sir, and thanks, again, for believing in me."

Unlike with the other boy, he didn't offer to walk me out. He faced his laptop, poised to type something up. "All right, gon' and get over to Briar Park, don't want to be late on your first day."

That moment, I made it a personal goal to always be on time or early for my community service, to show that I was taking it seriously.

The drive from the courthouse to the center wasn't long, thankfully, and I pulled into the lot fifteen minutes later. Immediately I could guess my job description. There were flowers planted along the borders of the lawn, sprinkles of trash here and there. I heard commotion behind the center, where

I figured their playground and skating area were, and I knew more trash awaited. Briar Park Community Center was outside the bounds of the quiet and clean setting of Briar Pointe.

A plaque out front said An Asylum for All. Beneath the inscription were two hands shaking in front of a solid heart.

I got out of my car and appraised the building, noting that, unlike a lot of the businesses I'd driven by on the way over, it was devoid of graffiti and had no broken windows, no sense of carelessness. This was where the lost became found.

At the front desk, I asked for Mrs. London. She was in charge of the center and oversaw the community service program I'd been placed in: Respect.

Mrs. London turned out to be a tall, gentle, but assertive-looking Black woman. She studied me silently before offering me a handshake and gesturing for me to follow her.

Before I'd left the house, Yesenia had slipped me a blue hair tie, para la buena suerte. Maybe I should've worn it in my hair rather than on my wrist like a bracelet.

No matter. This morning, I'd made sure to dress clean: powder blue button-down shirt, dark jeans, and white tennis shoes, along with a touch of cologne. In his younger days, Tío Matt used to be a lady's man. He told me that cologne was a great opener in all things; it aroused the senses and helped people warm up to you on first impression, sending a message of sorts.

I couldn't tell what kind of first impression I was making on Mrs. London.

She cleared her throat. We sat opposite each other at a long oval table in a conference room on the second floor. Mrs. London's stoic expression almost made me nervous, but then it didn't. With my own parents branding me American Psycho, nothing could get to me.

"The Respect program was established to teach juvenile offenders patience, responsibility, accountability, and most important, respect. We take in one to two probationers at a time to make this transition intimate. You will work here five days a week like a part-time job, nonnegotiable, and once you've been in our program for three months and have shown promise, we have an arrangement with the local Goodwill on Waterloo Road, where you'll spend your remaining time volunteering while the next probationer works here. Is that understood?"

It could be worse. "Yes, ma'am."

"The point is to rehabilitate you, Guillermo, to give you a shot at a better future. A lot of our probationers who've made it through the program end up finding employment at Goodwill, or at Henry's next door."

I knew the places she was talking about. The Briar Pointe subdivision was just off Waterloo Road, and before you turned onto a long route that led into little suburbia, there was a shopping plaza with a Mexican restaurant and the local supermarket, Henry's, and beside that, a Goodwill. One positive thing about this move was how convenient everything was; there was no need to leave this side of the city to wander back to where I'd come from, even though Rowling Heights was only twenty minutes away.

"Here at the facility you will answer to me, and if I'm not here, you can go to our co-lead, Daren Goldberg. He's usually on-site in the afternoons."

I noted she was in control. "Yes, ma'am."

"It says in your file that you just moved to Briar Pointe?" Mrs. London said this more as a question than a general statement. Her gaze held curiosity and…something I couldn't quite name. "At 226 Leona Drive?"

That must be my new address. I hadn't memorized it yet. I nodded anyway. "Yeah."

Mrs. London blinked and drummed her fingernails on the tabletop momentarily. "And you'll be attending Arlington High?"

"I guess that's the name of my new school," I said. "I start Monday."

"I see." Mrs. London procured the file in question and set it on the table in front of her. My answers to her questions seemed to have sparked a mood. Again, she cleared her throat. "I've read over your situation."

I almost chuckled at her wording.

"You think it's funny, Mr. Lozano?" Mrs. London arched a brow, challenging me.

I settled back in my chair, nearly wincing. None of this was funny. I tipped my head toward her. "My file says I'm a monster, and now I'm here to repay my debt to society—and him."

Mrs. London appeared thoughtful. "Do you think you're a monster?"

Flashes of the "situation" came to me. My fists caked in Shad's blood. The echoes of Tynesha screaming and crying. The sounds of the guys pleading for me to stop. The red haze of rage that had coursed through my body.

I could've killed Shad if the cops hadn't shown up and pulled me off him and thrown me to the ground.

Blinking, I came to. "Maybe I am."

Sympathy washed across Mrs. London's face. "While I understand you were provoked, what happened wasn't acceptable. But that doesn't mean it's the end of the line for you." She shifted in her seat as she leafed through the file. "Now, these three arrests leading up to here is what's concerning. After every incident, your behavior escalated. The loitering, the weed, and the violence—it's a very alarming path. You ever study Greek mythology in school?"

"A little bit." Not that I had paid too much attention.

"You're like Icarus, remember him?"

The name vaguely rang a bell. "Kinda."

"In the myth, in order to escape Crete, his father designs wings for him and Icarus, made of wax and feathers. His father warns him not to fly too low, to avoid the sea so water won't clog his wings, and not to fly too high, so the sun won't melt the wax. During the flight, while they're getting away, Icarus is feeling such a rush, he's so exhilarated, he soars higher and higher, and you know what happens? He gets too close to the sun. The wax melts and he falls into the sea and drowns." Mrs. London fixed me with a serious look. "Moral of the story? Don't be reckless, respect your limitations, and don't get too close to the edge. Don't get burned."

There was a chill in the air at the story's conclusion, an eerie sense of familiarity.

Before, all I'd done was wreak havoc with my friends, having no care in the world. We would hang out at this park after hours, horsing around and being stupid. Sometimes the other guys would drink a beer or two, or smoke up. The one time I tried a hit I got busted, hence Arrest Number One. Another time we were trying to sneak into a bar—not that I even drank, it was just something to do. The cops caught us, and this led to Arrest Number Two. And then came the Situation, aka simple assault, which led to Arrest Number Three.

None of my past could be filed under the fine label of "peer pressure." It was all my own doing; I just hadn't cared. I hung with guys who were questionable and troublesome, and I took part in their shit. My third arrest could've been avoided had I kept better company and made smarter choices.

My parents were already fed up with my shit by that point. Staying out late, skipping school, getting into fights, and being just a grumpy asshole, to say the least. This last Situation was just the cherry on top of the sundae of my screwed-up deeds.

My gaze fell to the tabletop. I thought about my time away, my fear of going back, of the loneliness that kept me up at night. *I can't do that again.* "Who I was before—I can't escape or erase that. Who I'm going to be is entirely up to me. I take full responsibility for my actions. I won't make the same mistakes—I can't afford to. I learned my lesson, and from here on out, I can only hope to right my wrongs and change opinions of me."

Mrs. London offered me a smile. "That's what I want to hear. Welcome on board our team, Guillermo."

She placed a beige tote bag on the table and slid it to me.

Inside were a couple of folded yellow T-shirts with the word RESPECT in all black caps. A peek at the tag showed the right size.

"If they don't fit, let me know and I'll go into our closet and grab you another size," Mrs. London said. "When you wear that shirt, Guillermo, you are not only representing this program and Briar Park, you are representing a goal—a goal to grow and have not only respect for the community and those around you, but for yourself as well. Is that understood?"

I looked from the shirts to Mrs. London. "Understood."

As she went over my responsibilities at the center, I told myself I could do this. That I could turn myself around and better myself. Knowing what was at stake, I had no choice but to silently swear this oath.

No shitty friends, no trouble, and absolutely no girls.

Regan

I had just enough time to eat a Toaster Strudel before leaving for the community center Saturday morning.

I was standing at the island, icing my strawberry strudel, when my father entered the kitchen, prepared to drop me off. I took a nervous breath.

"Good morning," I said, keeping my attention on my pastry.

"Morning," he replied.

He came to the counter and refilled his mug with coffee. I wrinkled my nose. The smell was always warm and delicious, but the taste was just plain bitter and disgusting.

My hand shook as I anticipated his next move. My gaze stayed glued to the packet of icing so I didn't make eye contact with him.

"So," he said, leaning back beside me, "how's accounting going?"

I swallowed the lump that had lodged itself in my throat. "G-good. Great."

At school, thanks to his pushing, I was taking a vocation in Accounting 101.

Truth was, I hated accounting, but I couldn't tell *him* that. Some parents wanted their kids to be doctors or lawyers. My father was very insistent on my becoming an accountant.

He nudged me, a gleam of joy in his eyes. "You keep at it. You ace the course and you'll breeze through college with no issue, and the next thing you know, you'll be working up at Sherry's firm with her."

Right, my aunt Sherry, his sister who owned her own accounting firm. Not only that, she was good friends with Clarence Jordan, Troy's uncle, who owned a bank.

My father was proud of his sister's success, so much so, he was determined to make sure I mirrored it.

He was just so passionate about the idea that, whenever I wanted to tell him I *didn't* want to be an accountant, I fumbled, unable to stomach letting him down. Unable to come up with an alternative path to forge.

Our dog, Tanner, sauntered into the room, wagging his tail with the happiest grin on his face. I reached into the cabinet under the sink and grabbed him a "Tanner treat," as we called them, and fed him the pepperoni stick.

We spoiled his six-year-old butt rotten, allowing him on the couch in the basement, and I let him sleep on my bed in my room. He was a tan mutt who was blind in one eye, and the tip of his tail was crooked. He even had his own signature scent of old dirty socks. We'd gotten him from a home giving away puppies, noticing him right away due to his tail.

Our other family dog, Kandi, hadn't taken a liking to him. Tanner was so friendly and always wanted to play, and even when a bad fight early on left him with the blind eye, he never gave up on her. I'd done a lot of research into training them to live together, and eventually Kandi had decided she could tolerate him. She was gone now, having passed away four years ago, and Tanner and I were as close as could be. Altogether his quirks just made me love him more.

I petted his soft fur coat while internally cursing the whole topic of accounting.

Tanner's food dishes were by the basement door and, seeing that he was getting low on water, I went into the fridge and grabbed one of the gallons of purified water I insisted we buy for him and filled up his bowl.

"Rey? Did you hear me?" my father asked from behind me.

There was no escaping it.

"Can't wait," I said to appease him, turning and giving him a tight-lipped smile.

I focused on shoving the Toaster Strudel in my mouth to keep from having to say more. Luckily, it worked, and before long he was dropping me off.

On weekday mornings, the Briar Park Community Center front desk was run by adult volunteers, and teens manned it in the afternoons. On weekends like this, teens were given the option of a morning shift. Even if it was almost 11:00 a.m., way too early to be up on a weekend for my taste, I didn't mind so much. Sometimes I used the center as a refuge, a place to get away from it all: my father and his love of accounting, and Troy and his love of that next step.

I entered the center with a faux cheerfulness. As much as I loved my job, I was dreading that evening's party plans. My best friend, Malika, wanted to go all out with hair, makeup, and outfits, but I feared giving Troy the wrong impression. There were always girls around Arlington High's star players who seemed full of confidence, aware of who they were, owning themselves, flirting with the boys and probably doing more than just kissing.

I was the only one being prudish, as far as Troy was concerned.

Honestly, if I had to go to the party, I would rather wear jeans and a T-shirt than show any skin and give Troy ideas.

After punching in at the center, I plopped down at the front counter, prepared to do a little more studying.

"Uh-uh." The loud arrival of my mother halted my plans. She came around the corner and over to the front desk with the echoing clicks of her heeled shoes. "Park duty, Rey."

I groaned. "Mom."

Our playground was situated behind the center, along with a skating area for the preteen and older crowd. Park duty meant babysitting and keeping an eye on the kids as they ran around, making sure no one got any scrapes or bruises. Way too loud and chaotic to get any studying done.

My mother arched a brow, and I knew not to test her.

Park duty it was.

With a heavy sigh, I left my books at the front counter and prepared to go out back.

"Troy nervous about the game this evening?" my mother asked.

I looked over my shoulder. "He was born ready."

My mother chuckled before going to collect the day's mail.

Riotous screams flooded my ears as I neared the side exit that led to the playground.

Park duty sucked.

As I opened the door, a trio of girls no older than seven rushed by, palms out as two boys chased them with something in their hands.

"Eww!" one redheaded girl cried.

"Gross!" another screeched.

Watching to make sure no one fell, I chuckled. That was a situation waiting to—

"Crap!" I yelped, stumbling over a heap of trash bags just outside the door.

Who in their right mind would block an exit like this? I squatted down and started picking up loose wrappers and empty soda cans that had fallen out of one of the open black trash bags.

Slowly, a pair of white tennis shoes and an old rake met my stare.

My gaze ran up dark jeans to a T-shirt, until it found who they belonged to. I paused, leaning back on my haunches, and shivered.

A boy peered down at me, an impassive look on his tan face. Stoic expression or not, he was gorgeous.

All I could do was stare as I took in his yellow RESPECT T-shirt, the special one all probationers in the outreach program had to wear while they worked at the center. He smelled like sweat and outside, with a faint hint of cologne.

The boy was athletically built, his grasp on the rake making the veins in his forearms bulge just slightly. His stance above me wasn't intimidating, but the sharp features of his face definitely were. Thick brows over serious eyes, full lips pressed into a fine line, and a small bit of facial hair that only highlighted how handsome he was. I could see he'd tied his dark hair back in a small bun at the nape of his neck. For some reason, it worked for him, complementing his hard image.

I was frozen, holding his gaze. One second I could've sworn his eyes were pure black voids, emphasizing his overall dark presence. And then, they became a pretty shade of brown, reminding me of the color of tea with lots of sugar.

The more he stared at me, so focused and intent, the more I forgot to breathe.

Whoa.

Guillermo

Damn.

She knelt before me, wide-eyed and frozen. *In fear?* I wondered.

I hoped not, because I did not want to be feared. Especially not by this girl.

Her long dark hair framed her brown face and fell just past her shoulders. She wore a cream-colored sweater with light blue jeans and white sneakers, and looked so innocent and clean that I wanted to tell her to get up. She was too nicely put together to risk getting dirty.

She nervously got to her feet. Then she smiled, revealing dimples in each cheek—dimples deep enough that someone might want to poke their fingers into them just because. There was a radiance to her.

Hermosa.

"I...I'm sorry," she stuttered, then released a light chuckle.

I swallowed, finding my words. "It's okay."

She peered up at me with what I thought might be wonder. "I'm Regan." Her gaze fell to my tee, where I wore one of those Hello, My Name Is… stickers with my name written on it. Seeing a crease of confusion on her forehead, I was tempted to step forward and wipe it away.

"Guillermo," I told her to clear things up. "It's Spanish for William."

Her mouth formed an O, and she bobbed her head. "Okay."

"Most people call me Memo." Most people being my family. Others had either learned to pronounce my name or opted to call me *Mo*. In juvie, there were even a few who had gone with my last name and shortened it to *Lo*, which I hadn't minded as my life had hit an all-time low.

Regan released her dimples once more as she grinned at my name tag. *"Gee-yehr-mo."*

I watched her mouth as she uttered the syllables, making each one sound pretty.

Bad idea, Memo.

Loosening up, I nodded. "Right."

Regan rocked onto her heels. "Well, Guillermo, it's nice to meet you. You must be new."

I wanted to make up some corny lie about volunteering, but I had an idea she knew what my T-shirt represented.

There was no pretending I wasn't a fuckup.

I glanced at my shirt, still wanting to explain somehow. "I—"

The back door opened and Mrs. London stepped outside. Her gaze went from Regan to me, her face instantly drowning in disapproval.

Regan blinked and ran a hand through her hair. "Mom?"

My gaze darted to Mrs. London, who was crossing her arms. There was a slight resemblance.

She cleared her throat. "Attend to the kids, Regan."

Regan conceded and offered me a wave before stepping around the trash bags and making her way toward the playground. Once she reached the blacktop, she peeked back at me.

"She's off-limits," Mrs. London announced.

I faced my supervisor. She would know, being Regan's mother and all.

"I just thought I would make it clear now, seeing that this kind of thing..." She trailed to a stop.

Seeing that *this kind of thing* was the reason I was on probation.

I got her message, loud and clear. "Understood, ma'am."

Mrs. London glanced at the trash bags. "You can come back to this later. For now, come with me."

After moving the bags out of the way so no one else could trip over them, I followed her back inside the facility.

"I mean no harm or malice, Guillermo," Mrs. London continued. "I just think it's best to set things straight right away. Rey has a boyfriend, and you're going forward, not back."

Maybe it was a cover for not wanting her daughter talking to a delinquent, or maybe she was looking out for me. I left it up in the air.

Going forward, I had bigger things at stake. Cleaning up my image was my number one priority. Regan was gorgeous and seemed nice, but no way was I getting mixed up with another girl, especially one who had a boyfriend.

"There's...something else." Mrs. London paused, holding up a finger. She turned and kept walking past the front desk while I shadowed her. We walked down a long corridor until we reached a set of double doors.

Mrs. London opened one for me to enter first.

Inside was a rec room, complete with a pool table, air

hockey, foosball, and couches, chairs, and a TV. A few empty tables were scattered throughout.

"This is where most of the big kids hang out," Mrs. London explained. "When they show up during the colder months."

"Nice," I decided to say.

"Come, there's more." Mrs. London turned off the light and we went back into the hall. She opened the door across from the rec room, revealing an in-house gym. "One positive way to channel aggression is to work it off."

A few people were using the gym, jump roping, walking or jogging on the treadmills, or lifting weights. The smell of sweat hung heavy in the room, mixing with the clinking sounds of the steel of the weights being raised and lowered.

Mrs. London led the way to a punching bag and patted it with her fist. "Know how to work one of these things?"

I was good at punching people; how hard could punching a bag be?

Tío Mateo was a big fan of boxing, especially cheering on contenders from Mexico. In the basement at his old house, he'd had an Everlast punching bag. It was so hard and intimidating, I'd never taken a swing at it for fear of breaking my hand.

I joined Mrs. London at the bag. Quickly, I fed my fist into the equipment. The sting of the punch burned, but it felt good.

Angst?

Aggression?

Anger?

Yeah, I had some of that.

Maybe it would do me some good to channel it elsewhere.

"You thinking what I'm thinking?" Mrs. London asked as she observed from the side. "Whenever you're free, you're more than welcome to blow off steam here, or hang out in the rec room. Rehabilitation isn't only about lectures and misery. You can enjoy yourself, too, as you get back into the swing of things."

I jabbed the bag, almost laughing at her. "'Enjoy' myself, sure."

She reached out and gently touched my arm. "You're not a monster, Guillermo."

Tell that to the system.

My parents.

Tynesha.

Mrs. London held my gaze, demanding my attention. "You. Are. Not. A. Monster."

She said the words with care.

I wondered how many times she would have to say them before I believed them.

My parents were unpacking the living room when I arrived home. Yesenia was bouncing around as my mother listened to an old album from her youth.

"Can we get a puppy?" Yesenia asked my father.

My father was dusting the fireplace mantel, where my mother was preparing to place our family photos.

I wondered if mine would be put on display. My parents had visited me only twice while I was locked up. That first visit, my mother had slipped me an old family photo, something I'd taped to my wall to look at on all those lonely days, grappling with despair.

My father turned to answer my sister and caught me lingering in the doorway. "No, mija." His dark eyes flickered over me. "You show up?"

"Of course, Papá," I said. "I'm not going to mess this up."

"Mmm-hmm." He returned to dusting. "Go and finish unpacking your room."

Yesenia frowned briefly before offering me a small smile. She still believed in me, still wanted to be close. She was innocent in that way. At thirteen, she still saw good in the world.

I envied that.

Up in my room, I didn't bother unpacking. Instead, I lay on my bed and put on my headphones, and soon I was lost in one of my favorite rappers' lyrics.

It wasn't long before I felt tapping at my leg, causing me to sit up. My mother was in my room, a box in her hands.

"This got mixed in with the living room stuff," she told me.

I took the box from her and looked inside. It was filled with my shirts, neatly folded with the care only a mother could provide.

She gazed around my room at all the boxes I had yet to unpack. "You gonna settle in and decorate?"

At our old house, my room had been sparsely decorated, but it'd had some touches of belonging. A thick block letter G, a gift from my mother, had hung on the door, and a few posters of boxers I admired had littered a wall or two.

Here, in our new home, I didn't see myself going that far.

"Kind of feels like I traded one prison cell for another, so why bother?" I said.

Her tired eyes held mine. "Memo."

She used to tell me I grew up too fast. Within a blur, it seemed, she went from tucking me in at night to bandaging my wounds from one of my fights—when I would let her.

Everything was different, but I was hopeful we could get it back.

I didn't want to disappoint her any more than I already

had. "I'm sorry." Because I didn't want her to go, and I was genuinely curious, I asked, "How's Abuelo doin'?"

Her hand fell upon her chest as she released a sigh of relief at the mention of her father-in-law. "He's doing much better. The doctors are hopeful he'll have a full recovery, gracias a Dios."

That lifted my spirits. His turn of good health engendered a sense of a new beginning, of possible and incredible things.

"Remember when I was a kid you used to let me help you make buñuelos?" A smile washed across my face at the memory of the fritters dusted with powdered sugar. The delicious treats reminded me of happiness. "Used to be my favorite dessert."

For just a second, my mother was with me, smiling as well. Then ever so quickly her full lips went flat, and her gaze fell to the carpet. "And now I work, and so do you."

Right, we were both busy, me with my community service and school, and her with her job at the dentist office doing HR.

My shoulders sagged and my head hung low, my pride evaporating.

Gently, my mother's hand lifted my chin so that I was looking into her eyes again. "I love you, *we* love you, but you put us through so much. It's going to take some time, mijo, for things to get back to the way they were."

"I won't let you down," I promised.

Her bitter smile said a lot. We'd been down this road before. "Don't, please."

She caressed my cheek, the bitterness slipping out of her smile, before she turned and walked away.

I fell back on my bed, my gaze on my ceiling. My heart

throbbed at my mother's kindness, for those little breaks in her tough love where she'd be delicate with me.

Briefly, a dimpled smile came to mind, and I was back at the center. Regan hadn't smiled again after our first encounter. I'd crossed paths with her a couple more times and hadn't seen her light up, not even once. When the kids had come inside from their play, she'd been patient and helpful, tying shoes and fixing loose braids. She worked with gentle precision, but she didn't smile.

Squeezing my eyes shut, I swore.

No. More. Girls.

Regan

I hated being a Trophy. It was a demeaning term the athletes had come up with for their significant others. Well, you didn't exactly have to be a significant other to be a Trophy; friends with benefits could get the title, too.

The moment I got with Troy, my position was set. I was expected to attend all the games, and *all* the after-parties. Being a Trophy was highly desirable for some girls, but for me, it could be a hassle.

For one, I didn't like being seen as an accessory. For two, I wasn't that crazy about sports or all the celebrating around it. Watching the boys get drunk and rowdy wasn't my idea of fun.

Still, I wanted to be a good girlfriend, so I sat in my bedroom with my best friend, preparing for the latest football party after yet another impressive win for Arlington High.

Malika Roy had been my best friend since our freshman year. She was everything that I wasn't in the confidence department. It wasn't that I had low self-esteem, it was just that

Malika was beyond outgoing, almost enough to make me envious.

During our freshman orientation, Malika had approached me in the back of the auditorium and asked to sit with me. I was nervous and by myself; all my friends from middle school were going to a different high school. Malika had appeared like a beacon of hope, and that afternoon we'd barely paid attention to the principal and the teachers speaking. We shared candy, cheered being able to go from mesh book bags to solid at last, freaked out over the latest Tinashe video, and checked out all the cute boys in the room.

We'd been together ever since.

Tonight, while I'd chosen a simple floral-print top paired with denim jeans, Malika had gone for a crop top and miniskirt, proudly flaunting her flawless body.

I sat at my vanity, letting Malika curl my hair. Her cell phone kept going off as we talked about nothing too important.

"Who's texting you?" I finally asked.

Malika answered her text with a shrug. "Nobody important, they just want to see if I'm going to the party."

I felt like there was more going on. "You can tell me, if you want."

Malika peeked at me before going back to my hair. "Calvin."

Oh.

Sensing my surprise, Malika went on as if it were nothing. "We bumped into each other at the mall, and he's been blowing up my phone ever since."

Calvin Evanson was kind of, sort of, her ex. This past summer, he and Malika and had hooked up, her first time. He hadn't acted romantic with her; it just kind of happened. A part of her hated him, and another still carried a torch for him.

I didn't want her getting hurt again. I offered a smile as I touched Malika's hand. "Is he bothering you? I can ask Troy..."

Malika's dark brown face fell flat. "No thanks. I mean, he seems sincere, but it's whatever really."

She left it there and I didn't push. I went back to skimming my timeline on my phone, liking pictures from the game.

"You think this'll be a long night?" I wondered.

Malika chuckled. "Damn, Rey, you sound about ready to come back, and we ain't even left yet."

Tanner trotted into the room and jumped on my bed.

"Y'all spoil this dog," Malika said, sitting on the bed and petting him.

"Of course we do, he's family."

Malika dug into her bag and procured a tiny jar that could only be her beloved banana baby food. "Gotta get a snack in before the party."

She'd been eating banana-flavored baby food for as long as I could remember. Discovering she'd stowed a jar in her bag wasn't surprising in the least. "You need help, you know that?"

Malika shrugged and unwrapped a plastic spoon, then un-screwed the lid. I had to admit, I was always curious why she liked it so much, but it was more fun teasing her than ask-ing for a taste.

Time was getting short. "I'm going downstairs to wait on Troy," I announced.

Malika rolled her eyes.

In a few short words: she hated Troy, and he wasn't so fond of her either. Almost every time we were all together, they ended up arguing. She didn't like the Troy Jordan Football

God vibe he exuded, and he didn't like her attitude. Having my boyfriend and best friend constantly fighting just added to the mountain of stress I carried on a daily basis.

Malika stood and threw away her empty jar before leading the way down to our family room. As usual, Avery was on the couch playing his handheld and listening to the TV.

Malika sat beside him, laying her legs across his lap. Avery's gaze trailed up her toned legs to her face. "Hey."

Malika smiled confidently, aware he was checking her out. "Coming to celebrate?"

Avery shook his head. "Nah, not this time."

"How are you ever going to meet a girl with your head in those video games?" she teased.

He blushed and fiddled with his handheld. "I don't know."

Feeling sorry for him, I stepped in. "'Lika, come on, leave him be."

"I'm just teasin' ya." To be even more of a pest, Malika leaned over and planted a big, loud kiss on Avery's cheek.

He furnished a dimpled smile. Along with being introverted, my younger brother was pretty bashful when it came to girls.

My dad came in, greeting Malika before turning to me. "I just got off the phone with Sherry, you oughta give her a call. She's looking for an intern a couple days a week. I mean, you've still got a ways to go, but who better to help her out than you?"

My stomach dropped. In my head, I was already planning to put the idea off for a while. My dad and I had been talking about accounting ever since I got to high school—well, *he'd* been talking about it. I mostly just listened, hoping one day he'd think to ask me if I *wanted* to do accounting in the first place.

Speak up, Rey! I yelled at myself.

Standing a little taller, I glanced at my father, ready to come out with it.

But then he took his attention from the TV and focused on me, and the weight of his gaze caused mine to slip to the floor. He must've been an amazing cop, keeping criminals in line with just one look. The only person I'd never seen cave to him was my mother.

Just like always, I clamped my mouth shut.

I would tell them I didn't want any part of accounting… as soon as I figured out what I did want. They wouldn't let me drop the class without a plan, and boy, did I need a plan.

"What about you, Malika?" my father asked.

"I just started the Early Childhood Education & Care program, Mr. London. They help set you up with a job your senior year even."

The doorbell rang, and I was quick to excuse myself to answer it.

Troy had arrived, saving me and Malika from my father's intrusive lecturing. For that, I instantly hugged him. "Thank God you're here."

He gave me a kiss, smiling at the comment. "For real?"

"Yeah, my dad's talking about me and accounting, *again*."

Troy's smile faltered. "Yeah, let's get out of here."

I went and gathered Malika, let my father talk to Troy about the game for just a minute, and then we were all out the door and on our way to the party.

Finally, some freedom.

You would've thought we won the Super Bowl with the way everyone was carrying on. Twenty minutes in, and I was ready to go home and let my father plan my future for me.

Pop Smoke blared throughout the house. With the song's infectious beat, I was almost tempted to dance, but I felt too out of place.

"Rey! Rey!" Troy was calling my name, pulling me from the kitchen island with its offerings of pretzels, Cheez-Its, and potato chips.

I meandered through sweaty bodies to meet my boyfriend on the back patio.

Troy took me under his arm and planted a big kiss on my cheek, prompting an "aww" from the group of girls standing around us.

With me in place, Troy faced his audience and raised his other arm in the air, showing off his Solo cup of beer.

"I just gotta thank y'all for supporting me these last four years, man," he began. Girls and guys alike hung on his every word. "This is my last season as a Panther, but it feels like only the beginning. Next year, we're thinking OSU, shit, maybe even Duke University, the sky's the limit, and I just want to let everybody know I wouldn't be here without your continued support."

People started clapping and I took that as my cue to join.

Troy regarded me next, a loving expression in his eye. "And I especially want to thank my biggest fan, my number one, my support system, Regan."

This drew another round of "awws."

I did as expected. I leaned up, offering my lips for Troy to kiss, ignoring the praise we were receiving.

Troy focused on his audience again. "Hell, let's have a great season. I'm ready to win another title!"

Everyone raised their Solo cups and cheered him on, and I managed to slip out of his grasp and escape into the house.

Troy was Akron royalty. He'd found his niche, only my

crown didn't quite fit. Being a potential football wife wasn't enough for me, but then that dreaded blank I came to whenever I tried to picture myself doing or being something else nearly made my mask slip.

Tonight wasn't about me, but about Troy.

Inside the house, the party was going strong. Another song that inspired hips to shake was playing loudly, and kids were getting down and dancing. I recognized a few girls from English and trig, but I wasn't in the mood to join in. Malika had disappeared, I noticed.

"Five-O! Five-O!" a crowd began chanting.

A look into the next room found Thomas Jordan—*Tommy J* as he preferred, aka Troy's younger brother—dancing with two girls. He had his shirt unbuttoned, giving the whole room a peek at his muscled chest. Tommy J was in heaven.

He was a year younger than me, but though he was only a sophomore, Tommy already held major clout at Arlington High. Not from being Troy's younger brother, but from his own massive talent on the field.

Tommy was nice and all, but he had an ego. He didn't get that much playing time yet, since he was the backup to Troy, but he always kept a harem of girls on his arms. With his perfect dark brown skin, handsome smile, and growing reputation, he was a certified charmer. He was already doing too much.

Sometimes I wondered if Troy would be the same if we broke up.

My cell phone buzzed in my pocket. Fishing it out, I found a text from Malika.

Don't be mad, but I ran into Calvin and he wanted to talk. Don't wait for me

I could only hope she was being smart about this.

BE SAFE. Love you

An arm snaked around my waist and before I could push whoever it was away, lips brushed my neck and made their way to my ear. "Let's go to my car, I wanna tell you something," Troy whispered. His hand was already steering me out of the room before I could respond.

Whatever Troy wanted to talk about, it beat being in attendance at yet another football kickback. When he reached for my hand, I let him lead me toward the front door. Along the way, I watched and waited each time someone stopped him to compliment his game or dap him up.

"Heading out now, Five?" Tommy J caught us as we made it to the door. Around his neck hung a gold chain with a number 50 pendant resting against his glistening chest.

In a way, Troy was humble in comparison. Along with his chain, Tommy wore a gold watch and a thick gold ring on his right hand. Troy had told me the watch was an heirloom from their grandfather.

Troy gave him a sly grin and gestured to me. "You already know."

I didn't like what he was insinuating, but I said nothing as the two brothers bumped fists.

Troy led me to his Nissan Frontier. He helped me into the passenger seat, but not without managing to feel my butt just a little.

I let it go.

Inside, I sat up straight, trying to breathe calmly. As soon as Troy got in and closed his door, the space felt small.

"So," I said, moving some hair out of my face. "What's—"

Troy crossed the space between us and practically shoved his tongue down my throat, taking my face roughly in his hands.

At first, it was awkward, and I told myself to relax, to just let go and kiss my boyfriend. But when his hand cupped my breast, giving a gentle squeeze, I froze.

"What gives, Rey?" Troy pulled back, wiping his mouth as he rested against the driver's door. I didn't miss the frustration on his face.

I couldn't look at him, I felt so wrong and embarrassed.

This kept happening.

I wanted to like it, I wanted to be okay with him touching me all over, but I just kept freezing up. Feeling weird and squirmy.

Facing the window to hide my shame, I said, "Can you take me home? I don't feel so good. I think I'm getting a migraine, I'm sorry."

Troy snorted in the driver seat. "Fine."

He put his keys in the ignition.

"A-are you okay to drive?" I made sure to ask before he risked more than just his potential scholarships.

"I only had one beer, Regan."

Troy was responsible enough not to be a major drinker, and I had only seen him drink *a* beer, as he said, so I let it go.

Troy's music played the whole ride to Briar Pointe. The tension between us was stifling, and I was all but ready to flee from the vehicle as soon as he pulled up in front of my house.

"Rey." His tone stopped me, making me fear the worst.

I found the courage to look at him. "Yeah?"

He seemed tired, then shook his head. "If not now, then when?"

I had a right to not be into it, but even so, somehow my stance felt wrong. "I don't know, Troy. I'm sorry."

He released a sigh. "I'll text you when I get home."

"Okay." Because I didn't want to leave on a bad note, I leaned over and kissed his cheek. "I love you."

I could tell the smile he gave me was forced. "I love you, too."

I couldn't have walked to my front door any faster. When I reached it, I turned and waved to Troy, indicating I was safe, and watched as he drove away.

Tanner met me in the foyer, and because I wasn't ready to go inside, I let him out and followed him down our driveway.

I took a seat at the curb as he sniffed around to do his business.

I felt like a child. Troy was only a year older than me, but he was so much more experienced and sure of himself. Tears prickled in my eyes as I thought of having to call Sherry about the internship. I didn't want to. I didn't know what I wanted, and I hated it. Hated feeling so powerless. Hated—

A bark caused my head to snap up just as a pair of Jordans came into my line of vision.

The boy from the community center was standing in front of me.

Guillermo.

Immediately I smiled at the familiar face, but he didn't return the favor as he gazed down at me.

His eyes were intense. One minute they were dark, the next they were light. The contrast reminded me of a comic book hero, teetering on the edge between good and bad.

"We gotta stop meetin' like this," he said, a hint of playful taunting in his deep voice.

My smile broadened. "It's you."

He smirked, nodding. "It's me."

Nothing else was said, and I took the time to study how he looked outside of the community center. He had a decent build, not too bulky and not too scrawny. He could hold his own in a ring, I figured.

Goodness, I was staring.

Blinking, I brought my attention back to Tanner, who was snuffling around Guillermo's feet.

Guillermo seemed to like dogs; at least, he held out a hand and allowed Tanner to sniff him.

"So, I guess we're neighbors?" He observed our surroundings before meeting my eyes again.

"What a small world, huh?"

"Something like that."

Tanner trotted off to find a spot to get down to business, leaving us be.

"What are you doing out here?" I asked.

Guillermo shot a look back toward what I guessed was his house—the one that had been for sale over the summer and recently sold—before returning to me. "The roof was caving in on me."

I got that. At times, it felt like my own walls were closing in. We all had our own crap to deal with.

I glanced up and down the street. An early September breeze lifted my hair, cool but refreshing. The temperatures weren't chilly just yet. It was dark, the streetlights illuminating the road, and no one else was outside.

I patted the spot next to me. "You can sit."

Guillermo's eyes fixed on my hand. He took a step back, tucking a lock of hair behind his ear. I hoped he never got the sense to cut it. "I, uh, I probably shouldn't."

"Why not?"

Guillermo gazed past me at my house. "Wouldn't want to give anyone the wrong idea."

"Wrong idea?" I arched a brow, and then to ease the tension, I teased, "Ohhh, you must've heard."

"Heard what?"

I leaned forward as if to tell him a secret. "My dad used to be cop, and he keeps a close eye on the neighborhood, so you better stay in line."

Guillermo's eyes doubled in size as his gaze raced to my house again. "Shit."

My father had been a cop for almost twenty years before he quit the force, citing a conflict of morals. He worked in the heating and cooling field now, but due to his years as an officer of the law, not to mention the conversations he had with my mother about her work, he was real strict about where I went and who I went with. Avery, too. During my middle school days, when boys had started hinting at wanting to hang out, I always had to decline. I wasn't allowed to date…until Troy.

I let out a laugh. "I'm kidding, it's no big deal. We're just saying hi."

Guillermo looked at me funny, as if there was something I wasn't getting. "I'll stand," he finally said.

"Okay."

"I'm not trouble," he seemed to feel the need to say.

"I…I didn't say you were."

"No, but it looks bad."

I suddenly got the sense he was talking about his service at the community center. Then I recalled the way my mother had looked at him when she caught us together, and I finally got his meaning.

"I'm not scared, if that's what you're talking about. My

mom is understanding, Guillermo. She wouldn't judge you either," I said.

Guillermo shoved his hands deep into his pockets, still seeming uncomfortable. "I better get to bed. Can't be late for tomorrow."

"Yeah," I said, rising to my feet. "Me, too."

Once more, Guillermo's gaze settled on me. "So I'll be seeing you?"

He was my neighbor, and he worked at the community center—there was a good possibility he'd be going to my school come Monday as well. "You going to Arlington?"

He tipped his head. "Yeah."

My lips drew up into a smile. For some reason, I liked this fact. "Yeah, I'll be seeing you. If you need help getting around school, or the neighborhood, I'm—"

Guillermo blinked, inching back toward his house. "Bad idea."

Although it was no big deal for me to extend a hand and show him around, Guillermo seemed intent on walking away. With a stiff wave, he left me to wait on Tanner alone.

Guillermo

Something good was cooking early Sunday morning, waking me up before my alarm. The spices lingering in the air had my mouth watering as I got ready for community service.

It wasn't just the scent that had woken me up; it was the sound of music, laughter, and the sizzling of food in a pan that caused me to stir. It reminded me of before.

My parents didn't work weekends, givin' them both the choice to sleep in or get up early. When I was younger, they'd get Yesi and me up and make a party out of preparing breakfast. Music would fill the background as tiny Yesenia stood on the stool at the counter, helping our father chop onions or peppers. She'd wear an apron to complete her look as assistant cook. Me, I'd be at the stove with my mother cooking the food and basking in the jovial atmosphere of my family.

That was a long time ago. Before high school. Before I started taking interest in being out with my friends as opposed to having "family fun" at home.

That was before, and this was after.

My therapist insisted that I could get it all back, that I could start over and regain a relationship with my family. She wasn't the one experiencing my father's cold shoulder. Shit was brutal when I already felt bad in my own guilt.

Still, after getting dressed for the day, I took a chance and went down to the kitchen to greet everyone. I had forty minutes before I was due at Briar Park Community Center.

The scene before me was pure nostalgia. The music was going and Yesenia was at the island whipping some batter in a mixing bowl as my father put together eggs and his famous chorizo—my favorite breakfast dish. My mother was at the stove, warming up the tortillas, and I could already taste what was to come.

"Can I help with something?" I asked.

My father had been smiling at Yesenia as she threatened to flick pancake batter on him. Now, as his attention shifted to where I stood in the doorway, his show of humor diminished.

He cleared his throat and refocused on his work. "You goin' in?"

There didn't even need to be a draft for the coldness that had seeped into the air. My chest tightened. "I've got time."

My father was no longer looking at me. "It's okay, we've got it covered."

Yesenia frowned, her big brown eyes wounded for me. Our father's constant reprimanding of me in front of her caused me more shame and embarrassment than ever before. I wasn't a role model, that was for sure, but each time he took a jab at me, I felt like shit. Like a worthless older brother.

I bowed out, knowing I wasn't wanted. "I'm just going to head in early, then."

My father grimaced, clearly not at all interested in me anymore. "You do that, Guillermo. Keep this routine up. Show them people you take this punishment seriously. And another thing—" his steely eyes focused on me again "—what did I tell you about cutting your hair? School starts tomorrow, muchacho."

My father was old-school, equating my long hair with being unprofessional and unpolished. He'd sooner I get a crew cut and wear polos to fit the image that I was turnin' over a new leaf.

My old group of friends, back home in Rowling Heights, they would've clowned the shit out of me if I ever showed up looking like some prep school dropout. Hell, I'd clown the shit out of me if I adopted a look like that.

For a moment, I wondered, though…if I did concede and cut my hair, would my father ease up on me?

Judging by the way he was shuttin' me out, probably not.

Without another word, I turned and made my way toward the garage.

"Wait!" Rushing down the hall behind me, my mother handed me something wrapped in foil. It was hot, fresh from the stove. She said nothing else before kissing my cheek and going back to the kitchen.

In my car I pulled my hair back into a bun. It wasn't exactly cutting it off, but it was a start.

It was still pretty early when I made it to the center. I wanted to sit in my car and sulk, but there was incoming traffic in the center already, despite it being early on a Sunday, and I felt too exposed.

Instead, I gathered my earphones, went inside and waved at the receptionist, then sat in the rec room. It was empty, no surprise there, and I was able to fully retreat into myself as I sank into a sofa cushion and plugged in my music. In moments I was drowning in waves of the music of my favorite hip-hop artists and eating the breakfast burrito my mother had slipped me.

Whenever Tío Mateo would watch Yesenia and me when we were younger, we'd listen to his choice of music, hip-hop and R&B, as opposed to my parents' preferred banda and Latin pop. He'd urge us to keep it un secreto, pressing a finger to his lips before playing songs from *Tha Carter III*.

Tío Matt's passion for the urban storytellers resonated deep in me, always catching my attention whenever I was browsing the radio or watchin' music videos. It sparked an obsession, because I went from tolerating my parents' musical tastes during car rides to getting my first iPod and filling it with the rappers Tío Mateo would play. The punch lines, the metaphors, the double entendres, the flows, I lived for that shit.

Listening to hip-hop was how I'd spent most of my time after the Situation. Gettin' lost in music was more therapeutic than talking. Some rappers were good kids from mad cities. Others, like me, were troubled kids from good cities. Their lyrics spoke to me, tellin' me I wasn't alone, tellin' me that there was a way through this rough patch. From my favorite rapper of all time, Jay-Z, to a lot of the newcomers, music held all the answers.

And I was so desperately seeking answers most days.

Soft fingers came down on my arm, and all at once the scent of berries and a hint of vanilla enveloped my senses, jolting me upright. I'd been in my thoughts, not even realizing someone else had entered the room.

Regan stood by the arm of the sofa, holding back a laugh.

I removed my earphones and got up, keeping my distance in case Mrs. London was around.

Regan seemed to notice. "I was just saying hi. You came in so fast and—are you okay?"

Concern crossed her pretty face, an emotion I didn't deserve.

We'd just met, but Regan had this way of looking at me as if she saw something worth looking at. My own family couldn't stand to look at me for five seconds. Who was this girl who so openly seemed to accept me, or at least, welcome me? The night before, she'd wanted me to sit with her. She'd even been kind enough to offer to show me around.

You're not a monster. Her mother's words echoed in my ears.

Yeah, right. I snorted to myself.

I balled up my empty foil and tossed it in the wastebasket behind her. *Kobe.*

Avoiding Regan wasn't going to be as easy as I thought. The world was too small. "I'm gettin' there."

Sympathy tugged on her lips as she offered me a smile. "I'm a good listener, if you ever want to talk."

I hadn't told her when she'd been on her curb last night, but I'd seen her the moment that guy had dropped her off. I'd assumed he was her boyfriend. The car had been dark, but the streetlights were bright enough for me to see their tension. The guy had appeared disappointed about something, and Regan had seemed eager to get away.

And then she was just sitting there on the curb, balled up and looking gloomy. An itch had drawn me over, too curious for my own good.

It was clear to me she had her own issues. Who was I to unload all of mine on top?

"So," Regan said. Her eyes lingered on my phone, clutched tightly in my hand. I was out of my element here, and for some reason she was making me nervous the more she studied me. "What are you listening to?"

"Old Wayne," I said. Specifically Lil Wayne's classic from *Tha Carter III*, "Tie My Hands." Through the song, I could almost believe that overcoming harsh times and persevering was possible, no matter the obstacles in the way.

"Talk about a throwback," Regan said.

I could sense she was trying, even though I insisted on putting space between us.

There was no denying Regan was a nice girl. I made an effort to appease her with a smile. "Thank you, though, for checking in on me. I'm really into lyrics, and I needed to get lost. Rough start this morning, you know?"

Regan groaned. "Aren't they all? I hate getting up early on weekends."

Her hand took mine with a gentle squeeze. The sensation melted a layer of ice inside me. "Let's get clocked in, we can endure this long day together."

I examined her hand on mine, the soft texture of her touch somehow so *her*, from what little I knew. My fingers twitched. If the wrong person saw us even breathing the same air, it would be bad.

One thing I could read from Mrs. London was that she didn't take any shit. She seemed almost as tough as Harvey. A friendship with Regan, which seemed innocent enough, was out of the question.

I could read between the lines: one, Regan had a boyfriend, and I was supposed to be taking steps forward, not back. Two, there was no way in hell I could ever start something with my supervisor's daughter—that was a risk I wasn't willing to take.

Being smart about it, I took my hand back. "Nah, I'm going to hang here for a second. Thanks, though."

Regan's smile dimmed, and she left the room without me.

I sighed. Seeing that light slip from her face was disappointing, and I didn't know why.

Regan

Long after my shift at the community center, where I'd avoided one moody boy who seemed to think I was a pariah, I was in my room trying to get homework done. This effort lasted all of an hour before Troy texted me that he was coming over.

Before, I would've loved hanging out, but with the way things had been so rocky lately, I just wasn't prepared for another fallout. I wanted to put it all on the back burner and focus on my schoolwork, but of course, because it was Troy, my father wanted me front and center to play my part as the loving girlfriend.

Amid the chatter of football, I wondered how Guillermo was doing. Earlier at the center he'd been so down, his dark eyes full of pain. Guillermo seemed guilty, like whatever he'd done had really left a mark on him. Weighed him down into eternal defeat. In time, I hoped he'd see himself in a new light. Some of my mother's probationers could be jaded and angry about serving time, and others were eager to change.

For example, Daren, the facility's co-lead, had once been a member of the program.

Anyone could come back from oblivion; everyone deserved second chances.

"You really threw down, Mrs. London," Troy said after dinner, bringing me out of my thoughts. Usually picky, he had dug into my mother's ham and collard greens, even allowing himself to indulge in the carbs of her homemade scalloped potatoes.

My mother seemed pleased with the compliment as she leaned back against my father on the love seat across from us. "I'm glad you liked it. Make sure to mention that my cooking made you nice and strong when you go pro."

Her remark caused everyone to chuckle.

Well, not everyone.

Avery wasn't really paying us any mind as he sat by the arm of the sofa on the floor, with Tanner at his side, lazily watching some movie on TV. He also had plans after dinner, but our father wanted us all around to entertain Troy. Sometimes it honestly felt like a full-time job with no pay when my father was around.

"You make sure you tighten up in the gym," my father warned Troy. "I'd hate to see you get too comfortable on that field. Your aim should be to win by ten more points than the last game each game."

That sounded easier said than done, but Troy was nodding along, not at all fazed by the challenge.

"For sure," Troy replied. "My biggest competition on that field is myself, sir. Next to that, it's Tommy. I just know he's going to be a problem by the time he's a senior."

To this my father didn't disagree. "Both you boys are going to make this city proud."

Talk of Troy's impending success always got old fast for me. It was inevitable; everyone knew he was going pro some-day. It was almost kind of boring to keep talking about it, at least to me.

My eyes found my mother, who was half-listening and half-watching the movie as she cradled her wineglass in her hand. She looked content, snuggled against my father as he spoke of football with his favorite person in the world.

I was settled under Troy's arm, but, as I admittedly didn't care for football, I felt more awkward than content.

"Regan's coming with me, all the way," Troy was saying. "She gon' be rich, probably become the team accountant or something."

I looked up at Troy, feeling my brow arch in curiosity. "Team accountant?"

"Oh yeah, you workin' for the best," he told me.

I opened my mouth—

"Just as soon as she graduates college and aces her account-ing programs. Hell, you're right, why stop at Sherry's firm when she can go all the way to the top? Buy us a nice retire-ment home, even."

They were laughing, and I was confused about where I'd said I wanted to do any of that.

"What if I just want to be small-time?" I questioned.

My father frowned, looking at me funny. "What if Troy decides to waste his talent? How much sense does that make, Rey? We don't believe in limits in this house—there is no ceiling for you."

"Absolutely," Troy was quick to agree.

Now they *both* were speaking for me.

Almost as if my opinion didn't count.

My gaze fell upon Avery and how he'd abandoned the movie to scour something on his phone.

I envied him his freedom of choice. Our father was pushy, but he never seemed to tell Avery what to do for a career.

"Read anything good, Ave?" I asked my younger brother.

He lifted his head from his phone and squinted at me. "I'm binging on *Bleach* right now."

Out of context, it sounded like he was chugging chlorine. I blinked, trying to connect with him. "I should get into that."

Avery's expression grew suspicious. "It's actually—"

"A waste of time," my father cut in. "What I tell you about getting out more? You conveniently missed the football try-outs *again* this year."

My mother drove her elbow into his side. "Cliff, stop, leave that boy alone and let him enjoy his reading."

My father appeared innocent as he held his hands up. "What? Why can't he read *and* play a sport?"

"Colleges do like extracurricular activities, ma'am." Troy tried to reason with my mother.

I bit my tongue to keep from speaking up about the fact that *I* wasn't active in sports at school. Outside of the center, I didn't do extracurricular activities.

My younger brother seemed to shrink within himself, and I felt guilty for putting him on the spot. I knew how he felt. I didn't want to let my parents down either, to do or say anything that would disappoint them.

I envied my mother's passion and zeal, her drive to seek change and help mold those who society would deem lost. The effortless way she ran the community center. Sure, I had my moments of enjoying my time at the center, but it wasn't *my* thing. Just like accounting. Chewing on my lip, I found myself back at square one as always: What was my thing?

"How many hours does Aunt Sherry work at her firm? Is she able to control her own schedule?" I blurted out, drawing the focus back to me.

At once, my father eased up. "Sherry works full-time, but I know her schedule's flexible. You gotta call her, Rey, don't let her fill in that internship before you do."

He started talking more about Aunt Sherry and accounting, with Troy chiming in with support.

Avery was safe, back in his game.

While my family and boyfriend were busy planning my future, I was lost in my own head, desperately trying to pin down who I was.

Guillermo

I didn't get much sleep Sunday night.

Instead of tossing and turning, I lay back staring at the ceiling, consumed with what was.

By morning I'd managed to amass a total of five hours of sleep—not bad, but not enough to make me want to pull myself from bed and prepare for my first day at Arlington High.

Yesenia was in the bathroom already when I made my way into the hall. She was humming happily along as she brushed her teeth. She'd be an eighth grader at Allendale Middle School, and there wasn't as much pressure on her as there was on me.

She caught me standing in the doorway, a gleam in her eyes as she smiled up at me. It slowly died as her brows furrowed. "Pasa algo?"

I shook my head. "No, no pasa nada."

Yesenia wasn't convinced; she came and squeezed my arm gently before giving me a hug. "Cheer up, Memo, this is a fresh start. Be optimistic, okay?"

For her, I'd do anything.

So I hugged her back and went into the bathroom to start my day.

Hair back or down? I briefly pondered. My father hated my hair, but I felt a bit insecure with this new and improved image I was going for. After raking a hand through it a few times, I decided to pull it all back into a bun.

A ringing sound made me leave the bathroom to grab my cell phone off my nightstand. I recognized my uncle's number flashing across the screen. It had been too long since I'd spoken to him, so I picked up right away. "Hey!"

"Is for horses," he responded. Wind in the background let me know he was more than likely in the car taking my cousins Melisa and Carlos to school.

I deadpanned. "Ha ha."

"First day. Nervous?" Tío Mateo asked me.

Being the new kid? "Not too much. Thanks for the car—I meant to call you, I've just been busy."

He hummed. "Yeah, workin' for the community, you likin' that?"

"Oh yeah, thinkin' about a permanent stay."

"Memo." His stern tone said he wasn't about to be my friend in this situation. Tío Mateo was never the strict type, but he could get on me when he needed to. I hated that he lived in Columbus now. "I won't be on here long to hold you up, but I wanted to hear from you. It's your first day—stay out of trouble and don't fuck this up. José moved mountains for you, and you better be grateful."

The weight and pressure of all the expectations grounded me in place. "I know. I have no intention of fuckin' this up."

"Language!" Even as he said it, I could hear the smile in his voice.

"Thanks, though, for callin', for reachin' out. I needed this," I told him.

"Always, you're my favorite nephew."

"I'm your only nephew."

"Semantics." Tío Mateo chuckled. "Have a good day. Stay up." He disconnected.

Staring at the phone in my hand, I thought of *her*.

The source of all my troubles.

In the beginning, my parents had debated getting me another cell phone. In the end, they had, with a new number. Not that I hadn't memorized Tynesha's. The phone was a test, to see if I'd give in and break the rules. Would I text her? Call her? Reach out in some way?

Images of the past haunted me, and I knew I wouldn't do anything like that. The brutal sting of betrayal had me squeezing the device tight in my hand.

She'd made her choice, as I had made mine.

I shoved my cell into my pocket. It wasn't constructive to blame her.

It was time to start school and get back to normal. New school, new start, possibly a new Guillermo. I didn't too much like the idea of changing who I was, but for my parents', and the court's, sake I would. No more mouthing off, no more fighting, and definitely no more trouble with girls.

One of the first things my therapist had asked me to do was to set a goal for myself. My first goal was to make new friends in this move. To seek out better association. After feeling isolated at home, I was ready to meet new people and find acceptance.

I made my way down to the kitchen, hoping for a quick bite of whatever it was my parents had made.

I was just rounding the corner off the kitchen when I heard my parents speaking in the dining room.

"I just want this to be our last stop, José," my mother was whispering. "He's been through a lot, and I'm not sure I can handle much more."

My father wasn't the least bit sympathetic. "Ese chico siempre estuvo mal."

It wouldn't be easy, but I would endure.

Instead of joining my parents, I grabbed a fruit smoothie from the fridge before making my way outside.

Yesi wanted me to be optimistic, and one thing I had learned from counseling was that to be positive, you couldn't surround yourself with the negative. Giving my parents space was good for all of us.

I'd left my car out front when I'd gotten home yesterday. On my walk down our driveway, I spotted a kid around my age two houses down. He was standing by the side of his house, smoking a cigarette and savoring it as if it were his last meal.

Not likely, given his athletic build.

The boy lifted his gaze and caught me watching him. He tipped his head toward me in acknowledgment as he released a stream of smoke.

I nodded back.

He swept a hand through his dark, thick hair, styled in a faux hawk fade. Seeing his olive complexion and features, I felt a sense of kinship, reveling in the fact that we and the Londons weren't the only families of color in the neighborhood.

"New?" the boy shouted my way.

My gaze flicked toward my house. "Yeah."

He scanned me over. "You play soccer?"

A bunch of my cousins lived for the sport, but I was never into it. I enjoyed the pastime of just listening to music.

"No," I told him.

"You should," he continued. "You look like a guy who could keep up."

Despite my disinterest, I *had* played soccer with my family before. But with my new stint in community service, I doubted I'd have time to revive my career. Still, I recalled my goal to make friends.

"I could hang," I said.

A corner of his mouth curled up. "You going to Arlington?"

"Yeah."

"Our soccer's the shit."

I wasn't ready to commit to anything, even though me playing soccer would get some sort of positive vibe from my father. He and Tío Mateo loved soccer. My tía Guadelupe, too.

"Raviv! You better not be out there smoking, mister!" a woman's voice screamed from inside the boy's house. Seconds later, a woman emerged onto their front porch, sweeping the area for her son.

Raviv pressed himself against the siding of the house, smirking at me. He raised a hand and pressed his finger to his lips as he stubbed out his cigarette on the bottom of his shoe. His mother huffed and went back inside.

I shrugged. It wasn't my business anyway.

"Need a ride?" I offered, since we were going to the same place.

Raviv peered around the corner of his house to his front porch and then looked back to me. "Nah, not today, my mom's already on that, but thanks."

It was time to get a move on, as I had to get to Arlington High early and meet with the guidance counselor about my schedule. School had been in session since after Labor Day, which was only four days, so thankfully there wouldn't be too much to catch up on.

I was one of the early birds and had to be buzzed in by the main office. The guidance counselor was waiting for me at the junior office door. She was a tall White woman with brunette hair and green eyes, and she had a friendly smile on her face. She read as the *nice* type, which was far better than my last guidance counselor, who had dubbed certain students as problems the instant they entered her door. Then again, as many times as I'd sat in front of her, I couldn't blame her.

"You must be Guillermo. I'm Mrs. Greer." The counselor beamed even bigger, sticking her hand out to shake mine. "So nice to have you with us."

We headed into her private office, passing an office worker along the way. I took the black plastic chair in front of her desk as she occupied the plush seat behind it.

She grabbed a folder and opened it up. *Here we go.*

"I read your file. It's quite colorful. Ten suspensions and countless detentions all in one year, Guillermo?" She looked concerned, letting me know a possible lecture was coming.

"It was *quite* a year," I said.

Mrs. Greer shook her head. "And quite a cry for help."

Please tell me she's not about to shrink me.

"This is my second chance. I intend to use it to its fullest." I spoke up to shut her down. "No more mistakes."

I already had to answer to my parents and to Harvey, not to mention my therapist and Mrs. London—I didn't have the endurance to face this shit at school, too.

"Now, let's just relax, you're only four days behind, not a

big deal." Mrs. Greer spoke in a soothing tone. It was easy to imagine that any kid would feel comfortable coming to her; she was friendly, gentle, assertive, but mostly, happy. "What electives were you looking into taking at your old school in Rowling?"

I tried to think and came up empty. It had all been a blur. During the career carnival my sophomore year, I'd cut the day to hang out in Mouse's basement with the other guys. "To be honest, I don't remember having an idea."

Mrs. Greer quirked a dark brow, her face saying what her voice wouldn't. "Let's run down some ideas and see what strikes you, okay?"

She listed the major options: accounting, hospitality, cosmetology, animal care and management, auto body, web design—

"Web design," I interrupted. Did I care about the course? No, but nothing else she listed grabbed me, and from what I knew of the other options, it was the most interesting of my choices.

We continued putting together my schedule, with me agreeing to certain classes that sounded interesting. Glancing around her office, I found that she was married to a Black man and had a daughter. Among the usual clutter of academic flyers and posters, she had awards and certificates hung up on her walls as well. There were senior photos on her bulletin board, and many notes of love and appreciation from students. She seemed more promising than my last counselor for sure.

"Foreign language?" Mrs. Greer asked, louder than needed, dragging me from my thoughts.

"What?"

"I said would you be interested in taking a foreign language?" she repeated.

I'd taken two years of Spanish, what more did I need? "I gotta take more?"

"If you plan on going to college, you'll need three years, and since you're more than likely going to college, let's set you up."

She said this with finality, as if there was no disputing it. *Great.*

"I'll take Spanish III."

She was back on her computer, silent for a moment.

"Okay, your schedule's good to go." Mrs. Greer leaned over, facing her open office door. "Hey, Avery?"

A student appeared in the doorway and gave Mrs. Greer his attention.

"Guillermo's new here, would you mind showing him around before school begins?" She glanced at her wristwatch, noting we had about fifteen minutes before the bell rang and the other students entered the building.

"Sure thing."

I stood up and accepted all the paperwork, student planner, and my schedule from her. "Thanks."

"Have a nice day, Guillermo. Remember, this is your new start, new you." There was that big friendly smile again. How could anyone be that happy?

I followed Avery into the hall. He was a little shorter than me, and a little scrawnier, too.

"Can I see your schedule?" he asked, holding his hand out.

I handed it to him, taking a moment to look around the hallway while he read it over. Judging from the Class Of photos on the walls, the school was predominantly Black, with some other ethnic groups and a sprinkle of White kids here and there. My old school had been mostly White. I hadn't had a lot of friends there. I didn't relate to the things they talked about and cared about, and the music and shows they tended to watch weren't my taste either.

Although I'd gone to a White school, I had lived in a predominantly Black neighborhood. Most of my friends had been Black, and of course I got along with the other Latinos, too, as my parents became good friends with their parents. The girls I'd dated had been Latina or Black, like Tynesha.

Seeing this new range of students made me hopeful Arlington High would be a better experience for me.

Avery took the lead, showing me to each of my classes. He was a quiet kid, not making much conversation. It didn't bother me. I took in the school; it was clean and the floors were all polished and shiny, and the school colors were obviously light green and purple. The lockers on the first floor were purple, the lockers on the second floor were light green, and I wasn't surprised when the lockers on the third floor turned out to be purple, too. From a few posters, I gathered that the school mascot was a panther, and that the sports teams did well. There was a glass case on the first floor by the main office filled with trophies.

"Nervous?" Avery asked as we paused on the third floor.

"Nah, not really. It's a good school?"

He shrugged. "It's my second year. It's pretty straight. My sister's a junior, and she's never really complained. You should be all right." He pointed to the door on my right marked 306. "That's where you have chemistry with Mrs. Renner." He glanced back at me, an odd smile spreading across his face. "Yeah, that oughta be good for you today."

I didn't understand. "Huh?"

"Nothing." Avery checked the clock that hung on the wall a few lockers down. "The bell's going to ring, better get you to homeroom."

He took me back to the second floor and stopped in front of a door marked 212. "If you have any trouble, Mrs. Greer is always there to help."

Sure.

I thanked him, then faced my homeroom, prepared to start my first day. Who knew what Arlington High had to offer?

Midday, I bumped into Raviv. He was with a girl I assumed was his girlfriend, a Latina who was no taller than Yesenia. She stood underneath Raviv's arm, smiling up at him like she was in a daze. He was looking down at her as if he could just eat her up.

The honeymoon phase was all bliss when you were in it, but annoying when you were watching it.

Raviv acknowledged me with a bob of his head. "Sup?" Glancing at the girl on his arm, he squeezed her a little closer. "This is my girl, Camila. Cami, this is... Actually, I never got his name."

"Guillermo," I offered.

"Where ya headed?" Raviv asked.

"Lunch," I read from my schedule.

"Need help getting there?"

"Nah, I think I remember the way."

Raviv left it alone. "Cool, I'll catch ya later. Keep thinkin' about soccer." His attention turned to a tall, lanky kid down the hall who was leaning his head against a locker as he dialed in his combination. "Heads up, Kayde!"

Camila smiled at me a little too long, angling her head in a funny and suggestive way.

Deciding I was being paranoid, I smiled briefly and went in search of the cafeteria.

They were serving cheeseburgers and fries for lunch, and

unlike my old school, it was real hamburger meat, not that soy meat crap I'd been forced to swallow for two years.

I didn't mind sitting alone—

My body lurched forward as somebody bumped into me. A look over, and I found a couple boys with trays in their hands walking by, one stopping and noting my glare.

"Problem?" he challenged.

"Yeah, mind sayin' excuse me, or watchin' where you're going next time?" I shot back.

"Man, what?" As if to intimidate me, he bucked at me, stopping only when his friend pressed a hand to his chest to push him back.

My fists clenched my tray. With everything in me, I wanted to throw the tray down and feed this dickhead's face to the linoleum.

"Hey."

A boy was beside me—Avery. He swept a nervous gaze from me to the two boys now walking away.

"Trust me, guys like that aren't worth it," he said.

That wasn't the point. Where I was from, you didn't just let people walk all over you. Screw that. "Here's how my fucks work—I don't give any."

Avery blinked and took a step back. "Uh, that's one way to look at it."

Seeing his unease made me freeze.

It was only my first day. I couldn't lose my shit this soon, this early. I practiced even breaths to calm myself down. This wasn't Rowling Heights—I couldn't let every asshole get to me. I knew I could handle myself, but maybe—just this once—I didn't have to prove it.

Running a hand down my face, I forced myself to let it go. "Sorry."

Avery shrugged. "I get it."

"I've got an issue with authority. The less I come into contact with people to answer to, the better."

A small smile tugged one corner of Avery's mouth up. "That's a good train of thought."

I glanced at the cafeteria, feeling a little antsy as I slowly came down from my anger. "If it's not too much trouble, can I sit with you?"

Avery bobbed his head, and together we went and grabbed an empty table for ourselves. Almost immediately he pulled a graphic novel from his bag and commenced reading it. With his quiet demeanor, he seemed like a safe choice to associate with, someone my parents and PO would approve of.

Two girls walked by with their lunches. Two girls with identical faces—twins, one wearing a blouse with teal polka dots and teal jeans, and the other wearing a blouse with pink polka dots with pink jeans. They were twinning to the max.

"Those are the Winston sisters, Britney and Briana, they wear matching outfits *every* day," Avery clued me in.

"Why?"

He shrugged. "Never asked."

This school definitely had its own character going for itself. The cafeteria was abuzz with chatter, some kids throwing things back and forth, and some playing music in various areas. As I looked around, taking the place in, I noticed a girl sitting alone.

Like Avery, she was reading during the lunch hour. She sat with her legs crossed and her nose deep in her book, not eating or paying anyone any attention. Even from this slight distance, I could read her Don't-Fuck-With-Me demeanor. The attitude etched on her face, just daring someone to approach her, caused me to smile.

My gaze ran up her golden-brown legs and settled on her face, which was pretty no matter the angry expression on it. As I studied her, I realized I recognized her from a couple of my earlier classes, trig and geography.

"That's Jenaya Omar," Avery said, clearly noticing my staring. When I faced him, he added, "She's...tough."

My eyes returned to the girl. *Jenaya.* Tough suited her, because even though I was new, I could tell from her body language that she didn't take shit from anyone.

I rose from my seat, grabbing my tray. "Let's go sit with her."

Avery blinked. "Th-that's not a good idea."

Maybe it wasn't, but I wanted to know the girl everyone else seemed to be staying away from. She was alone, and I was alone, apart from Avery. Why not?

"She's tough for a reason," Avery went on, taking a moment to observe her. "She's sorta got this reputation."

A reputation? That would piss me off, too. That made my decision final. "So do I, let's go."

Avery didn't have to join me, but he did, and we walked to Jenaya's table together. I sat across from her, and Avery stood beside her, looking nervous.

At once Jenaya stopped reading and glanced between Avery and me. For some reason, she gave me the mean look. "Can I help you?"

Up close, I saw that she had pretty hazel eyes. The tone of her voice was strong, too, letting me know she meant every word she'd ever utter.

Feigning nonchalance, I looked around before shrugging and opening my bottle of juice. "Nah, I'm good."

I didn't miss Jenaya narrowing her eyes. "There's a bunch of empty tables."

I couldn't tell you why I wanted to sit with this girl and befriend her, but something about her drew me in. "True, but I like this one. I recognize you from trig. I'm new, and I saw you sitting alone, so I figured why not eat together?"

She lifted a brow. "Not interested."

"No? Too bad. The cheeseburgers look good." I faced Avery, still standing uncertainly beside us. "Sit. I don't think her bite's as hard as her bark."

Jenaya lifted a brow. "Wanna try me?"

I met her sneer with a careless smirk. "No, not particularly."

She leaned over the table, as if to tell me a secret. "I don't have the best reputation around here, so I don't think you want to be associated with me."

I mirrored her movement. "I got an arrest record, *and* probation. One more strike and it's back to juvie for a *lonnng* time for me."

One of those finely shaped brows of hers arched upward. "No shit?"

I gave a nod. "Unfortunately, unless you got an arrest record, I beat you by a mile in the bad seed department."

She let it go. "Jenaya Omar."

"Guillermo Lozano."

Finally she peeked at Avery. "Hey."

He took that as his cue to sit down and join us.

Suddenly my skin prickled and I smelled the fruity scents of berries and vanilla. Before I turned my head, I knew who I'd see. Regan had walked up behind me and stopped by Avery. She looked between me and Jenaya suspiciously. "Everything okay, Avery?"

Avery looked up at her, frowning. "Yeah, Rey, just having lunch."

I looked between them, noticing their similar expressions, and I realized they were siblings.

Regan had been in my homeroom and study hall. She'd smiled at me and looked friendly, and I'd had to remind myself to shut it down. Now, here she was again.

I studied her soft, feminine face, admiring the protective, resilient look in her dark eyes. Each time I bumped into her, it felt like something new was revealed. There was Nice to Meet You Regan, Sullen yet Proficient Worker Regan, and now there was Protective Sister Regan. I wondered, foolishly, what Happy Regan was like.

She looked at me, those dimples coming out as she smiled. "Hey, Guillermo."

My name, wrapped in her musical voice, coming from her nice—

"You good?"

I snapped out of my haze and forced myself to focus on my burger.

Her boyfriend had come over.

Regan tucked some hair behind her ear. "Troy, hey, I just noticed Avery sitting here. You know Jenaya, right, she's a junior."

Troy tipped his head toward Jenaya. "What's up?"

Jenaya nodded his way.

Regan peeked at me, then back to her boyfriend. "And this is actually our new neighbor, Guillermo. He just moved in across the street."

I narrowed my eyes. She didn't mention the center. I caught the omission and wondered if she was being considerate, or if she didn't want to be publicly linked to someone like me.

Troy regarded me, as if obligated due to the introduction. "What's up, man."

I lifted my chin. "Sup."

A wave of awkwardness swept over the table, swamping all of us.

Regan opened her mouth, but Troy was quick, reaching a hand out and steering her in another direction. She glanced back at us and gave an apologetic frown as they went to another table full of students. From the size of the guys, I assumed they were athletes. Regan seemed out of place among them, and even more out of place with her boyfriend. Something about the way she looked so small and helpless under his arm made the picture kinda cringey.

I focused on Avery and the reveal.

He wasn't that talkative, and his quietness helped me see more of his resemblance to Regan. She seemed shy and innocent, and as I sat with Avery, it was clear he was, too. The only difference between them was that Regan was more outgoing when she approached people, whereas with Avery you had to start the conversation.

Jenaya was studying me, smirking just a little. She said nothing and went back to her book. Avery was into his graphic novel as well.

I ate my cheeseburger.

Right after lunch I had chemistry with Mrs. Renner. I waited at her front counter while she was outside on hall duty, looking out for any prohibited activity. I'd spotted several teachers doing this throughout the day, each carrying a pad in hand to issue citations if need be.

The bell rang and the teacher entered the room, closing the door behind her. She went and stood behind the front counter, meeting me with a joyful smile that reminded me of Mrs. Greer. Suddenly all the positivity didn't seem so great.

Please tell me the whole damn school isn't like this.

"Greetings!" she said, that big smile growing wider. She looked to be in her mid-to-late forties. She had very curly graying brown hair, some framing her face while the rest was clipped up at the back of her head, and she wore glasses. But nothing could distract from that big smile on her face. Whether she was tough I wasn't sure, but it was painfully obvious she was friendly. "You must be new."

For a second, I considered responding in Spanish, so that we wouldn't have to talk.

Instead, I bobbed my head.

"Excellent. Let's take a look at your schedule to see if you're in the right place."

I handed it over and eyed the room. Typical science decor adorned the place, with a focus on chemistry. Over the whiteboard behind the teacher hung a large poster of the periodic table, and chemistry posters littered the walls. The back of the room contained the actual lab, set off in three rows of black laboratory counters. To my right was a glass case, which looked to be housing little beanie babies.

I focused back on the teacher, who was staring at me funny. It was enough to make me uncomfortable and the class behind me laugh.

She handed back my schedule and glared at my shirt. "That's an interesting choice of clothing you're wearing, Guillermo."

Her comment made the class laugh more. I didn't get the joke, and I didn't like it one bit.

"Is something wrong?" I asked.

The question fueled the humor in the room, annoying me more.

"Well, Guillermo, my name is Mrs. Renner, and here in

Mrs. Renner's chemistry class, we do not take to the color orange kindly," she replied.

I looked down to take in my navy and orange tartan button-down and the orange T-shirt underneath. From a couple of my bracelets to my shirt, I was covered in orange. The look on Mrs. Renner's face said she was indeed serious.

I nervously swept a hand through my hair. "Didn't get the memo."

"We do very much like the color green. It's also one of our school's colors."

Looking around the counter, I spotted an orange highlighter lying beside her open binder. I nodded in its direction. "Your highlighter's orange."

Mrs. Renner glanced at the utensil. "Yes, I use it to highlight the tardies. I don't like tardies, Guillermo."

She was strange as hell. "Okay."

She walked to the left end of the counter and patted what looked to be a medium-size box turned into some type of creature with teeth. "This is Earl, our recycling bin. Whenever you have nibbly bits of paper, you're more than welcome to feed them to him. Bear in mind that Earl only eats paper, no wrappers or plastic."

I looked from Earl to Mrs. Renner, finding her to be completely serious once again. I blinked, unsure how to take the recycling bin and the eccentric teacher behind it. "I'll keep that in mind."

She walked back to her post behind the counter and took a seat on a stool. "After class I'll be sure to hand you our guidelines and syllabus and assign you a textbook. For now, let's get you seated." She reached for her binder and flipped it open to a seating chart. She looked up at the desks behind me and counted silently to herself. "You'll sit behind Regan London. Regan, please raise your hand."

I inhaled. Of course she was here. Turning around, I spotted Regan sitting toward the back, hand raised.

I gathered my schedule and walked to the seat behind the familiar face.

"You picked a great day to show up, Guillermo," said Mrs. Renner. "As I said last week, I'll be assigning lab partners, but we won't be getting into the lab until later in the grading period. Today we're doing icebreakers!"

Mrs. Renner truly must've found joy in everything except the color orange. She was so happy even Eeyore would've lost his damn depressive mood. Hell, I could just imagine her and Mrs. Greer in a contest to see who was more positive. *No, you're the happiest!*

She went through her seating chart, reading off pairs alphabetically, so I wasn't surprised when I got paired up with Regan. After she'd read the last of the pairs, Mrs. Renner grabbed a thick stack of papers and started passing them out.

Regan briefly turned and offered me a smile, capturing me with those dimples. "Welcome to Chemistry 101, where the color orange can be triggering," she joked.

I glanced at Mrs. Renner. "That shit's no joke?"

Regan shrugged. "Don't worry, most of us wear orange or bring orange things *just* to set her off."

The playful smile on her face allowed me to ease up on my feelings for Mrs. Renner. She was odd, but not so bad. The orange thing was a quirk I'd just have to get used to.

"I've never met anyone who didn't like a color," I said.

"I know, right? When I first got here, I thought her students were kidding, but she's for real. She's real sweet and fun, though. We have Mole Day in October, I'm really excited."

"Mole Day?"

"It's a day where we celebrate Avogadro's number, 6.022 x 10^23, or a mole. She'll explain it better when it's time. We get to make T-shirts, hand stitch stuffed moles, and bring food in."

Regan seemed excited at the idea. She must like school. "Cool."

Mrs. Renner passed out two worksheets. She paused beside us, her attention on me. "I told everyone on the first day, and now I'm telling you, this isn't a class that many pass with high marks. You don't want to miss a day, and if absence is unavoidable, I am here before and after school for any assistance you need." Mrs. Renner faced Regan. "Or, your lab partner could help."

Regan seemed to agree with a nod of her head.

Mrs. Renner walked on, and we got to work. The icebreaker was filled with trivial get-to-know-you questions, giving us an easy day in class.

I watched as Regan filled out her name, her handwriting thin yet curvy. She looked up and caught me staring. "How many siblings do you have?"

"One. Her name's Yesenia. You?"

"Just Avery."

"Favorite place to eat?"

"Taco House."

I wrinkled my nose, frowning as I wrote down her answer. "What?"

"Taco House is nasty."

"No, it's not."

"Yeah, it is. It's a sorry excuse for Mexican food."

Regan rolled her eyes, clearly not agreeing. "Taco House is the bomb, and it's only the *American* version."

"The American version sucks. The stuff they serve is insult-ing to the culture. You ever have authentic Mexican food?"

She shook her head, shy suddenly. "No."

"You try it once and you'll never go back to that dump Taco House."

How she could consume the crap Taco House called food was beyond me. One bite from one of my mom's famous al-bóndigas and Regan would be in love with authentic Mexi-can food.

Regan stared at me, seeming thoughtful. The next sec-ond, she was looking elsewhere, like she was hiding a blush. "Maybe someday I'll try the real thing."

At least there was hope for her.

"If you could have a superpower, what would it be?" she read from the list.

"Invisibility," I answered, thinking of the past summer, school year—my *entire* life. If I could, I would be invisible all the time at home due to the mess I'd made.

"Why?"

"No reason."

She squinted, probably thinking my reasoning was some-thing perverted.

I gave in and confessed, "Sometimes when life sucks, you just want to be invisible, so no one can see you, or even think of you. The power could come in handy."

Regan seemed to get it. She reached out and placed her hand on mine. When our eyes met, there was a level of un-derstanding in hers that let me know there was more to her than what showed on the surface. We shared a smile as she said, "Yeah, I know exactly what you mean."

Regan

Troy was at it again after school. He was all over me as we sat in his car in the parking lot of the community center. Well, *sat* wasn't the correct term; he was leaning over me as I was practically lying down on the passenger seat in an uncomfortable position. The radio was on, a suggestive song that seemed to imitate his intentions. It was 3:55 p.m., and I would be late if he didn't stop messing around.

"Troy, come on, I've gotta get inside." I sat up and straightened my clothes, then pulled down the mirror flap and fixed my hair as well.

Troy groaned and faced the steering wheel. "Every time, Rey."

Was he serious?

"Every time? Would you really like to have sex in your car, right here of all places?" He had to be kidding. There was no way I was giving up my virginity in his passenger seat in front of my mother's place of business.

"No," Troy said, annoyance dripping from the single word. "I mean… Just forget it."

I hated arguing, hated frustrating people. He had no clue how bad I wished it were that easy to just give him what he wanted. But the passion wouldn't come. It wasn't in me, for some reason.

Still, he was being rude.

"Quit whining, I'm going to be late," I told him as I ran my hands through my hair one last time. I could see that he was already beginning to pout.

"*I'm going to be late,*" Troy mimicked as he watched me finish fixing myself.

"Being an ass won't get you anywhere."

"Being a gentleman's gotten me nowhere."

"Troy!" I snapped at his blatant disrespect.

He winced. "Sorry."

Keeping my head down, I attempted to get out of the car, completely over it.

"Shit. Wait." Troy's hand found my arm, causing me to pause.

"Yes?" I asked.

"I got a surprise for you," he said, flashing me his handsome smile. "We gotta celebrate our one year."

It was sweet that he wanted to make a big deal of it, but part of me worried about his plans.

"What do you have in mind?" I asked.

"Dinner at House of Solé this weekend. It took forever to get reservations. Maybe some dancing at After Hours when we're done." Troy did a cute little move, making me ease up and grin.

House of Solé was *the* premiere soul food restaurant in the city. It was a family-owned restaurant that served classic soul food dishes and played throwback music from jazz to blues to R&B. My parents boasted about their food all the time.

"Wow." I couldn't hide my surprise. "House of Solé is a big deal."

Troy playfully jabbed my shoulder. "Anything for you. *This*—" he held my hand firmly "—is a big deal."

"Well, of course then." To show my appreciation, I came back over and gave him a hug and kiss.

I almost squealed when I felt his greedy hand squeeze my butt.

Quickly, I pushed against his chest and fled from the car, issuing a quick goodbye.

It wasn't until I was out of the car and away from him that I could finally relax. The cool air against my skin and the smell of the nearby flowers cleared my senses and psyche, and all was well.

Except…one look around, and I saw him.

Guillermo was in the yard in front of me, glancing my way and then at Troy's car. He'd been changing the nearest trash can's bag, and there was no doubt he'd seen the whole show.

Embarrassed, I ducked my head and rushed to get inside, pretending not to hear him call my name.

In the lobby, I stopped and closed my eyes. I told myself that the anniversary date would go fine. Maybe after eating and dancing, Troy would be too tired to try anything.

Hopefully.

A hand came down on my shoulder, and I shrieked as my eyes flew open.

Guillermo took a step back. "Sorry." He held up something in his hand. "You, uh, dropped this."

Relief spread through me. It was him.

In his hand was a folder of mine; I recognized the glittery red color I used for my math assignments. I made myself loosen up, slowly unwinding from the emotional aftermath of being with Troy. I allowed myself to breathe, basking in the warmth that radiated from Guillermo.

"Sorry, I'm just out of it, I guess." I took the folder and examined it, focusing hard on the glitter texture instead of Guillermo's gaze lingering on me.

"You okay?"

I ran a finger over the glossy folder. "Uh-huh."

Finally, Guillermo glanced outside. "I better get back to work."

He turned to go. Because he'd done something nice for me, I stopped him.

"Guillermo," I spoke up. "Thanks for returning this. God knows trig is hard enough, I don't know what I'd do without my notes."

Guillermo studied the folder I was clutching. "I sorta get trig. If you ever…" He stopped himself, shaking his head.

For once, he wasn't pulling away. Wasn't putting space between us. Wasn't making me feel wrong.

I stood taller, smiling at him. He was about to offer to help me out in math, and because I wanted to pass the course, I wouldn't let the chance slip away.

"I'd like that," I said. "The next time I'm stressing, I'll look for you."

Guillermo simply bobbed his head.

I wanted to say something more, to let him know that things were okay. I couldn't explain it, but a part of me wanted to be nice to Guillermo, beyond the fact that that was the human thing to do. Maybe it was the way he seemed to move so cautiously. He acted as though being near me was a crime, and I saw no issue with us being friendly.

Earlier, I'd seen him having lunch with Avery and Jenaya Omar. My younger brother was kind of a loner, so the sight had been a surprise, prompting me to say hi and make sure things were okay. I also didn't know Jenaya well—she was in my class, and she'd gotten a nasty reputation back in middle school that hadn't let up yet. Most people left her alone; she was tough because of her rep, often shooting people a cut-throat look that would have anyone shaking in their boots.

There was an icky part of me that was jealous Avery was the one Guillermo was comfortable enough to sit with, to talk to longer than a minute without looking over his shoulder. Avery *and* Jenaya.

At least he was making friends.

"Ahem."

My mother entered the lobby, glancing from Guillermo to me. "Guillermo, your tasks aren't going to complete themselves."

"He was only returning my folder, Mom," I said, waving it for emphasis. "It's my fault."

My mother didn't soften. "Get clocked in, you have work to do also."

Guillermo returned to changing trash cans, and I walked with my mom to the time clock.

"I want you to be very careful, Rey," she told me as she watched me punch in my number.

"He was just helping me." I faced her, unsure what she was getting at.

"Guillermo has a lot to focus on in his new world."

"And he can't have friends?" She'd never hovered before whenever I was friendly with one of the probationers. What made Guillermo any different?

My mother released a breath through her nose, practicing patience before responding. This was work for her, and she took her program seriously.

Finally, she asked, "How's Troy?"

Her question brought me back to his plans for the weekend. "Things are good." I focused my attention on my folder again. "He actually asked me to dinner this weekend for our anniversary, at House of Solé."

Instantly my mother brightened up. "Oh that's wonderful, baby. You're going to love it. The food is delicious." She came close, kissing my cheek. "Don't forget to tell your dad later."

She disappeared down a long corridor, leaving me be.

At the front desk, in the assorted filing system set up for each individual volunteer, I found my name and the day's tasks. I was on playground duty once again.

Sighing, I shifted my gaze across the room out the front windows.

Guillermo was in the yard, working with precision as he collected scattered trash.

I already had so much on my plate, and yet I was curious. My mother, being in charge and all, knew his situation, and I couldn't help but wonder what he'd done to have her shooing us apart every time she caught us together.

The more I observed, the more I could discern that, whatever it was he'd done, it had left him troubled and broken.

Everyone deserved a shot at redemption. I hoped Guillermo knew that, too.

Someone had to make sure he did, to show him it was true, and for some reason, I wanted to be the one.

Guillermo

Once a month, Tuesday meant one thing: therapy. I'd completed my anger management course over the summer in detention, but had to keep seeing a counselor for my rehabilitation.

Dr. Hart was okay enough. From our very first meeting, she'd showed no sympathy regarding my punishment. She didn't believe in violence whatsoever. I guess that left me a monster fit for her changing.

I attempted to go with it. At home, I was persona non grata; what more could I lose?

"Afternoon, Guillermo," Dr. Hart greeted me as I sat across from her in her office in a lush skyscraper in downtown Akron. The room was very white, from the couch I sat on, to Dr. Hart's chair, to the rug under the glass coffee table between us, to the bookcases lining the walls, and even to the walls themselves. It was all hyper clean, making me feel like a dirty little stain. "How's everything?"

"Everything's pretty much the same," I told her.

Dr. Hart frowned. She was never satisfied with simple answers. If it took our whole forty-five minutes, she would dig a proper response out of me before letting me walk out the door.

"Things still pretty awful at home?" she asked.

"Yup. I overhead my dad telling my mom I've always been this way. La semilla mala. He's got no faith."

Dr. Hart seemed to understand. "I said it in the beginning, and I'll say it again, this is going to be a long road you walk toward redemption. After all, this wasn't your first offense."

No, it wasn't.

"Let's talk about that goal I assigned you. How are things at your new school? Are you making any new friends?"

I thought about the question. Earlier that day at lunch, I'd eaten with Jenaya again. This time there was no protest, even when I'd sat by her in our shared classes.

During lunch, while Avery was still in line, Jenaya had taken one look at me and shaken her head. "I wouldn't if I were you."

"Wouldn't what?"

She gestured with her head toward the athletes' tables. "Regan London is off-limits."

Briefly, I glanced at our topic of conversation. Troy had his arm across the back of Regan's chair as he sat talking to a guy across from him. Regan seemed to be trying to keep up with their chatter as she sat with her chin resting on her fist and a slightly bored look on her face.

She'd looked bored that first day I'd noticed them sitting together, too. I wondered how she even fit into Troy's world.

"She's got a boyfriend, I noticed," I said as I brought my attention back to Jenaya.

"Uh-huh, and he's top dog around here. And even if she wasn't dating Mr. All-American, it'd still be a no. I used to hear guys complain all the time about asking her out and her turning them down due to her strict dad or whatever. So outside of Troy, Regan London is untouchable," Jenaya continued. "I just thought I should warn you, since you're already on probation."

"Thanks for the heads-up," I said.

Later, when I'd gone home to drop off my school stuff, I bumped into Raviv and his girlfriend.

"What are you about to get into?" Raviv had asked.

I was about to get into my Charger, which wasn't what he meant, but I couldn't miss how eager he seemed, giving me an idea of what he was building up to.

At his side, Camila stared at me with a look in her eye that caused me to focus more on Raviv. I suspected she was trouble, but until I got a good feel for Raviv, I would keep my thoughts to myself.

"I've got an appointment I'm due at," I said.

Raviv wasn't put off. "What about this weekend? I gotta see you on that field, just once."

This kid literally lived and breathed soccer. "I'll check my schedule."

He pretended to be exasperated. "Geez, this guy. What, do you already have plans? I saw you with Jenaya at lunch." The suggestive wiggle of his eyebrows made me defensive.

"It's just lunch," I told him.

"Be careful," Raviv went on. "People say she has a little… mileage."

His words irked me, although he hadn't been the only person to warn me about Jenaya. First it was Avery, and then during lunch a few guys had been looking our way and snickering. When I caught them in the hall and questioned them, they made mention of Jenaya being "a good time."

From what I knew, the girl was straight. I thought it was typical high school bullshit. At my old school, there'd been a few assholes who spread rumors on a girl or two because they couldn't get laid, or because they had.

Even if I were still figuring things out, I wasn't going to judge Jenaya.

I didn't want anyone judging me.

Remembering that exchange brought me back to my session with Dr. Hart.

"Things are moving along," I decided to say. "I think I'm making a few decent friends."

During our third period class, Jenaya had mentioned being a fan of a rapper I liked, and I knew I'd found a friend. Jenaya was super into hip-hop like I was, Avery seemed like a nice and quiet kid, and Raviv was still pending.

The one thing that truly mattered was that none of them were anything like my friends back home.

Dr. Hart made a note on her writing pad. "And girls?"

I kept any expression from registering on my face. "I think I've got a lot of things to work on before I attempt to see anyone."

This pleased her. "Good. Now, since you've been back in the States, have you had any contact with your old friends?"

Her question sent me back to six months prior, when I was with Tynesha, messing around in my bed as we skipped school while my father was away at work and my mother was out at the gym or shopping. Things like that had been no big deal, because if I wasn't skipping with Tynesha, I'd be skipping school with my friends. And her boyfriend.

I came back to now.

"Those bridges were burned a long time ago." Outside

of Tynesha and Shad, I'd left the others behind because they weren't good company to begin with.

I must've been saying all the right things, because Dr. Hart appeared very pleased.

"Guillermo, I must say, I have high hopes for you in this new move," she said. "It's good to see you're willing to leave the past behind and make new friends."

I nodded, hoping she was right. There was a lot at stake, and a lot for me to work on. With myself, with my family, and maybe even my new peers. The kids at Arlington seemed decent, but I wondered how much of myself I could share, how deeply I could let them in.

When it came to the Situation, I wasn't sure I wanted to tell anyone. I already saw the way my parents looked at me; I didn't need to stomach seeing the judgment in these new people's eyes.

When it came to girls, I could reflect only on my time with Tynesha in terms of being serious. Could I ever trust again? *No.*

I squeezed the armrest on the couch, telling myself it wasn't all on her. I'd played a part in my downfall as well.

Still, deep in my chest, my heart was heavy and cold.

"Now, how are you feeling about community service? What's that like?" Dr. Hart went on. "Have you been showing up on schedule?"

"Yes, I don't want to piss off anyone else."

Dr. Hart looked quizzical. "What's your supervisor like?"

I pictured Mrs. London and how steadfast she was, how businesslike and intimidating. "Serious."

"You get along?"

I thought back to our first day. "She's tough, but she's nice. She told me I'm not a monster."

"Do you think you are? What's the color of your self-esteem?"

My throat tightened. This conversation was making me think too much, feel too much, things I didn't like doing. I swept a hand through my hair, my eyes on the carpet as I gave a lazy shrug. "It's black. A cold and dark place."

Dr. Hart heaved a sigh, tapping her pencil on the notepad. "Maybe what you and your family need is a formal apology to start off this new beginning."

I had apologized, didn't seem like enough. "Sure."

"You need to mean it this time, show them that you are serious about changing your behavior. Before, you engaged in a cycle of saying sorry and then going out and finding the next thing to get into. This time, repent. Do you know what that means?"

"To feel bad?"

Dr. Hart shook her head. "To turn away from the old and to change one's course into something better. This time when you apologize, repent, *mean* it."

Maybe she was right. "Okay."

"Guillermo, I'm going to give you another assignment, another goal. Be. Happy. Forgive yourself for your past indiscretions and just be happy. We all deserve happiness, believe it or not."

Be happy.

I wondered, after everything, if that were possible.

Regan

"He's so fine," Malika was saying as she sank down into the sofa in her TV room Tuesday after school. She was talking about Guillermo, or really, she was *still* talking about Guillermo. She had first mentioned how attractive he was as soon as first period let out, and now here she was starting up again. "I can't believe *that's* your neighbor."

But really, I had to agree, because Guillermo was gorgeous. It was only a matter of time before some girl came along and cuffed him. A boy that cute would not be single for long at Arlington High.

Malika was babysitting her one-year-old cousin, a curious baby boy named Davion who needed constant attention from Malika. As she finally laid him down in his playpen beside the sofa for a nap, I was relieved for the break.

"Yeah," I said, trying not to make a big deal out of it. I thought of Troy and our issues; this could be a good time to get some advice. "But anyway, maybe you can help me with something."

"What's wrong?"

"Nothing, really, it's just that Troy wants—"

"Sex," Malika said, finishing for me like a clairvoyant, as she often did. "Of course he does, he's a boy."

"I'm just confused. He's trying to be patient, but I can tell he really wants it and he's getting a little frustrated." Or maybe a *lot* frustrated.

"Why are you confused? You love him, your parents love him—everybody loves him. You've got the butterflies and fairy tale, what's holding you back?"

"I do love him, but there's never been any butterflies."

Malika made a face, her eyebrows knitting together in a frown. "What do you mean?"

"He was always just..." *Troy Jordan.* I'd never chased after him or felt weak at the knees at the sight of him. I was flattered he was paying attention to me in the beginning, but to be honest, we weren't a thing until my father found out. When it came to Troy, a prominent member of the sports section of the local paper, my father all but pushed us down the aisle.

"So no butterflies?" Malika asked.

I shook my head. "No, but it's not that big of a deal, right?"

She sat back, like she was mulling it over. "You should wait until you're ready. You deserve to feel butterflies, so maybe you should think about this. If this thing with Troy is what you really want or not. On the surface, he seems like a pretty decent guy, but dig deeper."

"Yeah," I said, "he's amazing."

"You don't even sound convinced, Rey." Malika chuckled. "As your best friend, I gotta ask, have you guys done anything...*spicy*? You know, beyond kissing, under the clothes, et cetera, et cetera?"

I cringed. "Malika."

"I'll take that as a no."

"He almost showed me once, but I freaked out. I don't know, I guess I'm just afraid I'll be awful, or I won't like it."

"The first time's different for everyone, and if Troy is such a great guy, he'll help you and make sure you're comfortable so you can enjoy yourself and trust yourself. Guys can be selfish assholes, some only look out for themselves, and that's the type you wanna steer away from. You don't want a *situation* like I got."

Right. Calvin. "How are things with him?"

Malika lifted and dropped her shoulder, then went and gathered her phone. "We're talking, nothing serious or anything yet. This is his probation period with me." She sneaked me a look. "Maybe that's what Troy needs to be on if he keeps buggin' you."

Maybe.

"Yeah, but at least Troy's trying to be romantic. Hopefully the date goes well," I said.

"It better."

"I just hope…" I paused, trying not to put my fears into the universe. I just hoped my boyfriend kept it to dinner and dancing, not anything else. "To have a good time at After Hours."

"Shoot, I need to go, too. I ain't been in a minute."

"Maybe Guillermo will be there," I joked.

Once more Malika was all heart-eyes over the mention of the new boy. She lifted a brow, like she'd got a mischievous idea in her head. "Maybe he will be."

"But then, how do we know if he's single or not?"

Malika was silent as she scrolled through her phone. Then slowly, a Cheshire cat smile spread across her face, and she turned her phone around to me. She'd pulled up Guillermo's social media page. A few images of him were on display.

"Malika!" I don't know why I was embarrassed, as if he could somehow see us spying.

She waved me off. "Girl, stop. Ask and you shall receive. From the looks of his page, he hasn't posted in months, but he is in fact single. Lemme add him." She continued to search through his profile, her eyes lit with intrigue. "Plus," she went on, "he seems to be hanging around Jenaya, too, at school."

I didn't care if the rumors about her were true or not, but I did know one thing—Jenaya was tough. A toughness I envied, because if I had her strength, I bet speaking up to Troy, and my dad about accounting, would be a breeze.

"Do you think he's into her?" Nobody else ever approached Jenaya, and yet Guillermo had done so fearlessly. The boy barely looked at me in the classes we shared together, chemistry and English, but when it came to his lunch period with Jenaya or the times I'd caught them in the hall, he was smiling away.

Malika gave a careless shrug. "Who knows. They'd make a cute couple, though."

Looks-wise, I guess… Malika was right. Given their tough demeanors, I could see it.

I abandoned that thought, deciding it was simply nice that Guillermo was making friends.

Malika reached out, grabbing a jar of banana baby food from the coffee table in front of us. She caught me side-eyeing her, and shrugged. "What?"

"Please tell me you're not stealing that boy's food."

Malika appeared innocent. "Listen, my aunt knows to get him the other fruits by now. This is for me."

"Malika." I shook my head, watching in fascination as she

spooned up some of the banana-flavored mush and commenced to enjoy it.

Davion stood up in his playpen suddenly, his big eyes focusing on me.

Malika noticed and softened up. "Aww, I think he likes you. Wanna hold him?"

"Yeah, sure," I said, curious.

Malika gathered Davion from his playpen and carefully handed him to me. He was far from that all-too-fragile stage, able to stand on his own and hold his head up, so I wasn't completely hopeless as I cuddled him on my lap. He looked up at me, studying me, and soon he was reaching his little hand out to clutch a chunk of my hair. Thankfully, he didn't yank on it.

"I love babies," Malika gushed as she watched me with her cousin. "They're just too cute for words, man."

She was right, Davion was adorable. He smelled clean, like that baby wash sticking out of his diaper bag.

I wondered, then, could this be my thing? After volunteering at the center for almost two years, watching the kids at the playground, one could almost say I was a seasoned pro.

But babies were different.

The Briar Park Community Center didn't watch infants or toddlers, just the grade school kids from kindergarten and up. Unlike Malika, I didn't have any experience with babies. I was going to take health my second semester, and I knew the teacher, Mrs. Emerald, at one point had a baby project where kids took robot babies home for a day or for the weekend. Kids were able to partner up or do it solo, naming their babies and even signing a birth certificate. The project sounded like fun, although I'd overheard tons of kids complain about the realistic crying keeping them up at night.

Davion wasn't so bad, he was—

"WAAAH!" Davion let out the loudest cry. One minute he was just sitting there in my lap, fine as could be, and the next, his face was wet with tears as he screamed. His toffee-brown cheeks turned red as his mouth stretched wide-open, wailing.

"What's wrong?" I asked, panicking as I tried to adjust how I was holding him.

Malika didn't freak out. She simply accepted him back. "He's probably just cranky."

His baby teeth were on full display, as he cried on and on, the sound threatening to end my hearing for good.

"Can't you give him something to make him stop?" I asked desperately.

Malika wasn't fazed by the crying. "Doesn't work that way. He'll stop on his own, they usually tire themselves out."

Okay. One thing was clear. I might be all right with the kids at the center, but I had no affinity for babies.

"He could be hungry," Malika mentioned. "Hand me his bottle."

I found his bottle on the table in the next room and quickly came and handed it to Malika. She gave it to the shrieking baby, who stopped instantly. With the bottle in his hand, his dark eyes were on Malika, and then me. Was that it? Was that all he wanted?

Nope.

In seconds, the bottle was on the ground, the lid not having been screwed on tight. Milk spilled all over the hardwood floor.

Davion began screaming once more.

No. I wasn't cut out for this career path either.

Messes were not my thing.

Guillermo

I felt humbled as I pushed around a mop and bucket at Briar Park Community Center. It was a stressful task; every so often someone would walk through my clean floor and leave tracks, and I'd have to start over again.

I'd worked my way down from the third floor to the lobby area, so I was almost done.

One thing I was quickly learning through my stint in community service was that I hated picking up after people. There wasn't a day I came in to work that I didn't find the staff breakroom a mess. I had a newfound appreciation for anyone who worked in the cleaning field. After these six months were up, I was never again taking a job where maintenance was a requirement. From the kids to the adults, these people were messy, lazily leaving wrappers and trash wherever they saw fit, as if a walk to the trash can would kill them.

Pinche flojos.

"Slow down!" a voice yelled.

I looked up to see a couple young girls running through

the automatic doors across the lobby and around the corner. Chances were, they were going to one of the kids' camps that ran on Wednesdays.

Did I mention it was raining?

My gaze fell on their muddy shoe prints, and I sighed.

Mrs. London had mentioned an extra supply of rugs in storage in a back room somewhere. I made a mental note to go grab them after cleaning up the mud.

The automatic doors opened again. This time Jenaya graced the entrance. By the scowl marring her face, I guessed the two girls who'd run into the building were with her.

"Shania! Khadija!" Her yelling was futile; both girls were long gone.

Jenaya shook her head, then paused on the only rug at the entrance when she saw me. Embarrassment seemed to seize her, and she recoiled a little.

From the moment we met, there'd been a sense of understanding between us. Her with her rep, and me with my own shit. She didn't need to be embarrassed. The only person who should be embarrassed was me. *I* was the one who had to clean up after the girls.

Still, I lifted my hand to wave. "What's up?"

Jenaya rubbed her arm, fidgeting. "Hey." She looked at the tracks the two girls had left. "I'm sorry. I'll clean this up."

"I got it."

Jenaya inched toward me. "Please, it's no problem," she insisted.

She *was* embarrassed.

"I'll get in trouble if I let someone else do my work, so trust me, I got this. It's not an issue." To lighten the mood, I flashed her a smile. "It's been happening all day."

Finally, she exhaled. "I guess you really are on probation, huh?" Jenaya took in my uniform shirt and my work tools.

I examined my mop. "Yep." I looked up at her. "I got a break in ten minutes, wanna chill in the rec room?"

I'd had my eye on the pool table from the moment I first saw it. I didn't do sports, but I was damn good at pool.

Jenaya appeared thoughtful. "Why?"

"Why what?"

Jenaya looked around before refocusing on me. "First you hang out with me at school, and now here? Why?"

If I didn't know any better, I'd say she looked suspicious. "Can't I just want to be friends?"

"No, you can't," she responded.

Her guard was up again, and I didn't know why. Her sisters had just tracked mud into the building, not dog shit or something worse. "What's your problem?"

"Why do you care so much?" Jenaya snapped. Her defenses were up as she edged back toward the door.

I spread my arms, not sure why myself. "I just do, okay? You looked like you needed a friend."

She narrowed her eyes. "I'm not a fucking charity case!"

"I didn't say you were," I insisted.

"You don't have to—I can see it on your face. You think you know me, just like everyone else, but you feel sorry for me, and I'm telling you not to."

She didn't hear me out, just walked out of the center with her head held high, like she always did.

"Shit!" I threw my mop to the ground.

I didn't feel sorry for her. I genuinely liked her, shitty rep and all.

I sighed, then collected the mop and finished up the floor, my arms aching the whole way through. When the lobby was spotless, I placed the Wet Floor signs down and laid out the extra rugs near the other entrances.

Ten minutes later I took my break in the empty rec room. There was a stereo system set up where you could sync your phone via Bluetooth. I set mine up and soon was immersed in the sounds of J. Cole.

I sat back against the sofa, closing my eyes and trying to let the tension go. My mind had other plans, stuck on Jenaya, stuck on the hurt and anger on her face.

A knock on the door caused me to open my eyes and sit up. Jenaya stood in the doorway, nervously playing with her hands. My guard went up, cautious for round two.

"The boy at the front desk said you were back here," she explained as she came into the room. "I…I was kind of mean, I mean, I *was* mean. You've been nothing but nice to me, and I guess I'm a little skeptical."

"I *don't* know you," I acknowledged. "But I want to. I don't know what made me sit with you that day, but I don't care either. We like the same music and we get along. I don't need a huge reason."

Jenaya sighed as she came and sat down on the couch, folding her arms across her chest. "It's not you, it's just…*every*-thing. I'm not even supposed to be watching my sisters, but my grandma offered for me to look after them without even asking me."

I could see she needed to vent, so I kept quiet and let her tell as little or as much as she wanted. "I'm listenin'."

Jenaya faced me. "I got a lot of shit, Mo."

She'd taken to calling me *Mo* immediately when I told her my nickname. She'd told me people called her *Naya* for short.

I liked her full name. *Jen-nai-yah.*

I gestured to myself. "Not trying to have a contest with

you, but I'm on probation, remember?" I looked away. "My family hates me, so I get what it's like to have shit at home and at school."

My revelation loosened her up. "The school stuff is just bullshit. People have been calling me out of my name since middle school. I don't even care anymore, they don't got the balls to say it to my face."

I liked her strength. She was right, I could tell no one would challenge her face-to-face. I didn't have to know her well to discern she could hold her own.

"And home?" I wanted to know.

"Your folks really hate you?" Jenaya asked instead.

Something told me if I admitted my wrongs to Jenaya, she wouldn't judge. I didn't fear scaring her off, unlike… *Regan*.

There was an immediate difference between them the more I thought about it. Regan was shy and raised sheltered, and Jenaya held a story that left her resilient and tough.

"Three strikes should've had me out, but they pulled strings this last time and I'm on probation instead."

Jenaya studied me. "Must've been real bad."

I held out my hands, examining my scarred knuckles. "This last time was an assault charge."

Jenaya peered at my hands. "Was it worth it?"

I was enveloped in the memory of Tynesha screaming and me leaping into action and pounding into Shad's flesh.

Even if the outcome was the same, would I do it all over again?

"Maybe not," I said.

Jenaya was gentle as she ran a finger over a scar. "At least you learned. And you got out."

"Out?"

"Do you live around here in Briar Park, or do you stay up in Briar Pointe?"

"Briar Pointe." The little suburb of wonders.

Jenaya lifted her chin. "That's what I mean. I'd kill to live in a place like that."

"I don't know about all that." Even if my old neighborhood housed temptation, life in Briar Pointe didn't seem so appealing.

"Why?"

"I feel trapped." I leaned over and wrung my hands together. "This place just makes me feel boxed in, it's too much. Like I'm some defect that doesn't belong."

Jenaya placed her hand on mine. "Don't deny yourself a better shot because you messed up in the past. Your place is safer than my neighborhood. See, there's the right side of Brown Street, and then there's the houses and neighborhoods on the left side. I stay on Lovers Lane, and trust me, it goes down on the Lane. My neighbor's dog just got shot the other day for no reason."

Shit.

The Briar Park Community Center was located farther down Brown Street, near downtown. A ten-minute drive from home or five from the school, give or take the traffic. I drove by Lovers Lane on the way to the center, noting the businesses with graffiti sprayed on the side, the loiterers by the gas station, the abandoned Rite Aid, and all the trash. That's what I couldn't keep my eyes off, the litter. Litter like I was assigned to pick up around the center.

Jenaya sat back and frowned. "If anyone's defective, it's me. I'm the oldest of five girls and a little boy." She picked at the couch cushion absentmindedly, a touch of grief on her face. "It was bad, Guillermo, real bad."

I squeezed her knee in support. "How bad?"

For once there wasn't a look of resilience in her hazel eyes. "We lived in this house my nonna helped my mom get."

"Nonna?" I repeated.

She softened up, if only a little. "My mom had us young, and my grandma refuses to be called 'Grandma,' so she demands we call her 'Nonna' instead. She says *granny* sounds too old, *nana*, too. Clearly—" she gestured to her golden-brown skin "—we're not Italian, but she likes the sound of 'nonna' better."

"It's different, but I get it," I said.

Jenaya went on. "Anyway, the house was nice at first, until it wasn't. The place became a wreck. My sisters, they bad, and I wasn't any better I guess, but that house was trashed 'cause of them. They wrote all over the walls, broke windows and mirrors, too. My mom was never around to discipline us, hardly any structure was set, let alone someone to tuck us in."

Her situation had been far worse than I imagined. No wonder she considered me lucky.

"So one day I kindly insisted that my nonna take me in. I was tired of my mom not coming home for like two days, or until five in the morning at the earliest. My mom would rather be out messing with men than at home being a mom. My nonna mostly picks up the slack, and I'm tired of it. A lot of girls, they can go home to their moms and cry on their shoulders about being picked on, but I've never had anyone. My nonna takes care of me now, but she's not exactly the nurturing type either.

"I try to look out for my little sisters the best I can, but in some ways the damage seems done. My sister that's a year younger than me, Nakaia, she don't listen, and her influence has our sister Ayana acting up, too. I don't want my sisters

growing up and being like our mom, having babies with
dudes who won't stick around. We deserve better."

It was good that she got out but still went back to check
on her younger sisters. "I definitely feel you there. I've got
Yesenia, and I don't play when it comes to guys." I wasn't the
best example, but I knew there were guys out there worse
than me, and I'd gladly catch another charge if some pendejo
ever tried to play my sister. At thirteen, Yesenia kept her head
in books and didn't worry about guys yet, but I still cared
enough to be watchful.

Jenaya chuckled. "You seem like the type of guy that would
go crazy over your little sister."

I didn't deny it. "The worst mistake any guy could make
right now is talking to Yesi."

"I don't blame you."

I focused back on Jenaya. "I still don't get it. Why all the
hate on you at school, though?"

Jenaya frowned. "Oh that. Back in middle school, there
was this guy all the girls liked, and for some reason, he liked
me—or, I thought he did. We messed around, and the next
thing I know he's telling the whole school about what we did
and it's been over for me ever since."

In my lap, I felt my fist shake. Shit like that was unfair and
uncalled for. From home to school, she wasn't protected it
seemed, and it wasn't *fair*.

Jenaya wasn't even seventeen yet. With her tough home
life, school was the last place she needed more stress. It was a
lot for her to take on by herself.

I held my hand out. "I got your back, okay?"

She looked at my hand and began to smile a little. "You
don't gotta do that, Guillermo."

"I want to." Maybe it was my Achilles' heel, taking up for

girls in need, but I didn't like the idea of people picking on her over bullshit gossip.

I continued holding my hand out. "Friends?" To be corny, I smiled.

Jenaya laughed and slapped her palm against mine. "Friends."

I had about fifteen minutes left of my break. I stood up. "Cool, wanna play some pool?"

Jenaya stood as well. "Nah, I got a nail appointment. Nakaia should be swinging by to get the girls in an hour. Sorry in advance if they get in any trouble."

Her sisters and her life weren't a burden for me, and hopefully in time, I could show her that. "We should hang out more. What do you do for fun besides read?"

Jenaya perked up. "Actually, I've been thinking about starting my own YouTube channel. I'm in cosmetology, but I want to do videos beyond hair, maybe nails and makeup, too."

I wrinkled my nose. "On second thought, I'll just see you at school."

Jenaya shoved me for that.

I laughed, catching her wrist, and reveled when she allowed me to give her a hug. There wasn't much I could do, but I wanted to show I cared, and I appreciated her telling me her secrets.

I wasn't too sure about other things when it came to this new move, but I was sure about Jenaya.

It felt good to have a friend.

My parents were both home from work when I got in. The tension hadn't eased one bit since our move, and even if my word wasn't much, I wanted to speak up.

I hovered in the kitchen doorway. My mother was at the

stove, stirring something in a pot, and my father was at the island chopping peppers.

To make this place feel like home, my mother had started adding pieces of our old life. Throughout the house, she'd hung decorative words on the walls. Against one of the peach-shaded walls in the kitchen, she'd hung up Create; in our dining room, she hung up Eat; in the living room against the wall behind the sofa, she hung a sign that said Family; and in our TV room, she hung up Love. Cheesy, but the message wasn't missed. Her efforts to always provoke a sense of love were what made me *love* her the most.

This life they provided for us... I'd taken for granted.

Before, my father had managed to take care of all of us as a dentist. My mother stayed home while I was in middle school, enjoying the task of keeping our house together and going to the gym every morning. After my ordeal, she went back to work, taking an HR job at my father's clinic. My father hadn't liked that, saying that while my troubles had been expensive, he could still afford the lifestyle we were used to. My mother hadn't been satisfied and wanted to pitch in, to have money for a rainy day—should I ever fuck up again and they need it.

Thinking of my talk with Jenaya, I finally saw how good I had it. When I was facing time, my parents saw to it that I had a good lawyer instead of leavin' it in the hands of a shitty public defender. Even outside of the Situation, they'd always been good to me and Yesenia. They went above and beyond for us whenever we asked for or needed anything, they drove us around when needed, and my father had even negotiated with my tío Mateo to give me his old Charger. I stuck my nose in the streets, knowing there was nothing to find there, and time and time again, my parents were forgiving with me.

Unlike some parents, mine really gave a shit about me. I'd

made it hard for them, and there was no way I could ever truly pay them back for their pain and suffering.

"¿Qué quieres?" My father looked up from his peppers. His tone wasn't very inviting.

I wondered if there'd come a day when he didn't treat me like I was in the way, like he was merely tolerating me. I knew they both still loved me despite my faults; I was their son... but the warmth was gone.

Sweeping a hand through my hair, I hung my head. "Can we talk?"

"What about?" My father made a show of setting down his knife, as if this interruption was exasperating.

"José," my mother cut in, shooting him a stern look. "Ay, let him talk."

My father heaved a heavy sigh and gave me the floor.

I cleared my throat. "I know I've messed up too many times in the past to count, but I mean it when I say from the bottom of my heart that I'm sorry. You guys did a lot for me, gettin' that lawyer so I wouldn't be stuck in juvie. You work your asses off to provide for me and Yesenia, when some parents don't even give a shit. I took for granted how good my life is with you guys when I was out bein' reckless, and I see that now. Lo siento de verdad."

My mother looked touched, while my father stood silent.

"We've been down this road a lot with you," he finally spoke. He pointed at my mother. "She's cried rivers for you, and I cannot take any more of that. Mírame," he instructed, telling me to look him in the eye, "if you fuck this up, I'm done with you. I mean it, you wanna be out acting a fool, chasing tail, fighting over nonsense, you're out. You can go and stay with Mateo or Lupe."

It sounded harsh, but I understood. "I get it," I told him.

My father settled down, glancing at the meal he was preparing. "Lávate las manos." He said nothing further and went back to prepping.

A small sense of anxiety lifted from my shoulders, and I went upstairs to wash up for dinner.

Yesenia was peeking out of her room, her silver laptop abandoned on her yellow bedspread. She probably heard the whole conversation.

She didn't hide it. She came and hugged me extra tight. "I'm glad you guys talked, Memo. Please be good here, and don't mess up again."

"I won't," I promised as I held her.

For the first time in a long time, I actually had faith that things were on the way up.

Regan

Tanner was standing on his hind legs, sticking his nose through my blinds and whimpering. He must've needed to do his business. Whatever the reason, I could use a break from my math homework. Not that much was getting done when my mind kept drifting over possible outfits to wear Friday night.

I grabbed a leash to take Tanner for a walk. Anything to get out of the house.

I honestly believed my parents—especially my father—were more excited than I was about the impending date. You would've thought Troy had asked him out with the way my father was acting all proud.

"Hey," my father greeted me as he entered the room from the kitchen. He eyed me with the leash and Tanner who was wagging his tail beside me. "I was just about to do that before I started dinner."

I fiddled with the leash. "It's okay, I don't mind."

A corner of his lips curled up. "I know what you're doing, you're just trying to be his favorite. You ain't slick, Rey."

I chuckled as I leaned down and hugged Tanner close. "Trying? I am his favorite, right Tanner?"

My father watched as Tanner licked my nose. "Oh, I see how it is, boy. After all that I've done for you?" He pretended to be hurt before returning his attention to me. "I took out some salmon for tonight—what do you think I should pair with it?"

I loved when my father made salmon. I wasn't sure what he did, but he had a magical flare for making us all eat every bite until there were no leftovers. "Ooh, can you do the lemon-garlic asparagus?"

My father snapped his fingers and bobbed his head at the suggestion. "Yeah, I was thinking of seasoning the fish that way, I can do both, and maybe some roasted red skins on the side."

My mouth watered at the thought of all the delicious food. "Ah man, I can't wait now."

Tanner must really have had to go, as he was quick to walk over to the front door and paw at it.

"Here I come," I told him as I pulled my hoodie on.

"Thank you, Rey," my father said to me as he went back to the kitchen.

Tanner dragged me out the front door.

"Slow down, boy," I said.

Tanner was already sniffing around, and I was quick to check my pocket for a blue bag in case he did more than just pee.

"Regan! Wait!" a high voice called from across the street, and I looked up to find Yesenia Lozano coming my way, holding a book.

I'd officially met Yesenia Tuesday afternoon when I'd gotten in from school and then taken Tanner outside. Her mother had just picked her up from the local middle school, and Yesenia had all but abandoned her once she set eyes on Tanner. Yesenia was more upbeat than Guillermo. She was all smiles and super friendly as opposed to her brother's brooding demeanor. She'd been outgoing as she introduced herself and asked to pet Tanner. There was something cute and adorable about her that I'd liked instantly.

"Can I help?" Yesenia already had her gaze on Tanner's leash, and I couldn't say no to the longing look on her face.

"Sure." I handed the leash over and Yesenia accepted it, kneeling down to pet Tanner, who sniffed her.

"He needs a bath, too," I spoke up. "I was thinking of giving him one this weekend if you want to join me."

You would've thought I'd offered Yesenia the winning lottery ticket with how much she brightened at the chore. Then again, even if it could be a hassle sometimes, washing Tanner was fun. Taking care of him was fun. We'd had a couple dogs while I was growing up, and I was always in charge of bathing them and walking them. I never minded. Taking care of animals was calming.

"I wish we could get a dog." Yesenia sounded sad as she stood.

Nodding sympathetically, I took the book she'd been reading and idly examined it. From the couple on the cover, I assumed it was a teen romance. A purple circular sticker on the spine of the book drew my curiosity.

"What's with the dot?" I asked.

Yesenia glanced at her book. "I color code my books. Blue for books with sad endings, purple for books with bittersweet endings, and yellow for books with happy endings."

"How do you know how they'll end?"

Yesenia blushed. "I've read a lot of books, and I reread

sometimes, too. The blues aren't my favorite, but they're important."

"Sounds like you're a big reader," I said.

Yesenia nodded. "I've been into reading since kindergarten. When I graduate middle school this year, I'm asking for a gift card to Books-A-Million."

Her innocence was cute.

"The best job ever would be to work in books, like a librarian or something," Yesenia went on.

I didn't mind reading. Could that be my thing?

Thinking back on the summer reading I'd had to do for school, sweating over Ernest Hemingway and Arthur Miller, I cringed. I honestly hated the classics; the way they were written, from the language, the style, to the big words, they always lost me. Reflecting on my B average in English, I decided that maybe books were better left for the passionate, like Yesenia.

Mentally I penciled her request down, hoping to have formed enough of a relationship with her by then that I could get her a gift card, too.

She reminded me of Avery. My younger brother was always reading manga. He had a skinny bookcase in his room filled with volumes of the stuff. Avery even had a little Japanese dictionary for reference. His Netflix and Hulu profiles were filled with anime, too. My father thought it was weird.

"Why don't you ask for a puppy?" I suggested.

"I've *been* asking. They always say no." Yesenia shrugged. "Well, maybe now we can get a dog, since my parents aren't so mad at Memo anymore."

Guillermo's troubles must've caused a burden for their family.

I was becoming more and more curious as to what he'd done.

"It must've been hard," I said.

Yesenia didn't answer. She simply hung her head and focused on Tanner.

"I..." She started and then quickly stopped speaking. Instead, she gripped the leash tighter and looked down the sidewalk as wind blew through her long dark hair. Someone somewhere was barbecuing; the smell was delicious and tempting. "I love Memo, he's the best big brother, but he's behaved pretty badly. But, like, even when he was hanging around his old friends back home, he was still good to me. Who he used to be, before he went away, it made everything different at home. They never were in the mood for a puppy."

She seemed to need to vent, so I rubbed her shoulder. "It's okay."

Yesenia looked up at me, her big brown eyes distant for a second. "I must've read about a hundred books back then to avoid the tension between my parents and Guillermo. Even when he was gone at juvie, when my mom and dad were trying to find a new house, things were sad. Like walking through a thick fog after a storm and being unable to breathe.

"Now that's he back, I can tell he's different, he's changed. He used to not care, used to just do whatever he wanted despite our parents grilling him, but now, it's like he's better—he's learned his lesson."

Sensing she needed encouragement, I threw an arm around Yesenia to comfort her. "Well, this is a new beginning, so who knows, maybe you'll end up with a puppy, and Guillermo and your parents will start over."

My words might as well have been silk, enveloping Yesenia in a cozy bliss. She lifted her head to aim a smile my way. "Thanks, Regan."

"No problem. I'm always right across the street if you need me," I let her know.

She nodded. "Things were really bad before, but I think they're about to get better. I'll still come and hang out, though. I promise."

We paused as Tanner found the perfect place to do his thing, and then we made our way peacefully around the block. But inside, my mind was churning. The Lozanos were still growing and healing from whatever they'd gone through with Guillermo. My brain was too hung up on what.

Yesenia had needed someone to vent to. Maybe that was what Guillermo needed, too.

I handed over Yesenia's book and made sure she got inside safe, then brought Tanner back home. But before I went in, I cast a glance behind me, checking out their house. I hoped the grass was greener for them in their new move.

Guillermo

I decided to take Dr. Hart's advice and stop feelin' sorry for myself for one night. To be happy. Things were easing up at home, little by little, but still I felt out of place and jittery.

In truth, I didn't know where I belonged. But tonight, I had a plan to maybe start to find out.

I found my parents were in the kitchen, washing the dinner dishes together while they carried on a hushed conversation that halted at my arrival.

Nervous, I stayed in the doorway, hoping my request wouldn't arouse suspicion. "I wanted to go to the movies with a couple of friends from school tonight."

My mother faced me, evidently not having an issue. "Will you be out late?" She walked by me into the dining room and grabbed her purse. She collected her debit card and passed it to me. "In case you want a snack."

My father remained silent, making me fidget from one foot to the next. "Is it okay if I go?"

He glanced at me, his shoulders rising and falling with his sharp intake of breath. "Go ahead, but be good. I mean it."

So I was still walking a thin line. Perhaps his letting me go out was a test. While going to the movies was a normal thing, it hadn't really interested me before. Typical and boring hadn't been my style back then.

I accepted the challenge, desperate to prove I could be trusted. "I'll be good, I promise."

He said nothing as my mother rejoined him at the sink.

I squared my shoulders and headed out, focused on the house across the street.

It was Thursday night, and Jenaya had mentioned going to the movies during third period. It might take some convincing, but maybe Avery would be on board to come with us.

I crossed the street and knocked on the Londons' front door, hopeful of this endeavor.

After a minute the porch light came on and the door was pulled open, revealing a man I assumed was Mr. London.

He was big, definitely active. Intimidating almost in the manner of Harvey with his bulky arms and tall height, and I'll-break-your-neck demeanor. He was wearing a brown T-shirt with the words I Bleed Brown & Orange. Go Browns! on it.

In his features and face was the man Avery would someday become—of course, you'd have to add a few trips to the gym.

Mr. London gazed at me, looking confused and on guard. "Hello?"

I lifted my hand in a wave as I felt my stomach knot up. "Hi, I live across the street. I go to school with Avery...and Regan." Why did I mention her? "Is Avery home?"

After arching a wary brow, Mr. London leaned back into the house. "Avery!" He waved me inside. "Come on in. What did you say your name was?"

"Guillermo Lozano," I told him as I stepped inside.

Footsteps sounded down the hall and Mrs. London emerged around a corner. One look at me and her expression went on alert. "Guillermo?"

Mr. London clearly saw the recognition on his wife's face. He turned to size me up. "You know him?"

"He's in the Respect program at the center."

Mr. London frowned. "And he's friends with Avery and Regan?"

Mrs. London cleared her throat, her posture tall and firm. "As far as I'm aware, he and Rey have no friendship. Avery is another story."

I didn't bow my head, I didn't look away in shame. I took their disapproval on the chin. "Avery was my guide at school on my first day, and we have lunch together. He seems like a nice kid to become friends with."

Mr. London still looked skeptical, while Mrs. London seemed to be softening, so long as my friendship was with Avery.

"It's good to see you picking your associations wisely," she said.

Finally, Avery came down from the second floor, rescuing me from the interrogation. He buried his hands in his pockets and hitched up his shoulders as he looked from his parents to me. Honestly, I wasn't sure he had other friends. It felt like my arrival was a foreign episode in their home. "Hey, what's up?" he asked.

"Sorry to just drop by. You busy or anything?" I asked.

"Uh, no. You wanna play a video game or something?"

I was never that guy to get caught up in mindless games inside the house. I'd always thought of them as typical, boring. "Not really my thing, but I could try."

"Hey, Guillermo, you like football?" Mr. London cut in.

"The one with your hands or the one with your feet?"

Mr. London blinked before simply walking away. Mrs. London tried to no avail to hide her smile.

"Jenaya was talking about going to the movies tonight, and I was just stoppin' by to see if you wanted to join us," I said to Avery before facing Mrs. London. "If that's okay."

Again, a look of surprise swept her expression. She narrowed her eyes, regarding her son. "Up to you, Avery."

A tiny smile curled the side of his mouth up. "Yeah, just let me go put on my shoes." He was quick to race upstairs.

Mrs. London seemed prouder the longer she studied me. "Normally, I'd be apprehensive, but this is good for him. So do me a favor and don't let me down."

"Yes, ma'am." She was extending faith and trust in me. I felt light on my feet, my insides buzzing with energy, ready to be tested, ready to show I was goin' to do and *be* better.

A series of footsteps came from the stairs, drawing my attention to the sight of Regan and Malika coming down.

Surprise crossed Regan's face, and Malika wasn't far behind as she took me in as well.

"Hey, Guillermo." Malika greeted me first, coming over and appraising me. One thing about her, she wasn't exactly shy, a trait that had me on my toes. I'd gotten a notification from my social media page that she'd followed me, prompting me to follow her back. Her page was loud with her personality, cheerleading at games, going to After Hours with Regan and a bunch of friends, babysitting her cousins or just posting cute selfies.

The moment I'd felt tempted to click on Regan's page after seeing Malika had tagged her in a cute selfie of the two of them, I tossed my phone to the side and distracted myself with homework.

Regan hung back, looking cautious. "What's going on?"

"Movies," I told her, "with Jenaya and Avery."

Malika's eyes were glued to me. "Dang, we should go."

Regan blinked, opening her mouth.

"Aren't you two trying to find something for Rey to wear for her *date* tomorrow?" Mrs. London stepped in.

Regan tucked some hair behind her ear as she came off the last step and walked by me. "Yeah, we just came down to grab something to drink." She turned and locked eyes with me, and something tightened in my throat and down through my chest. But then she focused on her best friend. "Come on, Malika."

Malika shrugged before following Regan down the hall.

Avery rushed back downstairs and joined me by the door, wading obliviously through the tension. He faced his mother, waving goodbye.

"Need any money?" she offered.

"No, I'm still good with my allowance," he said.

"Be good then, and don't be gone too late."

I tipped my head at Mrs. London before following Avery's lead out of the house. We crossed over to my Charger in our driveway and he hopped in the back, already politely leaving room for Jenaya to sit up front.

"Sorry about my dad," he told me as we buckled in.

"What about him?" I turned to make sure the coast was clear and backed out.

Avery fiddled with the hem of his T-shirt, shrinking into the seat. "He's big on football, he could talk you to death if you let him."

Regan and Troy came to mind and I tried not to think about it.

I shrugged. "No big deal, man. My family's into sports, too, boxing and soccer mostly, but either way I'm used to it."

Avery was quiet on the way to Jenaya's house, something I didn't mind as I let the radio play. When I pulled up to the corner of McKinley and Lovers Lane, Jenaya was outside already, waiting on the devil strip.

"Hey!" She was enthusiastic as she quickly jumped shotgun. She leaned over and turned to the back seat. "Hey, Avery!"

We were going to see a movie, and yet Jenaya had gone all out. On her pretty face was a pair of sunglasses with blue lenses, some jeweled stars on one side. Her blue tank top, high waist ripped jeans, and chunky tennis shoes together created a whole look.

I reeled back, taking her all in. "Extra, extra, read all about it."

Jenaya swatted at me. "Stop! I wanna look cute when I go out."

"To a dark theater, huh?" She gave me a mean look that meant business. "Kidding, you *do* look cute by the way."

She settled down and buckled in, satisfied. "I know."

"This better be a good movie or you're banned from choosing until further notice," I warned as I drove us to the nearest theater. "Your top ten is definitely lacking."

We'd spent all of seventh period arguing over our top ten favorite rappers, and Jenaya's list just wasn't up to par.

Jenaya clicked her tongue. "Boy bye. Besides, Mike Epps is mad funny."

"Need I remind you that this is a school night?" Avery spoke up. "I'm with Mo, it better be worth it."

Jenaya wasn't fazed by our threats. Instead she bounced a little in her seat as I continued to drive. Something told me she needed this. Maybe we all did. Together we were an eclectic bunch. Avery was the quiet loner. Jenaya, a girl with a shitty reputation. And then there was me, the delinquent.

Being that it was a Thursday evening, the parking lot wasn't full as I pulled into the lot to Movietown Theater. We'd probably have an entire screening to ourselves.

"Thanks for driving, Mo," Jenaya said as we vacated the car and made our way to the entrance. "I haven't been to the movies in forever."

Yeah, we all needed this.

"The last movie I saw was *Atomic-Man: Origins*," Avery said.

I had to stop and think about the last time I'd been myself. "Yesenia dragged me to some movie based on these angels versus vampires books. She was Team Angel or whatever."

Jenaya chuckled. "I read the first book to that series. Vampires all the way."

Avery and I shared the same frown as we walked up to the ticket booth.

We bought our tickets and went to the concession stand. While the smell of fresh buttery popcorn was tempting, I was going to pass. My father's chicken tinga was still sitting heavy in my stomach.

"I think I'll just get a drink," I let them know. I let others go in front of me as I made up my mind what I was going to order.

"I only had cereal for dinner," Jenaya said. "I want it all."

"You can get it all, too."

I jerked my head toward the new voice. A group of guys was standing nearby, and one had separated from the trio to check out Jenaya. They were our age, or slightly older.

Whatever their age, I didn't like how this guy was looking at her.

He was sporting a red hoodie underneath a denim vest,

paired with a matching red cap and red shoes. He wasn't that big, but his presence was enough to send Jenaya stepping back. The way he was rubbing his hands together, licking his lips, and eyeing Jenaya as if she were edible had my temper rising to a ten.

"Ay, lemme get your number, miss," he spoke, offering a smile.

Jenaya recoiled, shaking her head. "No."

"Aw, don't be like that," he said, not letting up.

"I'm good," she insisted.

"You could be better."

In therapy, they suggested counting to ten when you were close to losing your shit. But I was a hothead, and counting never worked for me.

"What, you shy or somethin'?" he asked further.

One. Two. Three. Four…

He got too close, reaching to gather one of her hands to pull her to him.

Fuck it.

Some guys suffered from entitlement, as if they had a right to say, or worse, touch whoever they saw fit. Not on my watch.

I stepped in front of Jenaya protectively. "She said no."

He laughed in my face. "Who are you?"

"If you want to be able to *chew* that popcorn, I suggest you walk away now."

My comment erased the humor from Denim Vest's face. "Say what?"

I wasn't sure how much longer I could endure this train of conversation before handling it with my fists. Jenaya wasn't interested, and I was doing my best to shoo this fucker away without going there. "You heard me."

He smirked, sizing me up. He gestured to Jenaya. "I know that ain't you. Ain't no way you can handle that."

One, Jenaya wasn't a piece of meat to be *handled*. Two, it wasn't up for debate, and I was quickly losing my patience. My fists were balled and itching for me to swing and end all the talking.

Worse, it was givin' me the sickest feeling of déjà vu, of before, with Shad and Tynesha. Before, I hadn't been able to rein in my temper or anger, and I'd lost control.

Blinking, I tried to focus on the here and now. What were those de-escalation techniques I'd learned in anger management?

"Walk away," I instructed. "Now."

"Or what, you really tryna fight over a thot, my dude?"

My patience snapped like a rubber band that had been stretched too far, and my hands shot out before I could realize what I was even doing. In seconds, I had two fists full of his vest, his body seized closer to me.

Caught off guard, he shook a little.

"Have some respect," I demanded.

"Shit man, get off of me!" he snapped.

My hold tightened, my anger rose, and all I could see was red.

His friends took defensive stances, and it wasn't until they did that I noticed we had an audience. Business was still going on in the background, but more than a few had stopped to see if we'd fight.

"Hey! Is there a problem?" Security stepped up to us, glaring at me and Denim Vest.

I released him forcefully, sending him stumbling back.

With authority present, he backed down. "Nah, we cool, officer. We cool."

He went and joined his friends as they left for their screening room.

The security guard turned on me, his gaze full of judgment, and really, I couldn't blame him. "Look, we don't need your kind coming in here causing trouble."

Jenaya stepped up. "That guy was harassing me, sir."

Doubtful, the guard still focused on me. "Son, if I get any more out of you tonight, I'm calling the police. Do we have an understanding?"

"Yes," I answered, trying my best to level my tone.

He wasn't buying it as he rolled his eyes before walking off.

The atmosphere returned to a steady equilibrium, but I couldn't hack it.

"Hey, we'll meet you inside," Jenaya said to Avery.

She walked me outside into the fresh night air, giving me space as I walked it off.

Tilting my head back, I shut my eyes and practiced squeezing and closing my fists.

One. Two. Three. Four. Five. Six—

"It's okay, Mo," Jenaya insisted. "He was just a dumbass."

"We both know his behavior wasn't acceptable," I said, keeping my tone even so as not to lash out at the wrong person. "When a girl says no, it's not an open invitation for debate. No means no."

Jenaya came to stand in front of me, hugging herself. "I know. I'm just used to taking care of myself. No one looks out for me, and I'm used to guys like that. I used to carry pepper spray until I got scared what would happen if it didn't work."

I needed to hit the gym as soon as possible. There was a lot of steam left inside me, and I couldn't think of a better way to work it off than punching the bag for a few hours. All my anger management lessons and all my attempts to do good, almost lost within the blink of an eye.

My hands were shaking at the thought of losing it all just like that. I couldn't allow myself to backslide. I couldn't.

I glanced at Jenaya, noting that even if she held a hard exterior, she was still pretty soft, fragile inside. "No one's going to harass you while I'm around."

"I noticed." Jenaya was blushing. She wasn't used to having someone have her back, and it was a damn shame.

My probation was on the line, violence couldn't always be the answer, but I wouldn't let some dickhead touch or catcall her in front of me.

I was still learning, still vulnerable when it came to protectin' people, but I hadn't completely lost this battle.

Maybe there was a chance for me. Maybe I hadn't fucked up.

"You good, Lethal Weapon?" Jenaya teased, jabbing my arm.

I furnished a smile, feeling slightly better. "Yeah."

Jenaya came and hooked her arm around mine. "Good, now let's go laugh our asses off, we could use it."

Regan

Friday night came all too soon. It was all my parents could talk about, my mother with her tips on what to eat, and my father with his watchful eye on my and Troy's relationship. After picking out the perfect look with Malika Thursday night, I was all set. Still, I was nervous.

I wanted to have a good time, but I wanted it to simply be a good time.

Please, no sex talk, I pleaded silently as I finished primping in the mirror that night. All I wanted was to celebrate our one year together without any obligations.

That wasn't asking for too much, was it?

"Regan, he's here!" my father called up to me from the landing.

A text came through on my phone from Malika at the same time. My stomach momentarily stopped flip-flopping around, comforted at the sight of my best friend reaching out.

Have fun tonight with the quarterback ☺

All sense of anxiety washed away as I managed a chuckle. She knew Troy was a running back.

With one last look in the mirror, I forced a smile on my face to ease the tension. I had curled my hair, put on a nice dress and comfortable wedge heels that were suitable for dancing.

It was time.

"You look like this is your first date."

Behind me I found my mother entering my room, appearing amused at my nervous state.

If only she knew.

"This is a big night for you, relax, breathe, you've gone out hundreds of times before," she told me as she came over and assessed my look. "You look amazing, honey."

I stood back so she could really get a good look at me. "Is this too much?"

My mother waved me off. "Oh no, you are stunning. Troy's going to think so, too."

She went on downstairs as I finished checking my appearance in the mirror. With one final breath, I turned out my light and stepped out of my room.

Down the hall, I spotted the light on in Avery's room. He wasn't downstairs with my family and Troy. I took a moment and poked my head in, finding him lying across his bed, lost in a video game. Last night, he'd gone to the movies with Guillermo and Jenaya, which seemed completely out of character for him.

I'd been so wrapped up in planning for my date, I hadn't asked about his night. "How was the movie?"

Avery jumped, startled at my appearance in his doorway. He paused his game. "Intense."

"Intense?" I repeated, confused. "What did you see?"

He shrank back, his gaze going to the carpet. "Never mind."

Something was off. I slipped into the room, closing the door behind me. "What's wrong, Ave?"

He faced me, frowning. "Don't tell Mom, okay?"

Something *was* off. "Promise."

"At the movies, there were these guys," he admitted. "One was messing with Jenaya, trying to get her number. She said no, and he got mean."

Typical. There was nothing worse than guys who couldn't take rejection and did a complete 180 and turned into jerks. "Is she okay?" I'd seen her at school today and she'd seemed her usual self.

Avery wouldn't look at me.

"Avery?"

"*Promise* not to tell Mom?" he asked again.

I went closer. "I won't tell."

Slowly, he looked up at me. "Mo...sorta lost it. The guy called Jenaya out of her name and Mo...*snapped*. One minute the guy was talking, and the next, Mo had him yoked up." Avery shook his head. "It didn't get too far before security stepped in, but Mo definitely had the guy about to piss his pants."

I froze, unsure how to respond. *A temper.* Guillermo had a temper. Protective, sure, but this was something that would definitely be a red flag for my mother, if she knew he was lashing out like that.

"The guy was being rude, Rey," Avery went on. "I should've said something, too."

Avery was sweet to want to protect Jenaya's honor, and I guess, in a way, I understood Guillermo's reaction. It was nice he cared enough for Jenaya to step in on her behalf. Still, was this why he was on probation? For being violent? Yesenia had said he was bad before, different, enough to entirely disrupt the atmosphere of their household.

"I'm glad it didn't get crazy," I said.

Avery bobbed his head. "Me, too. Mo's no joke, that's for sure."

Guillermo always seemed so nervous, hesitant. Now, I knew why.

Should I tell my mother? For his own good? To keep him in check?

The image of his wounded eyes came to mind. His stiff, uncertain shoulders as he stood in my foyer the night before as I'd come downstairs and set eyes on him.

My breath grew wings and flew out of my chest. *Guillermo.* He seemed so lost, so unsure, so broken.

I couldn't tell. Nothing had happened, and hopefully, nothing else would.

"I gotta go," I said.

"Have fun on your date," Avery offered.

"Thanks."

Down on the first floor, Troy was waiting in the TV room. He sat with my father and mother watching something on ESPN. Tanner was asleep at the edge of the coffee table, a stolen polka-dotted sock of mine sitting under his paw. The thief.

At my arrival, Troy immediately stood. "Whoa, Rey, you look beautiful."

His eyes took in my figure in my little red dress, and I watched as they tripled in size. The dress was loose enough, but there was no hiding my cleavage or the amount of leg on display. When I'd been debating on what to wear, I'd feared the dress would make me look like a tease, but in the end, I decided that it was simply a cute dress and Troy would appreciate it.

"Ahem." My father cleared his throat as Troy made his way to me. "Pick your tongue up off of the floor, boy. And don't keep her out too late."

Troy recovered quickly and grinned. "No problem, Mr. London. I'm just taking Regan out to House of Solé, and then a little dancing at After Hours."

"You be careful," my father warned. "Some fools don't know how to act at these clubs nowadays."

His words brought me back to Guillermo. And suddenly, I was thankful for him, thankful someone cared enough to protect Jenaya.

Troy placed a protective arm around me. "Always, sir. Regan's in good hands, believe that."

I never questioned this. Troy was both strong and popular, I knew he could protect me physically if need be, and I knew due to his fame, no one would want an issue with him.

Troy took me under his arm and soon led me out of the house and to his car.

He opened my door for me, helped me inside before closing it shut behind me.

My nerves were out of control, and I desperately tried to tame them for fun's sake. It was just dinner and dancing, some well-deserved fun after our first year together. Nothing more and nothing less.

"Ready?" Troy flashed me a smile as he climbed in alongside me.

I nodded, trying to match his excitement.

He put on the radio, and I spent the majority of the drive trying to decipher whatever it was the rapper was mumbling around the catchy beat.

"I've been dying to go to this place," I spoke up as the downtown restaurant came into view. "Thank you, Troy."

My boyfriend sat back coolly as he drove for the parking area. "No problem. This night is special," he insisted, reaching out and squeezing my knee.

This night *was* special; my first boyfriend was taking me out to celebrate our first anniversary. A lot of kids, their relationships didn't last ten minutes at our school.

Maybe Troy was the one.

Continuing to be a gentleman, he helped me out of the car and held my waist as he steered us to the restaurant's entrance.

"Right this way," the hostess said as she gestured for us to follow her.

The restaurant was full of an older crowd, which I didn't mind. Soft jazz music played throughout, and portraits of iconic figures in the Black community hung on the walls, from Malcolm X, Dr. King to Louis Armstrong and more. Not only that, each portrait was done in the style of a newspaper article, making them look vintage.

"Oh wow, I love it," I commented as I took in the decor. The warm smell of soul food filled the air, reminding me of my grandmother's kitchen growing up during family visits for Sunday dinner.

Troy barely looked around before agreeing. "Yeah, it's nice."

We sat across from each other at a small, intimate table. Our server came and gave us a glass of water each with a lemon wedge. When she left us to scour the menu, I focused on what all House of Solé had to offer.

"Damn, it all sounds so good," Troy said. "I'm starving."

I was a mixture of hungry and nervous. On one hand, all the food sounded delicious; on the other, I was still on edge about where our date would go.

In the end, I settled on the chef's plate, a house special, while Troy decided on Harlem jambalaya.

"My mom keeps talking about having a big dinner and inviting you over," he said. His smile was fond, making me relax a little. Our families were close due to my aunt and his uncle's business connection. Our relationship was yet another link. His parents loved me, and sometimes Tommy J even referred to me as Big Sis.

"I do miss your mom's cooking," I admitted.

"Who you telling? Next year, when I'm in school, it's all I'm gonna be thinking about," Troy said as he sat back. "I've been on a few college visits and some of them places ain't cuttin' it. Or they're surrounded by fast food, and you know I only eat that once in a while."

Troy was a machine, built and trained to dominate on the football field. He didn't really drink, never smoked, and he barely ate greasy food.

The topic of conversation made me feel curious. "Have you decided where you want to go?"

He brightened under the spotlight I'd placed on him. "Miami would be nice, the beaches, the weather..." *The girls.* "It would be like a permanent vacation."

"That's a lot of distance." For the first time, I wondered if Troy would be faithful while he was away at school.

He was faithful now... I hoped.

He placed his hand on mine. "We can handle it. It's you and me till the top, right?"

"And once you get there?" I asked, playing coy, but seriously curious.

"And then we enjoy the ride. You're my backbone, Rey. I need you. Things won't be right without you in my corner."

It was nice to feel needed and appreciated, but something still felt off.

I forced myself to smile and let it go. "Can't wait."

Soon, our food arrived, and talk of the future went out the window as we dug into our meals.

We both agreed that House of Solé was more than worth the hype. The food was immaculate, spicy, but not too spicy, but what I liked most was that home-cooked taste. It felt like food your grandmother would make. True authentic soul food.

"Your dad's talking about me trying to get Avery to play football again," Troy mentioned as he picked up his glass of water, appearing amused.

This wasn't the first time my father had attempted to goad Avery into some sport. I sometimes wondered why Avery never hung out with Raviv Hadad, the cute boy from down the street. They were in the same grade, although Raviv was more outgoing than Avery. He was making waves on the soccer team and always hanging out with the upperclassmen. He had a pretty little girlfriend as well.

I guessed they just weren't a personality match. My brother was more introverted than most people. Sports didn't appeal to him; he'd much rather sit on the sidelines with his head in his manga.

"Avery doesn't like football," I told Troy. "I wish my dad would leave it alone."

"Your pops just wants Avery to get out there more."

Suddenly I felt defensive for my brother. If he didn't want to step out of his shell on his own, what good was it to force him out? There was nothing wrong with Avery choosing to read instead of play sports. "Let him be, he'll come around to whatever he loves in the end."

Troy made a face and said nothing, but even his silence irritated me. So Avery wasn't like Tommy J. There was no harm in being a loner.

I relaxed when I thought of Guillermo, how he and Avery seemed to have formed a bond as they continued to eat lunch together with Jenaya. Somehow, he'd gotten Avery out of the house. Avery had had the biggest grin on his face when I'd caught him racing up to his room to grab his shoes the night before.

Guillermo.

Protector of Jenaya and gentle with Avery.

A guy like that, there was no way he was a bad egg.

Dessert came, and I'd chosen peach cobbler while Troy hadn't wanted anything. He was Mr. Serious about his body, claiming that the jambalaya had been enough.

"Well, how is it?" he asked after I'd eaten a few bites.

The savory sweet tartness of the warm peaches and sugary, flaky crust was a perfect finale after the incredible meal. "Oh my God, it's amazing. Almost as good as your mom's." Mrs. Jordan's cobbler was to die for. I'd walk through ten miles of snow just to get a plate of her peachy goodness. But this was close.

"I'm surprised you haven't pumped her for the recipe yet."

I wasn't much of a cook, but that wasn't a bad idea. I moaned a little as I took my last bite. "This is heaven."

Troy sat watching me, purely entertained. "Doesn't take much to make you happy."

It didn't. All I truly needed was a peaceful escape most days from all the pressure and obligation I dealt with. I just wanted to be myself, and here with Troy, it felt possible.

The bill came and Troy paid quickly before coming around

the table and escorting me out of the restaurant and back to
his car.

He didn't have to drive far, seeing how After Hours was
located downtown as well.

It was the weekend, so the club was packed with college
students, kids from the various high schools in the area, and
some older crowd.

No one I knew was at the club, but several people recognized Troy.

"Aw shit, we got Number Five of the Arlington High Panthers in the building!" the DJ shouted Troy out over the mi-
crophone. Those closest to us gave Troy some love, slapping
his back and giving him dap. His celebrity never got old to
his supporters.

"What can I say, the people love me," Troy leaned in close
to my ear to say over the loud music.

It was no surprise. This would only get bigger in time when
his success grew in college.

The DJ put on an urban pop song and Troy and I took
to the dance floor. As the singer sang about being "too on,"
Troy held me close as we danced with my back to his front.
We danced through a few songs, until a sassy Beyoncé record came on.

"Nah, that ain't it," he said of the vibe the song gave off.

His distaste for the male-bashing song caused me to
chuckle. I was a future alumnus of Beyoncé University, where
I was fully intending to pledge Beyoncé Delta Knowles. After
watching her iconic *Homecoming* performance at Coachella
repeatedly, it was set in stone.

We made our way to the lounge area. As I sat back against
a plush sofa with Troy, a hip-hop/R&B song played in the
background. Finally we were alone.

"You look pretty," Troy said, leaning closer to my ear to whisper.

I smiled. "Thank you."

He took my hand in his. "I can't wait to get back to my place."

Suddenly my meal was threatening to come back up. "Why?"

Briefly Troy furrowed his brows, as if my question confused him. "So we can be alone and talk, Rey. My parents are out of town."

"And...and Tommy J?" I wondered.

Troy sneaked me a grin. "Don't worry about him, he's out with Isaiah and Dane. We've got the house to ourselves."

I couldn't meet his eyes, my mind going a million miles a minute, scared of what possibilities were back at his empty house. His parents being gone only led me to believe Troy wanted to talk about one thing. The three-letter word still hanging over our heads.

The last thing I wanted to do was go down that awkward path with Troy.

"Can't we talk here?"

"It's a little public and loud, don't you think?"

My twisting gut told me not to go home with him. I didn't want to see the disappointed look on his face when I froze up on him—again.

"I just wanna have a good time," he tried to reason with me.

"And this isn't it?" I asked sourly.

Troy made a face, almost as though he were exhausted with me. "Yeah, sure."

I narrowed my eyes, repeating what he said. "Yeah, sure? What's that supposed to mean?"

Troy opened his mouth and then shut it.

Trying to get us back on track, I asked, "Do you want to dance?"

Troy angled his head, taking in the current song playing before frowning in distaste. "Nah, not trying to hear no female talk about finessin' a guy for his money."

I moved away from him. "Don't say that."

"Say what?" he asked innocently.

"That word, 'female,' it's insulting."

Troy gaped at me as if I were delusional. "How?"

Ugh. Was it really that hard to get? "What would you call Mike?" I challenged, bringing up one of his friends.

Troy's brows furrowed, as if my question were silly. "That's my boy."

"And what about...that girl over there?" I nodded at some girl in a cute pink outfit.

"That's a female."

I scoffed. "See!"

"But she *is*," Troy insisted.

It went beyond being definitive. "You don't call guys 'males,' so don't refer to us as 'females,' it's insulting, Troy. Especially when it's clear you mean to say 'bitch.'"

"It's really not that deep."

Wasn't the fact that I was offended enough reason to not use it? "Well, it is to *me*."

Troy ran his hand down his face. "It's like you want me to be a simp or something."

"Ah yes, because being nice to a girl and respecting her is *simp*ly repulsive."

He glanced at me, studying me. "You really want to fight about this?"

I didn't. I didn't want to fight at all. I wanted things normal, happy, safe between us.

"Hey." Troy's determined voice brought my gaze back to his. "I'm sorry. I don't like making you mad or upset. I'll, uh, stop saying 'females' if it offends you."

My heart jumped at the mini-victory that was Troy agreeing to change. I leaned up and kissed him. "Thank you."

Before anything else could be said, some friend of his approached. "Yo, Troy, you ready for East tomorrow?" the boy asked, giving Troy dap and a hug.

Troy released me, turning and greeting his friend.

I took the opportunity to get up and walk away. We needed space. While we'd resolved one argument, there was still the never-ending big reoccurring one hanging in the balance.

Meandering through the club, I had no clue where I was going. The restroom came to mind, but once I saw the mile-long line, I knew it was out of the question.

SZA was singing about broken clocks and I felt my shoulders sag with the weight of the evening.

In the end, I decided I needed air, so I stepped outside to catch my breath.

I couldn't do it.

This was our anniversary, and Troy probably wanted to make it special by taking that next step, but I could feel a hard knot in my gut at the idea of it. The last thing I wanted to do was ruin our night, but I couldn't go back to his house with him.

I almost wanted to blame my dress, but I knew that even if I were dressed in a turtleneck and sweats, Troy would still want to go there.

A few paces from the club was a bar, and on the left side of the club was the long stretch of building After Hours occupied. I took a left and began walking down the block, aiming nowhere but to find peace of mind.

This was our anniversary night and we were about to spend it arguing over sex yet again.

The more I walked, the more upset I became. At myself. At Troy. At the entire situation. A part of me was sure I loved Troy, and another wasn't so sure of anything.

In the beginning, it had all been so simple. Scary at times, but simple.

Now—

Crap.

I looked around and didn't know where I was.

Spinning around, I did my best to swallow the fear beginning to take over. How many turns had I taken? Had I walked this way straight?

Businesses and bars lined the block across the street. Behind me were a café and a pool hall. A glimpse inside the pool hall window showed that it was busy with men and women playing a few games.

Before I could get out my phone and call Troy, I froze.

Inside the pool hall, among the dim lights and smoke in the air, was Guillermo.

He was up front, toward the middle, leaning over a red pool table about to make a move. What caught my attention was his hair. Instead of being secured by a ponytail, it hung free. It fell just past his ears, and it was thick and wavy. I liked it.

I chanced a look around me, figuring that maybe stepping inside to say hey to Guillermo would buy me some time before calling Troy. My boyfriend needed to cool off anyway, with where his head was at.

I slipped inside the pool hall and immediately felt out of my element. The lower back section was smoking approved, causing the odor to filter through the entire place. Beyond that, the rock music—or was it metal? Grunge?—also made me uncomfortable.

Guillermo was playing alone, but he spotted me instantly as I approached.

He rose from the table, his eyes drinking in my dress. "You shouldn't be here."

"I know. I got mad at Troy and took off. One wrong corner and I got lost," I explained.

Guillermo shook his head as he chalked his cue stick. "You two spend more time fighting than you do lovin'."

"You don't know us." But he was right.

Guillermo shrugged. "Just an observation."

His nonchalance prickled across my skin, sinking in, it felt like. "We're fine, he just—"

"Ran you off *again*." Guillermo looked elsewhere. "Just an observation."

Maybe he had seen me running away from Troy more than once, but what did he know?

The obvious, my conscience spoke up.

I hung my head. "I honestly just want to go home now."

I could feel Guillermo's gaze on me, but I didn't have the heart to face him. He was right about Troy and me, because deep down I knew that if I went back to After Hours, we'd more than likely fight over how I'd left in the first place, and inevitably about how I didn't want to go back to his parents' house.

"I can take you," Guillermo spoke up.

I lifted my head. "Yeah?"

"We're neighbors, it's no big deal."

My mood brightened as I smiled. "Thanks, really."

Around us, the atmosphere was heavy with the music,

smoke, and the tattooed patrons. Some men were arguing over a game they'd played, causing the bartender to grimace.

I faced the street outside, more than ready to go.

"Hey." Guillermo was standing behind me, leaning into the cue stick, his eyes devouring me.

"Yeah?"

"I didn't say the ride was free." A dangerous grin washed across his face and I struggled to calm my nerves.

Slowly, I walked closer to him. "Why are you playing alone?"

An arrogant smile took his lips as he gestured to a group of college-age guys at a table a few paces down. "Won some money from them and they no longer wanna play." Guillermo gathered the triangle and began racking the balls. "People don't like losin' money."

He must've been good. *Real* good.

"So, uh, what do you want for the ride?" In my clutch purse, I carried only my cell phone and a few loose bills in case of emergency.

He tipped his head. "Come play pool with me."

"Pool? Let's say…twenty bucks I'll win?"

Guillermo smirked. "I don't play girls for money."

I lifted a brow. "Oh really? What do you play for?"

The mischievous look that washed across his face should've had me stopping the train of conversation, but I was curious— and I liked the smile.

Guillermo shook his head. "Forget it, we'll figure it out."

I folded my arms. "Uh-uh, tell me."

"A lap dance."

My mouth fell open. "Perv!"

He chuckled, that sexy grin showing no shame. "You asked. Besides, that was the *old* me. I'm a completely changed guy now."

That daring gleam in his eye begged to differ.

"I don't know how to play pool," I told him. I knew what the object was when it came to the game, but as for the skills, they were beyond me.

Guillermo furrowed his brows. "Your friends don't play?"

"Malika doesn't. Troy might, I'm not sure."

Guillermo shook his head, mumbling something beneath his breath. "It's a shame. Don't worry, I'll teach you enough to play, but not enough to beat me." He winked at me, seeming playful and carefree for the first time. I wondered if he was aware of how good he looked. Actually, from his cocky smile, I was sure he was.

After setting up the balls, he came over to me with an extra cue stick, quickly chalking it up before handing it over.

He came closer, making me tense up at his proximity.

Breathe, Regan, breathe.

Guillermo paused, hovering just behind me. I wondered if he could feel the heat between us like I could.

"Is it okay?" he asked. "If I touch you?"

I watched as he held up his large hand.

"I..." My words got caught in my throat, and I lifted my eyes to his.

Funny, it was almost as though he were standing closer. "I only want to touch you with your permission."

Slowly, I swallowed. *Good lord.*

Doing my best to ignore the fuzzy sensation deep in my belly, I collected myself and swept some hair behind my ear.

"Yeah, it's...it's okay," I told him.

What I liked most in that moment was the fact that he asked to touch me. I didn't have to bury discomfort while letting him.

It was hard to explain, as he adjusted my posture over the table, but I felt powerful being in control like that.

With one hand on my waist, he used the other to demonstrate how to drive the cue stick toward the cue ball. Once he was sure I understood the game, he stood away from me, leaning on his stick and waiting for me to go.

"Can, um, we move the cue ball to get a better position?" I asked.

Guillermo frowned. "Don't ever play for money." He narrowed his eyes and glanced down my body. "Or clothes."

I was going to lose.

I bent over, slowly realizing just how hard it was to work the cue stick. Concentrating, I pushed it toward the cue ball and hit it just hard enough to break the balls but not enough to make them go into any pockets.

Guillermo was trying his best to hide his smile. "Good job."

I rolled my eyes. "So we're just playing for that ride home?"

He quirked an eyebrow and bit his lip, as if thinking.

Geez, he even makes thinking look good.

"Yeah, just a harmless game," he assured me.

I nodded, standing back to let him to take his turn.

He positioned himself, leaning over as he made his move. Four balls went into four separate pockets.

He grinned, knowing just as I did that he was going to win.

The game was pretty hard to play. I was terrible, and each attempt I made to hit the cue ball only gave Guillermo new opportunities to get creative stifling his laugh. It didn't take long until he was sinking the eight ball.

I wasn't sour about losing. It just made me want to learn more so that I could wipe the grin off his face.

He came closer, eliminating the distance between us, his

movement fluid with confidence. Waves of it overtook me as he came to a stop just in front of me. He rested his hand on the edge of the table and leaned, his muscles flexing with the weight. "Good game."

The grin he shot me was distracting. My eyes flickered to the wall behind him, where a dartboard was hung up. "Can... you play darts?"

He tilted his head, eyes fixed on mine, a lock of hair resting against his jaw. "Now what do you think?"

I swallowed. *I'll take that as a yes.* It was clear his hands were skilled at more than just arranging flowerbeds at the center.

"I will say, though, that was a funny game." Guillermo set the balls up for someone else to come and play.

"I want a rematch," I fumed. "And a better instructor."

He smirked as he waved a hand toward the exit. "Yeah, you do that, so I can beat you again."

I opened the door and led the way outside. It was getting chilly, and as I shivered, Guillermo placed a hand on my arm, offering warmth.

"You ready?" he asked.

My cell phone rang, the notification telling me Troy was calling. He must've finally realized I was gone.

Was I really going to accept Guillermo's ride and ditch my boyfriend?

Going back to Troy meant dealing with a potential argument.

I was done discussing sex.

Sorry to further disappoint you, but I caught a ride home.

Tucking my phone away, I faced Guillermo. "Yeah, let's go."

Guillermo

Hermosa.

An angel in red.

Or maybe la diabla.

I thought my eyes were playing tricks on me when Regan walked into Pete's, but once I set eyes on that nervous smile she'd given me, my interest in pool went out the window. God help me if I wasn't becoming addicted to that smile, those dimples, and the way they complemented the color of her skin.

I told myself to be smart about things and play it cool. She *was* my supervisor's daughter.

I led the way to the parking lot, lightly steering her with my hand on her back. Her phone was ringing but she made no effort to answer it.

It was dark out, and annoying boyfriend or not, perhaps Troy was worried about her. She looked amazing in her dress; I'd be worried, too.

"Shouldn't you let him know you're okay?" I asked.

Regan paused for a moment, thinking it over.

Whatever Troy had done to run her off had left her disinterested in communicating with him.

It wasn't any of my business, but something told me the guy was about to lose his girl. Thinking of the image of her playing pool, I almost felt bad for him. Regan was crazy cute when she was trying to win.

When we reached my Charger, she walked to the passenger door herself, but I made sure to step forward and open it for her.

Regan placed her hand on top of mine as she passed me to get into the car. "Thanks."

Her skin was soft but I chose not to reflect on it.

Every bit of her was temptation, a dangerous tug toward the past. Harvey would lose his shit if he knew what I was up to. Fuck, so would my parents.

It's just a ride, I told myself as I rounded the hood. Still, I found myself taking a few calming breaths before finally climbing in beside her. Suddenly the small space inside the car felt suffocating.

"Do you want gas money?" Regan spoke up.

That brought me back to earth. "We're going to the same place. You're good." I set my key in the ignition and paused. "Do you like hip-hop?"

Regan smirked. "Uh, yeah."

"Didn't want to play anything offensive."

She rolled her eyes playfully. "As long as I don't hear some guy telling me to pop a pill or shake my ass, we're good."

I chuckled. "I prefer the thoughtful shit anyway."

"Guess I'll never see you in After Hours, huh?"

I thought of the night club I'd heard about around school. Up north in Rowling Heights, we didn't have any clubs that let teens in. I'd never sneaked into one either, but the idea had been tempting. Maybe I would check out After Hours once I got more adjusted.

"You might," I said as I grabbed my phone and began sifting through music.

"Well, I'm a Beyoncé type of girl," Regan said proudly.

"Who isn't," I remarked. No wonder Regan had left ol' boy behind. Strong women inspired her. Yesenia was more into the younger pop singers, from what I'd heard her listen to, but a lot of the girls I knew were fans of Beyoncé.

Regan perked a brow. "Oh, you're not afraid to admit you like her? Troy always complains about her music."

I shrugged. "Doesn't hurt my masculinity an ounce to admit I like her." Both my mom and my tía Lupe had blasted her while I was growing up. She was iconic.

To get us on the road, I found a Beyoncé song in my music and pressed Play. It had Bey and it had Jay; it was a win for both of us.

I could tell Regan appreciated the gesture when she leaned over to turn up the tune while Beyoncé sang about being unstoppable and how everything was "nice."

I drove for home as Regan visibly got comfortable and relaxed beside me. I thought of how, at school, she always seemed so stiff and uncomfortable—especially under Troy's arm. At the center she was slightly more in control, but I could tell it wasn't her choice to work there.

It made me wonder what *she* wanted in the grand scheme of things.

Regan's cell phone rang a total of five more times on the way back to Briar Pointe, all of which she ignored. She bobbed her head and seemed to admire my choice of hip-hop as my music shuffled elsewhere from the Beyoncé song, but she stayed quiet, clutching her phone, clearly in her head about something. I didn't want to pry.

As I pulled into my driveway fifteen minutes later, Regan heaved a sigh as she pressed airplane mode on her screen.

Oh he's done for now.

We got out of my car and Regan stood there for a moment as she looked at her house across the street.

It really was a small world.

Bravely, I stuffed my hands in my pockets and walked over to her. "Something wrong?"

Her shoulders sagged. "I'm not ready to go back there yet."

"Afraid they'll ask about your date?"

Regan made a face. "You have no idea."

The sound of a car door shutting nearby caught our attention. One look, and regrettably I found Troy marching his way to us.

Shit.

His whole demeanor read pissed-off, and his determined stride to get to Regan had me going on the defense as I caught her inching back.

"So this is what you're doing?" he snapped at the sight of us together.

Regan hung back. "Troy, please."

"Please nothing, Rey. I was looking for you, and now I find you with someone else?"

I didn't like his tone, or the aggression in his stance as he faced off with her. It was his own fault she'd run off in the first place.

"Hey." I parked myself in front of Regan, speaking gently. "Lower your voice, you're scarin' her."

Troy's dark eyes shot to me, accusation in them. "And who are you again?"

"My neighbor." Regan's voice came out strong. In seconds, she walked around me, standing firm and unafraid. "You know what, just leave, Troy. I'll think about if I want to talk you in the morning."

Troy snorted. "It's like that? After all that I set up tonight?"

"I'm sorry you think I owe you something, but I don't," Regan responded.

Troy held up a finger.

"Please just walk away before I say something we'll both regret."

His jaw set. I was ready, in case he couldn't take the hint. Luckily for Regan and me, he backed off. He stalked to his car and climbed in, slamming the door shut before driving up the street, hitting a U-turn, and taking off with a short screech of tires.

In front of me, Regan expelled a heavy breath.

"Nice guy," I remarked.

She peered back at me, the sadness in her eyes glimmering with unshed tears. "Yeah."

My gaze fell on her house and then my own. I wasn't ready to go home yet either.

"Wanna go for a little walk?" I suggested. "I don't want to go home yet. Although…I don't think your mom would like it if she saw us together."

Regan kinked up her nose at the thought, but we started walking down the street anyway.

"I don't get why my mom gets all bent out of shape about us being near each other," she confessed. "It's embarrassing. I mean, I work at the center, it's not like I haven't interacted with her probationers before."

"Yeah, but it's probably the nature of my crime." It wasn't something I wanted to outright admit to Regan, but there was no hiding who I was as I wore that yellow shirt every time I worked at the center.

Regan appeared thoughtful, and I feared I'd scared her away. I didn't want to scare her away.

She bit her lip. "Avery told me about last night." She looked my way. "He said you snapped on a guy who was being mean to Jenaya."

Throughout the movie I'd been antsy, unable to forgive myself for the slip. Avery was a good kid, and I hadn't meant to lose my temper in front of him. His mom thought I was a potential good influence, and I'd quickly proved her wrong.

"He was being rude, makin' Naya uncomfortable, and I just got fed up. That's...sorta my problem," I confessed. "Losing my head over bullshit. Swingin' instead of takin' a moment to think things through. It's all I've ever done. It's how I got *here*."

"Sometimes people lose their tempers. It's not like you killed anyone, right?"

I hung my head in shame. "Almost."

Regan didn't flinch, but I noticed the slight pause in her posture. *"Oh."*

"Yeah," I went on. "It's not like I'd hurt you, but maybe that's why she freaks out."

Regan lifted her eyes to mine. There was no sign of judgment, only curiosity. "Can you tell me what happened, before?" She lowered her gaze. "If it's not too personal or harsh, I mean."

I hadn't talked about it in full detail in months. My therapist and Harvey, as well as Mrs. London, knew it all in writing, but trying to say it out loud...it was hard to articulate.

When my family and I lived in Rowling Heights, I'd been

wild, fearless, and selfish. One night, it caught up to me in a frenzy of sirens, screams, and lots of blood.

I guess I knew where to start.

As we walked down the sidewalk, passing Raviv's house, I began to paint the picture of my past, hoping my shot at redemption wasn't slipping away. "I'm from up north, Rowling Heights."

"Oh," Regan noted. "Real suburbia."

I snorted. "Nah, *this* is suburban hell, dimples."

"Dimples?" Regan angled her head, eyeing me funny.

Without thinking, I poked her indentation. "They're cute."

"How do you say it in Spanish?"

"Hoyuelos," I told her.

I watched as she mouthed the word, almost hypnotizing me.

I was getting distracted, so I went on with my story. "Anyway, Rowling Heights wasn't so bad, but I chose to be in the streets. It wasn't like I was out sellin' dope or nothin', but I hung around a bunch of questionable characters."

"Did they sell drugs?" Regan asked.

I shook my head, thinking of Shad, Kent, Mouse, and Eduardo. "Nah, my friends didn't sell drugs either, but they did smoke and drink. It was never my thing, but I hung out with them anyway," I said. "We used to loiter at this park so much that people would see us and call us 'park rats.'"

Regan chuckled a little at the nickname.

"We hung out after curfew, they'd drink and smoke, and we'd all mess around with girls."

Regan appeared quizzical. "Girls, huh?"

My friends and I, we had a little rep and it made us popular. People knew who we were and what we were capable of. We all wore battle scars from various fights, and that made our image that much grittier. And the girls had loved that shit. I guess you could say we were all handsome, because gettin' a girl's interest had never been an issue for any of us.

This was something my mother disliked about me. She'd witnessed quite a few girls come and go. Carmen, Kayla, Monique, Selena—the list kinda went on. It was all about fun, no one got hurt, and none of it meant anything. Except for Tynesha.

"Yeah, girls." Reflecting on it, I said, "It's kind of the whole reason I'm on probation."

The truth was, I'd broken the Bro Code.

My third arrest was as my much own fault as anyone else's.

"One of my best friends, Shad, he had this girlfriend, Tynesha." I stopped to whistle and shake my head. "She was as bad as they come."

Beside me, Regan rolled her eyes. "Hmmph."

"Nah, I mean it, she was so pretty, her hair was always done, and her outfits always fit just right. Tynesha had it going on," I continued. "You're not supposed to look at your friend's girl, but I wasn't blind either. But the thing was, Shad wasn't even good to Tynesha. He cheated on her all the time, and he was mad disrespectful. He was my best friend, but he was a dickhead."

"What happened next?" Regan asked.

"Tynesha texted me one day because Shad had done something to upset her, and we linked up and hung out. One thing led to another, and I ended up messing around with her. It wasn't lust for me, I really liked her. She used to fill my head up about wanting to be with me instead, and I fell for it."

Regan's brows crumpled in confusion as she stopped walking. "She was lying?"

I stared ahead of us down the block as the rest of the events replayed in my head. My fists clenched at my sides. How oblivious had I been? "At the time, it felt real. Like she was really about to leave him for me. She would text me complainin' about him, tellin' me how I was so much better—I should've known it was all a lie. I wasn't that much better, I was a mess, too."

Regan reached out bravely, placing her hand over my fist, and I jumped. Then I reveled in her soft touch, calming down just a little.

"It's okay," she told me gently, "go on."

"We were all at the park one day, and Shad was gettin' on Tynesha's nerves, and that's when she blurted it out. 'That's why I'm fuckin' with Mo!' It was the way she said it, the look on her face, like she'd done it to get back at him," I reminisced. "Shad looked at me and he could tell it was true. He blew up, started yelling at Tynesha and getting in her face. One minute he's yelling, and the next he's smackin' her hard and shovin' her down to the ground."

In the heat of the moment, I'd been hurt as I realized Tynesha's game, but then, without even thinking I'd sprung into action. "I took Shad down and started whaling on him. I couldn't stop. He'd hit her, and I just fuckin' lost it."

The other guys, Mouse, Kent, and Eduardo, they'd tried to get me off him, but to no avail.

It took two cops who'd been on patrol to come and pry me off of Shad.

In the end, it didn't matter that he'd hit Tynesha. There was so much blood that I got arrested. Shad was really fucked up, broken nose, swollen eyes, hell, I think they mentioned a missing tooth.

"What really tore me up was walkin' into that courtroom and seeing Tynesha there by Shad's side. Through it all, she was with him. I guess I can't be too mad, because she did admit he hit her. It was my third arrest and it was a violent act, but I managed to get on probation and into the program with your mom. I'm lucky my parents got a good attorney, or else I'd still be in juvie right now."

We reached the end of the cul-de-sac, but we had a long walk back.

Regan just stood there, looking up at me without a hint of fear or judgment in her eyes.

She still had my hand in hers—in fact, she went as far as to grab my other hand and swing them a little. "I don't blame you for what you did. Shad's a punk for hitting Tynesha, and she is awful for leading you on like that. I'm not afraid of you, Guillermo. What happened happened, and what's important is you learned from it."

I felt a warmth spread through my chest. She didn't judge me. Her response, much like her touch, was soft. Soft Regan, gentle Regan, was nice.

What I'd done was something I would carry with me for the rest of my life, something I would never forget. That day, I'd relinquished my freedom over a broken heart and a messy situation I'd placed my own self in. I had selfishly ripped my family's world apart.

Nunca jamás.

"Hey." Regan got my attention. "I don't care what my mom says, let's be friends. I look at you and see Guillermo Lozano, and I want you to see me as Regan London. Before doesn't matter."

Her words sank in, and I hadn't known how much I needed to hear them until then. Or how much I didn't want this girl to see me as a monster. To know that I wasn't a monster.

Regan London wasn't just any girl. As long as there was

a boundary there, a fine line I would not cross, maybe, just maybe, nothing bad could come from being friends.

I squeezed her hand, ignoring the jolt in my chest at the sensation. "Friends?"

She squeezed back, and I wondered if she felt something, too. "Friends."

Regan

Troy was the last person I expected to bump into when I opened our front door Saturday morning. Especially after how we left things in Guillermo's driveway.

He was standing with his hands in his pockets, shoulders hunched and a forlorn look in his eyes. Nervous waves of energy streamed off him, making him seem jumpy.

I wasn't sure what I felt toward him, but I now knew what I didn't.

"Hey." His wounded eyes drank me in. "Can we talk?"

Folding my arms over my chest, I stood my ground. "I'm going to be late."

Troy sighed. "I was worried about you, and then when I come to check on you, you're with another guy?"

"I got lost walking around, and Guillermo was nice enough to take me home. That was it."

"But that's just it, Regan. You couldn't tell me what was wrong before taking off?"

Here we go again. My heart ached at the fact that this was it. That long gone were the happy moments, replaced with constant grief and arguing. It felt like the end wasn't near, but it was already here.

"Troy." I heaved a sigh, not wanting to do this now, not wanting to possibly break up before my shift at the center. "I gotta go."

Troy stepped back. "Come on, I'll take you."

Just then, because the universe clearly hated me, my father stepped into the foyer from the kitchen. His face lit up.

I was a goner.

"Troy!" My father could see Troy every day of the week and he still would act as though it was a pleasant surprise to see the boy.

"What up, Mr. London?" Troy reached out and embraced my father.

"Nothing much this morning. I was just about to take Rey for some food before her shift," my father replied.

Troy placed his hand on my shoulder. "If you don't mind, I'll take Regan out and see her off."

There was no arguing against that. When it came to Troy, my father was too enthralled by his majestic image.

Sighing, I gathered my things and followed Troy to his car.

I glanced across the street, wondering if Guillermo were up and if he'd be working today. His story had stayed with me through the night, and even though my mother was against it, I wasn't backing off; I was going to be his friend. Guillermo *was* a good guy.

I could see the lesson learned in his eyes. He was wounded, being branded a delinquent. Some kids, they wore their yellow Respect tees with pride or ease; Guillermo wore his in shame. The path he walked was a weary one, but I respected his intent to improve.

Troy stopped at Freeze, the local café most teens from

Arlington High hung out at because it was just around the corner from the school and across the street from the local public library.

As we got our food and grabbed a table, I spotted a few kids from school, either working or eating.

Jenaya Omar was one of them. She was sitting by herself, reading a book and eating some ice cream. Seeing her on her own should have been normal, and yet I looked around for Guillermo and Avery. I'd gotten used to them being together.

Bad record or not, Guillermo seemed to be having a good influence on my younger brother.

"So, about last night," Troy began awkwardly as we sat across from each other.

I pulled my strawberry soda close—only the best from Freeze—and took a hearty sip as I searched for words. I couldn't figure out why it was so hard to begin. I bet Jenaya would have no qualms speaking her mind.

"I'm sorry," Troy said. "For driving you away."

Bravely, I met his eyes. "I'm just not ready for things to go there, Troy."

I watched as he swallowed, his attention falling to his bottled water. His hands shook as he held on to it. "You're scared, I understand."

Scared wasn't the word for it.

"No." I put in effort to sound serious. "I'm not scared. I'm just not ready to have sex. Fear has nothing to do with it." I'd thought about it overnight, and I just couldn't see myself going all the way with Troy. The thought made me squirm. Perhaps we just needed more time?

Begrudgingly, Troy nodded. "Okay."

"If we're going to move forward—"

"If?" Troy reached out and took my hands.

It was such a sweet gesture, but I felt nothing as I held on to my resolve.

"I mean it, Troy. If you can't accept that I'm not ready, then we're done." There, I was standing my ground.

Troy frowned and squeezed my hands slightly in his. "I can't lose you, Rey. If you're not ready yet, okay. I'll wait." The desperate look in his eyes held me in place as his fingers ran across my hands. "I don't want to lose you, I love you."

Love.

It almost reminded me of a song.

I guessed that was enough.

"I love you, too," I told him.

And I guessed I did.

Guillermo

Saturday morning, I was finally giving in to Raviv's constant requests that I play soccer with him.

We'd hung out after school once, and I'd decided he was straight. Seeing him around and how he moved, it was easy to determine that he was smooth. He liked R&B and pretty girls, and outside of smiling at a few, he seemed faithful to his girlfriend.

The jury was still out on if that was mutual.

I wasn't a huge fan of soccer, unlike most of my family, but I could hang, and since I had the morning off, I decided to loosen up and hang out with Raviv.

His father, Raz, let me inside, greeting me with a friendly smile and hug once Raviv introduced me. He spoke with a thick accent, and through my curiosity, Raviv clarified that his parents were both from Israel. His father had lived there for most of his life, whereas his mother's side of the family had come to America when she was a baby.

"You going to show this one how it's done?" Raz asked me as Raviv sat on the floor putting on his cleats.

Raviv puffed up his chest proudly. "Doubt it."

To be honest, I doubted it, too. His heart was in the sport; mine wasn't.

Raz reached out and patted my back. They seemed to be an affectionate family. "Keep an eye on him, he needs to be humbled."

Raviv rose to his feet. "Not happening, old man."

"The mouth on him." Raz snorted, shaking his head as he walked away.

Raviv followed me to my Charger and hopped in shotgun, then found a station that played his music of choice. As the featured rapper spat his guest verse, I drove to the nearest playground with a large field for recreational use over in Briar Park.

"We meeting anyone?" I asked.

Raviv sat back as he gave a shrug. "Just Andy. Kayde said he might come through. He's known to flake, so we'll see. This is just a scrimmage—one of our players twisted his ankle, and like I said, we could use the practice and I know you know how to play."

From what little I knew, Raviv and his best friend, Andy Cowell, were soccer prodigies at Arlington High. Both had made the varsity team during their freshman year. They definitely didn't need "practice" if they were that advanced.

A pack of cigarettes was sticking out of the hoodie Raviv was wearing, highlighting the irony in his athleticism. "How the hell do you manage to play so good with all that damn smoking you do?"

Raviv smiled, showing me his surprisingly pearly whites

as a cocky gleam lit his olive green eyes. "Just goes to show that you can do anything you set your mind to."

"How can your parents just let you do it?" My parents had had conniptions apiece when they found out about the weed I'd tried *one* time.

"They don't. My mom's always sneaking into my room and throwing away my pack. But I just get someone to buy me more. My dad's more low-key about it, he says I'll burn out or give up eventually." Raviv grinned, looking my way. "So we're going with that route."

I shook my head. Cigarettes smelled awful. Not as bad as weed, but they were up there. "How can Camila stand it?"

I recognized the arrogant smile that washed across Raviv's face at that moment; it was one I often wore when I was about to brag about something. "I'm a very fun person to be around, smoke and all, Memo."

Sure.

"Why don't you just vape?" It sure as hell would be more tolerable than the stench of his cigarettes.

Raviv scrunched up his face. "Vaping is for douchebags."

"So it's your calling?" I quipped.

Raviv chuckled as he reached out and shoved me. "Easy, man."

At the park, he pushed a headband through his thick hair, then stretched on the side of the field while we waited for his friends.

I took in our surroundings and almost chuckled at how completely normal this all was. Me, about to do something clean-cut like play soccer in my free time. None of my boys back home would believe the sight. Shit, they'd clown me, and I'd let them.

This was better, though. Safer.

Things were shaping up.

"There you go," Raviv was saying.

I turned, catching a tall, lanky boy I recognized from school approaching. His thick black curls blew in the wind as he squinted to get a good look at us.

"I told you I was comin'," he spoke up. His accent said he lived in a Spanish-speaking household.

Raviv gestured from me to the boy. "Guillermo, Kayde. Kayde, Guillermo."

Kayde was wearing a plain T-shirt, exposing a deeply tanned arm with a growing sleeve of tattoos. He was close enough that I could smell he'd waked and baked.

"You bring any?" Raviv asked, alluding to Kayde's scent.

"You know I did."

Raviv faced me. "You smoke?"

I shook my head. "Can't afford dirty piss."

"You're really on probation, huh?" Raviv took a moment to observe me.

"Yeah."

He lifted his chin at me. "What for?"

After talking to Regan, I didn't feel so bad stating the facts. "Assault."

Kayde blinked while Raviv whistled. "Don't fuck with this one," Raviv said.

"New start, you know? I just can't mess up," I went on. "I never smoked or drank before anyway."

Raviv accepted this. "I do!" he said proudly as he grinned at his friend.

I was only a year older, but after the shit I went through, it felt like more. The me one year ago was probably like these guys—no, he *was* these guys. For their sake, I hoped they weren't out of control elsewhere.

Andy showed up ten minutes later and we paired off two and two with Kayde on my team.

I wanted to take it easy, but it was clear once the game started that Raviv did have an ego, one Andy matched.

They ran fast and hard, scoring their first four goals effortlessly.

Kayde was an adequate teammate, and because I knew he was on the soccer team, too, I put in more effort.

Running back and forth, aggressively attempting to steal the ball or keep it, was physically demanding.

Funny thing was, it was actually fun.

Forty minutes later we called game, with Raviv and Andy coming out victorious. Even though we'd lost, neither Kayde nor I wore our loss with bitterness.

"You've got what it takes," Raviv was saying as we sat along the field hydrating.

"Yeah, man. You're a natural," Andy insisted.

Kayde was lying on his back with his arm over his eyes, resting quietly.

Organized sports just weren't my thing. "Must be in my blood, practically my whole family plays. I *have* played recreationally growing up."

"That should tell you something," Raviv said.

My only interest was in finishing my community service and staying out of trouble. Joining the soccer team just didn't appeal to me. "Nah."

They let it go as Raviv's cell phone pinged. By the way his face lit up, I knew his girlfriend had texted him, or sent him a photo.

Andy regarded me curiously. "You seeing anyone?"

I focused down at the grass. "Nah."

"At least not yet," Raviv chimed in, elbowing his best friend. "I've seen the way girls look at you."

His remark made me wonder if he'd seen his *own* girlfriend's wandering eye.

"Girls and I don't mix right now," I told them.

"I see you still hangin' around Jenaya," Raviv said, once again being suggestive.

Really, Jenaya was cool, but much more on a friendly level.

For some reason, Regan crept into my mind, and I tried to block her out. The image of her in that dress the previous evening was stuck in my head, that and the feel of her skin, the sight of her smile, the sound of her laugh, the look of frustration when she sucked at pool…

No, girls and I did not mix at all.

The trouble with girls was they were fun, they were wild, and they were so damn fine.

For my parents' sake, and *mine*, I was putting on my own little chastity belt.

San Guillermo.

"I already told you that wasn't a thing. Naya's a friend," I clarified. "She's actually a good person once you get to *know* her."

Raviv held his hands up. "Easy. I was just sayin'. There's more options out there, though." His attention was back on his phone. "*So* much fun you could be having."

Kayde was dead to the world, while Andy was rolling his eyes.

"Don't listen to him," Andy spoke up. "Someone oughta take that phone from him and talk some sense into him."

Raviv made a face. "You'd have to pry it from my cold dead hands."

"I bet." Andy smirked. "Especially with all the filthy pictures you've got in there."

Raviv took the remark as a compliment and I found myself shaking my head. "Be careful, Raviv," I said. "Have fun, sure, but you don't want to be too crazy. Being bad isn't all it's cracked up to be. Before you know it, your parents won't be able to look you in the eye anymore, and the girl you really like won't want anything to do with you because you're so screwed-up and risky."

Raviv stood, dusting himself off and looking around the park before meeting our gazes with a careless shrug. "No problem, Guillermo, I'm good. Matter of fact, I'm going to go see Camila in a little bit and we'll keep it PG just for you."

From the weed to his girl, I hoped Raviv kept it all under control. He wouldn't want to walk this road I was on. No one would.

Raviv made good on his word about meeting up with his girl. As soon as we made it back, he rushed inside to shower and take off once again.

Camila must've been sending him some pretty tempting pictures.

I'd never sent a nude, but I'd received my fair share of them. At a time, Tynesha had been that ballsy.

The thought of her had me getting back into my Charger and driving to Briar Park Community Center for a little one-on-one with a punching bag. After nearly losing my shit in front of Jenaya and Avery at the movie theater, I needed a good round or two.

When I walked inside, I paused and sucked in a breath. Regan was at the front desk, and she wasn't alone.

Troy was leaning over the counter, staring her down and

saying something that had her forcing a smile on her face. Just like she often did at school, Regan seemed to dwindle before him. Troy didn't notice.

She spotted me, her smile turning genuine as she lifted her hand to wave.

I merely tipped my head toward her, not wanting to intrude.

Troy turned, catching sight of me, his demeanor less than friendly.

"You working today?" Regan asked.

"Nah, I figured I'd punch the bag a few times."

"Oh," Regan said. "There's a few people in there, but it's mostly empty today. Have fun."

Her boyfriend's gaze was fixed on her, but she seemed oblivious.

"Thanks," I told her before making my way toward the exercise room. Or, at least, I tried to.

"Hey." Troy called out to me, causing me to stop and turn around. He was still leaning over the counter, a cold look in his eye. "Thanks for taking *my* girl home last night."

If he kept being such a dickhead, she wouldn't be his girl for very much longer, whether I helped her out or not. I opened my mouth, wanting to ask him what was up.

Footsteps sounded down the hall, and I froze at the arrival of Mrs. London. Her face lit up at the sight of Troy, a warm smile stretching across her lips. "Troy! Good to see you."

His features quickly morphed into happiness as he focused on Regan's mother, going over to hug her.

"How was your anniversary date?" Mrs. London asked.

Troy was grinning, his gaze going to Regan, then to me. "Great."

I buried my annoyance and went into the gym. Sure

enough, a few older guys were on the machines, lifting, jogging, or working with the battle rope.

The punching bags were free, though, and I welcomed the task before me.

There was a trainer in the room overseeing an elderly man who must've been recovering from surgery. He helped me bandage my hands, then left me to work off my aggression.

I quickly rid myself of my tank top, then plugged in my wireless earphones. With the loud rap in my ears to motivate me, I approached the nearest bag and sized it up.

The first punch I landed into the mass of leather felt good. But the pain stinging in my fists and arms after an hour's worth of punching wasn't enough to stop the ache deep within my chest, in my heart.

I threw more and more blows into the bag, wishing I had more free time, wishing I could take boxing and have someone to spar with. As the thought of Tynesha came to mind, I wished for a speedy year and threw a lethal blow.

All the while fighting off the temptation of a certain dimpled smile.

Regan

For the first time in a long time, I was having fun with Troy. Sunday evening, he came and took me to the last night of a local carnival. We were double dating. Or, according to Tommy J, "hanging out" with him and a girl from his sophomore class, Jasmine Cooley.

I knew her only in passing, since she was a year younger and she hung in a different crowd than Avery, but she was always extra nice to me, possibly due to my affiliation with Troy. Jasmine was a very pretty girl with big silky 3B hair, and her dark brown skin always seemed to radiate with a glow most would envy.

"Yo, we needed this," Troy said to me.

Ahead of us Tommy and Jasmine were eyeing different rides and booths. They weren't holding hands like Troy and I were.

"We did." In a move to be affectionate, I snuggled close to him.

"I care about you, you know?" Troy said to me. "I know I've been acting impatient and rude lately, but I do care about you."

I put a smile on my face, ignoring the impulse to point out

you didn't treat people terribly when you cared about them. Troy was trying, and for that I tried, too.

"Never again, okay?" I said.

He squeezed me close, holding on to my gaze and what felt like my heart, too. "I can't lose you, Rey. I don't want to be that guy. I like going out, but no girl can replace you. No other girl could put up with my rants about football, no girl could make me laugh when I'm pissed or argue with me about stupid stuff. We'll do things your way."

There was no reason to be upset or fight anymore. "Okay."

"Hey." Troy perked up. "I've got a college visit coming up, you should come with me and check out their accounting programs."

Accounting. The bane of my existence. "What if I don't like accounting?"

His brows knitted together in confusion. "What do you mean? You're probably just nervous and psyching yourself out."

Wrong. If there was one thing I was certain of these days, as I tried to figure myself out, it was that I *wasn't* nervous about accounting—I hated it. I hated math. I didn't want to spend my life staring at numbers all day.

"Actually..." I finally had time to confess how much I *loathed* my vocation, how much I couldn't stand walking into Accounting 101, how much my ears wanted to bleed whenever my dad brought up his daily question about it. "I'm not too—"

"Bet you can't do it, Five."

We'd come to a stop behind Tommy and Jasmine. They were studying a game that tested your skill in knocking down empty soda bottles. Tommy puffed up his chest.

Troy rolled his eyes. "Bet."

Maybe we'd talk later.

One thing about Tommy and Troy, there seemed to be an unspoken competition between them. Tommy specifically chose the number 50 for his jersey because he swore he was ten times better than Troy. I was never sure who was the best of the two of them. Still, as the boys got ready to compete, I made sure to stand by Troy's side.

He looked back at me and grinned.

"Which prize you want, JC?" Tommy asked Jasmine.

She eyed the array of stuffed characters hanging on the wall of prizes to claim. "Ooh, Stewie from *Family Guy*."

"Say less."

There were so many iconic cartoon characters on the wall. If Troy won, I wanted the enormous stuffed Clifford the Big Red Dog. I loved the color red and I loved dogs; it was a win-win.

I stood back to give them room and Jasmine did the same. The guy behind the counter counted down from three and the boys immediately commenced their game.

Their first attempt saw them both as losers, prompting them to shovel out five more dollars to play another round. By their *third* try, I tapped out and found myself wandering away to people watch.

Couples and kids with their parents were lining up by the vendor offering fresh French fries, hot dogs, nachos, and ice-cold drinks. I drifted across the walkway from the boys and leaned against the railing to watch parents ride the carousel with their children. I'd always had a thing for carousels. When I was a kid and my parents would bring me to the mall, it was a must that I rode it. Sometimes, I questioned the age limit and still wanted to ride.

Even with all the commotion from the rides, games, and

chatter in the air, I could still hear someone playing their radio loudly nearby. An old Taylor Swift song was on; she was singing about sparks flying whenever she saw some guy. It was a sweet love song, but hearing it, and seeing girls my age walking hand in hand with their guys with glitter in their eyes, I couldn't relate.

I swallowed this thought. Troy and I were on a new path, a *better* path; we were content and okay.

"Hey! There you are." Troy materialized beside me. "Don't tell me you didn't see it?"

I put on a chipper face, ignoring the pop tune still playing. "See what?"

"Me kick Tommy's ass."

Peeking back at the booth, I could see Tommy playing against Jasmine. At least he wasn't a sore loser.

Troy tapped my shoulder and when I returned my attention to him, he held up the big stuffed Clifford the Big Red Dog. "For you."

A huge grin spread across my face. "Oh my God!"

"I know you like dogs, so I figured you'd love this," Troy reasoned.

I stood on my toes and kissed him repeatedly. "I do, I love it, thank you."

Troy just stared at me, a softness in his eyes. "You make me feel like a winner, Rey. I wanted to win something special for you."

My heart swelled as I hugged Clifford to my chest. With all Troy's football accolades, it felt good to know that I made him feel like a winner, too. "I'll love it forever, I promise."

"Let's go ride the Ferris wheel," he suggested. He took me under his arm and led me to the ride. The smell of fresh elephant ears drifted to me, and the sight of a little girl carrying a huge powdered sugar–coated elephant ear had my mouth watering in envy. I had to get one as soon as we got off the ride.

Once on the wheel, I stayed snuggled up to Troy, trying to keep the mood.

"You and me, Rey, to the top." He pointed high above. I didn't doubt for a moment that he would reach such heights; it was written in the stars. "Just you and me."

Him and me.

People liked Troy and me together. We were goals to them. Trouble was, I just wanted to be normal. I wanted to be Regan, but I knew deep down Troy could never just be Troy. He was Troy Jordan, MVP of the Arlington High Panthers, soon-to-be college football star on his road to the NFL. He wasn't the first promising baller out of Arlington High; there were a couple other boys who'd gone into the league from previous classes. But he was the most watched, the most loved, and the most rooted for. He would never have normal.

I stared into his eyes, putting a smile on my face as I hugged my stuffed Clifford close. "Yeah, you and me."

Troy grinned, coming close and pressing his lips to mine in a sweet, chaste kiss.

There were glowing lights all around us, but as I looked on, I didn't see any sparks.

Troy dropped me off, obliging me by not walking me to the door. It was better this way, so I didn't have to watch my father trip over himself with praise and admiration as he so often did at the sight of Troy.

Instead, I kissed him good-night, thanked him for Clifford, then slipped into the house. With my back against the door, I breathed, long and deep.

"How'd it go?" My father was in the TV room. *No surprise there.*

Entering the room would instigate a full-on conversation, so I only poked my head in, finding him watching a football game as he sat back with a glass of water. The earnest expression on his face made my heart clench—it was like a child was looking at me, expecting the world of me, and I had to come through.

"It was great." I held up my gift. "Troy won me this."

My father cracked a smile. "Nice of 'im."

"Yeah. I'm going to go shower and catch up on homework before bed," I said.

He waved me off, and I carried myself across the foyer to the staircase. I should've gotten into acting, I was so good at it.

I was so in my head that I nearly ran into Avery as I made my way up the steps. The forlorn expression on his face pulled me from my own troubles. "Hey, what's up?"

He lifted and dropped his shoulder. "Just getting ready to watch football with Dad."

I narrowed my eyes. "Since when do you like football?"

Avery pulled a face as if the answer wasn't already obvious. "Come on, Rey."

"Want me to say something?" Honestly, when would our father realize that Avery was just not that into sports?

He frowned and kicked at the carpet. "I don't need you babying me. I can handle a football game, no big deal."

He went on down the steps and I felt my shoulders sag. I might not have been able to fix my own messy world, but making things easier for my brother would at least make me feel better.

"Hey, Dad?" I called out.

"Yeah, Rey?"

"Do you mind if Avery helps me with something? The shelf in my closet needs to be adjusted." It was yet another small lie, but this was for the greater good.

In another moment, Avery was coming back up the staircase, looking at me funny.

I tossed my brother a smile, tilting my head toward his room. "Go on, in another minute he'll be too caught up in the game to notice you're taking too long."

Avery smiled a little as he walked by me and disappeared into his bedroom.

It wasn't much, but at least one of us was free.

Exhausted, I quickly went up to my room to change so I could take Tanner for a walk.

Guillermo

"Do you think things will be like before?" Yesenia asked me Sunday night as we sat out on the porch swing.

"Before was bad, remember?"

"Like…*before*-before, when everybody was happy and you weren't always in trouble." She held one of her books in her tiny hands. She'd put it down when I came out and joined her after dinner.

"I'm hoping things will be better than ever, yes," I told her truthfully. "I can't run from my past or let it consume me either."

"Well, I think things will be best," Yesenia declared.

I envied her optimism and positivity. I wasn't sure what was in those books she was always reading, but I admired the way they gave her hope.

Even still, she was another person I owed an apology, too.

"Hey, I'm sorry, okay?" I spoke up. "I know the focus has been on me, but you lost a lot of friends in this move, and it's not fair."

A frown tugged on Yesenia's features, and her gaze fell to the porch. "It wasn't fair, Memo. I didn't do anything, and I had to pack up my whole world because of what *you* did, and they never even asked me how I felt."

Guilt swept through me, making me feel worse. I pulled her in close for a hug. "I'm sorry. I'm here, okay, if you want to talk or vent."

Yesenia leaned into me. "I get it, I do, but starting over was hard on me, too."

"I'll make it up to you, I promise," I swore. Somehow, someway, she deserved something to compensate for uprooting her life for me.

The front door opened and our father poked his head out. "You good?"

Yesenia bobbed her head merrily, standing from the porch swing to go inside. "Yes, I'm going to finish this in my room. It's getting too dark out here."

My father stepped outside as Yesenia went by him and into the house. He leaned against the pillar on the porch, pocketing his hands and peering up at the night sky.

"How's school?" he asked of me.

Standing, I went and leaned against the pillar opposite him, going and watching the same view. "School's pretty decent so far."

"Friends?"

"One of the new kids I'm hangin' with is actually the son of my probation supervisor."

My father faced me. "Yeah?"

"She's cool with it. He's kind of quiet and awkward, I'm almost certain I'm the first guy he's hung around. I guess that's not a bad thing anymore now that I'm turnin' a new leaf." I gave a loose smile, hoping my father believed me. I wanted to make him proud, wanted him to see that I was eager to change and make things right here, at Arlington High and with my community service. No more backsliding.

My father appeared thoughtful as he bobbed his head. "And the girl?"

I swallowed, confused. "What girl?"

"The one you saw a movie with."

"Jenaya? She's also a new friend. She's single and clean," I was quick to clarify. "She's also the reason I realized I messed up a good thing here. Not everybody has a home life like this, and I took that for granted, Papá. She's tough, because she has to be, but I'd like to be there as a friend for her."

My father smirked, unable to hide his smile as he shook his head. "You wear a cape so well, Memo."

I rubbed the nape of my neck, feeling uneasy in case he was alluding to Tynesha. "This isn't like that."

"I know," he agreed. "You don't got that look in your eye."

"What look?"

He grinned at my ignorance. "You were so dopey over that other girl. Even if she was leading you to hell, you were ready to burn for her. You speak of this new one, Jenaya, like you speak of protectin' Yesenia. Careful, though, not everybody's fight can be fought. Don't take on more than you can chew, you're still findin' yourself here. If she needs help, help her, but don't throw yourself over the coals if you don't have to, okay?"

He was giving me the okay to be there for Jenaya if needed, and that felt good. Rewarding. *Trusting.*

"Yeah." I faced the sky again, suddenly feeling a weight lift from my shoulders. Yeah, we'd be better than before, I was sure of it. "There's a kid down the street I played soccer with. You want to talk about obsessed, that's all he talks about."

"You give 'im a run for his money?" my father teased.

Athletic or not, there was no beating a pro like Raviv. "Nah, he bested me, but it was fun. I'm not interested in joining a team, but maybe every once in a while, it wouldn't be so bad to kick back and play. Maybe we could start a game with Tío Matt sometime."

My father stood away from the pillar and checked the time on his smart watch. He released a yawn. "Don't remind me, he's talking about training for next summer's 8K."

"Yeah," I agreed. "I don't see that going well for you. Eres todo un vejestorio."

"Hey!" He laughed as he smacked the back of my head.

The sight of him smiling, lightening up, made me feel good. To be like this, laughing and joking around, it felt like a dream come true.

"Listo?" he asked as he went for the screen door.

I buried my hands in my pockets, hunching my shoulders as the September air nipped at me in my T-shirt and jeans. "Nah, give me another minute."

My father went back in, telling me not to stay out too late seeing how I had school in the morning. While I was never an honor roll student, I did want to apply myself more at Arlington High. Hell, I even wanted to ace Mrs. Renner's chemistry class, eccentric teacher or not.

The thought of class turned my mind to Regan, and I glanced at her house just as the front door opened. Regan herself appeared in the doorway before stepping outside with her family's dog.

The smart thing to do would've been to turn around and go inside. But I told myself I was just being friendly as I crossed the street. I told myself I was just going to say hi. But once

Regan smiled at me and I set eyes on those cute dimples, I knew better than to keep lying to myself.

"Late-night walk?" I asked as I spotted the leash she had in hand. The dog was sniffing me again, and I didn't mind even if Regan insisted on tugging him away.

"I've sorta taken on the dog care role in my family. It's okay, I love dogs. Besides, my dad has a history of losing our dogs ever since I was a kid. He once lost Tanner, and that was an awful week without him."

I leaned down and rubbed Tanner's head, admiring the playful look on his face as he panted. "That sounds rough."

"It was. But this walk is more for me than for him," Regan confessed. "Want to join me?"

It was probably a bad idea, but I was curious about this girl and what had her always running, from her boyfriend and now from her own house.

We started off down the sidewalk, walking away from her house and mine, side by side.

"My dad's in there watching football, and there's only so much sports I can take, you know?" Regan groaned as she focused on Tanner trotting ahead of us.

I tried to understand her angst, but I didn't get it, especially considering Troy, Arlington High's football god. "Football seems to be a big part of your life."

Regan frowned, and I tried not to think about why that made my chest twist. "Does your family like football?"

"Not Americano."

Regan snorted. "Lucky you."

"Bet he's mad happy you're seeing Troy, huh?"

"You have no idea." She sounded tired.

Still, it didn't make sense. "How'd you two meet and become 'Troy and Regan'?" I asked.

"Troy started pursuing me and my dad found out and he's a big fan." Regan made a face.

I wagged my finger. "That may be my favorite love story of all time."

My sarcasm had her rolling her eyes. "You wouldn't get it."

"Probably not," I agreed.

Regan sighed. "Do you ever just wish to be someone else?"

I nudged her, flashing her a smile. "If I had a superpower, I'd choose invisibility, remember? Although, I'm startin' to like being me again." I looked into her dark eyes. "There's always time to start likin' who you are and bein' yourself."

Regan bit her lip and I had to stop myself from noticing. "Again, you have *no* idea."

I stopped walking and faced her, not wanting a riddle. Red flags were flying, telling me this was Pandora's box and I was getting way too close, but then deep down, I had a feeling she wasn't trouble. That this wouldn't be like *before*, should I get to know her more. From Troy, to her community service gig, to her home life, nothing seemed to make her radiate happiness.

If it wasn't so late, I'd dive completely headfirst into stupidity and offer to take her out for a game of pool to ease her mind.

I really should've turned and walked away.

But I didn't.

Her cell phone rang and broke our trance, and she looked away as she dug it from her red hoodie. One glimpse at the screen had her sighing and turning back for her house. "Duty calls."

I felt my brows furrow. "You make it sound like a job."

She peeked back at me. "Some days, I'm not sure it isn't."

"Maybe you should change that," I suggested.

Regan only stared at me, then shook her head as if *I* didn't get it.

A deep need tugged inside me to find out just who she was and what she was all about beneath the surface.

Yep, I definitely needed to stay away from this girl. My father was wrong, I wasn't wearing a cape. I had wings, and like that Icarus guy, I was getting ready to fly too close to the sun.

Regan

Everything was in chaos. We were beyond busy Tuesday afternoon at the community center. Somehow, we'd double-booked our banquet room for a women's leadership conference and a business seminar. A large party had shown up for each, and everything was a royal mess as the leaders of both groups argued about their deposits and receipts.

Daren and my mother were being yelled at as they frantically checked the registry and calendar at the front desk.

"I honestly don't understand how this could've happened," my mother was saying as she tried to soothe Miss Andrews, the woman in charge of the leadership conference. My mother shot Daren a look. "Who took down the events?"

Daren started typing into the reservations on the computer. "One of the volunteers might have—we've had issues with a few not paying attention to the dates."

It sounded like Daren was throwing one of the teen assistants under the bus, but in his defense, a few of them had absentmindedly booked things on the same day before. Running the front desk was an easy job when all you had to do was sit and hand out passes, take money, or answer calls and book events. Some of my coworkers were careless about their job, and it showed, as the man from the business seminar, Mr. Walton, started chewing Daren out.

My mother kept her calm, though I could see her taking an easy breath before stepping in to help. "I think I have a solution to accommodate you both, and my further apologies for the delay—"

A loud scream sounded from outside. A child's cry.

My mother sighed, reaching up and briefly massaging her temples. "Regan, please go and see what's going on and fix it. I don't care how, but fix it."

"Unbelievable." Miss Andrews harrumphed.

My mother stepped around the front desk and faced her problems head-on. "Miss Andrews, go ahead and set up your conference in the banquet room."

"What? What about me?" Mr. Walton exclaimed.

My mother appeased him with a friendly smile. "I've got an idea for you, since your group isn't as large. Both of you will be treated to deli platters and fruit trays on us."

I watched as my mother spoke in a soothing, yet commanding tone that held the attention of the room. As she began to work her magic, I hustled toward the playground exit.

The screaming had ceased, but in the distance I could see a small crowd gathered in the grass away from the playground equipment, looking down at something. As I drew closer to the group, I spotted Guillermo. He was kneeling down and through the gaps between the kids I could see animal fur, causing me to quicken my pace.

"What's going on?" I asked.

There, lying on the ground breathing slowly, was a dog.

His light brown coat made me think of Tanner and my heart tightened as I knelt near Guillermo to assess the situation.

The dog was calm despite the crying group of kids around him.

"I think his leg is broken or something. He seems sick, too," Guillermo said.

The dog, probably a mutt, appeared to be a mix between a golden retriever and a Lab. It was thin to the point of starvation, and one of its hind legs was swollen.

"It can't die!" a little girl cried, tears soaking her brown face.

I gently rubbed the dog's head to comfort it. "Emma, honey, calm down."

Guillermo removed his lawn gloves, swearing beneath his breath as he swept a stray hair behind his ear. "He needs attention now."

"Let's go get an adult," Emma begged.

"They're busy with their own crisis right now," I said. "Plus, animals aren't allowed in the facility."

I sat back on my calves, trying to keep my own self from breaking down. Guillermo was right, the dog needed help right now.

On the playground I could see April, one of my coworkers, sitting on a swing texting on her phone. She was in charge of the group of kids outside playing while Mrs. Bloom took care of the younger kids inside in our after-school classroom. The adults were busy; it was up to me to navigate this situation, scary or not.

I faced Emma and offered up a smile. "Do me a favor? Go and take the others to April. I'm going to take care of the dog and get him help, okay?"

Emma wiped her face before gathering the other boys and girls and leading them back to the playground.

"What now?" Guillermo asked, looking at me steadily.

"I need a favor," I began cautiously, in case he rejected me. "There's an animal hospital fifteen minutes from here, it's where my dad takes Tanner."

"Go on," Guillermo insisted.

I looked into his dark eyes, noting his stoic expression. "I don't want to wait—can we take him in your car? I'll find a way to pay you back or clean—"

"Won't your mom be mad we left?" he interrupted, already standing up and tucking his gloves in his back pocket.

The last thing I was worried about was my mom. "We'll worry about that later. I'll take the heat if we get in trouble."

Guillermo fished in his pocket, procured his keys, and tossed them to me. "I'm going to pick him up and put him in the back seat. I need you to open the door for me."

"Be careful," I instructed. I hoped moving the dog wouldn't cause more damage.

But Guillermo was gentle as could be as he bent down and scooped the dog to his chest, then carefully lifted him up. The dog whimpered just slightly as he rested against Guillermo.

There was no time to cry at the sound of the dog's pain. I raced ahead to Guillermo's car where it sat in an employee parking spot. I unlocked the back door and held it open, waiting for Guillermo to make his way over with the dog.

He set the dog gently across the back seat before accepting his keys from me. He rounded the car and was quick to climb behind the wheel. I grabbed the handle to the back door, but Guillermo leaned over. "Shouldn't one of us stay?"

"I'm coming with you." I jumped in without a second thought and allowed the dog to rest his head on my lap.

My mother was busy weathering her own storm. I could handle this—after all, it was what she had told me to do.

Guillermo cranked up his car and took off for the animal hospital, following the instructions Siri was giving him from his phone.

The dog was breathing heavy now, his eyes closed tight as he whimpered.

My chest ached for his pain. *Poor guy.*

"It's going to be okay, boy," I told him. I faced the road, crossing my fingers and wishing things would be okay.

Guillermo pulled up to a red light, then stole a glance at me in the rearview mirror, his dark eyes measuring me. A thick brow raised curiously.

"What?" I asked.

"You okay? You're not freaking out."

I smirked. "Should I be crying?" I sure wanted to.

He snorted and turned back to the road ahead of us. "I don't know, I'm losin' my shit over here. I was cleanin' the yard and I saw all those kids huddled around and I raced over thinkin' someone was hurt, and it was a dog limpin' around. He fell over and that girl, Emma, screamed."

I reached out and squeezed his shoulder. "I'm freaking out, too, but I'm trying to be strong, for the dog."

Guillermo removed one hand from the wheel and seized mine in his, squeezing gently.

The light turned green and he drove on. It wasn't much, but the shared hope between us was enough to carry us to the animal hospital.

At Waterloo Animal Clinic, I opened the back door for him to gather the dog, then led the way inside.

The receptionist, whose name tag read Sarah, took one

look at the dog in Guillermo's arms and her face fell awash with sympathy.

"Aw, what's wrong?" she asked as she sat up in her seat.

"I think he's real sick," Guillermo explained. "His leg is swollen and he whines whenever I move him."

Sarah frowned as she gathered some paperwork. "Poor guy. What's his name?"

Guillermo opened his mouth but I stepped up. "Simba." I gave him a casual shrug. It was better than sending the dog off into the world without a name. Everyone deserved a name. "We found him at work, he was limping around the playground."

"So he's not your dog?" Sarah clarified.

"No, we just found him," Guillermo said.

Chances were, if we didn't help, Simba would be put to sleep. Panic set in, and I whirled around and took in the pooch's face. He had to be a year old at the most, far too young to die.

"I'll pay for his medical attention," I said, facing Sarah. Then my stomach dropped. "Oh God." My book bag with my wallet and emergency debit card was back at the center, and I had a strong feeling the hospital wouldn't take Apple Pay.

"I can pay." Guillermo's strong and confident voice comforted me. "Can you guys help him?"

Sarah handed me some paperwork to fill out as a nurse came and helped Guillermo place Simba on a gurney.

I filled out the paperwork as best as I could before sitting in the open waiting area. In the center of the room was a large fish tank with a bench beneath it. I sat there, finding the luminescent blue water tranquil. In the row of chairs to my left, an elderly couple waited. The man held an empty carrier in his lap.

The news was on the large flat screen TV hanging in the corner of the room, but I paid it no mind as I stared at the floor as my hands shook in my lap.

Guillermo came to sit beside me. He pulled his ponytail holder from his hair, and he ran both hands through it, then exhaled as he leaned over. "Say something, I don't want to think about Simba not makin' it."

"Thank you," I told him. "For offering to pay. I can pay you back. She said something about giving us a discount, thank God."

Guillermo shook his head. "Nah, I've got so many wrongs to right, this is nothing."

I could tell my mother was against us being friends, but I didn't care. I jumped through hoops for everyone and didn't get a say in anything, it felt. Because I wanted to be Guillermo's friend, I reached out and rubbed his back. I sniffled as tears came to my eyes. "I think we just saved a life, and there's nothing righter than that."

Guillermo peered at me, cracking a small smile. He raised a hand, about to wipe my eyes, but stopped himself, as if he were crossing a line. Instead he set his hand in his lap and squeezed and opened his fist. "Maybe we found our calling."

I sat back against the fish tank case, staring ahead at the news. "Accounting is my calling." Whether I liked it or not.

"You already got it all mapped out? What school you goin' to?" Guillermo asked me.

College was tricky. Sometimes Troy would hint that he wanted us to go to Ohio State together, but while the thought was nice, I just wasn't sure.

"I don't know. I must've watched Beyoncé's *Homecoming* a dozen times. I get more inspired every time, and for a while I was really set on going to an HBCU. We have Central

State here, but Akron U is closer and convenient." My cheeks warmed and I looked away. "I know it's dumb to get motivated to go to a school because of a singer, but I don't know, it just makes me feel pride in my skin, you know?"

Guillermo frowned. "I don't think you should apologize or feel weird that a Black singer inspired you to feel good in your skin and want to educate yourself. I'm proud to be Brown and nobody can take that from me, and whenever one of us wins, I feel it deep in my chest." He pounded his heart for emphasis. "Being of color, especially Black in America, ain't a joke, so if Bey lifts you up, you stay up. Even if you don't go to an HBCU, I'm sure you can find a club dedicated to Black students to thrive in."

I loved that he was supportive. If only my own parents—my father—could be the same.

When I began to feel chilly, Guillermo didn't hesitate to take me under his arm, first asking if the gesture was okay. I nuzzled close to him, enjoying the faint scent of his rich spicy cologne.

"Guillermo Lozano?" A doctor came into the waiting area wearing a long white coat over her baby blue scrubs. Her brunette hair was pulled back into a ponytail, and her young and friendly face didn't hold an ounce of defeat. Perhaps we weren't about to receive bad news.

I stood along with Guillermo. "Yes?"

"Hi, I'm Dr. Meyer." She held her hand out and Guillermo and I both shook it. "I just wanted to let you know that Simba appears to be dehydrated and malnourished, and he's suffered a broken leg. It's a good thing you found him when you did, I'm not sure he would've made it another day out there."

Leaning into Guillermo for support, I felt my heart leap into my throat. "Is he going to be okay?"

"I want to keep him here overnight for observation, but with plenty of fluids and some food, he should be fine. Do you intend to keep him?"

A sense of excitement flooded through me at the idea of keeping Simba. Of watching him heal and grow.

But then reality came crashing into me.

Tanner was a friendly dog, but more than likely my parents wouldn't allow us to take Simba in long-term. If Guillermo's family wouldn't take him, where would he go?

"My family already has a dog." I looked to Guillermo. "Will yours let you have him?"

He shook his head. "We're still gettin' settled, I'm not sure my dad's up for it right now."

"Well." Dr. Meyer cleared her throat. "Our sister clinic, Kind Paws, also has a rescue service. I'd be more than happy to send Simba their way as soon as he's more comfortable with transportation."

I breathed a sigh of relief, unable to stop the tears from rolling down my cheeks. "Oh my God, thank you." Overcome with joy, I hugged Dr. Meyer. I couldn't take Simba in, but he wouldn't be euthanized either. Surely someone would adopt him; he was too cute not to be loved.

Dr. Meyer gave me a gentle hug before pulling away. "It's not a problem. We typically send unclaimed animals their way. All animals sent to Kind Paws are rescued and adopted—they are one hundred percent a no-kill shelter."

"That's a relief," Guillermo commented, and went to pay at the front desk.

It was getting late, and a glimpse at my phone found a couple of missed texts from Troy and Malika, but not my mother.

With Simba in good care, I promised to return the next day and followed Guillermo to his car. I wasn't sure what lay ahead of us back at the center, but I felt bubbly inside. We did it. We had saved a life.

In the parking lot, not caring whether anyone was around, I did a little victory shimmy just to let out the butterflies.

Guillermo was grinning at me over the hood of his car, squinting just slightly. "What was that?"

Unashamed, I stood tall and proud. "My happy dance."

Guillermo chuckled as we climbed back into his Charger. "That has got to be the most interesting thing I've ever seen."

I elbowed him. "Don't hate."

"I'm not. It was cute." Guillermo gathered his ponytail holder and brought his hair back into its usual bun.

I liked his hair loose, but I didn't say that to him.

The ride back to the center was a much happier one than the one to the hospital. I couldn't explain it really, but I felt proud of myself. I was in control. I'd seized the moment, and I'd gotten Simba help. Nothing could take that from me.

"Shit."

I came down from cloud nine at Guillermo's curse.

He pulled into his parking space while my mother stood in front of the center's door with her arms crossed, as if she had sensed our arrival. The look on her face let me know she wasn't in a good mood.

"Let me talk to her," Guillermo insisted.

Bad idea, *he* was on probation. "No, let me."

He grimaced as we got out of the car and prepared to face my mother's wrath.

"Just where have you been?" she demanded immediately, marching up to us.

"There was a—"

"Inside." She cut me off, looking to Guillermo for answers.

"No." I stepped up. I didn't want him getting yelled at

for driving me to the hospital, especially when he had done a good thing. This was my fault for dragging him into the rescue.

"Regan." It was a warning my mother was losing her patience.

"It's my fault, ma'am," Guillermo said.

I didn't back down. He was not about to play martyr for me. "No!" They both faced me, Guillermo wishing me to be quiet with his eyes, and my mother breathing in through her nose to calm herself down. "There was an injured dog and it had the kids crying. You told me to fix whatever was wrong, you said you didn't care how, so I had Guillermo take me to Waterloo Animal Clinic. That's where we've been."

My mother softened just an ounce, then turned her attention to Guillermo. "Is that what happened?"

"The dog was starvin' and he had a broken leg. He must've been on the street for days. I didn't see a collar, so I don't think he has an owner." Guillermo looked my mother in the eyes, standing firm. "Regan stepped up and took charge, ma'am. She saved his life. She's a hero."

My mother rolled her eyes, but she lost her resolve. "You have a lot of work left to do, Guillermo, please get to it." She shifted her gaze to me. "As for you, you could've called."

"You were handling World War III, and I just wanted to deal with it as best as possible, like you would've done." My mother hadn't been remotely overwhelmed by the disaster earlier; she'd managed it all with poise.

She sighed. "Come on, there's some fruit and deli sandwiches left if you want some. You can tell me all about your little rescue mission."

I let her go ahead of me to the front entrance so I could

have a final moment with Guillermo. His mind seemed to already be elsewhere as he put on his lawn gloves once more.

"I didn't mean to get you in trouble." I hoped my mother wouldn't hold this incident against him. I'd needed him and he'd been there for me...again.

Guillermo focused on his gloves, keeping his distance "Like I said, I've got a lot of wrongs, what's one more?"

"Well, like *I* told *you*, I don't see any wrong in what we did."

"Do you always see the good in everybody?"

I wasn't a total optimist, but my gut told me Guillermo wasn't someone to count out. "I do when I look at you."

He blinked. "I'm not in trouble, so we're good."

I started to go after my mother, but turned to look back at him one final time. "Thanks for helping me today."

Guillermo looked at me, his full lips curling into a smile, then he gave a little shrug. "No problem. I'd be happy to drive the getaway car for you anytime."

I smiled back, deeply. We'd run off together on a rescue mission, done something amazing for Simba, and now he'd live to see another day.

No, there was no shame in that.

Guillermo

Flying was nice. No, really—since I was acting like Icarus against my better judgment, a part of me understood the beauty of flying toward the sun and her gorgeous rays. Some might have called Icarus an idiot for taking such a risk, leading to his own demise, but they didn't understand. It wasn't about getting burned. It was about that tiny moment of being so close to something so beautiful that the end result didn't matter, because that one moment was worth it.

That was what I was telling myself as I got chewed out by Mrs. London after clocking out Tuesday afternoon. My little rescue mission with Regan had served a great deed, but Mrs. London wasn't entirely impressed.

"I'm sure you had good intentions, but honestly, Guillermo, what were you thinking?" Mrs. London stood in the doorway, making it impossible to leave without hearing her full reprimand. I knew it was coming, despite her daughter's best efforts to smooth things over.

While Mrs. London had been surprised to see I'd formed

a friendship with her son, she had no interest in allowing the same to happen with Regan. Avery was the quiet, introverted loner, but with me and Jenaya, he was slowly coming out of his shell. I was a good influence in that department, she couldn't deny that. With Regan dating the football god, there was no way Mrs. London would look at any type of relationship with me as anything other than a downgrade. If she only knew.

"Simba was in pain and hurting, I only thought about gettin' him help," I said.

"Simba?"

"Regan named him." I faced Mrs. London with a sheepish smile. "She's a real sweet girl that way."

"I'm aware." Mrs. London shook her head, disappointment rolling off of her in thick waves, flooding the space between us with shame. "Your purpose here is to give us your time and hours to right your wrongs. You owe it to the state and to Shad." *Fuck him.* "And how fair would it be if I let you slide when it comes to the time you missed when you were going off with Regan playing Mr. Hero? No one else gets to just come and go as they please."

"It wouldn't be fair at all," I agreed.

"Harvey sent you here in good faith, and honestly, Guillermo, I'm starting to think that maybe he spoke *too* highly of you." Mrs. London folded her arms.

I stood strong, looking her in her eyes. "I wasn't trying to do anything bad, I just wanted to get Simba some help."

She wasn't convinced. "And you didn't think to get ahold of Daren, or me for that matter, before taking matters into your own hands?"

"We thought you were busy."

Mrs. London dug into her pocket and pulled out her cell

phone. She held it up. "I'm obligated to call Harvey when something like this happens. Because if *I'm* not getting through to you, maybe he will."

My stomach dropped and my heart along with it. Shit. Harvey, just like Mrs. London, wouldn't care about the circumstances surrounding Simba's rescue. He would be on my ass about this, and worse, he'd talk to my parents, my father. I wasn't ready to face his wrath, wasn't ready for him to give up on me and think of me as nothing but a failure.

"Please." I held my hand out as Mrs. London was scrolling through her contacts for Harvey's info. "Regan's got a good heart. *I* wasn't thinkin', I should've known better than to leave without tellin' you or Daren what was goin' on. It won't happen again. My next shift, I'll come an hour early and I'll stay an hour late to make up for the loss of time. I'll do whatever you want, just please, don't call Harvey."

Mrs. London sighed, her phone still clutched tight. "I expect a lot out of you, Guillermo. You seem like a decent kid who just made a lot of poor choices. I don't want to see that behavior manifest here. As a member of the Respect program, you need to take it seriously. I want you to show up on time and stay on campus, or at least alert one of us when there's an emergency.

"When it comes to my daughter, I'm not saying stay away, but *be* smarter. Don't be alone with her, or put yourself in situations where something can happen. What if Troy had seen you two arriving together? We're not trying to repeat history, remember? Think about stuff like that." She studied me, her face softening slightly. "Otherwise, it was a good thing, what you did for that dog. Just be more responsible next time."

Mrs. London left me alone to make my exit. Regan was

already long gone, making it easier to walk out of the center and think no further about the day's events.

No matter how much the image of her sitting beside me in my car was burned into my head.

Mrs. London didn't want me to stay away from her daughter, but she wanted me to stay away from her daughter. I could read between the lines pretty well. So when I went home Tuesday night, I didn't think about Regan on the way, I didn't think about her during dinner with my family, I didn't think about her while Yesenia prattled on about some book that had just come out, I didn't think about her during my shower, and I definitely didn't think about her as I closed my eyes and lay in bed, trying to find some sleep.

I didn't think about Regan London. Not those dimples, not her radiance, not that cute little happy dance she'd done in the parking lot, and not that look of triumph that had washed across her face when Dr. Meyer said that Simba would more than likely be okay.

Wednesday in homeroom, I forced interest in catching up on my homework. Staying away and ignoring Regan was my best option, I told myself.

"I'm free this afternoon, what are you doing later?" I asked Jenaya as we sat at lunch.

Avery was lost in some manga, oblivious to those around him.

Jenaya rested her elbow on the tabletop and pouted. "I think I gotta watch Brooklyn."

"That your baby brother?"

She nodded. "I think he's going to be the good one. He's only four, but so far he's real quiet and tries to be helpful."

Even if I hadn't known her long, I could tell Jenaya didn't want sympathy or pity. From what I could see, she could hold it down just fine on her own. But there was nothing wrong with a little help every now and then.

"You can bring him to my place," I offered. "I'm sure we got some kiddy movies lying around. Hell, one look at this kid and my mom might just snatch him."

Jenaya tried to hide her blush, but it made her look that much more cute. "Really?"

"My mom loves kids. When I was younger and Tío Matt and Tía Jacki had their twins, my mom would spend her days helping out. She never wanted to leave. She's a sucker for babies mostly, but cute little kids are up her alley, too."

Jenaya softened. "You really don't gotta do that for me, Mo."

I pretended to be offended at her making it seem like a chore as I rolled my eyes. "What are friends for? You'd be doing me a favor by hanging out with me."

Jenaya didn't protest as she mouthed a thank-you.

A tray smacked onto our table as a chair was pulled out and the smell of a hot slice of pizza greeted us. Raviv had actually broken away from his clique and joined us. He sat opposite Jenaya at our square table, with me on his left and Avery on his right.

"What's up?" he said, nodding at us all.

I was sure he knew Avery since they were in the same grade and lived on the same block, but it was more than clear he didn't know Jenaya. If we were going to be friends, he had to respect her and know what was up.

"Raviv!" I said with faux enthusiasm. "You remember my good friend Jenaya, don't you?"

Jenaya narrowed her eyes and looked from me to Raviv. "Is he one of those idiots who think we're dating or something?"

Raviv visibly cringed at being put on the spot. "Actually no, I may have put my foot in my mouth a few times, though. I'm sorry about that. It's nice to meet you officially. Any friend of Memo's is a friend of mine."

Jenaya pursed her lips and sized him up. "What makes you think I want to be friends with *you*?"

He blinked, seeming at a loss for words.

Jenaya cracked a smile. "I'm kiddin', just don't go puttin' your foot in your mouth anymore and we cool, okay?"

Raviv bobbed his head as he reached out and pounded his fist against hers.

"Did you guys have plans or something?" she asked, nodding toward Raviv.

"You probably just saved me from him invitin' me to play soccer," I let her know.

Raviv made a face, then looked to Jenaya. "The guy is good and should really be honing his skills."

"Maybe he should," she seemed to agree. "He could use the distraction."

He grinned. "I think we're going to be *best* friends."

Now I was rolling my eyes. I did need a distraction, but joining Raviv's soccer team was not about to be it.

"Hey."

Her voice sent me on alert, and the feel of her presence next to me had me losing my cool.

Regan was standing beside me. She made sure to greet everyone else before focusing on me.

The table got quiet, even Avery set his book aside, as they all looked from Regan to me. Then, because he was a pretty decent guy, Raviv cleared his throat and asked Jenaya a question, drawing the attention away from us.

I stood and walked with Regan into the aisle between our row of tables, out of the others' hearing. "What's up?" I kept my distance, trying to be nonchalant.

Regan was her usual self, smiling up at me all friendly. Oblivious to the effect she had on me. "I was actually going to stop by the hospital after school and see how Simba's doing. He's such a cute dog he'll probably be adopted fast, so I wanted to see him before he's gone. I was wondering if you'd come with me."

In my peripheral vision, I could see Troy sitting at their usual table, staring our way. The annoyed look on his face confirmed all that Mrs. London tried to tell me the day before.

Regan meant no harm, but distance was safe. "I've already got plans with Jenaya."

Her smile died, then she frowned a little. "Oh, okay."

I didn't want to come off like a dick, and because I did care about Simba, I loosened up. "But you can come tell me how he's doing when you get back." I inched back, shoving my hands in my pockets. "And send him my well wishes."

Regan nodded solemnly, offering me a small smile.

I watched her go back to Troy, and I returned to my table, trying my hardest not to look behind me.

Regan

It stormed all Thursday morning through the afternoon, making my shift at the community center long and tedious due to the lack of people stopping by. I didn't have park duty, because the after-school crowd stayed inside with the staff, who'd put on *Wreck-It Ralph.* By now, most of the kids had been picked up.

With nothing to do but answer the phone and properly schedule appointments, I was enjoying a little me time as I worked on homework and did some reading for English. My mother was even off for the day, so it was like a break from everything and everyone. No accounting talk, no football talk, no hovering, and no smothering.

And it was nice.

Malika: So he put the S on his chest and came to the rescue?

I'd had to tell someone about saving Simba with Guill-ermo. About the way it felt to save a life. About the trouble I hoped I hadn't landed Guillermo in.

Me: Malika!

Malika: What? He dropped everything to take you, coulda got you an Uber or somethin

Me: He was worried too

Malika: Still, he risked getting in trouble to help you. Says a LOT

It did, it really did. And now we were back to square one with him being so distant. I'd thought we were friends.

The sound of whistling pulled me away from my phone. Daren came around the corner, a little pep in his step as he approached the front desk. He glanced outside and shook his head before returning to me. "Gotta love the weather in this place, huh?"

A steady sheet of rain fell from the sky. I feared getting wet when it was time to go home. Even with my umbrella and hat, it looked unrelenting.

"Do me a favor and do last call for me on this floor," Daren said. "I'll check upstairs, but it's been pretty dead since the kids left."

It was seven thirty and we'd be closing in an hour. I had to do a round of checks in each room to let everyone know. Due to the storm, not many people had showed up that evening, but still I went from room to room on the first floor, not surprised to find them empty.

The lights in the rec room were on as well as a TV. When I poked my head into the fitness center, I saw one lone figure going at it with a punching bag.

Guillermo.

He viciously fed his fists into the mass of leather, bobbing and weaving as if his opponent was swinging back. From the lethal blows he was sending, I had a feeling a real person wouldn't stand a chance against him. No wonder that guy, Shad, hadn't been a match for him.

The door slammed loudly behind me, alerting Guillermo to my presence. He stopped what he was doing, turning and facing me. His dark hair was wet and wild from perspiration, his breathing uneven, and his dark eyes stared at me.

"Uh, last call," I let out, a little uneasy.

Guillermo nodded, shaking out his fists. "Yeah, I was just finishing up."

"I didn't see you come in."

"I've been here for an hour. Daren was up front when I came in. I thought he had the place to himself."

It was tempting to stay and talk, but I didn't want to bother him during his workout. I took one last look at the equipment in the room and turned to go.

"Regan," Guillermo called. He was watching me when I faced him, a hint of amusement on his face. "What do you do when the walls start closin' in on you?"

When weren't the walls closing in on me? "Suffer and endure."

He cracked a smile and shook his head. "C'mere."

The husky way he said it, the cocky little grin on his face, should've told me to reject him and leave. But I dared to go closer, all too aware that the topless boy in front of me was looking better and better the closer I got. Sweat rained down his fit and tan frame, and his skin glistened.

It wasn't until I was right in front of him that I saw it.

On the right side of his rib cage, a tattoo in lowercase script read *reckless*.

Oh wow.

It was…sexy, fitting his image effortlessly. I wanted to trace my fingers over it, feel the skin there and be just that. *Reckless.*

"Yeah, don't be like me." Guillermo chuckled as he looked down at himself. "I got this after my second arrest. I was feelin' really badass and one of my friends knew a guy, and this happened. My ma cried for weeks."

"I've seen way worse basement tattoos at school. This is good," I said.

"Wanna touch it?" he offered, noticing my continued stare.

I knew better, but I was too curious to say no. Timidly, I reached out to touch his tattoo.

The feel of his hot flesh beneath my fingertips caused goose bumps to prickle across my skin, and a weird sensation tingled through my body. I couldn't explain it, but I suddenly felt giddy.

His hand encircled my wrist, taking the lead. "Know how to punch a bag?"

I faced the black punching bag, intimidated. "No."

"Let me show you." He moved closer. "If you're going to be out walking around in the late evening to get away from that boyfriend of yours, at least let me show you how to defend yourself, *hoyuelos.*" His voice was like honey—sticky, sweet, enveloping me in a spell. "I want you to be safe when you're on your own. Okay?"

"Uh-huh."

Guillermo grinned, disappearing behind me and placing his hands on my waist as he steered me in front of the bag.

"I…I've never even been in a fight," I admitted.

"Of course not." His voice hummed in my ear, causing me to suck in a breath. I was fully aware of him in that moment. "Square up for me, get in your best fighting stance."

I made two fists and did my best impression of one of those

tough women from the few action movies I'd seen. If I looked ridiculous, Guillermo didn't say anything.

"What you're going to want to do in any situation is be calm and rational. Don't react—wait, and respond. Impulsive equals sloppy, got it?" He backed away and I found myself pouting at the coldness I felt at his absence.

I eyed the punching bag. "Do I just punch it?"

He held the bag and shook his head. "Nah, you gotta get in the zone."

"In the zone?"

"Whatever bullshit problems you have, make it this bag. Your dad. Stress. Expectations. Punch it away. *Own* this bag." He raised his fist for emphasis. "Make it yours."

Suddenly, all I could see was my dad yapping away about accounting, Troy and his greedy hands, everyone else and their expectations of me.

I threw my first punch hard into the bag. Pain accompanied the blow, but it felt good to release energy like that. I threw another punch and then another. Soon, I was grinning like a fool, proud of myself, even though I hadn't really done anything major. I'd thrown my first punch, and I was proud.

"I did it." I couldn't stop smiling as I examined my fist. I needed lotion now, but still, I felt accomplished. Tough even.

I gotta do this again.

Guillermo observed me like a proud parent. "You should keep practicing."

"I will."

He studied me, angling his head for a moment before rolling his shoulders and shaking out his hands. "It busy out there?"

"It's dead."

"I'm going to shower. Want to play a game of pool before closing up?"

I'd never cared for sports or games, especially with the way my father got so animated over football. But after losing pool to Guillermo before, I wanted to give it another go. I had to beat him, just once.

"Sure."

"Meet you in...ten, fifteen minutes?"

I nodded, then forced myself to keep it together and calmly walk back to the front desk—who was I kidding? As soon as the door to the fitness center shut behind me, I raced back up to the front and found Daren shrugging on his leather jacket.

"Can I take an extra break?" I asked.

Daren took a look around, noted no one who was still in the center, and nodded. "I'm about to sneak a cigarette, so sure, why not? Just don't tell your mom."

I raised my finger to my lips. "Our secret."

Daren slipped out into the rain and stayed close to the front windows for the slight protection the roof gave.

I didn't go to the rec room right away. I hung back, watching and waiting to see if the phone would ring or if anyone would stop by.

With my own cell empty of notifications, outside of a few likes on my social media page, I pocketed my phone and made my way to the pool table. The triangle sat in the middle with the balls racked and ready to go. I was slightly intimidated, but mostly eager to play again.

Running my finger along the royal blue felt, I imagined myself winning and wiping the smirk off Guillermo's face.

You can do it.

With my cue stick in hand, I tried to take a nonchalant warrior's stance.

A few minutes later Guillermo entered the room freshly showered and changed into a long-sleeved thermal underneath a red flannel top paired with dark-wash jeans. The smell of his bodywash danced into the room as he came to the table. Even with his clothes on, I could picture that tattoo gracing his skin.

"Ready to lose?" he teased as he chose his own cue stick and began chalking it up.

"You should be asking yourself that," I told him.

Guillermo whistled. "Famous last words." He reached up and pulled his hair back into a bun and secured it at the nape of his neck. It was a shame really.

"Before I forget…" I dug my phone out of my back pocket and scrolled through my photos in search of—there it was. "I got a picture of Simba before he goes to the rescue center."

Dr. Meyer had been optimistic about Simba when I'd stopped by after school to see him on Wednesday. She'd told me he was eating and drinking, and estimated he was about six months old. Despite my best efforts to keep it cool, I'd gotten all misty-eyed when I saw the pooch in his little cage. There was a cast on his hind leg, but he was otherwise doing better. When I'd gone home on Tuesday, I'd immediately gathered Tanner into my arms and just breathed him in.

Guillermo took my phone and examined the photo of Simba, a smile forming on his lips. He passed my phone back. "I'm real glad he's doing better. Yesenia about bawled her eyes out when I told her what happened."

His sister was so sweet. "Too bad your parents aren't ready for a dog."

He shrugged. "Give it a little more time and they'll break. Now that things are better, there's only so much longer they're going to be able to resist Yesi's puppy dog face. She's the cute one."

Liar.

I concentrated on placing my phone in my back pocket, ignoring the urge to compliment him.

Guillermo grabbed the triangle from the table and placed it on the wall where the cue sticks hung. "All right, let's make it happen."

"Will there be a prize?" I asked.

"Of course." He rounded the table, coming close like a hunter stealthily approaching prey. "Prizes equals stakes, and stakes make things fun. Do you want to have fun?"

Somehow, he'd managed to drip just the right amount of taunting into his tone as well as something that caused me to take a breath and tell myself to relax.

"Y-yeah," I told him. "I'm game."

The little smirk on his face should've let me know I was in for trouble.

He leaned against the table. "Ladies first, think you can break?"

Guillermo was looking at me and I was caught up watching him. I had no idea what he meant until it hit me. The balls, he wanted me to be the first to break them from their triangle.

"Sure, I got this," I boasted.

He smiled softly and stood away from the table. "Have at it."

I faced the table and vertigo threatened to end the game as anxiety set in.

Easy, you got this, Rey.

I mumbled motivating chants in my head as I bent down with the cue in my hand and positioned myself comfortably. It would probably take a few more games before I developed

a preferred method of handling the cue; even as I gripped it
and practiced sliding it through the tunnel of my thumb and
index finger, I didn't feel too confident. But I didn't let this
psych me out as I locked onto the cue ball, determined to
break and knock a ball into a pocket.

Letting out a breath, I released the cue stick with just
enough force and sent the cue ball rolling straight toward
the triangle. The balls went flying across the blue felt and
I watched with excitement as a solid ball and a striped one
went into two pockets.

Guillermo hung back, looking impressed. "Take your
pick—solid or stripes?"

"I'm pretty *solid* that I'm going to win, so I'll stick with
that," I gloated.

Amused, he chuckled. "Oh we gotta make this interesting. What's the prize?"

I'd be satisfied with beating him, especially after finding
him at the pool hall playing alone after hustling college guys
for their money. "I don't know. What do you want?"

Guillermo blinked and took his bottom lip into his mouth.
He soon looked elsewhere, an impish grin washing across
his face.

I narrowed my eyes. "Let me guess, winner gets a lap dance?"

A heavy look swept through his dark eyes. "I was considering going easy on you. Now, I might wanna win."

A fuzzy sensation erupted in my belly. "If I win, I want you
to post on your page that you are no longer the pool champ,
that Regan London owned you."

Guillermo snorted. "Yeah, that ain't happenin'."

"Better get those fingers ready, mister."

He sized me up, that cocky demeanor taking over. "Can
you even dance?"

The thing about Guillermo, I was coming to realize, he was every ounce a hot-blooded male. He stood there, gripping his cue stick and staring at me in such a way I felt my palms begin to sweat. I had to fight to concentrate on the task at hand.

"Uh-huh, but it don't matter. I'm going to win," I declared.

A brow arched. "Oh?"

"Yep, I've been watching YouTube videos."

Guillermo flashed me a cute grin as he laughed. "Ay, no, I'm playin' with a pool shark."

His sarcasm made me blush. I would probably lose, but I wouldn't go down without trying.

Determined, I gathered my cue stick once more and tried to line up another shot.

My palms were too sweaty. My grip slipped and my attempt to make a shot ended with me weakly grazing the tip off the cue ball and hitting nothing.

Crap.

Guillermo was nice enough not to mock my failure as he came around the table for his turn. Like the seasoned pro he was, he scanned the table, seeming to envision possible moves, planning his victory shot by shot. He leaned over the table, eyes trained on the cue ball before sending the stick toward it harshly. Two striped balls went into a corner pocket. Not done, he rounded the table and found a new angle to secure another ball into a side pocket.

I shouldn't have, but as if I were studying for an important exam, I found myself thinking through every detail about Guillermo. From the way he wore his hair back and how his shoulders would sag when he was feeling low and guilty, to the way he was careful whenever touching me, to his strong silence, or even the way he'd goof off with Yesenia whenever

I saw him about to take her somewhere. I especially admired his choice to go against the grain and befriend Jenaya, and include Avery in his private circle.

It was hard to believe he'd ever been a troublemaker. He seemed so incredibly kind and controlled.

He played pool meticulously, concentrating as he lined up each shot. He won the game in a matter of seconds, and it felt like he'd gone around the table in a calm blur.

I couldn't look at him when he was done, I was too busy pouting. How was he so good?

I felt him come up beside me, his presence demanding my attention. A look found a playful gleam in his eyes. "You were saying?"

What could I even say? He'd won, quickly and brutally.

"Fine." I pretended to huff. "What do you want?"

Guillermo looked thoughtful, and soon he was pulling out his phone and swiping the screen. Seconds later, an old familiar song began playing. It was "The Hokey Pokey."

Confused, I asked, "What?"

"I want to see you dance." The devilish grin he tossed me almost made me laugh, but I could tell he was serious. He held his hand out. "Give me your phone."

I took a step back and Guillermo took a step closer. "Huh?"

"You wanted me to post my loss on my page, but since I won, I want to post *you* doing a little dance for me."

My mouth dropped open. "You're not serious!"

He fiddled with his phone. "I won, and one thing about me, Regan, I *always* collect."

The atmosphere electrified and the humor was gone. I swallowed, unsure what I was feeling or how to react to it.

Guillermo furrowed his brows, losing his smile. "On second thought, you should go."

"Why?"

"Because I want to do something *really* stupid right now."
He spoke directly to my lips.

"Stupid, huh?" My brain told me to leave, but my legs
stayed planted where they were. Curiosity had me ready to
risk it all.

His arms circled my waist and my feet left the ground as
he lifted me up and set me on top of the pool table. *Oh.* He
came close, inches from my lips. I could feel his breath across
my skin. "Very stupid."

It felt like gravity wanted us closer, and I could feel us hovering just centimeters away from something that would be
mind-blowing.

Reaching out a shaky hand, I caught a loose strand of his
hair, coiling its silkiness around my finger.

Closer.

We were hypnotized by the charge between us and I could
almost close my eyes.

Closer.

I'd been kissed before, but this was something I wanted to
know about. What would kissing Guillermo Lozano *feel* like?

We were chest to chest, sharing the same breath, thoughts—
this moment. His hot hands singed my skin, boiling my blood,
sinking down to the bone. His devilish full lips were tempting, too tempting.

Closer—

I snapped out of my haze, suddenly remembering one major
thing: Troy.

Jerking away, I rushed off the table and was halfway to the
door when Guillermo shouted from behind me. "Regan,
wait! I'm sorry!"

I didn't stick around to hear him out. I flew back to the

front desk, where Daren was just coming in from his cigarette break.

"You okay? You look a little flushed." Daren slowly removed his jacket, looking over at me.

My cheeks felt hot as guilt washed over me. How could I have lost my head like that? "Yeah, I'm fine."

I issued a convincing smile before excusing myself to go to the restroom. I steadied myself against the edge of the sink, trying to calm my rapidly beating heart.

It had been so easy, so fluid, so fun and so natural—but so wrong.

The trouble was, I found myself questioning how could something so wrong *feel* so right.

Guillermo

The one good thing about the rain? It washed away everything—well, almost everything. When I stepped out of the community center Thursday night, I'd gotten soaked walking to my car. At the time, I hadn't cared. I let the rain come down on me, hoping it would wash away my sins.

It didn't.

I had almost fucked up, and I couldn't shake the unease.

The plan had been to stay away from Regan, but then she'd stepped into the fitness center and I got caught under her spell. When she'd appeared in the doorway with a halo of light coming down on her from the hallway, I could've sworn I was looking at an angel. The closer she got to me, the more my common sense went out the window.

She wasn't even my type, but there was no denying the truth: I had it bad for her. Against all logic and reason, I went along with her to play a game of pool, I teased her, I watched her—I flirted just a little. And then I lost it and almost fucking kissed her.

She'd fled from the room, and as much as my feet were

itchin' to chase after her, I didn't. It was better this way. We should stay apart.

I didn't eat dinner that night. I avoided my family as I went up to my room and forced myself to go straight to bed.

Bad idea.

As soon as I closed my eyes, I was enveloped in the sight of her. I could feel her soft skin, smell her pretty perfume, hear her cute little laugh, remember the bravery she'd had when she took charge and rescued Simba.

Needless to say, I didn't get much sleep Thursday night and as I pulled myself together to get ready for school Friday morning, I was more than a little cranky.

"You don't look so good." My mother caught me down in the kitchen. She frowned as she placed the back of her hand to my cheek. "You feelin' sick?"

She had no idea. "Just didn't get any sleep."

She took a motherly stance, hand on her hip. "You shouldn't be out so late in the rain like that. You might be coming down with something."

Catching a cold was my due after the events of the previous evening. Because even as I felt guilty, another part of me ached to know what Regan London's lips felt like. Beyond those damn dimples I admired so much, she had pretty lips with a perfect cupid's bow that I wanted to—

Fuck!

"Trust me." I focused on my mother. "I won't be doing that ever again."

Satisfied, she backed off. "Good, you missed dinner."

Missing a meal was like an insult in my family. The fact that my absence bothered her caused me to smile. We really were moving forward, my family and me. I couldn't mess that up.

I promised that I'd be home in time for dinner after my

shift at the community center, then slipped out the door and took a gulp of the fresh morning air. The happy sound of birds chirping brought my attention to the new day ahead of me; another shot at redeeming myself and starting over.

"Memo!" Raviv shouted to me from down the sidewalk as he made his way over.

I slapped my palm against his and reeled him in for a brief hug and pat on the back. "Sup?"

"Don't worry." He flashed me a smile and held up a hand. "I'm not about to rope you into a game of soccer. Cami and I were thinkin' about going to see that new Frank Grillo movie tomorrow, I think he's a cop in this one. You down? You could invite Jenaya and we'll make it a group thing."

He was really making an effort after his suggestive comments about her. I liked that about Raviv—he could admit he was wrong and move on and not let ego get in the way. Jenaya was great, and I was starting to see that Raviv was, too.

"Think we can squeeze in Avery?" I asked. He was a self-confessed homebody, but when he'd gone to the movies with Jenaya and me the week before, he'd had fun, letting loose and laughing alongside us.

Raviv didn't give this a second thought. "Sure, let me know what they all say and we'll figure out a time."

He went back to his house while I made a mental note to ask Jenaya and Avery if they were free Saturday evening. I was off from the center at four, so my night was pretty much free.

Across the street, the Londons' front door opened, and it was just my luck that Regan came outside. Would we play it cool and pretend it never happened? Or would she avoid me like I planned to do with her?

There was no hiding, being out in the open like this. Instead of playing awkward, Regan evidently decided to cross the street and come right over to me.

Despite the fact that I wanted to do what was best and leave her alone, I knew I owed her an apology. I should've known better and done better. Mrs. London had warned me, and I hadn't listened, but I would do better now.

"Hey." She didn't get too close, standing back on the sidewalk while I stood in my driveway beside my Charger. "Can we talk?"

I buried my hands in my pockets and dared to take a step closer. "I'm sorry about last night."

Regan frowned. "Don't be."

"I lost my head," I insisted. *I was caught up in your energy, drowning in intoxicating waves of you.* "I never want to feel like I'm takin' advantage of you or makin' you uncomfortable."

"You didn't, and it wasn't like that for me." She wouldn't look me in the eyes. "I wasn't uncomfortable, Guillermo."

Maybe she was lying to save face, but I still didn't feel too good. "It won't happen again."

Regan tentatively nodded. "I'm sorry, too, I…I know better, but I wasn't on my best behavior either. Let's just forget it happened, okay?"

With that, I disagreed. I would forgive myself for nearly slipping up, but I wouldn't forget.

"Listen…" I rubbed the back of my neck. "We can't do this anymore. We should just not be cool."

A wounded look crossed her face. "What? Why?"

"You've got problems I can't fix."

She looked at me incredulously. "I didn't ask you to."

"That's just it—this is my weakness, pretty girls with issues," I said. But even that didn't sum up Regan. "You're more than just a pretty girl, you're smart, you're innocent,

you're brave, you're silly when you want to be, you're nothing like what I'm used to, and I like that. I *can't* like that. I
can't like you, even as friends. You're distracting. We almost
kissed, and it's all I can think about. I don't like almost. The
more I think about it, the more I want it, and I can't want it."

"Guillermo—"

I took a step back, putting much needed space between us.
"You got a good thing going with your boyfriend, don't waste
time on me. I'm no good, but I'm tryin' to be."

As the morning wind rushed through her hair, I forced
myself to stay where I was and not brush it out of her face. "I
understand," she said at last.

"I'm going to see you around, so it's not like I want to be
enemies, okay?"

Regan nodded, hugging herself as she looked toward her
house. "I better get going before my dad sees us." She didn't
look at me as she turned away. "Goodbye, Guillermo."

"Bye, Regan."

I didn't watch her cross the street. Instead, I got behind the
wheel of my Charger and buckled in. But when I checked
the rearview mirror, I saw her stiffly approach her father's
SUV and climb into the passenger seat. It didn't feel too
good, but this was for the best. Regan London needed to be
in my rearview.

Regan

Two hands covered my eyes, blinding me as I attempted to shove my books into my locker at the end of the day. The hands were distinctively male, I could tell by their size and rough texture.

"Guess who."

I recognized his voice instantly. "I don't know, is it…Troy?"

He released me, stepping back and allowing me to turn and face him. Smiling, he handed over a gold metallic gift bag. "Here, I cut last period to get you this."

I accepted the bag and dug inside to find a brand-new folded gray fleece, a mini basket filled with movie theater candy from Skittles to M&Ms, and a card.

"What's all this?" I asked, looking up at him.

"It's Friday night, I figured we could head to that hill at Goodyear Park and watch the sun set, and if it's not too late after maybe we could go to my house and watch a movie." Troy held his hands up. "Don't worry, my parents are home."

There was a fat glob of hope in his eyes that the slightest prick of a possible *no* could burst.

How could I say no when it was the sweetest gesture?

I shut my locker and let Troy take me under his arm. He walked me down the hall, leading the way to the nearest exit so we could go to his car. Or at least, we tried to.

"Ready for tomorrow's game?" A science teacher caught him on the way down the hall.

Troy puffed up his chest. "Definitely."

I took the time to open and read Troy's card while another teacher jumped in to question him about the upcoming game.

The front cover was a watercolor image of a Black man and woman, tangled up in each other like some sort of human yin and yang symbol. Inside, Troy had written a short, but romantic note.

Just because you're my biggest support, my truest friend, and the apple of my eye. I love you, Rey, to the moon and back—Troy

He was still talking, but I didn't care as I rose on my toes and pressed a kiss to his cheek to show my appreciation. It reminded me of the beginning, of him letting that football ego go and just being Troy while he pursued me.

When his fan club finally let him go, he settled down with a shake of his head.

"You nervous?" I wondered.

He made a face. "It's Garfield, we got this in the bag."

Once we were outside, we bumped into Avery.

"Hey, I was thinking we should hang out sometime. Maybe throw the ball around or watch some of those cartoons you're always watching," Troy said.

Avery awkwardly looked to me and back to Troy. "Anime?"

"Yeah, that."

I couldn't help but grin at the supportive effort Troy was putting forward.

"Uh, sure. You ever hear of *Fullmetal Alchemist*?"

Troy blinked. "No."

"One Piece?"

"Nah."

Avery sighed. "You gotta at least know *Dragon Ball Z*."

To this Troy was quick to lighten up. "Hell yeah, my cousins used to watch that."

"Guess we have a winner," Avery responded.

"Need a ride?" Troy asked as he reached out and slapped Avery's shoulder. It didn't look hard, but Avery still flinched and moved a step back.

"Nah, I'm riding with Mo," he said.

Guillermo.

Just like that, all sense of joy washed away as the uneasiness I'd felt that morning came rushing back. He'd told me we couldn't be friends, and I couldn't understand the knife-like twist in my gut at the idea. Even as I'd stood right next to him, it had felt like miles were between us.

We'd almost kissed yesterday, a fact that made me feel guilty as I held Troy's hand. But still, we hadn't. I'd caught myself before I lost it.

I forced myself to glance down at the pavement, to avoid looking around the parking lot for Guillermo. To possibly catch further rejection in his dark eyes.

Troy let Avery go and we got into his car, my mood disturbed for no reason other than some strange bout of selfishness.

"So how about it?" Troy asked me five minutes later as he pulled up to my house and parked. He didn't turn the car off; he wasn't coming in.

It was Friday, a perfect night to bond and chill with my boyfriend. The boy I loved.

I let all thoughts of that morning go as I faced Troy. "Yes, I'll text you later when I'm all ready."

Troy leaned over, his face softening and an unmissable twinkle in his eye. He pressed his lips to mine and I returned the kiss, closing my eyes and trying to get lost in the moment.

My head was all over the place, but as I climbed out of the car and waved goodbye, I finally managed to breathe.

Inside, my father was ending a phone call as he stood in the front foyer. A vivid look of worry was etched on his face.

"What's wrong?" I asked.

His shoulders sagged and he released a sigh. I watched as he ran a large hand down his face, then uttered three words that cracked my world in two. "Tanner ran off."

My chest felt like it was caving in. My heart swelled with emotion, my throat threatening to close up permanently. *NO*.

"I let him out, and I came in for just a few minutes…"

His words seemed to become a foreign language almost as my gaze bounced into the next room, looking for my tan dog, down the hall, hoping to see the crooked tip of his tail, to the staircase, thinking maybe he'd slipped back in somehow and was up there napping on my bed.

I abandoned my book bag and Troy's gift at the front door and raced up the steps to my room. Nothing. I checked Avery's room. Nothing. My parents'. Nothing. The bathroom and the adjacent closet connected to it. Nothing.

The basement! My mind was determined, believing Tanner was in the house and my father hadn't looked hard enough. I ran to the basement, searching the finished bathroom, the rec room, and the laundry area. Nothing.

Panic started to set in as the reality that he was not in the house hit me.

My thoughts guided me to the backyard, in case he had meandered out there and was resting in the green grass. It wasn't fenced in, a hedge separating our yard from our neighbors on both sides. It was all too easy for Tanner to walk up the side of the house to the front to roam around if he wanted.

In my jeans my cell phone buzzed and I fished it out with shaking hands to find Troy texting me.

Troy: It'll be nice to get out of the way, just the two of us

The last thing I wanted to do was watch the sun set when Tanner was missing.

Me: OMG, Tanner ran away!!

Troy: Again?

Troy: Shit, I mean, are you sure?

Me: I looked around the house and outside and I don't see him. Please, help me find him?

Over on Troy's end, a series of ellipses bubbled up, as if he were typing his response. Then they stopped, nothing coming through. And in another moment, they started back up again.

Troy: Yea, let me change first

I circled back up to the front yard, finding my father on our porch eyeing me with shame and pity. "Rey…"

His words faded in the background as my head spun.

I scanned the block on both ends, looking for a sign of my dog.

"Tam*wahs*." My voice trembled as I called the name we used whenever we baby talked to him.

Nothing.

Guillermo

It was a good day for buñuelos, it had been too long. Marc Anthony was playing on the stereo in the living room, my mother singing along as she prepared the fritters. I was off from the center, and the idea of staying in and cooking food with my mother sounded all too good. It was nice to just relax and do something so normal and carefree without any grief attached for once.

My mother was swaying around the room, being loose and silly. She grabbed my wrists, trying to goad me into dancing with her.

"Vamos a bailar, mijo!" she insisted, swinging my arms.

I chuckled, fighting her grasp. "I'm good."

She pouted. "You too good to dance with your ma?"

It was just us. My father and Yesenia were in the family room watching a movie. So why not?

I gave in, entwining our fingers as I pulled her close before twirling her out. I sang along as loudly as she was, getting lost in the moment.

With the current cease-fire with my father, my mother had aged backward a decade, seeming to breathe easier now and smile more. I loved the sight of her giggling and being so carefree. I loved that she believed in me, had faith in this new chance.

Ding dong.

Jabbing a thumb over my shoulder, I said, "Front door."

My mother let me go, returning to her solo moves as she checked the oil in the pan.

"Regan?" At the sound of Yesenia's heightened voice, the amount of concern packed in it, I quickly headed to the foyer.

Yesenia and Regan stood in the front doorway. Unlike this morning, Regan was in disarray, her hair up in a messy ponytail, her yellow top and white jeans replaced with a plain navy T-shirt and varsity shorts. Her usually chipper face was flooded with worry, her lips quivering.

My guard switched to a protectiveness I couldn't trace, and I stepped closer until I was right behind Yesi. "What's wrong? Are you hurt?"

Regan wiped at her glistening eyes. "T-Tanner ran away earlier. I just… I just wanted you guys to keep an eye out for him."

Yesenia's hands rushed to her mouth. "Oh my God, are you guys looking for him right now?"

Malika was down at the sidewalk, texting on her phone, dressed in biker shorts, a large T-shirt, and tennis shoes fit for the task of searching the neighborhood.

Regan nodded. "Yeah, I looked earlier with my boyfriend, but I wanna keep trying."

"Can I help?" Yesenia was all too eager, not even wasting time to hear Regan's response before she raced to ask our parents for permission.

Regan lowered her gaze to our front porch and didn't speak.

My tongue felt heavy in my mouth. My hands lay limp at my sides. My legs wanted to move, but my brain stopped them, putting a halt to acting stupidly. *Let her find her own dog, Memo.*

In no time Yesenia was back and grabbing her hooded jacket from the coatrack by the door.

"I'm coming with you," Yesi insisted.

I gritted my teeth, accepting what was. "Be careful." With my eyes on Yesenia, I spoke to both her and Regan. "Call me if you need anything."

I watched them link up with Malika before crossing the street and approaching a parked Rio.

My stomach full of dread and regret, I went back to the kitchen, no longer hungry.

Regan

It became a routine, a vicious never-ending cycle: go to school, go to the center, look for Tanner, call and check the rescue centers for any sightings, go to sleep and repeat. It went on for days, and then weeks.

I ran my hand over the missing dog poster, willing myself not to cry for the millionth time. It had been a tough few weeks since my father lost Tanner, weeks of agonizing hell.

Everyone was raving about the amazing football season, and Troy was excited about all the press, and then there was me, moping about my lost dog. Some would consider it pathetic, but I didn't care; Tanner was always there for me at the end of the day, and now he wasn't.

It wasn't the first time Tanner had run away, but it was the first time he'd been gone for this long without a trace. The last time he ran he'd been gone for two weeks, and he came back so skinny, the thought of what even longer of not eating properly could do to him—

Swallowing, I stopped my mind there. I refused to be negative about the situation. As much as I wasn't a big fan of the idea,

I relied on the hope that some nice family had found Tanner and taken him in. None of the local animal shelters had seen or captured him, and none of the vet clinics had a mystery dog patient. No one we'd talked to had spotted him on the streets.

I let out a whimper, on the verge of tears again.

In less than a month, I'd be seventeen. Troy wanted to do something special, and I had a troubling idea what that meant.

Though he'd calmed down since our talk at Freeze, it hadn't stopped his overall intention of bedding me. There were still moments where he'd touch me and I'd clam up, and kissing always got too heated too fast now.

It was such a tiresome back-and-forth that I didn't care to argue anymore. Especially after my near slip with Guillermo. I hadn't told Troy, because it was a mistake that neither of us were intent on acting on. None of us needed the drama that would ensue if Troy did know.

Troy wasn't concerned about Tanner, and I got it, Tanner wasn't his dog, but his lack of support burned under my skin. He'd gone out looking with me the second night, too, but even then he'd cared more about the events on his timeline than focusing his flashlight in every bush and shadow we came across.

My mother thought it was useless, sadly, as our subdivision was much too simple for Tanner to get lost in and for us to not see him. Meaning, he'd probably strayed farther outside of Briar Pointe.

The thought brought my mood down as I came into the community center that Tuesday afternoon. I clocked in and read my tasks for the day and prepared to get distracted by work.

Troy had a big game Friday, his final of the season. This year, our team wasn't going to the postseason city series championship, but Troy wasn't completely bummed. He was still being hounded by scouts regardless.

My boyfriend was going to be huge someday.

I was happy for him, really I was.

Pressure pulsed in my temple and I did my best to massage it away.

Relax, Regan, just breathe.

I tried to pump myself up for Friday's impending game, even mentally penciling in going shopping at some point to find something extra nice to wear for Troy. I just knew the party that evening was going to be epic.

I pushed myself into my work, first watching the kids on the playground before coming inside and answering the phone for an hour.

Around six, my mother came into the lobby, giving me a brief smile before sifting through the day's mail. "Hey, Rey."

"Hey, Mom," I replied.

"Friday's the big day," she continued. "Think we'll get a win?"

I didn't care. If we won, we won, and if we lost, maybe Troy would be unbearable.

Forcing a smile, I said, "Of course, Troy and Tommy J are unstoppable. You know that."

My mother clearly agreed. "It will be an interesting season next year, that's for sure."

"Tommy's a great player, he's going to own that field."

Because there was nothing worse than getting stuck in a sports conversation with my parents, I quickly stood from the front desk and gathered my schoolbag.

"Well, I'm going on break," I told her, then slipped away. I rushed up the corridor and around the corner before anything else could be said.

Usually, I hid away and did my schoolwork in the conference room on the second level. Call me a punk, but in the past Troy had stopped by to surprise me—and mess around. He'd never think to check upstairs for me, no one would.

I also loved the design of the conference room. One wall was large windows that overlooked the playground area. On the back wall hung a large forty-inch flat screen, and one wall held wallpaper filled with inspiring quotes and words.

It was here that I could truly escape from it all—Troy, my father, and sometimes my mother, too. Here I could unwind and let myself breathe, and be whoever *I* wanted to be. The room always provided me security and peace of mind.

Except, when I pushed open the door to the conference room, the light was already on. Not only that, someone was sitting at the large conference table.

Guillermo.

He had his school books laid out around him, letting me know he was also studying.

I wasn't sure how to approach him anymore. He had become distant since that night we played pool and almost lost our heads. The next day, when he'd said it would be best to stay away from each other, he'd meant it. He was still friendly with a wave or a "hi," but he no longer paused to carry on a conversation.

With one month down and five to go, it was clear Guillermo was making progress with the Respect program. At school, he kept to his group of friends, Jenaya and my brother, and sometimes Raviv from up the street. He was probably being extra cautious so as not to mess anything up. He was making smarter choices, but I didn't like that avoiding me seemed to be one of them.

Couldn't we just be friends?

Rejection was supposed to hurt, but the way Guillermo had done it stuck with me. He'd built me up just to walk away, but I couldn't stop hearing him count my attributes on his fingers. He thought I was brave? I couldn't even tell my father I wanted my own future. I couldn't even figure out my relationship with my boyfriend most days. *Brave* was the last thing I was.

"Hey." I decided to test the waters as I entered the room, smiling at him.

Guillermo looked up from his notebook and studied me for all of a second before scooting back from the table.

His movement alerted me—I was interrupting him.

Maybe I'd just go back down to the rec room, no sense bothering him. "I usually sneak up here to get away for a bit. Most of the kids just stick to the gym or rec room. I'll let you—"

"No." Guillermo stood and gathered his things. "You stay."

I held my hand up. "No harm in sharing, right?"

Guillermo stood there, weighing his options, obviously leaning toward leaving.

Why were my feelings hurt?

"Please." I tilted my head. "I promise I'm not contagious."

Guillermo snorted and covered a grin. "I'm tryin' to be good, dimples."

Dimples, his little nickname for me. At least we had that.

"So, be good." I edged into the room. "It's just a little studying, right? And if I say hi to you in class, you don't gotta be afraid to hold a conversation."

Guillermo shook his head, but he sat down regardless. "At least close the door. If your mom catches us, it's *my* ass, not yours."

Right, that was the first step in perfecting my hideaway.

Quickly, I closed the door, then grabbed a seat at the table. I ended up sitting across from him and two chairs down.

I pulled out my chemistry homework, dreading it the most. Seriously, why did they insist on torturing us with this crap? Where in life would I ever need to balance chemical equations? I was really tripping when I thought taking chemistry was a great idea.

"Having trouble?" Guillermo spoke up.

I'd spent a good ten minutes attempting to understand what the heck I was supposed to be doing. "I suck at numbers. Throw in letters and I'm a complete disaster."

"Trig?"

"Chemistry actually."

His gaze lingered on the worksheet before coming up to me. "I could help. I went to see Mrs. Renner after school about it."

Feeling playful, I flashed him a smile. "Can I copy your answers?"

He rose from his chair, making a face. "But then how would you learn?"

I held my breath as he came around the table. Instead of focusing on the smooth way he walked, I tried to take an interest in the first equation:

$$P_4O_{10} + H_2O \longrightarrow H_3PO_4$$

Guillermo took the seat next to me, not shying away from me like usual. I realized, oddly, I had missed the comforting warmth of his nearness. All thoughts of chemistry went out the window as I watched him scoot closer, angle his head— *exist* next to me.

"Chemistry is *so* not important," I came out and said.

A ghost of a smile swept over his lips, his dark eyes studying my face before burning into mine. "Some might say chemistry is the root of everything."

My breath hitched in my throat. "Y-yeah?"

He leaned close, teasing it seemed. "Yeah."

My brain scrambled and I blinked to come back to earth. "Okay."

"It's really easy once you learn the process of balancing out the reactant side and the product side," Guillermo explained, producing a sheet of blank paper. I watched as he wrote the problem down in his thick handwriting. "First, let's write down the number of each atom on the reactant side, we have *four* phosphorus atoms, *eleven* oxygen atoms, and *two* hydrogen atoms..."

Guillermo broke it down further, writing the amount under the reactant side of the equation.

$$P_4O_{10} + H_2O$$

P = 4
O = 11
H = 2

He lifted his eyes to mine. "With me?"

I bobbed my head, loving the gentle yet strong sound of his voice, the sight of his game face as he took the role of teacher seriously. "Yeah."

Guillermo looked on for a beat more before going back to the sheet of paper. "Okay, so let's look at the product side. There's *three* hydrogen atoms, *one* phosphorus atom, and *four* oxygen atoms..."

$$\longrightarrow H_3PO_4$$

$$H = 3$$
$$P = 1$$
$$O = 4$$

As he explained, I stared at the equation, chewing on my pen, still confused. And then…something clicked and I did a little mental math.

"If I add a six coefficient to the H_2O molecule, and add a four coefficient to the product side, it'll balance, right?" I asked.

Guillermo read over the problem without having to work it out himself. "Yep, try the next one."

$$CH_4 + O_2 \longrightarrow CO_2 + H_2O$$

I followed his instructions, managing to balance the equation quickly. "Add a two coefficient in front of the molecule O_2 on the reactant side, and then add a two coefficient to the molecule H_2O on the product side?"

He glanced at the equation before flashing me a smile. "You got it."

To my disappointment, he stood and went back around to his side of the table.

"Thanks," I told him.

Guillermo bobbed his head. "No problem."

I went back to my homework, managing to solve the next six problems on my own. Oddly enough, it was almost fun now that I understood what I was doing.

"Can I ask you something?"

My gaze darted up from my work, and I sat straight, my ears drinking in the welcome arrival of his voice. "What?"

He seemed confused, his gaze going from my books to me. "Why are you in accounting if you don't like working with numbers?"

I snorted. "It's my dad. He's got it in his head that I'm going to follow in his sister's footsteps and join her accounting firm one day."

"What's the big deal with his sister?"

"Nepotism, you know? Like when there's a family of doctors and it's assumed that their kids will become doctors, too. It's sorta like that. Aunt Sherry started something, and they want to keep it in our family. I mean, even my grandma used to be an accountant. It's destiny to them."

Guillermo furrowed his brows, looking thoughtful. "Why not tell him you're not interested?"

"You wanna do that for me?"

"Can't be that hard."

It wasn't that my father was crazy controlling, but it wasn't like he *wasn't* either. From Troy to accounting, he was pushy on a lot in my life, grooming me to live up to whatever image he had in mind.

"I was supposed to call my aunt about this intern position, but I've been 'conveniently' forgetting. There's only so much longer I can do that. I've been thinking of alternatives, but nothing's sticking. I mean, we can definitely cross chemist off the list." Chemistry was way too stressful. No, this wasn't it for me either. "I don't know, my dad gets to talking and I just shrink. The words get stuck in my throat." My gaze fell to my homework. "It's like that with a lot of things lately."

"You're so busy pleasing all these other people. Who's pleasing you?"

I blinked, wondering if he'd caught his own double entendre. "No one, I guess."

Guillermo wasn't satisfied with this response. "What does Regan want?"

It was like he was the first person to genuinely ask that. The touching thing about it was that he truly seemed concerned.

Smiling bitterly, I said, "To find my dog."

I could see an internal battle written across his face, his gaze moving from me to his notes and back again.

In the end, Guillermo returned to his notebook. "Well, I did get a good look at the guy, so I'll keep an eye out."

He didn't have to, but the fact that he cared meant something. "Thank you."

"Don't mention it." Suddenly he was holding back a laugh. "If anything, it's also for Yesi. She loves that dog."

Yesenia had come over more than once to play with Tanner when he was out in the yard sniffing around. She seemed to love playing fetch with him, and he had never really been a fetch type of dog before she moved in across the street. His sister was sweet.

We worked on our homework in silence for another ten minutes before we both had to get back to work.

"Let me know if you have any more trouble," Guillermo said as we walked side by side down to the lobby. "I'm right across the street if you need me."

Even if it was just for studying purposes, it felt good to have his offer.

Up ahead of us, leaning against the front desk, was Malika.

"Hey, Mo!" Malika waved a little too enthusiastically for my taste.

Guillermo lifted his chin at her. "What's up with you?"

She came over and he wrapped an arm around her. "Nothin', I just got out of cheer practice."

Their exchange, ever so casual, prickled underneath my skin.

"Malika, you need something?" I spoke up, halting their chitchat.

My best friend suddenly noticed me. "I was just stopping by, Rey." Her attention went back to Guillermo. "You going to the game Friday?"

He smirked. "You know I don't care for football."

She smiled, almost as though they'd had this discussion before. "Well, you oughta come through After Hours or something this weekend again. It was fun last week, wasn't it?"

Guillermo didn't deny this. "Yeah, it's all right."

"You've been to After Hours?" I hoped my voice was even, not at all giving away the slight irritation I felt that he and Malika were so buddy-buddy.

"Yeah, Naya wanted to go and I had the night off," he explained.

My heart sank, and I tried to shrug it off. It bothered me Malika knew things about Guillermo that I didn't. I shouldn't have cared, and I had to look elsewhere to try to conceal that I did.

Fortunately, Avery stepped into the center just then. He tipped his head at me before burying his hands deep in his pockets and facing the boy beside me.

Guillermo assessed him knowingly. "Cliff?"

Avery nodded.

Guillermo gave Malika a quick squeeze as a goodbye before walking to Avery. "Come on, I've got some stuff to do outside. I'm sure your mom won't mind you tagging along."

Together the two exited the building and I stared after

them, left with a ton of questions. The only *Cliff* I knew was my father.

I wondered if things were all right.

Avery and I, while only a year apart, weren't that close. It wasn't that we didn't get along, and I always tried to include him in things, but he always opted out for his beloved manga or video games.

"You two are chummy," I mumbled, grabbing Malika's attention from watching Guillermo and my brother disappear outside.

She faced me, shrugging her shoulders as if it were nothing. "Mo's the homie—he and Calvin have web design eighth period and sometimes I cut my last class to hang out. Ms. Jones is cool about it."

Of course, Guillermo only wanted space from me, not the people around me. First my brother, and now my best friend. Why did I hate this?

"He so fine." Malika shook her head, humming. "I wonder what's keepin' him."

"What do you mean?" I asked.

She made a face as if I were simple. "Every girl at school has been eyeing him, but for some reason, he just won't bite."

It would be a lie if I said I hadn't noticed. Girls did flock to Guillermo, who would simply be his friendly self and not take anything further. The only girl he ever hung out with was Jenaya, and they kept it friendly from what I could see.

I didn't really want to think about him with other girls. He said he had a past of messing around with them, but for some reason, I hoped he was turning a new leaf in that department as well.

Internally I cringed. I shouldn't be thinking about who he'd date at all.

I pushed all thoughts of Guillermo to the side. They were too distracting. "Come on, Malika, let's look online and see what I can wear Friday."

Guillermo

Harvey showed up at our door Wednesday after school.

After our first two initial meetings, our usual check-in consisted of a phone call. Catching him in person made me nervous. It had been a month, and I'd made sure I'd dotted every *i* and crossed every *t*.

At least, I thought I had, before Harvey's arrival.

He was in our living room when I came downstairs. Yesenia was entertaining him, fussing about some book she was waving in her hand.

A part of me would always envy her innocence. This was her world, tripping out over the latest young adult novel and nothing else. She'd made one questionable friend since our move, a girl named Leticia Rodriguez. For the time being she hadn't outright proven to be trouble, though I suspected she would be in the long run, with her constant talk of boys and calling Yesi's books boring.

I trusted Yesenia, though, so I didn't speak on my dislike of her first and only friend.

"Harvey," I said as I stepped into the room.

He turned from Yesenia and found me in the doorway.

"What's up?" he greeted me, studying my position. He seemed amused by my obvious trepidation. "I was just in the neighborhood."

Doubt that.

"Nice of you to stop by, then," I said.

Harvey chuckled. "Relax, you're not in trouble. Unless…" He let the cliff-hanger linger in the air, causing an uncomfortable silence.

"I've been straight," I said.

"How straight?"

"As straight as can be."

"Any girls, G?" His gaze bored into me.

Thankfully, the truth was the truth. "No."

"Mentiroso," Yesenia whispered, calling me a liar.

Harvey lifted a brow at my sister. "What's that mean?"

"It means no," I lied.

Yesenia scowled, and Harvey wasn't convinced. "Yeah, I'm thinking about initiating an English-only clause here."

I shot Yesenia a pained look. "Leave me to him, please?"

She sighed and grabbed her book. She looked over her shoulder on her way out of the room, peering at Harvey. "Don't forget to read it, okay?"

Yesenia was as sweet and as pure as they came, and Harvey was wrapped up under her spell. "I'll get me a copy as soon as I leave here, I promise."

Satisfied, she left us alone.

Harvey returned to me. "So, what's the story?"

"I'm friends with a girl, but it's not like that," I said, thinking of Jenaya.

"That's it?"

I thought of Regan and neglected to bring her up. She was all things off-limits, even if she kept slipping into my mind.

"I'm good, Harvey," I insisted with a little more bite to my tone than needed.

He didn't press the issue. "How's that temper?"

On some days, it was perfectly in check, and then on others, whenever someone tried to get handsy or mouthy with Jenaya, I felt tempted to slip back into my old ways. I was protective. It was what I did best, protect.

"I...I went to the movies with my friends. Some guy was being rude to my friend Jenaya and things got heated, but I didn't completely lose my cool. It was scary, being so close like that. I've been extra cautious ever since. I think working out in the gym helps a lot."

"I'm happy to hear that. If it was a test, you passed. I talked to Gloria London...she speaks highly of you. She thinks you have potential to be another success story. She says she admires your willingness to take responsibility and work hard for your rehabilitation."

This was news to me.

Mrs. London was tough on me, not letting up an ounce since our first encounter. If she saw greatness in me, she didn't let it show, but hearing her thoughts from Harvey was comforting. She wanted the best for me, hence her strictness. I could only respect that.

"I'm just trying to move forward," I said.

Harvey took me in, clearly deciding if he agreed or not. "I see potential in you, G. I mean it, don't fuck this up. Be watchful of these girls, and don't let these guys influence you one bit."

He didn't have to lecture me on that; it was the one thing I was set on during my transition to Arlington High and the

Briar Park/Briar Pointe neighborhood. As far as guys went, I was close with Raviv and Avery. Jenaya was probably my best friend through and through. She had my back as I had hers; we'd clicked like that from the start.

Outside of my friends, I would flirt here and there with girls who flirted with me first, but none of it meant anything and I never followed through.

Until I met a girl who made my heart race and I knew I could run the risk of trusting her, I was going to play it solo.

"I'm trying," I swore. "It's an everyday struggle that's getting easier and easier."

Harvey seemed to accept that as he stood and passed me on his way to the front door. He was just about to reach for the doorknob when he pivoted on his heel and faced me. "One more thing."

Shit.

"Listen to anything good lately?" he asked curiously.

I breathed a sigh of relief. "J. Cole just dropped a new freestyle. That new Meek Mill is probably my favorite on repeat, though."

Harvey bobbed his head. "I'll get on that. Stay good, Lozano, I'll be in touch."

He opened the front door and saw himself out.

For once I didn't feel too much weight on my shoulders. This was all starting to get easy.

A full minute hadn't gone by before the front door opened again and my father stepped into the house. He acknowledged me with a nod.

"Hey, Memo," he said as he shut the door. "Everything good?"

"Yeah, Harvey was just checking in."

"Anything new?"

"Mrs. London thinks highly of me. They think I have potential."

"You do," my father surprised me by saying. He paused to reach out and touch my shoulder. "When we first got here I had my doubts, but I've been watching you. You go to your community service, and you're always in on time. This move was the best thing for this family. I'm proud of you."

My heart swelled. There was a time I thought I'd never again see him look at me without shame in his eyes. Here he was, telling me he was proud of me. "Thanks, Pop."

He patted my back and went toward the kitchen, probably to start dinner. "Keep it up."

I would. Seeing that gleam in his eye was far better than living with the disappointment that had been there for so many months.

I was in a good mood now, and oddly enough, I felt like paying it forward. I went and found Yesenia in her room, lying across her bed, nose deep in her book.

"Hey." I knocked on the wall to get her attention.

She perked up at the sight of me. "What'd Harvey want?"

"To tell me I'm doing good."

"You are, Memo."

"It's good to hear." I buried my hands in my pockets. "I was thinking about going and hanging posters for Regan's dog. If you help, we'll get ice cream."

My little sister lit up, abandoning her book with no fight. "Really?"

I'd swiped a handful of posters from the community center. I didn't want to examine why, but I felt for Regan. I hadn't been able to get her out of my head since our talk Tuesday. She'd looked so lost and sad. Everyone dumped on her, from her pops, to her boyfriend, and all she wanted was her dog.

She'd saved Simba, something I hadn't forgotten, and she didn't deserve this. I'd wanted to help right from the beginning, but it wasn't in my best interest—it *still* wasn't in my best interest, but something had to give for Regan.

Yesenia was on board. She took half the posters and made a few suggestions about where to hang them as we made our way to my car.

The closest places near Briar Pointe were Arlington High, the Briar Park library, and a few other businesses.

"Think this'll work?" Yesenia asked as we pinned a poster to the bulletin board at Freeze.

"Hope so," I said. We'd already gone to the library and the mini-mart across the street, and though we'd hung the posters anyway, no one we'd talked to had seen the poor dog.

Deep down, I was hoping Tanner had been taken in by a loving home instead of winding up dead on the streets or at a kill shelter.

"Maybe if Dad sees how thoughtful we are, he'll let us get our own dog." Yesenia was hopeful. She'd wanted a dog for as long as I could remember.

Before, our parents had been too busy cleaning up my screwups to be bothered with Yesenia's lingering wish. Now, things were significantly different.

Our next destination was Igloo's ice cream. Yesenia was ecstatic about getting a pint of their blueberry cheesecake flavor after hanging the last of the posters.

"We gotta go downtown one day," she was saying as I skimmed the menu. I was debating trying their nondairy peach champagne flavor or going for just vanilla.

"Why's that?" I wanted to know.

"There's this place where they wrap books in brown paper and only write descriptions on them, that way you buy them based on their plots and themes and not their covers or titles. It sounds really neat."

I would forever admire how much of a bookworm my younger sister was. "Sounds great, Yesi."

I half listened as she prattled on about the bookshop until something caught my attention.

There, scattered across the countertop, were flyers advertising a club event at After Hours. Two beautiful girls were posing, one with her back to the camera emphasizing her round butt, and the other, posed front and center with her perky breasts on display in her small crop top. Both were givin' sex appeal in their outfits, and their makeup was on point, something that would impress Jenaya for sure.

Yesenia peered at the flyer, a look I couldn't decipher in her eye. "Memo, what kind of girls do you like?"

Fuck.

My eyes flickered toward the flyer once more.

It was a trap. If I said I liked girls like the ones on the flyer, I was superficial and asking for too much. If I said I liked girls who were makeup free, hair tied up, and in sweats, well, I was being cliché and pretentious. To be honest, I just liked girls, didn't matter if they liked makeup, hair extensions, or were more natural. Who gave a shit?

But this was my younger sister, wasn't I supposed to set an example? If our mom were with us, I knew what my answer was supposed to be.

Still, I went with honesty, the best way to set Yesenia straight.

"I like girls who aren't afraid to be themselves," I told her. "Whatever you like or feel, be that, and that's what I'll gravitate toward."

It seemed like a fair answer.

The corner of Yesenia's mouth curled up. "Thank you, Memo."

The guy behind the counter handed us our ice cream and I paid him as Yesenia grabbed a table for us.

I'd gone with plain vanilla. Across from me, Yesenia was eating her ice cream, but there wasn't a hint of joy on her face.

"What's wrong?" I asked.

She frowned. "This isn't working. Tanner's been gone for so long, and we've already hung up his picture in so many places."

Seeing her just as down as Regan ate at me. I wished there was something more I could do, but there was no denying the time that had passed.

I licked my cone, thinking. "I mean, you've pretty much been all over this side of the city at least twice... What if we checked some of the shelters on the west side?"

Hope raised Yesenia's mood. "Okay!"

I pulled out my phone and began looking up animal clinics. The first one on the list was Kind Paws, on the west side of Akron. The name rang a bell, making it as good a place to start.

Yesenia and I dropped off her leftover ice cream at home and told our parents what we were up to. Unsurprisingly, they approved. She and I were going on an adventure, something that boosted my energy and caused me to smile. Going above and beyond to look for Tanner said a lot about my sister. Her eagerness to help Regan made me love her more.

At Kind Paws, we showed the receptionist our flyer, hoping to spark a memory.

"He's been missin' for about a month, any chance someone brought him in?" I asked.

The receptionist eyed the glossy image, no hint of recollection on her freckled face. "I haven't seen him."

Yesenia pouted, her tiny shoulders sagging.

The receptionist, whose name tag said Felicity, noted her defeat, and sympathy colored her green eyes. She leaned back in her chair, angling her head toward the open door behind her. "Hey, Leonie?"

A girl walked out in lavender scrubs, her box braids up in a bun and a purple headband around her head. "What's up?"

"They're here looking for a missing dog. Mind showing them the pets in case one of our rescues is theirs?"

Leonie perked up. "Absolutely." She came around the front counter, which was covered in photos of dogs, cats, kittens, and puppies. Colorful hearts were taped here and there for added effect.

The smell of animals was prominent as Leonie took us to where they kept the dogs. The bright room had sparkling white floors and clean steel cages, offering a sense of hope. A male volunteer, a tall Black boy, was walking around strumming an acoustic guitar, playing for the dogs, bobbing his head, and grinning at each one.

If Tanner was at a rescue clinic, I hoped he was in a place like this.

"What's your dog look like?" Leonie asked me.

I handed her a flyer. "He's got his own look goin' for himself. Cute guy."

Leonie agreed and began scanning the cages as Yesenia did the same. I took off, too, seeing all kinds of dogs but no Tanner.

"Memo! Look, there's puppies." Yesenia was at the end of the room, kneeling down at one cage and sticking her finger through the chain link.

"One of our rescues was a pregnant black Lab," Leonie told me as we walked over to Yesenia. "Her puppies are ready to find their forever homes."

Inside the cage a mom was resting while five black Labrador puppies were caught between eating, playing with squeaky toys, or entertaining Yesenia's finger. She'd wanted a dog for so long, and I hated to wave this in front of her.

"How much are adoption fees?" I wondered. I had a little of my stash from my trip to Mexico and from before left. I definitely needed a job once my community service gig was up.

"Puppies are a bit on the pricey side versus dogs seven months and up," Leonie warned me. "We're talking $350 and up. There's an application and interview process as well."

Looking at Yesenia being so gentle with the puppies, I knew the idea was priceless.

I started to get closer, but something in the next cage caught my eye. A familiar face. My heart threatened to explode out of my chest.

"Yesi," I said, not taking my eyes off him, "call Mom, she's about to kill us."

The biggest smile lit up her face, and I knew there was no going back.

Regan

Between struggling with my accounting homework and feeding Troy the attention he came over for, I wasn't sure which was a more tiring task.

Probably Troy. I just couldn't focus on anything he was saying.

My mother came into the kitchen to check on the oven. She'd baked fish, yet another meal that wasn't to Troy's taste. He wasn't alone; my mother always had to fry certain fish for my father or he wouldn't eat it.

"You helping that girl with her work, Troy?" my mother asked as she opened the oven and peeked inside.

Troy eyed my work, spread out before me on the kitchen table. "Nah, I'm not the math genius like Rey here."

I blinked. I was far from a math genius. Not that anyone ever asked. Not that I ever found the guts to speak up.

I had to do better.

"Tomorrow's the big day, you nervous?" my mother asked him.

The idea of having nerves made Troy snort. "Nah, we gon' win and end it on a good note."

My whole family, apart from Avery, was going to support Troy's last game. His family was talking about meeting up, and I was cringing at the pressure both parties would present. I had to act like his biggest cheerleader when they were around.

My shoulders sagged at the weight of it all.

Ding dong.

The front doorbell was a welcome distraction. I rose from my chair and led the way to the front door, my mother and Troy filing behind me.

At the door, to my surprise, was Guillermo. Goose bumps lit my skin on fire at the sight of him standing on our porch, saving me from my stress.

Blinking, I realized he wasn't alone. Yesenia stood beside him, holding a tiny black puppy. But my focus wasn't on her long before I noticed the leash in Guillermo's hand...and who was attached to the other end of it.

Simba.

Guillermo almost seemed to be blushing. "We went to a rescue clinic to look for Tanner yesterday, and Yesenia was lookin' at puppies. That's when I saw this guy." He leaned down and petted Simba's head, earning a tongue bath that had him wrinkling his nose and grinning. "I'm not trying to replace Tanner, and I'm sorry if this is oversteppin', I just know how much Simba meant to you. It felt like fate, seein' him again. I thought...you might want him."

My heart melted into a pool of awe.

He'd gone out of his way to do this for me. When I was at my lowest about all my expectations, he really came through to cheer me up.

There were no words.

"Guillermo!" Without even thinking, I threw my arms around him and embraced him tightly. He stumbled just a little as I mumbled thank-yous into his chest. For just a sliver of a moment, he wrapped his arms around me, and it felt oh so cozy.

He soon stepped back and handed over the leash. "All you."

I knelt down and hugged Simba, instantly hit with his dog-shampoo scent. He was here, he was clean, and his leg was healing nicely.

"He's so much better," I let out.

Yesenia reached down and petted him. "I named mine Smokey. Smokey and Simba, they gotta be close, Rey, like us."

I loved the idea of that. Yesenia had been going on and on about a dog, and now she had one of her own. Playdates were definitely in our future.

My mother cleared her throat. "Well, this was thoughtful, Guillermo."

Troy said nothing as he stood taking in the scene. His gaze lingered where I held Simba against my chest.

Guillermo stepped farther away from me. "This is the dog Regan and I rescued that day. I know how much he meant to her, and I thought it would make her a little happy while the search goes on."

"How big of you," Troy commented dryly.

I was hoping no one caught it, but it seemed as though Guillermo did. He angled a thumb over his shoulder. "We should get going."

"You got him a collar," I said, spotting the strip of fabric around Simba's neck.

"Red's your favorite color, right?" Guillermo said.

I couldn't contain my smile. *He noticed.* "Right."

"How'd you know that?" Troy asked.

Guillermo tipped his head toward the red furry slides on my feet.

Troy glanced down, examining my shoes. "Huh."

Guillermo's eyes met mine, and then they were on my mother. "I hope you don't mind, ma'am."

My mother offered a smile. "Regan's been so gloomy over Tanner, and it's nice to put a face to the name Regan's been talking about ever since *that* day."

Guillermo's gaze flickered to me. "Glad I could help."

My mother came past me, standing in front of me as she reached out to shake hands with him. "And it's much appreciated."

He faced his sister. "You about ready?"

They took off for their house across the street, and my mother shut the door behind them.

She looked curious as she turned and faced me. "How nice."

I tucked some hair behind my ear, hopeful she was being sincere. The last thing I wanted to do was cause trouble for Guillermo when he was doing so well in her program. "You've had a good influence on him. The program has."

With my mother's sternness, and Daren's backing, the Respect program saw a good success rate. There were those few who didn't adjust and went back to their previous ways, but a lot of the kids took to my mother, warmed up to her approach of believing in them, and owned up to their mistakes when she held them accountable. I was glad Guillermo was another success story.

"That's what I'm here for." She said no more as she walked by me, but the look in her eye let me know she wasn't exactly thrilled about what Guillermo had done.

I hung back with Troy, putting off facing my mother until after he left. It was more fun to think about what I might need now to take care of Simba.

He had to be about seven months old now; I wondered if the dog food we had for Tanner was okay for him. We would definitely have to go out and buy him his own things, because Tanner was coming home. He had to.

Troy was standing casually where he'd been ever since I'd opened the door. He watched me unleash Simba and stroke his fur. "That was nice of Con, wasn't it?"

The name didn't register. "Con?"

"Con, you know, short for *convict*. Ain't that what ol' boy is?"

I narrowed my eyes. "That's not funny, and no, he isn't."

"Oh, word? Then he's just volunteering his time at the center then, huh?"

Troy was being a jerk and I wasn't in the mood. "He's not some two-bit criminal, Troy, these are kids who made mistakes. We *all* make mistakes."

He rolled his eyes as his full lips formed a careless smirk. "Anyway. Let's just focus on Friday night."

"The party?"

He stepped closer, placing his hand on my shoulder. "Yeah. Wear something sexy."

His hand fell from my shoulder, measuring me out, caressing my curves gently.

It made me want to squirm.

His request was simple, but I wasn't comfortable. I felt safer with the idea of wearing something cute.

I buried this discomfort and pasted a smile on my face. "Okay."

An easy grin spread across his face. "Good. And make sure Con doesn't get you anything else. Matter fact, dead that, ain't he friends with Jenaya? He need to be gettin' *her* dogs and shit."

He cupped my chin, lifting my face to give me a kiss.

Only, when his lips pressed against mine, I didn't respond. Now he was telling me who to hang out with?

Troy didn't seem to notice my attitude as he made his exit, promising to text me later before slipping through the front door.

My brows furrowed as I scowled.

Simba was more than just a dog; he was someone Guillermo had helped me save. Something that would never leave my heart. My first real victory in life.

Who was Troy to tell me to *dead* anything with Guillermo?

Avery came down the steps just then and I let it go as he set eyes on Simba. "Whoa."

"This is the dog Guillermo and I rescued at the center last month. He actually found him again while he was out looking for Tanner," I explained as Avery approached.

He knelt down, hovering his hand over Simba's head, hesitating so as not to scare him. "Mom and Dad cool with this?"

Our father was at work, but given *he* was the cause of Tanner being lost, his say didn't too much matter to me. "Mom seems cool with it."

"We're gonna have two dogs now, huh?"

My heart ached. "Yes, we will."

Avery stood. "I'm going to Mo's."

I nodded and tried to ignore how I wanted to go with him. Instead, I gathered Simba and led him into the kitchen, where I intended to finish my homework.

My mother turned the stove-top eye off as she finished cooking. From the look and smell, it was some sort of butter-and-herb rice. "Guillermo is thoughtful." There was no missing the way she was side-eyeing me as she made this remark. The way her gaze bounced to Simba and back to me.

"Yeah, I'm glad he cared. Troy's being a jerk about it." I filled Tanner's water dish in case Simba was thirsty.

"How is he supposed to feel when a cute boy shows up at your door offering presents?"

"You think Guillermo's cute?" I found myself asking.

There was no denying it really. Why did he have to be so gorgeous? It wasn't just his physical appearance either, all his trash talk while we played pool was sorta cute, too. Really, his whole presence was downright electrifying.

I wasn't supposed to think Guillermo Lozano was cute, but he was.

There wasn't a hint of humor on my mother's face.

I rolled my eyes. "It's not that big a deal."

She angled her head, studying me. "Just how close are you and Guillermo?"

Her curious gaze caused my cheeks to get hot. "Outside of class, we barely talk. We're more acquaintances than friends even."

"Yet he's coming over with a dog." She wasn't convinced.

"Mom." I groaned as I massaged my temples and rested my elbows on the tabletop. "Yesenia's been wanting a dog forever, and Guillermo was just trying to be nice by pleasing us both. Okay?"

"I'm going to have a talk with him about boundaries. As soon as I saw his address, I was worried this would be an issue."

"So he can't be friends with Avery?"

My mother paused. "Usually I would be against it, but there's no denying the positive influence Guillermo has on your brother."

These days, Avery would often go to the Lozanos' house, or Guillermo would come by our house. They seemed completely different, but unlike Troy and my father, Guillermo wasn't trying to make Avery be anything other than himself, and I appreciated him for it.

"Please don't be mad, Mom," I begged. "Guillermo barely speaks to me any other time. I've just been bummed about Tanner and he wanted to step up and help. Honest, he's not relapsing or whatever."

My mother gave me a smile as she joined me at the table. "Well then, on that note, I'm happy you're happy."

Happy. Was I happy? Tanner was still gone. I was still in accounting. I was still stressing over it all.

I gathered my homework and frowned at what all was left. "Would...would you totally hate me if I dropped out of accounting?"

"And have you break your father's heart?"

Her sarcasm took me by surprise.

She gave me a *come on* look. "Regan, the only person who talks about accounting in this house is your father. I've been holding my breath waiting on you to say *anything* about it."

"Dad's just so pushy," I confessed.

"That's his way. He wants the best for you."

In my life, my parents dictated so much, from accounting, to my volunteering, and even to my relationship with Troy. To make my own decisions based on what I wanted would be a dream. But knowing my reality, I was better off accepting that not all dreams come true.

"I know, it's just that I can't get into it. I'm trying, but my heart's not there." Accounting wasn't the only place my heart wasn't, but I kept that to myself for now.

"So what are you going to do?" my mother asked.

"You wouldn't be upset if I dropped the class?"

"*I* wouldn't," she said. "I want you to choose a path *you* enjoy."

My gaze fell on my accounting book and the ugly home-work that still lay before me. "I'm not sure what I want," I admitted.

"Then it's important you figure it out, on your own terms, because that's what's most important, Rey."

I didn't have any answers, but to know I had my mother's support gave me hope.

Guillermo

Turns out our mother didn't kill us over my impulsive choice to adopt not one, but two dogs. She'd showed up at the clinic Wednesday, heard me out, seen Yesenia's puppy eyes, and caved.

But not without warning us that pets were a big responsibility.

The sound of Smokey whining Friday morning was a taunting reminder.

"Yesi!" I called as I nearly tripped over the tiny black Lab on my way out of my bedroom. "I gotta go pick up Jenaya, it's your turn to take Smokey out."

We'd established a system taking turns letting him out in the mornings and evenings to do his business, and we'd gotten a baby gate to fence him in the kitchen while we were all gone during the day. I didn't mind the night walks or trips to the backyard, and Yesenia was all too eager to get up early to walk him in the mornings. Our father had even softened up and said he'd chip in on weekends.

Yesenia came out of her room, her face lighting up at the

sight of Smokey. I loved seeing her happy. To have finally gotten something she'd wanted for so long. "Smokey Midnight!" she cooed his first *and* middle name. Smokey Midnight Lozano.

Briefly, I wondered if Regan had given Simba a middle name.

Yeah, I had to get a move on.

I told my sister goodbye and quickly fled the house and jumped in my Charger.

On some mornings, Jenaya would let me take her to school. One thing about Naya, she was proud to the point of fighting you about letting her do for herself. In short, she'd rather take the bus than let me come out of my way too often to get her.

On some days I won the battle, and others I had to give in and let her have her way.

Friday morning was a day the battle worked in my favor.

"Want to stop for anything?" I offered as she climbed in alongside me.

A part of our arrangement was that I wasn't supposed to come to the front door of her grandmother's house. I was to wait in the car and text her when I arrived.

Jenaya had a few simple rules, and because I respected her privacy and space, I didn't question her much. Anybody not living with their birth parents had to have it rough, especially when it was by their own choice.

"I'm good," she said, declining my offer as she always did.

We arrived at school and I found a good spot in the student parking lot.

I was low-key dreading the day ahead at school for one sole reason. Arlington High was a big football school; there was no buzz around the other sports the school offered, even if Raviv swore their soccer was the shit. No, student after student and teacher after teacher would go on and on about football. And the name on everyone's tongue was Troy Jordan. Apparently, football was in his gene pool, because his younger brother was also a talented player making waves as well.

Tonight would be the last game of the season, and everyone was a mixture of sad and excited.

I was just anxious for everyone to shut up already.

"You going to the big party tonight?" Jenaya asked as she took in a group of students crowding around a Jeep Wrangler sporting purple-and-light-green varsity jackets. *Go Panthers!*

I wrinkled my nose. "I'm off at eight, I'll think about it."

Jenaya shrugged. "I could get out. I might go."

"Text me if you need a ride."

"Yo! Con!"

Shouting drew my attention to where Troy emerged from the crowd of athletes, coming my way.

"Con?" Jenaya repeated.

"I have no idea," I responded. I stood back, waiting for him.

Troy came closer, visibly sizing me up.

Jenaya went on the defense, slowly stepping in front of me.

The effort was cute, but I could handle myself.

"What's up, Troy?" I lifted my chin at him, going for nice.

"What up, Con." Troy came and slapped my palm before reeling me in for a hug and pat to my back. I reciprocated the motion, noticing at once how much strength he was using in his grip.

This couldn't be good.

"Who's Con?" I asked.

Troy grinned, his eyes sweeping me over once more. "You are, *convict.*"

I blinked and Jenaya stepped closer.

This was one pissing contest I'd have to sit out. Judging by Troy's demeanor, there was only so much patience I was going to have with him.

Putting a safe space between us, I scratched at my jaw, trying to compose myself.

"It's Guillermo," I told him.

"Sure it is."

"Jenaya," I said, keeping my eyes on Troy, "I'll meet up with you in a second."

She made no move to abandon me. "You sure?"

Behind Troy, I could just make out Raviv on the school lawn. He was tugging on Camila's arm, and she was pulling back. They seemed to be fighting, their expressions mirroring conflict more than harmless fun.

"Yeah, see if Rav's going to the party, I may link up with him," I said. Avery wouldn't go if I asked, but I knew Raviv would. Besides, it looked like he could use the distraction.

Jenaya begrudgingly left my side and walked over to Raviv. Camila stalked off, but Raviv cooled down enough to focus on Jenaya. We were an odd group, but Raviv and Jenaya got along just fine.

I settled back on Troy, hoping things weren't about to go left.

He stood all suave and collected, but the arrogance oozing from his person caused me to stay on guard. "What's up with you and that?"

"*That* is Jenaya, my best friend," I said.

He didn't seem convinced. "Word? She's pretty bad, ain't she?"

Jenaya Omar was beautiful, curves for days, pretty face, and a mindset that kept you on your toes. But we were just friends. I respected the hell out of her, and after our short while of knowing each other, I valued our friendship too much to get caught up in the idea of becoming something more.

"You wanted something, Troy?" I said, trying to get this confrontation over with.

He let Jenaya go. "You've got good taste. I say that because I seen you eyeing my girl."

"It's not like that, she's all you."

He grinned, but it wasn't friendly. "See, now you're being disrespectful. I *know* she's all me."

"Is this a warning?" Because it sure as hell couldn't be a fight.

"Nah, you smart, you know better," he said. "I mean, I've been thinkin', you one of Mrs. London's kids, so I doubt you'd be stupid enough to cross that line. Although, showing up after our date was one thing, but now a dog?" He cupped his chin, appearing thoughtful. "Shit makin' me uncomfortable, *Mo*."

The dots were lining up to connect a not-so pretty picture if Mrs. London found out how close Regan and I had gotten before I pulled away. "It's nothing."

"Of course not," Troy responded. "But let's talk. See, I've got this friend who recently became available because her dude was acting funny. I think it's time she meets a real one."

"And that's where I come in?" We weren't even friends. I couldn't grasp why he'd come to me of all people.

Troy shrugged. "Possibly. She's a senior. Her name's Sofia Rios, she's gorgeous, you should check her out."

"Maybe I will."

He rubbed his palms together as he came closer and nodded off into the distance. "She's right over there. See her?"

I spotted the Latina amid a crowd of blondes and a single redhead. "Uh-huh."

"She cute, right?"

Even with the distance, I could see that Sofia was indeed pretty. "Yep."

"I'ma let you take that. Go talk to her, ask her out, she cool."

The nerve of this guy. "Wow, didn't know she was your property to give away."

Troy chuckled. "Nah, it ain't like that. But what *is* like that, is Regan, that's all me, so why don't you take this one." He boldly reached out and patted my chest. "She's all you, playboy."

"How considerate of you," I decided to say.

"Yeah, well, her ex played her, and Rey's always talking about how nice you are. The next time you feel like getting a dog, get one for Sofia."

Regan was standing among the group of athletes hanging out by the Jeep Wrangler, bundled up in a hoodie as she talked with Malika. She glanced my way, her eyes widening, her posture freezing as she took in her boyfriend and me standing together.

Troy cut into my line of vision, picking up on where my attention had moved, catching Regan looking back to Malika. "You got a problem with my girl, man?" He kept advancing toward me, making me question if hitting him would land me in juvie.

Probably.

I took a deep breath, trying to find my sanity. "No."

"See, I don't want to tell Mrs. L about how uncomfortable you makin' me about my girl and you."

Shit. "Like I said, it's nothing."

"You want clarification?" He was taunting me, daring me to try him.

The old me wouldn't have backed down, but the new me, unfortunately would have to. "I don't want any static, Troy."

The little smirk on his face, as if he'd won, ate at me.

Vete a la verga.

Things were supposed to be easier here, and because I didn't want to repeat history, I conceded and backed down.

"I'll think about Sofia," I told Troy. "Good looking out." To push it a step further, I reached out and patted his shoulder, using more effort than necessary as I met his angry eyes. *Yeah, two can play at this game, asshole.*

I went around Troy and headed over to Jenaya, who was waiting for me on the lawn where Raviv had been.

"What was that?" she asked as the first bell rang.

"Troy wanted to let me know a friend of his is single now," I told her as we made our way inside the building.

She made a face. "Why is he telling you of all people? Since when are you guys cool like that?"

"We're not." I deadpanned. "I may have gotten Regan a new dog, and he was there when Yesi and I dropped him off."

Jenaya blinked, raising her hand and looking at me sideways. "Are you dumb?"

"I'm starting to think so."

She shook her head. "Mo."

I knew she was trying to be helpful, but no one knew the odds against me more than I did. "This girl is linked to the one person who can tell my PO if I'm fucking up or not, trust me, I'm on my toes with her. I just felt bad about her losing her dog."

"Hate to sound inconsiderate, but people lose their dogs every day. You have to move smarter."

It wasn't that simple, at least, it didn't *feel* that simple. Jenaya didn't know what it was like seeing Regan smile, seeing her face light up, those dimples in her cheeks, the glow in her eyes—and she didn't know the disappointment in seeing Regan frown. Of seeing her defeated. I couldn't control how it made me feel. It was upsetting.

I hadn't told anyone about that night at the center where I almost messed up.

For almost a month I'd tried to distract myself from Regan London, but hell if it wasn't hard. For starters, we were chemistry partners, neighbors, and coworkers. She was everywhere, and so was that smile.

I was good, though, at keeping my hands to myself and not lingering too long around her.

She wasn't the old Guillermo's type. Good girls who colored in the lines had always been off my radar. But looking at her and talking to her, I just knew she was real. Like, no games or bullshit. Something told me that, if I texted her, she wouldn't wait five minutes to an hour to respond back, she was either all in or she wasn't.

Jenaya shrugged. "She cute." *Talk about an understatement.* "And kinda bougie."

I sighed. "Jenaya."

She wasn't backing down. "I'm just saying."

"Yeah, well I thought *bad and bougie* was in."

She rolled her eyes. "Anyway, who did her *boyfriend* set you up with?"

"Know a senior named Sofia Rios?"

Jenaya bobbed her head. "Yeah, she's in the all the honors classes with the preppy bunch, why?"

"That's Troy's friend."

Jenaya narrowed her hazel eyes, shaking her head and releasing a whistle. "He set you up."

"How you figure?"

"Y'all not even friends. He called you 'Convict,' trying to be slick. I mean, let's face it, you organize your Jay-Z albums by most lyrical to decent, you scour hip-hop pages like the Bible, and you can't deny you been peepin' his girl. Troy doesn't know a thing about you. He chose a super preppy girl for you all because you're too close to his girl. This was a soft warning to tread lightly, Mo."

Passive-aggressive or not, I was on Troy's radar. This could go only one way if I kept being friendly to Regan.

Forward, not back.

Shrugging my shoulders, I made up my mind. "Oh well, Naya."

"So you're really going to do it, ask her out?"

The way I saw it, I wasn't looking for anything, and maybe Sofia wasn't either. Perhaps what we both could use was a night out. A night of meaningless distractions.

Surely there was no harm in that.

Regan

My mother's words circled in my head all day as I sat in my classes.

I couldn't focus in any of them. I was a nervous wreck about the game and the party, and I was anxious over what my father would say when I brought up dropping accounting. But I was determined. For once it would be nice to do something *I* wanted to do, instead of being programmed for other people's molding.

Trouble was, I still had no clue what I wanted to do. I just knew I couldn't pretend it was accounting anymore. It was too dull, not to mention numbers made my head hurt.

"Earth to Regan." Malika waved her hand in my face. "Um, hello, I asked which was cuter. This top or this one?"

We were at the mall after school doing some last-minute shopping to get ready for the game and after-party.

One top Malika was holding up almost resembled a tiny skirt. It was square, black with white lines forming cubes. The other choice was a white satiny long-sleeved shirt. She would look great in either.

"The white," I suggested.

Malika examined the top and wrinkled her nose. "Nah, white is too good and wholesome, this is a Regan London number. *I* wanna look risqué. Calvin's been on his best behavior."

Her words made me pause, but before I could call her out on it, a girl I recognized came over.

"Hey!" Jasmine Cooley waved as she walked up to us. I saw that she, too, was going for fun with a suede halter top in her hands.

"Y'all getting ready for the game?" she asked, looking from Malika to me.

"More like the after-party," Malika quipped.

Jasmine chuckled and slapped Malika five. "Heard that. Regan, you should sit with Ebony and me. It'll be fun."

"Can't," I told her. "My family's sitting with Troy's."

Jasmine seemed to understand. "Tommy's parents wanted us to sit with them, too, but then I couldn't act up like I want."

"You get all into it?" I asked.

She waved me off and rolled her eyes. "Girl no, I just have fun when we score, especially Tommy and Troy."

I sighed. It would be a lot more fun to watch the game with the girls versus being under my parents' thumb, playing my role.

"I'll be on the field cheering, but I'll see you at the party, assuming that's what Calvin wants to do," Malika spoke up.

"Definitely. I'll be with Ebony, Smiley, and Tiana," Jasmine said. "I'll look out for you." She gathered her top and waved to me before she took off toward the shoe section.

I followed behind Malika as she put the white shirt back. I felt pathetic for secretly liking the shirt enough to buy it.

"You and Calvin are seeing each other officially?" I wanted to know.

Malika bit her lip, refusing to look at me as she sorted through a rack of skirts. "I mean, he's my first, Rey. You never really get over your first."

Troy was nearly my first everything. I wondered if I'd become more attached if we went there.

"You sure?" I asked gently. Above all else, I wanted her to be careful with this second chance she seemed intent on extending.

"He apologized. We're seeing where things are going. Don't worry, Rey, we haven't even hooked up again. I wanna be like you and Troy. The next time should really mean something, you know?"

She was being smarter and more on guard than before. Though I wished she hadn't compared her and Calvin to me and Troy. We were still arguing over *that* topic.

"Yeah, me and Troy," I replied.

"Don't tell me you're on the outs again."

I groaned. "We were talking the other day about, you know, and all I could think about was how I'm going to deal with accounting."

Malika cocked her head, looking confused. "Wait, he over there thinking about sex, and you thinking about accounting?" she asked, shock dripping from her tone.

"I know, it's bad. But I might want to drop accounting, and that's more important than *that* right now."

"It gets you a lot of money."

"Yeah, but shouldn't I be looking at jobs that I'll *like*?"

"Work a job you'll like and be broke, or work a career that'll put food on the table and keep the lights on, hmm, tough call." Malika lifted and dropped each hand.

Her sarcasm made me laugh and I reached out and shoved her. "Sometimes it's like I'm making moves for everyone but *me*."

She took that in. "Well, what does Regan want?"

Her question made me think of Guillermo. *Guillermo*. He had been the first to ask me that. He'd helped just a little by getting me Simba, but it was still up in the air what *I* wanted.

I glanced outside the shop, across the traffic walking through the mall, and caught sight of the pet store. When we were kids, our parents would let Avery and me go inside and pet the puppies. Back then, Avery had always drifted to the reptiles, but I'd been obsessed with the furry pets. We'd be allowed in the shop for only so long before my mother would complain about the smell.

Whether the smell was foul or not, taking care of animals seemed like the *best* job.

I brought my attention back to Malika. "Right now, I'd just like to be free to explore my likes and dislikes. I know what's at stake as far as my grades are concerned. I've got too much on my plate to screw up now, but I wish I had the chance to try something for me."

"Rey. You've got a dad who loves you so much he wants you to have a stable career, and a boyfriend who loves you and just wants to show you in the next big way. I mean, it could be worse. Hell, you could be like me and have no dad around telling you what to do."

Malika lived with her mom and a string of her mother's boyfriends. She always said I had it better than her, but I still didn't think I lived the perfect life just because I had both of my parents together in a good marriage. We had our problems, just like anyone else, but I could see Malika's point. Perhaps I was just overthinking.

She soon plucked up a leather miniskirt, tilting her head to examine it.

My mind drifted to the offending white top that had been no good for her taste.

"Do you really think I'm boring and wholesome?" I asked, fiddling with the sweatshirt I'd picked out.

She heaved a sigh and faced me. I didn't miss the way her eyes briefly lingered on the shirt in my hands. "No, your style's cute, Rey. You always look cute. If you ever wanna step out of your comfort zone, you know I'm here for you." She reached out and swatted my hand. "And there's nothing boring about you. Just because you're not walking around with a boob out doesn't mean you dress like somebody's grandma."

I almost laughed, but still, I felt out of place with my fashion sense. *I* liked my sweatshirt along with the denim skirt I'd chosen to go with it, but this was a party.

Girls like Malika and Jasmine, they weren't afraid to dress flirty and sexy. They were comfortable in their skin, whereas I felt awkward and on display. A part of me wanted to dress up, too, but another feared Troy's reaction. It was his night, but I wasn't in the mood to fight him off and argue over going all the way.

A knot formed in my stomach and I hugged myself.

Malika chose her outfit and made her way to the register. After a two-minute debate, I paid for my clothing, too, hoping my choices would be enough.

"Touchdown!"

It was the final game of the season and one of our players had scored a touchdown against our rival, Moorehead High. On the field, Tommy J jumped in the air and bumped his chest against his best friend Isaiah Rhodes's chest. The boys were on fire, and we were up 49 to 37.

"Go on, Zay!" Mrs. Jordan was on her feet and shouting after Isaiah's impressive touchdown.

"Yeah, he better hurry up and win this for us," my mother was quick to agree. She was hugging herself as if she were freezing. It was a little chilly out. "I wanna get home before the storm begins."

Annnnnd it's going to rain?

I was more grateful than anything for my chosen outfit for the night. Despite the fact that I was wearing a skirt, my sweatshirt provided warmth against the breeze.

Avery had been allowed to stay home due to his genuine disinterest in the game. Not that our father hadn't fussed the entire ride about how disappointed he was. Still, he hadn't made Avery come, and I envied that as I sat with my mother and Mrs. Jordan on my left and my father and Mr. Jordan on my right.

We were seated in a reserved area near the field among other parents and family of the players. It made me feel like a VIP, although a reluctant one.

"That boy can run," my father mused, watching the action.

"Can't he?" Mr. Jordan agreed. "He might be faster than Tommy if Tommy keep playin'."

"Man, get outta here with that bullshit, ain't nobody faster than the Jordans," my father said.

"Them boys keep a fierce regimen, I tell you that." Mr. Jordan looked proudly down at the field.

"Avery's about to hit his growth spurt soon and he's just going to waste it sittin' on that damn couch all day watching cartoons and reading comic books," my father complained with a shake of his head. "He oughta be training to try out."

"He better do it soon. Tommy and his boys gon' own that team after Troy leave. Avery has a long way to come if he's going to join."

"Avery'll find his way, Dad, give him time to find what he likes and loves," I spoke up.

My father faced me with a proud look in his eye, reaching out and patting my knee. "I just want him to be passionate about something other than anime, like you and accounting."

Passion. Accounting. Right. I sank in my seat, counting down the minutes till the game was over.

"How are things with you, Rey?" Mr. Jordan leaned over to get a good look at me.

"Good," I told him.

A gleam shone in his eyes. "You doin' all right in that accounting class? Yvonne was on the phone with Sherry the other day."

My current C on my interim report said I was doing just average in accounting, but by the way my father was watching me, I knew I couldn't admit that. Our families were trying to join and build a legacy, whether I liked it or not.

It shouldn't have felt like a difficult task to speak up and say no once in a while, but it did. With everything. It was a shame I felt guilty wanting control of my own life. But I didn't have the tongue to say all that.

"It's going great, sir." I put on a big smile to sell the point.

"Good. Someday you can be Troy's accountant. I always tell that boy to keep his circle small and the people here now close with him at all times," said Mr. Jordan.

My father's large hand fell heavy on my shoulder. "Rey's gon' see him through. They're a perfect match."

"Regan!" Mrs. Jordan was shouting for me next. "You

gotta come by for dinner. I'm planning a big meal next week-end for Sweetest Day, and I want you and Jasmine to come."

It wasn't like I could say no with all eyes on me. And at least I could look forward to Mrs. Jordan's famous peach cob-bler. I pushed out all discomfort as I faced Troy's mother with that same phony smile. "Yes, ma'am, I'd love to."

Guillermo

Despite it all, Friday evening before the football game, I found myself standing outside the gym watching the volleyball team, trying to get a look at Sofia Rios.

She moved with grace in her purple-and-light-green uniform, whether serving the ball or sending it back over the net.

An ache singed in the back of my mind the more I took in the beautiful senior. Tall, athletic frame with a touch of softness, olive skin, dark brown hair, and a face that could send any guy to his knees.

As soon as the team took a break, I entered the gym and approached her, catching her friends' attention instantly. They looked at me and smiled, one blonde taking the liberty of nudging Sofia as I stood behind her.

From the moment she opened her mouth and I took in her personality, I knew exactly what Jenaya meant when she said Sofia was preppy.

"Omg, hi!" she exclaimed. Her face brightened with excitement. "Guillermo, right?"

So Troy had talked to her as well?

I ignored the setup. "Yeah, that's me."

"Troy told me about you," Sofia had said. "And I agree, you're cute."

I blinked. "Troy thinks I'm cute?"

She laughed, swatting at me playfully. "No, silly. He said you're the new guy every girl's buzzing about."

I bet he did.

Their break was only so long, so I kept it short, asking her if she was interested in going to the after-party the football team was having. Thankfully, and with no pressure, she agreed to meet me there so we could feel each other out and have some fun.

As I got dressed later that night, a gnawing in my gut told me to text her and back down. But then, maybe a night out with a nice girl would be fun. When I allowed myself to check out After Hours with Jenaya, it had been a blast. The music was dope, the atmosphere was safe and chill, and it was no issue hanging out and talking with girls. Perhaps this party would have the same feeling.

Jenaya insisted she was catching a ride with someone else since it was located on the west side where her mother lived. Since she was checking on her sisters and brother, she'd already be in the vicinity. A quick text from Raviv found that he wasn't even going.

Nah. Cami and I got into a fight. Waiting for her to cool down

Trouble in paradise.

One glimpse in my mirror, and I found myself at a crossroads about the whole thing. Nervously, I pulled my hair back into a bun. I removed it, then retied it once more. Anxiety was creeping up on me.

"Going somewhere?" My father hung in the doorway, studying me as I battled with my appearance.

"There's this football after-party for Arlington's final game," I told him. "I'm supposed to meet a girl there."

His brows lifted. "What girl?"

I shrugged in an attempt to be casual. "Just some girl from school."

He made a face as he came into my room, looking around. "It wouldn't be the girl from across the street, would it?"

Regan.

The last thing I needed was her on my mind. "What makes you think that?"

His expression went flat. "You got her a dog."

"Because hers ran off."

"So?"

"Dad."

"I'm only saying this because I've seen that novio of hers. We're not here to repeat the past, Memo." He said this with a gentleness that let me know he was only looking out for me. "She's probably a nice girl, unlike that other one, but still, take it easy here."

He was right to warn me.

What do they say about the more you can't have something…?

"Nah," I spoke up. "It's some other girl, I swear."

"You being careful?"

"Yes, I'm taking extra precaution here." Maybe it was best to put that wall back up with Regan. I could tell she'd been hurt when I was distant during our study session in the conference room. But it was for the best. I was trying here, I really was.

My father folded his arms across his chest. "You know, we never had the condom talk before."

Oh God no.

"Ay no!" I groaned as I covered my ears.

He held back a laugh. "I don't want any nietos anytime soon runnin' around here."

"Trust me, I'm condom savvy." I was a firm believer of no glove, no love.

"So long as we have an understanding," my father said. "I'd rather you be embarrassed now by this conversation than come to me later with some news I'm not ready for."

"Yes," I quickly agreed.

At least we were on good terms.

My father let me go, and I decided to wear my hair down. Maybe I was overthinking things.

Outside I caught a glimpse of Raviv leaning against his house, smoking. From his sagging posture, something told me the fight with Camila had been epic.

The sky above me was a dark gray, signaling an impending storm. Perhaps it would serve as an excuse to leave the party early should the night turn into a dub.

"Want to talk about it?" I offered as I walked toward him.

He shrugged, taking a drag from his cigarette. "She'll get over it. I've got Kayde coming to cheer me up. This ain't cutting it." He lifted his cigarette.

Something about Kayde turned me off, but I didn't bring it up. "These things happen. Give it a day, you two will be stuck like glue again in no time."

He smiled bitterly. "I hope so, man."

"Maybe you should come out to take your mind off it," I suggested.

He declined. "Nah, it wouldn't be right to go out when we're fighting and she's probably at home sulking."

I could only respect that. "Well, all right. Text me if you need me."

Raviv nodded, and I got in my car and took off, aiming to have a normal night.

The party was in full swing by the time I got there. Apparently, our team had lost due to a last-second field goal, but the score had been so close that people still wanted to celebrate. A lot of drunkenness soaked the air as I stepped into the two-story house. Red Solo cups could be seen all around as inebriated smiles and laughter set the tone.

I had come quite the distance from Briar Pointe to get to the west side, and I was already feeling claustrophobic and out of place, not seeing anyone I knew.

Scratch that—as I entered the entertainment area, I spotted Camila talking to some guy, a Solo cup in her hand. It didn't seem like a casual conversation, their smiles read more flirty than friendly.

I thought of texting Rav, but part of me didn't want to stir up any drama.

Would you want to know? I asked myself.

Knowing that I would, I pulled out my cell phone.

"Mo!" Malika came out of nowhere and wrapped her arms around my middle. One thing I liked about her was how bubbly she always was.

Regan was behind her, and I fought a smile to no avail. Where Malika showed out with her tube top and skinny jeans, Regan kept it simple in a sweatshirt and denim skirt, lookin' warm and cozy.

"You go to the game?" Malika asked.

I made a face. "You know I didn't. I'm just here to feel the place out. You seen Jenaya?"

Malika shrugged and looked to Regan. "You?"

Regan shook her head.

With my phone still in hand, I typed a quick text to my missing friend. "This place is pretty packed. You'd think we won or something."

"Tell me about it. Moorehead's our rival and they usually win, but this time we came pretty close," Regan explained.

My cell vibrated with Jenaya's response.

Got stuck babysitting 😣 Story of my life, right? Have fun w/ Sofia tho

I snorted and went back to the girls. "We always lose?"

"Mostly, although since Troy's been at Arlington, we won his sophomore year, not to mention he's got two city titles under his belt, and with this being his last game for our school..." Malika sorta shrugged. She craned her neck, peering past me. "Ooh, there go Jasmine, let me say hi."

She ran off, leaving me with Regan.

We stared at each other, and I didn't know what to say. Regan seemed to be keeping her distance from me, which was almost amusing. We both should walk away, but that didn't feel like any fun.

"You look cute," I told her.

Regan studied her outfit down to her white sneakers. "You think so?"

"I don't say things I don't feel."

I had a dangerous feeling a guy could never get tired of seeing Regan blush. I liked how she was dressed. It might look conservative to some, but it seemed fashionable to me. I loved the way her hair was styled, the way her legs looked in her skirt, the way the color of the sweatshirt complemented her skin tone. Old me *and* new me just wanted to reach out and hug her. Even with my attempt to break the ice, she was distant.

"Oh, we actin' iffy now?" I teased, folding my arms.

She loosened up, chuckling, and shook her head. "No, it's just—"

"Hey!" Sofia materialized beside me, chipper as ever. "I've been looking all over for you."

Regan gave a tight-lipped smile and issued a quiet little "hey" before stepping away from us. It was the right thing to do. But internally, all of me was more interested in following her like some lost puppy than staying and getting more acquainted with Sofia.

"Did you just get here?" Sofia was smiling from ear to ear. From her perfect white teeth and button nose to her glossed lips, she was incredibly pretty.

I made sure to greet her properly with a hug, since we'd come for each other.

"Yeah, seems like the whole city showed up." It was loud with chatter, but the music was louder. A Migos song had a few people bobbing their heads while a few girls danced into their boyfriends.

"Of course, we lost but Troy always plays an impressive game." Sofia spoke like everyone else did when it came to Troy, highly and loyal. "His fan base has been growing since middle school. You a fan of football?"

"Nah, I'm not a sports guy," I confessed.

She stood back and examined me, clearly liking what she saw. "Doesn't look that way."

Old Guillermo would've made a muscle and flirted. New

Guillermo felt rusty. "I've played with family, but organized sports aren't my style. You ever want to box, I'm your guy."

"Boxing, huh? That's kinda different. Where are you from again?" She eyed me over the rim of her cup as she took a sip.

"North side, Rowling Heights—more so the neighborhood than the suburb." Rowling Heights was known for its upscale suburbs, where most of my former schoolmates had lived. At one time, my parents had been workin' on getting a place among them, but I probably would've hated them. The neighborhood held more personality, more culture—and trouble.

Sofia wrinkled her nose. "I hear things aren't so nice outside of the suburbs, like they don't even have a Starbucks."

How tragic. "You must be a big fan."

"Are you kidding? I *live* on Starbucks, it's the only way I made it to senior year."

I didn't even like coffee.

"Hey, maybe we could get into the ring sometime! I'm super strong from volleyball." Sofia raised her hand and attempted to make a fist. It was all wrong.

I chuckled as I circled behind her. Leaning close, I said, "You punch someone with that, and you're going to hurt yourself more than them." I took her hand in mine, freeing her tucked thumb. "You'll break your thumb that way."

Sofia shivered in my arms and leaned closer. "Show me how to do it."

I enclosed my hand over hers and molded it into a proper fist. "When you throw it, make sure you put just enough force into it, not so much that you'll go flying if they dodge it."

Sofia turned back around. "Thanks." Her gaze lowered to my lips.

Cute girl or not, I wasn't feeling it, not enough to kiss her so soon. Old Guillermo was fine with a random, meaningless hookup, whereas New Guillermo wanted more.

Thankfully, by the grace of God, she soon moved away, groaning as she dug into her pocket. "He keeps texting me."

"Who?"

"My stupid ex-boyfriend." Despite her protesting tone, Sofia still read his text. If she were truly over it, she would've blocked him from the start.

"Looks like he isn't ready to give up on you," I said.

She softened as she read his text again. "Yeah, well, he should've thought about that."

I realized I had the perfect shot at a clean getaway. A perfect excuse to leave her alone. I was doing the right thing by avoiding drama.

But I wasn't going to make it obvious.

I placed a hand on the small of Sofia's back, ushering her out of the room and into a quieter area.

"So what's up? What went wrong with him?" I asked curiously.

"We always said we'd go to Akron U together, but he applied for Toledo and got in. He told me space would be good for us," she explained. "So I broke it off. We had a deal."

It was time to play Dr. Phil.

"Maybe—hear me out—maybe he's right about space. Just because he wants to go to different colleges doesn't mean he doesn't love you or want to be with you. Following your partner to college isn't the best idea. Sometimes things happen and you split, and then you're stuck there sharing a campus that gets smaller and smaller each time you bump into them. Trust me, I've got cousins and I've heard it all.

"So don't look at space as a bad thing. It gives you a chance to explore this new venture in your life on your own, and you can figure things out as you go. Plus, you get to miss your boyfriend, which makes weekends when you link up much more special."

Sofia seemed to soak that in. Then she frowned. "You must not be into me."

I wasn't; my mind was elsewhere, someplace it shouldn't be. Curious no matter the weight of the risk.

"You're a gorgeous girl, but I'm not looking to be a rebound right now. Your heart's still with this guy, you're just upset he didn't communicate with you," I told her gently.

Sofia pouted. "You're right. I just wish he'd told me."

"It's not too late to talk this out."

Her cell must've vibrated again, as she peered down at the notification on her screen.

"Looks like he's trying," I said.

Sofia squeezed her phone tight and gazed up at me, completely vulnerable. For a moment, she reminded me of Yesenia and how trusting she was when she needed me for something. "You know, you're a good-looking guy and you seem really nice, but I'm not ready to give up on Jesse right now. I still love him."

Whew.

I stepped to the side. "Don't let me stand in the way."

She smiled wryly as she patted my chest, then walked out of the room.

As I took in the ongoing party around me, I realized Sofia and I were more alike than I'd thought. We'd met here tonight both knowing we wanted someone else.

Regan

I found Malika in the kitchen grabbing something to drink with Jasmine. The atmosphere around me was rich with excitement and Panther pride, but I couldn't shake the sensation of being disappointed. It felt thick and cold, and my shoulders were sagging as I joined the girls at the island counter.

"Where's Mo?" Malika craned her neck, looking for him behind me.

"With his *date*." I hoped she didn't catch the bitterness in my tone. Sofia Rios was a senior friend of Troy's. I hardly knew her, except that she was pretty, smart, in the nursing program, and apparently single and ready to mingle, too.

Malika cringed, bringing her can of Coke to her lips. "Yikes."

Jasmine appeared thoughtful. "Guillermo?"

Malika nodded. "Cute, right?"

Jasmine shrugged. "I guess. He's no Troy, right, Rey?"

Troy was handsome as could be, but Guillermo was still incredibly—

"Speaking of Troy, Mrs. Jordan wants to do this whole big dinner for Sweetest Day next Saturday," I brought up instead.

"Yeah, Tommy told me."

"I didn't know you two were serious."

Jasmine was quick to wave me off. "Tommy's my best friend and all, but we mostly only benefit from our friendship, nothing too deep."

"Oh."

Jasmine grinned at my reaction. "It's cool, Rey. Not all of us can be like you. You and Troy always look so good together. You're like the ideal couple from Arlington, a real dream."

"But dreams aren't real." I knew she was trying to be sweet, but Troy and I didn't really live up to our image. It stopped being storybook when his impatience gave me anxiety.

"Well, yeah, true, but I don't know, you two are just perfect together."

Perfect, right. "Yeah," I agreed. I grabbed a can of soda from one of the coolers lining the island. Anything to distract myself.

"Hey!"

Malika's shriek drew my attention. Calvin had wrapped his arms around her and was nuzzling her close.

"Excuse the lovebirds," Jasmine mumbled. She tossed me a look before leaving the room.

"What up, Rey?" Calvin greeted me with a bob of his head.

In his arms, Malika was giddy, glowing, happy. Sometimes, second chances were worth it.

"Hey, Calvin," I said to him.

"Mind if I steal my girl right quick?"

"*Your* girl, oh, we claiming now?" I teased.

Calvin grinned proudly, squeezing Malika closer. "Hell yeah, this all me."

Malika's blush had me happy for her. She deserved to be happy. We all did.

I stepped away, giving them space. Usually, I hung out with Malika at these functions. Among the sports crowd, she was my ace. There were other girls I was acquainted with, but Malika was my *best* friend. She belonged in this world more than I did, and being with her made enduring it all easier. Still, as I meandered through the party swallowed in my unease and claustrophobia, I decided to let her breathe. She was boo'd up with Calvin, on cloud nine, and I wasn't about to interrupt.

I hadn't seen Troy yet. It was an hour into the party, and he was nowhere to be found.

"Oh wow." Ahead of me, I spotted a couple making out in a corner. The boy was much taller than the girl's tiny figure, but upon closer review, I recognized her instantly. I'd seen the sophomore coming and going from Raviv Hadad's house many times. I'd just seen her with him that morning, now that I thought about it. My heart plummeted for him, as he was nowhere to be found while his girlfriend was kissing some other guy.

"There you are!"

The shout caused me to turn, and I was instantly crushed in a massive hug as Troy's body collided with mine. He'd had more than his usual one beer, and his weight nearly took me down as he embraced me a little too tight.

"Hey, baby." I let out a giggle at how unsteady he was. "Good game. I'm sorry we lost, but you were amazing."

Troy gazed down at me with affection in his eyes. "The scouts are happy."

"That's all that matters." In the end, it didn't matter if Arlington lost; Troy's playing had been impressive as usual, enough to get the attention of more scouts. Rumor had it they were looking at Tommy already, too.

"Ah, man, you're gonna kill it next year at OSU, bro. They need a player like you." One of Troy's teammates came and dapped him up, admiring Troy like the football god he was.

Troy proudly puffed up his chest. "You already know, they don't call me Mr. All-American for nothing."

His teammate ate it up. "You about to go pro, shit, Tommy, too."

Troy tried to play humble before taking a sip of whatever he was drinking in his Solo cup.

His teammate moved on, but not a second later, another took his place and chatted him up. Oddly, I noticed the more praise Troy received, the more he drank, and the more his smile seemed to be as fake as the one I wore whenever I talked about accounting...or when I was with him.

"Finally." Troy breathed a sigh of relief in between fans. The room was still full of people, but for the time being, no one was worshipping the ground he walked on.

"I swear your fan base gets bigger with every game. I saw a guy with the other team's colors on bragging about you even," I said.

I thought this would impress him, but instead he gave a tight-lipped smile and downed the last of his drink. "Pressure makes diamonds, right?"

Pressure. There must be a lot on his shoulders, the weight of expectations on him heavy.

"It was a good game, and you played your best," I told him. "It's called a team for a reason—it's not all on you."

His mood didn't lift too much. "Still would've been nice to win my last high school game. Shit, what do I have if I don't win?"

I moved closer, offering my support. "People will support you whether you win or lose, Troy. Because they love *you*. I know I do."

He cracked a smile. "Thank you. I mean, at least it was close and we gave 'em a show, right?"

"Right." I relaxed, seeing him visibly calm down. "So, OSU?" Ohio State University was a popular school. Other football players from Akron had even gone there and later joined the NFL.

Troy shrugged. "I'm just weighing my options, Rey. I think I'd rather go to OSU than Syracuse or Miami. My family's here."

"Plus me," I chimed in as I elbowed him on the sly.

"Plus you." His gaze ran down my body, and his smile lessened a degree. "Nice top."

It wasn't what he'd requested, but it felt like me. I touched the material as I tried to explain, "It's going to storm later."

He wasn't satisfied. "Just for one night, you couldn't dress sexy for me?"

I'd known he'd be a little disappointed, but the look of sheer annoyance he was trying to keep from his face set me off. "Why can't you accept how I dress? I like my outfit."

Troy's focus went elsewhere as a muscle in his jaw tensed. "Whatever, Rey."

It was his night, and I didn't want to spend it arguing. I reached out to touch him. "I don't want to fight, Troy. Let's have fun."

He still wasn't paying me any mind and I was starting to get upset myself. I shouldn't have to beg for his attention or apologize for my choice of clothing. A petty part of me was ready to leave and let him have his fun with his beloved fan base, but I pushed to be supportive.

I buried my pride as I tried again to make things better. "Maybe we could go out and—"

"Hey, sexy!" Out of nowhere a girl slid in between us, giving Troy a hug that felt more intimate than it should've been.

I took in her look for the night, a body suit that emphasized her flat stomach, curvy waist, and perky chest. Her hair was long, hanging past her shoulders, and she'd applied body shimmer to complement her brown skin. She was pretty, and she smelled like a sugary blend of vanilla and honey. Troy was entranced—I all but disappeared as his stare locked on the showstopper before him.

"Yo, Genesis, chill," he said with a shaky grin as he held her away.

Genesis stood back and flipped her hair over her shoulder. "Why ain't you in there dancin' with me?"

As if he suddenly remembered I existed, Troy's gaze flickered to me. "I'm with my girl right now. It's not like that tonight."

His words upset Genesis and confused me. What did he mean by it's not like that *tonight*?

She scowled. "You need to hurry up and dead that so you can come and have some fun with me."

Her name was Genesis, but there was nothing holy about her. Not with the way she wasn't holding back from giving me the stank eye, as if *I* were in the way of *her* fun with Troy. Beyond the fact that she was being blatantly rude, I had a bigger issue with Troy letting her.

I crossed my arms and eyed Troy. "What's going on?"

I watched as my boyfriend nervously ran a hand behind his neck. "N-nothing."

"Doesn't look like nothing, Troy. Who is this?" I demanded. I knew most of his senior friends, especially the girls. Genesis didn't look familiar at all. Did she even go to our school?

By now we had an audience, and embarrassment prickled under my skin.

Genesis didn't care. "You know where to find me, Troy." She walked away, but not without smirking at me as she passed by.

"Troy," I let out. "What's going on?" I wanted him to tell me everything was okay, even though I knew in my gut that something was very wrong.

Troy blew out a breath. "Listen, I…I fucked up, but it was just one time."

I could barely hear the gasps and commentary from the small crowd around us. I had tunnel vision for the boy standing in front of me.

"What?" I needed him to be clear. I needed to hear him say it.

Troy couldn't even look at me. "I hooked up with ol' girl, but it didn't mean anything. I was just tired of waiting."

"So you *slept with someone else*?" I asked incredulously, stepping away from him.

"It was supposed to be our night, our anniversary dinner, and then you went ghost on me at the club and got a ride from *him*. You ain't want me, so I found someone who did."

My eyes tripled in size. His words echoed in my ears, my pulse thudding so hard that my head hurt. "Are you kidding me? You freakin' cheated on our anniversary?"

Instigators were quick to chime in.

"*That's cold!*"

"*Dudes ain't shit.*"

"*I hope she don't cry.*"

"It was just one time, Rey," Troy tried to reason as he came closer. "I slipped up, I was in my feelings, and she came out of nowhere."

It was everyone's fault but Troy's.

My heart started to hurt, my back stiffened, and I could feel the freezing ickiness of being stared at by what seemed like *every*one in the room. A part of me wanted to hit Troy, but I knew it wasn't worth it.

Tears pooled in my eyes. "You don't even have the decency to control your groupies. You got her looking at me all crazy because *you're* out being dumb."

He tried to reach for me. "Rey."

The last thing I wanted was his hands on me. "Don't touch me."

He frowned before casting angry looks at those watching us. "Let's just go somewhere so we can talk."

"Talk? You can have your groupies!"

Sure, I could've heard him out, but what could he truly say? I'd put up with so much from him and he had the nerve to try to excuse his cheating over the one thing I wasn't ready for. As if it were my fault for not just lying down and spreading myself open for him when he wanted.

If his cup weren't empty, I would've drenched him with it.

Instead, I turned my back on him and took off. People stepped aside for me, watching my exit with pity and amusement.

A crowd was dancing in the next room. My vision blurred as I attempted to seek out Malika. Or anyone I knew with a car. All around me was a pit of nameless faces lost in celebration.

I took out my phone.

Me: I need to go NOW!

"Move!"

Some girl shoved me out of the way as she held up her phone and smiled toward its camera for a selfie, probably to show off her cute outfit and the people enjoying themselves in the background. She was trying to capture a moment that didn't exist—at least for me anyway.

Nobody really cared.

I gave up on Malika as I reached the front door and slipped outside.

The first breath of fresh air cleared my senses, but my belly still swirled with butterflies. I was really doing this, walking away. There was nowhere to go, I was far from home, but going back inside wasn't an option.

Hugging myself against the chill, I stepped into the night, waiting on a heartbreak that didn't come. My feet hit the sidewalk and I pushed forward.

Maybe it was my fault. I'd done everything expected of me, and here I was, alone and miserable. I hated accounting, but I kept my mouth shut. I hated Troy's greedy touch, but I put up with it. My misery was my own doing.

A roll of thunder startled me, and a second later rain began sprinkling down drop by drop.

Yes, just rain on my parade.

"Regan!"

A car was coming up the street. I could barely make out its make and model as I stood back and waited.

Oh my God. I relaxed.

It was Guillermo. He leaned over the passenger seat to see me out the window.

"Hop in," he instructed.

The rain would only get heavier, not that it mattered. With him was where I wanted to be, so I climbed in beside him.

I wiped at my face, not wanting him to see what a mess I was.

"Troy's a dickhead," Guillermo told me.

Great, even he had already heard the news. I sniffled and faced the window. "Don't."

Beside me, I could hear Guillermo turn so his whole body faced me. "You deserve better than this. You deserve a guy that understands you and wouldn't pressure you into anything you're not ready for. A guy that wants the best for you like you'd want the best for him. Most importantly, you need a dude that's gonna let you do you, and even if he doesn't like you being friends with other guys, he wouldn't give you shit about it, 'cause at the end of the day he trusts you. You especially deserve a guy who wouldn't hurt you and not have the balls to run after you when he's wrong."

My heart dropped at the reality that Troy wasn't that guy. He never had been for me.

I was so embarrassed. "Don't worry about me, I don't want to ruin your thing with Sofia."

Silence fell, and for a moment I debated stepping back out into the rain.

Guillermo sighed. "I'm not feelin' her. Besides, I think she's getting back with her ex."

It was all messed up.

"Do you want to go back?" he asked.

"No," I said.

"You're on the other side of town, how were you going to get home. On foot?"

"I don't know."

"You gotta be careful, you shouldn't be walking the streets alone. It's not safe." He raked a hand through his hair and shook his head. "Troy should've come after you, even just to see you off in an Uber or something."

It continued to rain. Guillermo was right, I would've been

a goner out there on my own. It would've been smarter of me to request my own Uber instead of walking away.

"Let's get you home, dimples, it's been a long night," Guillermo said after a moment's pause.

His words warmed me. They were simple and soft, enveloping me in a sense of comfort I had come to find that only he could give.

"Thank you," I told him. "For helping me."

"It's never a problem. I'm beginning to think this is what we do best."

Because Troy had a habit of running me off. The signs had always been there, I had just chosen to ignore them.

I focused on Guillermo, who looked concerned and genuine. "I wanna give you a nickname, too."

"Most people call me *Memo* or *Mo*," he told me as he started driving.

No way did I want to be aligned with *most* people. "Nah, I wanna be different." I bit into my lip, thinking it over briefly. "How about *G*?"

He chuckled. "How creative."

In my pocket my cell phone vibrated with what could only be Troy's call. I didn't try to dig it from my pocket to hear his crappy apology. There was no going back, and I was high on the feeling of walking away for good.

"Wanna listen to some music?" Guillermo offered.

He put on some rap song on by DaBaby and I leaned back and listened.

"I hate takin' the highway, but I want to avoid the storm," Guillermo said as he aimed his car for the nearest expressway.

As if the universe had other plans, it began to rain harder, the water coming down like bullets on the windshield. It was so thick I could barely see, and if I couldn't see, I knew Guill-ermo couldn't. We weren't going to make it to an expressway.

"Fuck," he swore beside me. His jaw clenched tightly as he glared at the road.

It was raining too hard for the windshield wipers to clear the view.

"We gotta get off the road." Guillermo sat up, doing his best to see through the windshield. "I don't even see a place to stop."

A horn blared at us as two headlights whooshed by too close for comfort.

This wasn't safe.

We'd left the residences behind, and closed businesses lined the streets on either side of us from what I could distinguish.

Pressing my face against the window, I could just make out a lit-up sign in the distance.

"Let's stop there." I pointed ahead, and Guillermo did his best to get by without getting hit.

He pulled the car into the lot and found a parking space. Through the rain, I could just see that we'd found a motel.

He leaned against the wheel, staring at the motel and sigh-ing.

I hugged myself, feeling weighed down by my wet clothes.

I hated Ohio weather.

Guillermo looked at me seriously. "You're shivering. Do you feel comfortable going in there with me?" He studied me carefully, reading me for any signs of a breakdown. "Or we can stay like this in my car."

My heart fluttered. "Yes, we can go inside. Thanks for asking."

I looked out the window to hide my foolish smile. It was

such a small thing, like before when we'd played pool, but once more, I admired how he'd asked me.

Oddly, I felt safer going into a motel with Guillermo than I would've with Troy. Troy never asked; he just went ahead and did what he wanted. It was as if respecting my boundaries was easier for Guillermo.

He returned his attention back out the window. "You ready?"

Ready to run out in the rain? No.

But I agreed anyway and pulled up enough courage to open my car door and get out.

Not only was it raining hard, it was freezing. I didn't stand in surprise for too long before running alongside Guillermo up to the motel.

We burst inside, where a man sat behind a counter reading the paper and listening to the forecast on TV. He took one look at us and a humorous smile spread across his face.

"Got a little wet, didn't ya?" he tried to joke. He seemed friendly and nice, and as we came closer, I prayed he was nothing like Norman Bates from those old *Psycho* movies my mom would watch.

"Yeah, we did. It's too dangerous to drive in that," Guillermo said. "How much for a room?"

The man glanced past us outside and shrugged. "Nah, no charge." He leaned over and grabbed a key card and set it on the counter. "Just don't trash the place, and you can wait out the storm, got it?"

Guillermo looked back at me, smiling for the first time. "Yeah, we got it."

There was a set of vending machines in the lobby, and the sight of them reminded me that I hadn't eaten much tonight.

I dug into my pocket, finding loose bills. "Well, since you provided shelter, how about I splurge on a late-night snack?"

Guillermo walked up to examine the vending machines. "Deal."

The selection offered just about everything to suit any type of sweet or salty craving.

"Pretzels?" I asked.

"Fine by me." Guillermo pulled his wallet from his jeans. "Thirsty?"

"I could go for a Tahitian Treat."

I bought the pretzels and Guillermo bought the soda, and together we dipped back out into the rain to find our room.

Even if the walk to No. 2 lasted all of a second, we still got even more soaked.

"Ugh, I can smell my relaxer," I groaned as we stepped into our room. My hair was ruined.

"Yeah, I didn't want to say anything," Guillermo teased as he set the snacks on the dresser.

Embarrassed, I smoothed back my hair as best as I could, trying to perform a miracle on it out of thin air.

Guillermo went into the bathroom, running a hand through his hair, shaking it out as best as he could.

I tore my gaze away and looked around the room. It was nice and cozy, with one bed covered with the typical floral bedding that no one in their right mind would pick out at home. The TV was directly across from the bed, giving us something to do.

Guillermo handed me a towel before rubbing another one over his hair. He looked like a lion by the time he was done, his mane wild and disarrayed. I was tempted to touch it, to see if it was soft. I'd never cared about long hair on guys, but Guillermo was an aesthetic.

He'd been wearing a button-down over a plain white tee, but he'd laid it out to dry as he toweled off as best as he could.

I was probably being creepy just standing there watching him, but I couldn't turn away.

"So how's accounting?" he asked as he tossed the towel to the side.

My father wasn't around, so there was no need to pretend. "Can I swear?"

Guillermo shrugged as he held his hands out in front of the heat register. "You can do whatever you want."

Of course I could.

Why is the one guy I'm supposed to stay away from the only one I feel comfortable enough to be myself with?

"Accounting's shit. I was thinking about working with animals. I really like animals, even cats."

His full lips curled into a smile. "My *abuelita* had a cat down in Mexico, meanest beast alive. Cute, though."

I loved the sound of his accent when he spoke Spanish and the way he pronounced Mexico. *Meh-hee-co.*

Working with animals would be a lot more fun and interesting than accounting. I *liked* animals, and no matter the pay, I thought careers should be chosen based on genuine interest and enjoyment. Life was too short to spend it on work that made you miserable.

"The cat liked Yesi, though," Guillermo added. "You can't not like Yesi."

This was true. "Yesenia's a great girl."

He agreed. "Yesenia's special to us. In some ways, I don't blame my parents for keeping her from me when I wasn't at my best."

"You don't?"

"Yesenia's that rare breed of good people, she's innocent

and kind. We just wanna protect her at all costs. It's kinda like with Avery, that kid has to be protected."

His words took me by surprise.

I blinked to conceal how I was trying not to cry. I loved that Guillermo saw something in him, something pure like his sister, that he wanted to defend and shield.

My father and Troy could never.

"Hey, you okay?" Guillermo came close.

He studied me and I tried to hide that I was upset. Avery was innocent and good in all the ways that Yesenia was, and instead of embracing it and wanting to save him, my father and Troy judged him for his interests.

"I'm okay," I told Guillermo.

He could see right through my lie. "No, you're not. You're all wet." He shook his head but offered a smile as he took my towel from me. "Can I?"

I had barely attempted to towel off since we stepped into the room. "Yes, thank you."

He brought the towel to my hair and rubbed it gently. While he focused on his task, I got lost watching him and all his majesty. He looked so serious and handsome as he concentrated on drying my hair. The way his brows tipped down and how just for a second he bit into his bottom lip.

As I stared, I slowly accepted that I'd had a crush on him for quite a while. Perhaps since the beginning, when I first laid eyes on him after tripping over the trash. Guillermo wasn't just a cute boy, he was everything—mature, safe, and respectful.

His movements slowed as his dark eyes locked with mine.

My mind began to wander. Those strong arms of his, what would they feel like around me? Holding me? Caging me in, in all his safety?

We were a breath apart and seemed to shift closer and closer.

He was like fire, and I thought if I touched him, I'd get burned, but I didn't care. Looking at him was like watching scorching hot amber flames dance and sway, hypnotizing with their moves.

I *wanted* to get burned.

Guillermo froze with his hands in my hair. I shivered as he brought one hand to my cheek and ran his thumb over my skin.

Guillermo.

His lips brushed mine, and all my curiosity and desire brought me on my toes as I leaned in, allowing this moment to finally happen.

Slowly, he pressed closer, kissing me gently and languidly so that my heart burned as my soul set on fire. He cradled my head and tilted it back, going deeper, letting loose all his built-up want for me, too. My hands grasped the material of his shirt, fisting it as I struggled to contain myself.

He pulled away, taking a step back.

"That's not what I brought you here for," he let me know, his breathing jagged.

He didn't have to explain himself to me. Somehow with him, I just knew. "I trust you, Guillermo."

He shook his head. "We shouldn't do that."

Frowning, I didn't like this idea. "I want to. I wanted to before."

He stared at me, long and hard, before running a hand down his face. "As much as I would love to, as much as I can admit I think about you way too much, and that there's something about you, I can't risk that. We can't even be friends, not while you're seein' Troy. It's too much like before, and I want us to be us with a fair shot at something—a friendship, more, whatever—without the bullshit of repeating my mistakes."

He thought about me, more than he should. He liked me. He wanted to kiss me.

But he stopped.

Because he was respecting the risk, because he wasn't selfish, because he wanted us to be "us" with a fair shot.

It was a lot to process, but of one thing, I was certain. "You're right."

"I wasn't givin' you an ultimatum," he was quick to clarify. "I was just sayin'."

"And I said you're right. I put up with a lot of stuff that no kid should. I'm a robot, a puppet on a string, my painted smile is wearing off, and I'm *so* tired. I'm not heartbroken over Troy, because I'm just not that into him. I started dating him in the first place for my dad, just like I studied accounting, and I need to start doing things for me. I felt bad for almost kissing you, and he'd already cheated on me without a second thought."

Guillermo sat on the bed. "You've got some stuff to clear up."

"I do, but I'm ready now." Instead of heartbreak, I felt liberated by Troy's cheating. It hurt, but I was free.

A look at my phone revealed a series of notifications, several from Troy, a few from Malika, and a ton from random classmates who were either concerned or being nosy.

I put my phone facedown on the dresser.

Troy and the universe would have to wait for another day.

"Crazy weather or not, we shouldn't tell our parents about this," Guillermo said.

He was right. I was sixteen and in a motel room alone with a boy. I doubted my parents trusted me *that* much.

"Definitely," I agreed.

"I really mean it about us not being friends right now," Guillermo said with a frown. "It's not you, it's Troy—he really is a dickhead, and I know he's going to be an issue if we keep being friendly."

"I can tell." Troy had been jealous over Simba. He'd probably be unbearable if Guillermo and I turned into more. Guillermo couldn't afford that.

"And I don't want to be a rebound," he went on. "I know you're nothing like Tynesha, but I need that to be clear."

"You would never be a pawn to get back at Troy. You deserve more than that, Guillermo."

He accepted that. "Take some time and figure it out. Not for me or us, but for you. That's what's most important here—what *you* want."

What I wanted was freedom, with all aspects of my life.

I sat beside him. "So what now?"

"Now..." Guillermo shrugged. "We're just a boy and a girl stuck in a motel room, sharing pretzels and soda."

If only the rain could last forever. "And then we go our separate ways."

He seemed to blush as he said, "Just think of Bowie."

I didn't get the reference. "Huh?"

"David Bowie, he's got this song called 'Heroes,' and he's talking about how just for one day, we could be a hero. We could be anything. This reminds me of that."

I needed to listen to that song. "We could be heroes."

"Yeah, we could."

We linked hands, entwining our fingers.

Just for one day.

Funny, I had a feeling we both wished it could be for more.

Guillermo

I liked the feeling of her soft hand on my scarred one. Early Saturday morning as I worked at the community center, I reflected on my night with Regan. Last night, where I'd slipped up and crossed the line.

I had been in denial for a while about my growing feelings for her, and all it took was being in too small quarters for me to get caught up. She was no Tynesha—I knew for certain that I wasn't a pawn to get back at Troy—but staying away was the best thing for both of us at this point. At least until Regan cleared things up with Troy. Until she was stress free and could make a choice without other grief clouding her head.

Regan should've been off my radar, yet somehow she slipped through. I couldn't explain it if I tried. My heart raced when I was around her, and for some damn reason I didn't want to look like a complete idiot. With Regan London, I was always trying to be nonchalant and cool. Ever since she first set eyes on me and I was wearing my yellow Respect tee. The same T-shirt I was wearing as I cleaned windows Saturday morning.

Together Regan and I had stayed at the Keep Inn Company Motel for a good hour while we waited for the storm to pass. My biggest concern had been making sure she was comfortable. We were alone, and the last thing I wanted was for her to think I was going to try anything.

Before, with other girls, I'd known what they wanted from me. Now, with Regan, I could read that she was unsure, and I didn't want to pressure her into anything she wasn't fully in the mood for. Had I wanted to mess around with her then and there? Hell yeah, but the circumstances were chaotic and I wanted a fair shot. I was curious about this girl and I didn't want there to be any bullshit lingering—and Troy was still very much lingering, as her phone had kept lighting up with notifications.

Once it was clear that this was the final time we'd hang out, we piled onto the bed, eating the pretzels and drinking the soda as we caught an episode of *Law & Order: SVU*.

"Thank you," Regan had said to me after a while.

"For what?"

She focused on the bedding. "For being there for Avery. It really means a lot to me."

When I'd mentioned that Avery needed to be protected, she'd looked as if she were about to cry. Avery vented to me about a lot of things, so I could understand Regan's concern.

"No problem." I placed my hand over hers. "I got his back."

The real Regan was vulnerable, shy, and eager to live her own life. Accounting and Troy weren't cutting it. She deserved more.

I should've minded my own business, but I wanted to see Regan excel at what she enjoyed. I wanted to see her smile—the real one, not the phony one that didn't reach her eyes whenever she hung around the varsity jackets at school or when she was running the front desk at the center. I liked the one I saw when we played pool and she sucked, or when I brought Simba back to her. It had been like watching the sun rise on her face. She'd opened the door all sullen and tired, and then she noticed him and she brightened into a whole new person.

I wanted the real Regan, not the robot.

"Nice job."

My hands jerked. I wasn't sure how long she'd been standing behind me, but Mrs. London's arrival sent a chill down my spine. I was certain that what I'd done with her daughter Friday night was written across my face.

Mrs. London didn't seem happy to see me, despite her compliment on my work. I'd been cleaning windows all morning and as her gaze lingered where I was kneeling on the floor, I wondered if I'd messed up.

"Let's go have a talk in the conference room. There's a meeting at eleven, so we'll keep this short." She turned on her heel, not even waiting to walk with me to the second floor.

Harvey insisted she spoke highly of me, but while he wasn't one to lie, Mrs. London hadn't eased up at all since the day we met.

As I followed her to the conference room, I racked my brain on what all I could've done to upset her. Regan had promised that our stay at the motel would stay between us, which left me to believe maybe I had slacked somewhere in my cleaning at the center and Mrs. London had come to reprimand me.

She sat at the head of the table, crossing her legs and steepling her fingers as she waited for me to take a seat.

I sat a few chairs down from her on her right. "Yes?"

Briefly, the corner of Mrs. London's lips curled up. "Tell me, Guillermo, once you've finished your required hours with us, will you be continuing your services here at the community center?"

I stared at her, confused. That…was not what I'd expected her to say. I thought about my answer. As much as I didn't mind my duties, I wanted to be as financially independent as possible. "I do like it here, but I'm hoping to find work at Henry's."

Mrs. London seemed to find humor in that, but then within the blink of an eye, all joy disappeared from her face. "Simba is quite the cute little pup, isn't he?"

Shit.

Like Troy, Mrs. London wasn't so pleased with my gift. When I'd shown up to volunteer Thursday, Daren, the facility's co-lead, had been in charge for the day and things had been normal. I'd thought maybe Mrs. London would let it go.

Now I could see that she wouldn't. "I was just getting my younger sister a puppy. I saw Simba and I couldn't let the moment pass me by."

Mrs. London's stoic expression caused terror to settle in the pit of my stomach. "It was a thoughtful thing to do. My husband's just as taken by the dog as Regan and Avery."

The thought made me smile and loosen up. Maybe this wasn't a bad confrontation.

But Mrs. London didn't let me think that for long. "While it was thoughtful, it was inappropriate. As I told you before, Regan has a boyfriend, and there are certain boundaries that need to be respected."

I almost could've laughed. She clearly hadn't spoken to her daughter about last night.

Mrs. London arched a brow. "Is something funny, Guillermo?"

I sobered. "No," I told her. "I'm sorry."

"As I was saying, Regan has a boyfriend, one she's very happy with. The last thing you should want to do is to come between them. High school can be complicated, troublesome, and screwed up, but only if you make it that way. You're on a good path, Guillermo. I want more for you, but I must warn you again to keep your distance from my daughter."

She and her husband knew very little about their children. They had no clue how they were smothering one and neglecting the other. It wasn't my place to speak up, even if it was laughable thinking that Troy made Regan happy. It just proved my point even more that I had to leave her alone. I didn't need to be in the picture until she was able to be up front with them.

"You think Troy's better for Regan because you like Troy, or because he's not the one on probation?" I found myself asking.

Mrs. London appeared thoughtful. "Your circumstances aren't malignant to the point where I want my children to stay away from you. You're friends with Avery and I admire that, but understand, Regan already has a boyfriend, one who she loves and is happy with."

She kept repeating that idea. I had to look elsewhere to keep from losing it. Troy's image was so pristine and built up, I doubted either of Regan's parents would handle their breakup well. The guy was the king of Akron, destined for prime time, and I was just some kid on probation for simple assault.

"Guillermo," Mrs. London continued. "Is there something I don't know? Because you look like you find my comments about Regan amusing."

I sat back in my seat and looked her in the eye. "I'm not at liberty to say, ma'am."

This didn't please her. She narrowed her eyes. "Tell me something, do you think Harvey would like it if we had a phone call about this scenario?"

Harvey would be on my ass. "No. It's not necessary, Regan and I aren't friends and I won't be in contact with her anytime soon."

"Really?" Mrs. London asked.

I knew who held the power here, and I knew to stay in line. Calling Harvey would be a world of shit, but calling my parents would be worse. "Can I be honest?"

Mrs. London shrugged. "Certainly."

I leaned over, becoming extra serious. My future was on the line. "Regan deserves better. Who I was in the past was never 'better.' I may not be better now, but regarding Regan, *she* deserves better. At the end of the day, it's up to Regan to say who and what makes her happy. She's incredibly beautiful and intriguing, and she deserves *better*."

I rose to my feet and tipped my head toward Mrs. London. "Consider Simba my last gesture of goodwill toward your daughter. As long as Troy is in the picture, I won't be a problem. I promise."

I walked out of the room, leaving my false bravado at the door.

Regan

I couldn't understand a word they were saying. The actors on the TV screen were speaking fluent Spanish, and though I couldn't follow their speech, I was hanging on to their story.

Thank God for subtitles.

From the English commentary, I gathered that Pilar was in love with Manuel, a resident at a hospital, but he was engaged to her snobby cousin. Each time they talked, the chemistry was intense, and Manuel saw her for more than just the baker at her family's *panadería*, and I could tell he wanted her just as badly as she wanted him.

Saturday afternoon I stayed home in bed and found myself finally viewing the foreign films Netflix had to offer, or really those from Spanish-speaking countries. Both of my parents were gone and Avery was playing a video game. It was just me, Simba, Pilar, and Manuel.

"Oh, Manuel, get it together already!" I groaned as I watched him reel Pilar in just to push her away for the ump-teenth time. Sure, he was with her cousin, but he still had time to wise up.

Beside me my cell phone buzzed. I knew it was Troy before I looked at the text.

I miss you & I'm sorry

He at least had the decency not to use a corny frowny face. All of the other texts he'd sent me were also void of emojis. He had been switching between texting and calling for hours, with no sign of letting up.

At one point, he blamed it on jealousy, and then another he blamed it on being lonely, and finally he came to the conclusion that he was just stupid. His attempt at self-pity was lost on me, because cheating was intentional, as was his continued disrespect leading up to it.

I focused on the movie, admiring the handsome actor who played Manuel. His dark tan complexion, strong build, short curly hair, handsome face, and tempting crooked smile had me swooning right along with Pilar.

Get it, girl.

Malika came sauntering into my room, loudly introducing herself by way of the heavy step of her boots and the jingle of her chandelier earrings.

"Hey, Rey, what's—" She took one look at the screen and scowled. "Girl, if you don't stop playing games and just go talk to Guillermo already." She came and sat beside me, eyeing the screen while shaking her head.

"What? I'm just watching movies." I tried to feign innocence but my best friend wasn't fooled.

"Oh really? Since when do you like foreign movies?" She gestured to the TV. "I peep game, Rey."

"Spanish has always interested me, Malika."

"Bull."

I wouldn't deny Guillermo's influence was one reason I was watching the films. I loved the sound of his voice when he spoke Spanish. But it was genuine intrigue that had me up watching a telenovela after my hair appointment Saturday morning. That and some of the passionate-looking romance the films offered. There was a part of me that had always admired the Spanish language, even if I wasn't too fluent at it in school.

Loud screaming brought my attention back to my TV screen where Pilar was bickering with her cousin Maya. Manuel looked stuck in between.

I sighed. "Ugh, no!"

Malika clicked her tongue and began scrolling through her phone. "Guillermo's across the street."

I ignored that. "You know what I hate?"

"When people tag you in pictures knowing damn well they caught you at a bad angle," Malika replied as she stared at a picture on her phone.

She wasn't even with me. "No, I hate the idea of obligation. Just because you're one way doesn't mean you have to date someone who's the same. Opposites can attract."

She set her phone to the side, facing me. "Say what, now?"

"I'm just saying, Pilar gets dumped in the beginning of the movie by some jerk, and then she meets the perfect customer who's hot, funny, charming—and engaged to her cousin. But Maya's such a snob, and Manuel actually *gets* Pilar. It's not fair."

It was clear Malika was still confused. "Yeah, Rey, you need to go across the street."

I rolled my eyes, annoyed that she didn't get it.

Back on the screen, Manuel and Maya's wedding was taking place, and Pilar was standing behind Maya as her maid of honor. Maya was sporting a baby bump, obviously carrying Manuel's unborn child.

Pathetic.

Of course fairy-tale endings weren't real, but still.

My cell phone went off again and I quickly read Troy's newest text.

"Oh wow," I said, rereading it.

Malika leaned over my shoulder to read. She rolled her eyes. "I swear those are Trey Songz lyrics."

"No, it's a football thing."

"O-kay, whatever you say."

The ending credits were rolling and the movie was over. I closed Netflix and heaved a sigh. I wasn't in the mood for another sad Spanish film, not after watching Pilar lose the love of her life and end up alone.

Maybe I was deflecting.

"Have you heard from Troy?" I faced Malika, ready for some real advice.

She set her phone aside again and leaned back with a shrug. "Uh-huh, he came crawlin' to me, trying to get me to put in a good word for him."

"And?"

"And like I said, I peep game."

I played into her taunting. "And just what does that mean?"

"Troy cheats on you, and you're not up here watchin' *All-American*, but a telenovela. How did you get home last night?"

It was supposed to be a secret, but this was Malika, my best friend.

"I just got home," I said, refusing to look her in the eye.

"I was across the room, trying to get to you, but you rushed out the front door. A second later I saw Guillermo going after you. It wasn't hard to figure out what happened next, especially with you actin' like you can't text nobody back. So basically," she went on, "you're up here watchin' movies that remind you of Guillermo, which means you're not even hurt over Troy, which also means you've been developing feelings for Mo for a while, which—"

"Malika," I groaned.

She crossed her arms and angled her head to look at me. "You a sneaky ho."

I snorted. "That's your conclusion?"

"What other explanation is there? You had a side dude this whole time, which explains why Mo's been single. What, you still keepin' Troy and just rotating 'em when one gets out of line?"

Malika was dead serious, which made her theory even funnier. Me juggle two guys? I could barely handle Troy, and I wasn't the two-timing type.

"Guillermo deserves more than being a side piece, 'Lika. You're right about Troy, though, I'm not hurt as much as I am disappointed. This was a long time coming."

"So it's done-done?" Malika clarified.

Is it?

All over social media I was getting messages to forgive Troy. Hell, even Tommy J had sent me a DM on Troy's behalf.

JustJordan50: Come on big sis, big bro messed up. Y'all too good together to not talk it out

It sucked that girls were expected to forgive their guys when they stepped out on them. When it was the other way around, from what I'd seen, guys weren't so forgiving.

It didn't just stop at social media. I'd gotten text after text about forgiving Troy. Some were genuinely rooting for us, and others were thinking of the bigger picture, aka, what I'd be giving up if I walked away before he went pro.

I never cared about Troy being some famous football player. I cared about him, and he took me for granted.

"I haven't wanted to be with Troy for a long time, Malika. I don't want to be in his shadow. He's a great guy when he wants to be, but I just can't get into it. He doesn't make me happy, he just makes me feel all wrong and stressed out. Guillermo's a breath of fresh air."

"You don't *need* any guy, you're fine on your own, but if you want a guy, you definitely deserve to be with someone who makes you feel safe, comfortable, and respected. And it looks like you know exactly who that is," Malika said as she rubbed my shoulder in support.

She was right.

Guillermo gave me something no one else did: freedom. Freedom to make my own choice about what to do in the aftermath of the party with Troy. He could've just told me to pick him, and I probably would've, but I understood what he was doing. I was emotional, and my next move needed to be carefully thought out and rational. Guillermo hadn't given me an ultimatum, but respect and peace of mind.

When we'd been in the motel room together, he hadn't tried a thing. Guillermo was all about permission, which I admired and loved. I was empowered by that, the little sense of control I felt with him. If I said no, it meant no. It wasn't about debating or trying to change my mind.

But this wasn't about being with another guy, it was about me, and what all was weighing me down. The whole school—and my father—would probably hate me for dumping Troy and moving on with my life. And my father would probably be incredibly disappointed in me for ditching accounting after the effort he'd put into brainwashing me into liking it.

I had so much to finally speak up for, if I could speak up at all.

Guillermo

Apart from being with Regan, one thing that really stuck with me about Friday night was seeing Camila hanging with another guy. Maybe it was nothing, or maybe it was something. Whatever was up, Raviv had a right to know. He'd avoided the party out of respect for Camila, and she had gone and flirted behind his back.

Nava Hadad let me in later that afternoon when I stopped by after my shift at the community center. Looking at Nava, I could see that Raviv was a perfect blend of both his parents. He had his mother's olive green eyes, the same dark brown hair, and he was practically the spitting image of Raz.

The thing I liked most about the Hadads was their warmth. They embraced anyone attached to their son wholeheartedly. Once I came by with Jenaya, and they took to her as quickly as they'd taken to me. Raviv was lucky to have this support system. His parents were loving and open-minded, giving him a sense of freedom without smothering him, but weren't afraid to step in when it was needed.

If only Regan's parents were the same.

"Hey, Guillermo!" Like her husband, Nava was extra affectionate and she greeted me with a hug. "It's good to see you. Raviv isn't feeling very well today actually."

I had a feeling I knew why. "That's why I'm here."

Nava smiled as she patted my arm. "Good, he needs a friend like you right now."

"I'll talk to him," I offered.

"You want anything to eat? I was making Rav some oxtail soup and basbousa, just a little something to cheer him up. There's plenty." Like my mother, Nava was big on feeding people. In their eyes, a *little something* was usually a good spread of food.

"No, that's okay, but thanks," I told her before making my way up to Raviv's room. Chances were, she'd make me a to-go plate anyway.

I found Raviv laid back on his bed, catching and releasing a soccer ball.

Lazily, he rolled his head my way as I entered his room. "I told her no visitors."

"Yeah, well, tough shit." I grabbed a chair and took a seat by his bed. "How you holding?"

He scowled and went back to tossing his soccer ball in the air. The muscle in his jaw tensed, illustrating how pissed he was. "Let me guess, you saw it, too?"

I tilted my head. "So what's the verdict?"

Raviv caught the soccer ball and squeezed. "She hooked up with some football player. Andy saw her and texted me, and when I confronted her at two in the morning, she was still with the douchebag. She didn't even deny it. There go my plans for Sweetest Day. No chocolate covered strawberries. No roses. No date. No fucking girlfriend."

His calm tone didn't quite hide the storm brewing inside of him.

"I'm sorry, Rav," I said. "I saw her talking to the guy. I meant to text you but I got caught up."

He didn't pay this any mind. "I was good to her."

From what I'd seen, Raviv was loyal. Being loyal just to get burned sucked big-time. Talk about wasted effort.

"You'll find someone better in time," I encouraged.

He frowned. "Girls are nothing but trouble, man. They're not worth it."

Maybe a few months earlier I would've agreed. Now, I could see it wasn't that simple.

"Did you hear about Regan and Troy?" I asked.

"Dipshit cheated on her."

I leaned over and caught his eyes. "Yeah, he did. Guys suck, too."

Rav smirked. "People suck."

His cell phone let out a chime for a text message. He sat up and dug his phone from his pocket and was quick to read it over. "Kayde to the rescue."

Bad association spoils useful habits, mijo. My mother's words rang in my ears as I watched Raviv text Kayde Warren.

I was only a year older, not an authority figure. It wouldn't feel like I was smothering him if I offered guidance. Like Raviv, what I'd needed a year prior was a mentor, someone to set me straight and offer up no bullshit about my stupidity. Being angry at the world and smoking weed wasn't the way to go about it.

"Listen, I know what you're going through," I started to say.

Raviv shot me an annoyed glare. "Sure you do."

"Remember *I'm* the one on probation," I said. "I got in a

fight over a girl, and the funny thing is in the end I was betrayed, too."

He eased up and sat back, willing to listen. "Yeah? What
happened?"

"I was messin' with my best friend's girl—"

"You're a dick for that."

"Noted," I said before going on. "She had me thinking that
what we had was real, and when it all came to the light, I realized she was just using me to get back at him. I was angry, I
was hurt, and I hated her for the longest time. But you know
what, things got better when I allowed myself to learn and
grow from that situation. That's what you gotta do. Learn
from it, grow from it, and become stronger. Camila's the one
who fucked up and missed out on a good thing. Don't sit here
and beat yourself up over it, it's not your fault."

Raviv hung his head, pouting just a little. It would take
more than my encouragement to lift his mood. But I wasn't
going to give up on him. Channeling his anger into something active would benefit him more than sitting around getting high and moping.

Because I really liked him, I threw him a bone. "Hey, if
you're ever feelin' down or stressed, hit me up and we can
play soccer or whatever."

This caught his attention. For the first time since I joined
him in his room, he lightened up. "Really?"

Some things were bigger than you. "Yeah. Who knows,
maybe I'll get good enough to beat you."

Gone was the melancholy as arrogance washed over him.
"Not a chance, Memo. I'm scoring on you every time."

I shook my head. *Athletes.* "Jenaya's meeting me at Freeze
in a little bit, I should get going. You wanna come?"

Raviv was back in his phone, staring at some photo I

couldn't see clearly from my angle. It would take some time to get over Camila. She was a cute girl and they'd been inseparable.

But for a time, I'd thought I was heartbroken over Tynesha, and yet slowly I came to accept that it wasn't right or worth it. Raviv would get there, and I'd see him through.

"Nah, I really need what Kayde's got right now," Raviv declined.

"Weed's not the answer."

"Says you."

"Let's just say that 'just say no' shit in sixth grade really moved me." Until the time I'd tried it myself at sixteen. Wasn't a fan in the end.

I stood from my chair and set it back at his desk. "I'm serious about soccer and hanging out, though. You don't always gotta drown your sorrows in weed. I'm here if you want to talk."

Raviv lifted his head to look at me. "I know, and I appreciate it, man. Right now I just can't deal. Cami played me."

"It hurts now, but it's not the end."

Raviv clicked out of his photos. "I should join you, anything to avoid Andy."

"What's up with Andy?"

Raviv gave me a flat look. "His girlfriend Danielle's already having him mention this girl named Stacy to me. She's not my type."

"Who knows, sometimes those usually be the ones who work out best for you," I said.

I hadn't really liked nice girls before, probably because I wasn't a nice guy. I'd liked them mean, with attitude, sass—trouble. Now, now nice worked. I liked nice, and I liked being nice, too.

Raviv wasn't convinced. "Pass. The only girl I need is Mary Jane."

I rolled my eyes. "You know, Raviv, one day, and maybe not tomorrow, but one day, you're going to run into a girl who's going to flip your world upside down and you won't be able to be that heartless stoner you are right now. And when it happens, I won't only say I told you so, I'm going to revel in that shit."

Raviv's doubt was evident. "She better have on some nice shoes, 'cause she's gonna do a lot of chasing."

He wasn't ready to hear me, and for that I tipped my head at him and went to the door.

"It's a shame about Regan, though," he spoke up once more. "She's a nice girl. Sometimes good people just get burned."

"And sometimes stronger people are there to help them rise from the ashes," I told him.

Regan was strong enough to stand up for herself and speak up. Rav, he would need a hand to cling to. I'd been down before, but like a phoenix, I'd managed to rise again. With my support, Raviv would rise, too.

Regan

Commotion outside my bedroom window woke me up Sunday afternoon. After staying up all night watching foreign films, I wasn't surprised to find myself getting up at 3:00 p.m. the next day. From what I'd watched, a lot of the foreign films had bittersweet endings. No one really got what they wanted.

Story of my life.

My favorite would have to be *Three Steps Above Heaven*, a Spanish version of an Italian film and novel.

Babi was awful and just undeserving, but H. was gorgeous and easy to swoon over. I could watch their love story over and over, it was so good. By the time I fell asleep, I was obsessed. Enough so to go online and buy the English adapted novel.

Given the noise just below my window, it was clearly time to get up. I climbed out of bed and went to the bathroom to wash up before going downstairs to see what was going on.

It was a big mistake.

Our front door was open, and creeping over to peek out, I stumbled on the sight of Troy tossing a football around with

Avery. My father was standing back, coaching Avery on how to grip the ball right and throw it.

My stomach dropped.

What the heck?

I ripped my scarf from my head and quickly ran my fingers through my hair to undo my wrap and make myself look presentable before marching outside.

Troy turned his attention to me and still caught Avery's incoming throw immaculately. *Darn.*

"What's up, Rey?" Troy asked casually. As if it were no big deal he was at my house, playing catch with my brother like it was a normal occurrence.

We were not on speaking terms. Not now, not ever again.

"Don't just stand there, speak," my father encouraged.

This was an ambush.

"What's going on?" I looked from my father to Avery.

"'Bout time we teach Avery how to throw a football," my father said. "If he's going to join the team next year, we gotta get a move on."

Avery was clenching his jaw, his unease palpable.

I gaped at my father sideways. He couldn't be serious. If it wasn't accounting with me, it was football with Avery. Enough was enough.

"Avery doesn't even like football, just like how *I* hate—"

"Nicole," my father interrupted, saying my middle name in a stern tone. "If Avery has a problem, he can say so himself."

Avery stood where he was, awkward with the attention on him.

My younger brother was like me in that he was very much nonconfrontational. Standing up to our father probably gave him anxiety, too.

Before, I was weak, easily going along with my father's demands. Now...now I was fed up.

"Avery doesn't like football, do you, Avery?" I prompted.

"He just needs to come around, that's all," Troy insisted.

"Shut up, Troy," I snapped. The last thing Avery needed was Troy speaking for him. "Avery, tell them."

Our father was getting irritated, I could tell by the way he looked as though he wanted to wring my neck.

Avery had the floor, but instead of answering, he did one better. "I'm going to Mo's."

He turned and went across the street, leaving us for Guillermo.

My father's face twisted as he waved my brother off. He went back inside, stomping almost like a child throwing a tantrum.

Troy shook his head. "Wow. Guess everybody lovin' Con, huh?"

He had tap-danced on my last nerve. "Why are you here, Troy?"

He frowned. "I need to talk to you."

"There's nothing to talk about."

For a moment, he looked pitiful, his shoulders sagging in defeat. "I'm sorry."

"Is not enough," I let him know as I folded my arms across my chest. It felt really good to stand up for myself, and even Avery, for the sliver of a second it had felt like I got a victory there.

Sorry wasn't good enough, not when Troy clearly didn't understand his error. This was bigger than his cheating, and I could see that he didn't get that.

Troy hung his head. "My mom invited you to dinner and you said yes."

"Tell her I'm declining." I liked Mrs. Jordan, but things were different now.

"Rey."

"We're not together anymore."

"Come on, don't say that. Don't embarrass me like that. My mom loves you, she wanted to go all out for Sweetest Day this year by having you and me, and Tommy and Jas. Don't make me—"

"What? Don't make you have to look her in her eye and tell her *you* messed up? I'm not protecting you on this. You did this, not me. I don't owe you anything, much less my compliance to fit in your happy little picture."

Troy looked shaken. Perhaps some other girl would forgive him for cheating—I was still very much expected to, per my social media notifications. But I didn't want to be that girl. I had a backbone, and it was about time I used it.

"Just…please, think about it. My momma love you, Rey. It's this Saturday night, and all I'm asking is for you to think about it. Think about us. I messed up and I'm sorry, but I don't want to walk away."

"I'll do it for you. Goodbye, Troy." I turned my back on him and went back inside, shutting the door behind me.

I didn't allow myself to feel sorry for him and how awful he looked, didn't allow myself for a second to rethink my intentions and plans going forward. I had only dated Troy to please my father, and I was never going to make that mistake again.

"What's gotten into you?" My father was waiting for me in the family room, arms crossed, eyes zeroing in on me.

"Nothing," I told him. "I just don't think it's right to force football on Avery when he doesn't care for it."

"Let him say that. He wasn't complaining when it was just

him and Troy," my father said. "Speaking of Troy, what's got you being so rude to that boy like that?"

He probably would never see the truth for what it was. All he cared about was me being an accountant and Troy's future wife. It was good for business, not to mention Troy was the son my father had always wanted, making him the perfect man for me. Little did he know there were fingerprints all along my body from the many times Troy had touched me despite how I wanted to take it easy.

There was no strength in silence.

Thankfully, my mother's arrival with Simba at her heels interrupted the tension brewing in the room.

"I'm thinking about a roast for dinner. Unless you want chicken," she said.

My father tore his gaze from me and turned to my mother. "Chicken, I'm in the mood for some dressing."

They began to discuss dinner and I quickly escaped up to my room to safety and solitude.

Dinner was awkward. Quiet. Impersonal. My father kept eyeing Avery in disappointment, and me with suspicion. My mother was oblivious.

It would be so easy to fall in line again and appease my father, but that wasn't going to happen. Surrendering my rights and choices hadn't equated to happiness.

"Troy can finally relax now that he's in the off-season," my mother spoke up. "I'm guessing you two will be spending more time together."

He could use all his free time to woo Genesis, for all I cared.

"He was by here earlier inviting Rey over to dinner,"

my father chimed in. "We should reciprocate that sometime soon."

"I broke up with Troy," I announced.

You would've thought I dropped an atomic bomb by the way everyone froze.

My father gaped at me. "Is that why you were being so rude?"

"Rude?" I challenged. "I broke up with him and he shows up at my house, Dad. Some call that stalking."

Avery snickered and stopped once my parents looked his way.

My mother approached me softer. "What happened?"

It was so hard to put into words how I felt. It was like there was a mountain of things unspoken in my head that I needed to get out, and they were threatening to spill from my lips all at once.

"I just decided I want something different," I said in the end. It was a weak explanation, but all I could gather being on the spot.

"What—"

"Cliff." My mother hushed my father before he could say anything further. "Let her breathe."

I kept my face even as I rose from my seat at the table. I usually loved my mother's dressing, but I couldn't enjoy it with the current conversation. "I'm done."

"Me, too." Avery was quick to take his plate into the kitchen with me.

I scraped our remains into the trash before placing our dishes in the sink. Avery stood beside me, watching.

"Need something?" I asked.

He shrugged as I gathered the dish detergent and sponge. "You didn't have to speak up for me earlier."

"Yeah, I did."

He rolled his eyes. "I'm your brother. I should've kicked Troy's ass instead of being so chummy with him."

It was cute he was trying to be protective, but I was the older sibling; I could protect myself. Now. "No, you shouldn't have. It wasn't your place."

"He cheated on you, and then he comes over like he owns the place. I should've wiped that smile off his face with my bare hands."

Even Avery knew about Troy and me.

As much as I loved his loyalty, it wasn't his place to get involved. "Avery—"

"I've been working with Mo in the gym at the center. I'm not some little kid anymore, Rey. Troy doesn't own you, and neither does Dad. They don't get to just walk all over you and have you smile and ask for more. What about you, what about what you want, or what any of us wants?"

"Avery—"

"You know what, screw you, Regan."

He shouldered past me as he stormed out of the room.

He was upset with me, and I didn't know why. It all added on to the mountain of stress I was already dealing with, and I couldn't hack it.

I set the dishes in the sink and went up to my room to call the one person I should've been avoiding.

Thankfully, we must have been on the same page. He answered immediately.

"Hey." The sound of Guillermo's voice eased all my tension.

I sat on the ottoman at the foot of my bed. "Hey."

For a moment we shared a calming silence. Even the sound of his breathing was a relief. Yes, it was a good thing we'd officially traded numbers after our rainy stay at the Keep Inn Company Motel.

"So, I know we're supposed to stay away from each other, but I could really use a friend right now," I let him know.

"So you want to be friends?" His taunting reply made up for all the drama I'd dealt with that day.

Did I want to be friends when all was settled and squared away?

If I were being truthful, it had stung when Sofia Rios popped up out of nowhere at the party and Guillermo went off with her. It wasn't my place to be jealous, but I was.

Focus, Rey. "No."

"Okay."

"I'm still figuring things out, but I know what I felt in that motel room with you and it was real. I don't have friendships with people I want to kiss."

"Likewise," Guillermo agreed. "So what's up? Avery mentioned a certain visitor stopping by earlier."

"He and my dad are unbearable." I groaned, rolling my eyes to the ceiling. "I told Troy we're not together anymore. Gosh, it feels so liberating, standing up for myself."

"I can tell, I'm proud of you."

He couldn't see me, but I made a muscle to show myself I was strong, too. "Thanks."

"So he knows it's over?" I could hear Guillermo sitting up. "Avery said he was there, I assumed to grovel, but he for sure knows it's over?"

"Yes. I told him we weren't together anymore, and I walked away." I let out a laugh, feeling triumphant. Sure, I still needed to sit down and talk with Troy once we both cooled off. I needed him to understand that what he'd done was unforgivable. It was more than the cheating, it was everything that

I'd stomached from him. My father would have his share as well. Avery was right—it was about what I wanted. "My dad's stressing me out, but I feel good right now."

"You should get away for the night, have some fun," Guillermo said. "You up for After Hours?"

I leaped at the invitation. "Yes!"

His husky laugh sent butterflies to my belly. "Let's get it then."

We agreed to meet at his house an hour later, giving us both enough time to get ready.

I rushed around my bedroom driving myself crazy as I second-guessed what to wear. What to do with my hair and face. I wanted to have fun, but I wanted to look pretty. I wanted Guillermo to think I was pretty.

It wasn't until I'd moved rack after rack of clothing in my closet that I found the perfect outfit: a black bandeau top with matching high-waisted pants. There would be cleavage, and my belly button would be on display. It was far from the safe and boring looks I usually wore. It was perfect.

I took a quick shower before getting dressed and sitting in front of my vanity. I wasn't too into makeup, but I made do with some eyeliner and mascara, and I even went a little extra by applying highlight on my nose and cheekbones. Once I dusted myself off with perfume, I was good and ready to go.

I felt giddy. I was finally doing something for me, and no one could stop me.

A knock at my door caused me to jump.

Okay, scratch that. There was no way my mother or father would let me go out with Guillermo.

Hastily I stood from my vanity and tripped over myself to grab my fluffy red robe from my closet. When I was sure

I was nice and bundled up, I sat at my vanity and faced my bedroom door. "Yes?"

"Hey." My mother entered my room, her gaze immediately taking in my face and hair. "Going somewhere?"

Nervously I ran my hands over my robe, not wanting to lie, but having no choice. "No, I was just trying a look I saw online."

"Hmm." I expected questions, but she didn't ask more. "I'm here if you want to talk about Troy."

I smiled. My father would take our breakup hard, but it felt like my mother would be on my side no matter what. "Thank you. When I'm ready, I'm glad I can come to you."

She studied me once more. "You look cute by the way."

"Thanks, Mom."

She was out the door, having bought my lines.

Before the guilt could sink in, I thought over my plans with Guillermo, relived that annoying moment seeing Troy in the yard earlier, and knew I needed this. A break from how hectic everything was getting.

When the coast was clear, I took off the robe, turned off my lights after stuffing enough clothes under my comforter to fake like I was there sleeping, and crept out of my room. I felt antsy sneaking out. Like I was alive for the first time, as a rush took over my body.

Echoes of the TV let me know my parents, or at least my father, were still up watching something. Whoever it was, they were oblivious as I crept through the kitchen and sneaked out the back door.

Out of sight, out of mind, I quickly raced to the front.

Guillermo was just coming out of his house when I arrived. He took one long look at me and whistled. "Big late-night drip."

I spun around, modeling my outfit. "You like?"

His mouth made a perfect O as his brows furrowed. "You look one in a million for sure."

I was smiling so much it hurt. "Let's get out of here, my parents don't know I'm gone."

Guillermo's dark eyes tripled in size as they went from me to my house. "Regan—"

"Shh." I pressed my fingers to my lips, giving him a reassuring smile. "I spend so much time doing what they tell me to do, it's about time I do something for me."

"And that's sneakin' out? You feelin' wild, huh?"

"Yes." I took a step back. "Or should we walk over there and tell them what we're doing so they can drag me back inside?"

For a moment, he just stared at me. I loved the way his gaze lingered on my outfit, excitement to be found in the depths of his soul. "Nah, you look way too good to see you walkin' away. Fuck it, let's go."

The whole ride over to After Hours, I was a grinning fool. Guillermo was polite, opening and closing my door for me. Holding my hand as we crossed the parking lot to the club, and even standing in front of me protectively as we navigated traffic. It was the weekend; more people were here to blow off steam before work or school on Monday.

"Want something to drink?" Guillermo leaned close to ask, surrounded by the sounds of Big Sean over the stereos.

I met his eyes and bobbed my head.

He held my hand and steered me to the nonalcoholic bar, where he ordered himself a Coke and let me order a virgin daiquiri.

A couple of guys standing at the bar looked at me and admired my outfit, one even tipping his head at Guillermo as if he'd won something.

I liked that Guillermo was quick to shake his head at the gesture. I wasn't a Trophy to him.

He came close to my ear to say, "You really do look good. I see you managed to tame your hair." He was smiling, holding back a laugh.

I ran a hand through my bone-straight hair. "My hairstylist squeezed me in yesterday. No more rain for me."

The bartender handed over our drinks and I accepted mine from Guillermo, who refused to let me pay for it even though we weren't on a date, just having a night out to escape the stress life was providing at the moment. Either way, I was happy I was with him of all people.

We found an empty spot among the many lounge areas the club had to offer. Guillermo nursed his Coke as he nodded to the beat of the rap song that was playing. He'd kept it simple in a white Champion tee and dark jeans. His hair, his lovely hair, was down, free for me to admire.

"You look good," I leaned close to let him know.

His lips curled into a smile as he blushed. He touched his chest delicately. "I feel good, too."

"You do?"

He nodded as if it were a silly question. "Oh yeah. This girl I've had a thing for recently dropped some deadweight. I'm kind of hoping I got a shot now."

I knew my dimples were on full display. "Who knows, you might even get to take her out."

Guillermo clasped his hands together as he pouted. "I'm prayin' on it."

He was so cute.

"Let's see where the night takes us," I said.

"No pressure, I just want to see you win and have some fun. Honestly, whatever you truly want to do, I'm with it. Whether you want to be an accountant, a dog rescuer, a football wife, a person who cleans porta-potties—whatever, I support you."

I snorted. "*Porta-potties?* A real friend isn't going to let me do something so gross!"

"Shh." Guillermo brought me into his chest, smothering my protests. "It's about what makes you happy."

"You make me happy." I dared to flirt with him.

He quirked a brow, taking in my face and biting his lip in a way that made me envy his teeth.

Could this be it? A simple life with him and me being myself? No obligations to make appearances, no pressure to do or be anything I didn't want?

That sounded heavenly.

A new song came on in the club and it happened to be an R&B title I was obsessed with.

I set my daiquiri down and tugged on Guillermo's hand. "This is my song, we gotta dance."

He chuckled, but he set his Coke down and came along with me to the dance floor.

"I sure hope you dance better than you play pool," he teased in my ear.

My mouth fell open, and I spun around and faced him. "Hey, I'm ready for a rematch at any time."

Guillermo stepped back and scratched his impressive jawline. "I don't know, once I get in my bag, it's over. I once made five hundred bucks in a single night playing suckers."

I feigned confidence. "Yeah, well, I'm willing to bet money I'll win our next game."

He appeared thoughtful. "I don't think I want your money, Regan."

The flirtatious tone sent my heart fluttering. "It's on."

"Noted."

We found a space on the floor where people were already getting down.

Guillermo raised his hand in front of me, his eyes locked on mine. "Show me the boundary."

Heat swept through me. He was asking me to show him where he could touch me.

Guillermo was different, more considerate. I decided to be bold in this night of freedom. "You can touch me, it's okay."

I knew in giving him permission he wouldn't cross the line. We could dance all night and he wouldn't grope me if he thought I'd let my guard down. I trusted Guillermo.

The beat took over as he held on to my waist and I danced into him. A part of me was afraid, and another was excited. I didn't want to fall too fast for him, but he made it so hard not to.

All I knew was that I could be myself with Guillermo, and he supported my wants before anyone else in my life. He gave me butterflies when I was feeling insecure. He was way more than friend material, especially after we kissed. I couldn't forget it, and I wanted to do it again.

He leaned forward, his warm breath sending tingles down my spine, his touch electrifying my skin. I was going to melt. He whispered, "We could be heroes."

No, I didn't want just one day. I wanted as long as possible. Screw what anyone else thought.

I looked him in the eye, mentally confessing all that I felt for him.

As if he were clairvoyant, his gaze lingered on my lips, a look of hard concentration in his eyes. He came closer, tilting his head, pausing to look up, as if to ask if it were okay.

Here it was, the line, the boundary between us we weren't supposed to cross.

Giving in, I nodded, having no care left in the world.

And then Guillermo's mouth was seizing mine, sending a wild mixture of fireworks and confetti to my heart. I had already fallen for his caring way, had begun to crave his touch, and now I was dying a splendid death over the feel of his lips uninterrupted.

I could tell he wanted to go slow by the sweet way he kissed me, but it quickly became a wildfire as my head tipped back and he poured himself into me. Our connection was wrong in the eyes of our parents, but it felt so right. In that moment, with the music and our fellow partiers fading into the background, nothing else mattered as I got lost and wrapped up in Guillermo Lozano.

Guillermo

I could've danced with her all night. I could've kissed her all night. But like Cinderella, Regan had to get home while the coast was still clear.

She sat beside me in my car, fanning herself despite the chilly October night. She'd worked up a sweat dancing—we both had. She was beautiful, hair clinging to her neck, a glow rising from her brown skin, and an infectious smile across her full lips.

I didn't want this moment to ever end. Being with her was worth all the shit that led me up to here.

Though, I was really hopin' her parents hadn't noticed she was gone. If we got caught, that would not be pretty.

The thought made me shake my head.

"What?" Regan prompted.

"I can't believe we did that."

She grinned. "Yeah, you've got me breaking all the rules for you."

"You didn't *have* to sneak out. You could've asked."

She gave me a mischievous look. "Yeah, but what fun would that be?"

I took one hand off the wheel and reached out, grabbing hers and squeezing it. "Yeah, you're feelin' wild tonight. Must be in the air, because I'm feelin' it, too."

"So," she began. "What's your verdict on my dancing?"

I thought she'd be shy, but she was in control on the dance floor. Sexy, flirty, and a bit of a tease at times. She really let go with me, metaphorically letting her hair down. She wasn't afraid to dance on me or let me touch her.

Regan trusted me. Something I didn't want to fuck up like Troy had. Like Yesenia, like Avery, Regan deserved to be protected as well.

"You exceeded all expectations," I let her know.

She did her goofy little dance as she sat next to me, making us both laugh.

The distance from After Hours to the subdivision where we lived wasn't far enough, even if I tried to catch all the lights.

This thing with her, it was easy, no real pressure, and I wasn't ready to let it go. She had broken up with Troy, but there were bigger obstacles in the way. Her parents would be a hassle, as well as my own. Not to mention the crowd at school.

"Thank you," Regan said softly, sounding serious. "For taking me out."

There was no avoiding the inevitable as I drove past the Welcome to Briar Pointe sign in front of our subdivision. We were home and the fun was over.

Even Regan's energy lessened as I pulled into my driveway.

We got out of my car and met at the trunk. She cast a forlorn look over her shoulder as she gazed at her house. Her glow was diminishing, and I wanted to savor it for a little while longer.

"Hey," I said, capturing her hands in my mine. "Tonight was great."

She smiled bitterly. "No matter what happens next, it was."

"Your parents will never approve, but that's okay."

Regan appeared thoughtful. "Would you? If Yesenia was linked to a boy like you, would you approve?"

Her question was thought-provoking, and I had to pause and question whether I even believed in second chances. I could plead on my knees for Regan's parents to see something in me worth dating their daughter. But would I really want to see my own sister dating some delinquent, even a "reformed" delinquent? "I'd be a hypocrite if I said I'd rather she be with someone like Avery over me, but I've really changed, and if Yesi met a guy who was trying to walk a new path, then I guess I'd embrace him. I mean, she'll be twenty-five then, so I'm sure she'll be mature enough in her choices."

Regan's mouth fell open. "Twenty-five!"

"Yeah, after high school, college, grad school, a few years into her career path, so maybe thirty in the end."

"I cannot with you," she said. "She's going to meet boys way before thirty."

I grimaced. *God forbid.* "Can't wait."

She folded her arms. "To think I was going to kiss you again."

My mood quickly switched over. "Yeah? Out here in the open. You livin' dangerous tonight, huh?"

She played coy, shrugging her shoulders. "We could be villains."

A grin spread across my face. I couldn't get enough of this girl. You ask me why *this* girl before the tons of others at my school, and I'd be a sucker to admit that she was the textbook "good girl," and I was a former bad boy dying to be good enough for her.

I stepped up to Regan, towering over her. Her mouth was calling for me, a fountain of refreshing pleasure waiting for me to take a sip.

She kissed me like she would miss me, and it made leaving her ache more.

As if to torture me, Regan pressed one last soft kiss on my lips before pulling away. "Think about me later?"

I tipped my head back and released a smile. "Yo, you're going to get me in trouble."

She giggled and ran her hand up my arm, her touch killin' me. "I'm sorry to be a bother."

"Dimples, for you I'm willin' to endure a lot of problems."

She softened up. "I'm going to set my parents straight. Whatever happens from there won't stop how I feel about you."

I took her hand one final time and placed a kiss on it. "Until next time."

As much as I wanted to get back in the car with her and talk some more and hang out until the wee hours of the morning, I let her go and turned to head inside.

I was just beginning to smile to myself about the thought of her when I looked up and noticed my father standing in the doorway. My heart went into overdrive. How long had he been there?

"We should talk," he said, pocketing his hands.

We sat across from each other in the living room. My father watched me carefully, as if reading my entire being.

"So this thing with the neighbor girl," he began. "I thought we had an understanding."

He'd caught me, and there was no denying where things were now with Regan.

"Her name's Regan," I spoke up. "Regan London."

My father opened his arms out. "I care about that."

"Papá, por favor entienda," I begged. "She's not a game to me, and this isn't like before. She broke up with her boyfriend."

My father sat back, looking unconvinced. With my track record, I didn't blame him for doubting me. He eyed me suspiciously. "What do you see in her?"

I pondered that. Sure, Regan was beautiful and I liked what I saw when I looked at her body, but it was beyond that.

It was the dimples. The kindness. The innocence. The strong backbone when needed. The way she was shy. The way she actually looked forward to Mole Day in chemistry. The way she looked when she was trying to be mad or sassy. The way she said certain things, letting me know how inexperienced she was and how she was just begging to be properly educated. The way she played pool and completely sucked in an adorable way. The way she was willing to play again to try to kick my ass. The way she danced with me at After Hours. The way she felt in my arms and trembled when I pulled her close.

It was a lot of things.

Regan London was a breath of fresh air after I was finally learning to breathe again.

"She's a nice girl, smart, beautiful, goofy, and someone Yesenia can even look up to. She's incredibly sweet and supportive, and I like that I can be those things for her as well. She's never looked at me like I'm a monster, even when I wasn't deserving of that. But as much as I like her and am intrigued, I told her we can't be friends until she cleans up a lot of situations in her life, and she understands that. I like her, I'm interested in being with her, and I want it to be right this time," I confessed. "She makes me want to be normal and just happy. I wanna go on rescue missions with her just to see her take charge and be brave."

I wanted to get to know Regan, but only if the path was clear for takeoff. This was my second chance, and I really was trying.

For a while my father was quiet, his gaze on the wall where our family portraits hung. His attention seemed locked on an old photo, one of a six-year-old me and a three-year-old Yesenia sitting on his lap as our mother leaned in from behind us. It was probably one of the last times I was innocent in my father's eyes.

"Her ex-boyfriend is going to be a problem," I added. "He's an ass, but I won't give in and fight him if he tries anything. It's not worth it and it'll be a lose-lose situation. I won't pursue anything with Regan until he's out of the picture."

"So you've learned your lesson," my father observed. "I'm not happy this one also has a shady situation going on, but I'm happy you're smart enough this time to excuse yourself from the equation until she figures it out. Regan seems like a nice girl, Yesenia talks about her all the time."

I loved that my little sister admired Regan. "She *is* a nice girl, and you should meet her, in time, to know that this isn't a repeat of before."

My father seemed to take that in. "In time, that would be nice. In the meantime, I hope you're still focusing on more than just girls, Memo."

I thought of Raviv and Avery, and even Jenaya, and how they were important to me, how rebuilding with my friends was a big part of my appreciation in this fresh start. Some of us were strong, and some of us were just gettin' there, but it didn't matter. We'd be there for one another, lifting each other along the way if one of us fell down.

"I think this move was more than just a fresh start. I think it's been the *best* start," I said. "I'm gettin' a sense of who I am and what I want to do with my life, and I don't think I had a clue before. Thanks for savin' me by moving here."

The look of affection mixed with gratitude that took over my father's face let me know I was on the right path.

"Thank you for making the most of this," he told me. He stood from the sofa and appraised me. "I'm proud of you, mijo. Keep it up."

I felt myself smile. For the first time in a long time, things were better than perfect.

Regan

Going to school sounded dreadful Monday morning. I went about getting prepared slowly, anxiety making my stomach churn.

Troy had texted me as soon as he woke up, but I hadn't bothered to read it. As much as I wanted to block him, I intended to keep his contact available for just a while longer until it was time to text him so we could gather closure.

I was still receiving messages from others urging me to take him back, to consider what I'd be giving up. The idea of Troy Jordan seemed to outweigh his actions.

The thought of seeing Guillermo was what loosened me up enough to finally make my way downstairs. We'd kissed. We'd danced. We'd talked. We'd been together, if only for a little while. I'd never felt a rush like that, and I'd never feel it again if I didn't change course. Everything about my life was dull and agonizing, but dancing on the edge, walking that line, had been fun, thrilling, all mine. I deserved mine.

My mother was in the kitchen pouring coffee into her travel mug, waiting on me so she could take me to school.

Sometimes Avery preferred to carpool with Guillermo, or even take the bus.

"Morning," I greeted my mother as I stepped into the room.

She leaned back against the counter, blowing softly into her mug to cool down the coffee. "Good morning. Did you sleep well?"

I'd dreamed of Guillermo. "Yes."

The way she was looking at me, watching me, let me know something was up. "Did you call up Troy to talk it out?"

"Troy and I are done for good."

"Hmm." She showed no surprise as she set her mug down. "And you're sure about this?"

"Yes. He's not someone I'm comfortable being with anymore." It felt like a weight was finally lifted from my shoulders as I let the truth out.

"Who does make you comfortable? Oh, let me take a guess, tall, dark long hair, looks incredibly cute in yellow T-shirts," she said with a stone-cold face. "Because the answer is no, Rey, I can't approve. Jumping from one relationship to another is very unhealthy."

"I'm not emotionally attached to Troy," I said. "I thought I was, but I'm honestly relieved I've got a way out. I deserve better, Mom. I deserve— I have rights. I'm almost seventeen, and I can't even choose my own steps without you both coddling me."

My mother arched a brow, eyeing me carefully. "Just what was wrong with Troy? The last time I checked, you two were happy."

Of course she would question it, the same way my father had. The same way my peers would.

Staying silent got me in this mess in the first place. "He

doesn't treat me like a boyfriend should. We've been together for a year, and he feels ready to have sex. I'm not, but that hasn't stopped him from hounding me about it. He acts like I'm a prude for waiting, and I'm sick of it, Mom."

Why continue to protect Troy when no one was protecting me or my interests?

"I don't want to be with Troy, and I don't want to be an accountant, but I put up with it for so long to make you guys happy, and all I've gotten in the end is overlooked and hurt. Troy cheated on me because I wasn't giving him what he wanted, and now I'm supposed to bottle it up and pretend it's okay and go to his house for dinner because he's 'Troy Jordan, the next big thing out of Akron.'"

My mother softened up. "Oh, Rey."

It felt like I might cry, but I didn't. I stayed strong, because crying wouldn't fix a thing—action would. "If I go to dinner, I'm saying it's fine, Troy can cheat on me and treat me like shit. You're so quick to judge Guillermo as bad for me, probably because of his past, but Troy's the golden boy around here and he treats me like a piece of meat. Guillermo respects me in a lot more ways than anyone I know. He *asks* to touch me, he asks to be alone with me. Troy just takes and takes, and so do you and Dad. Guillermo was the first to ask what *I* want, and all I want right now is freedom. Freedom to make my own choices, with school or the boys I decide to let take me out."

My mother came over to me, pulling me into her arms protectively. "I didn't know things with Troy were so bad. I'm so sorry."

I didn't feel like going on about being groped or how awkward it made me feel. When I danced with Guillermo the night before, I'd appreciated how he asked me to show him where he could touch me. I'd given him freedom in his actions, and he hadn't let me down. He'd touched my hips, but he hadn't grabbed my butt or grazed my breasts. Other couples on the dance floor were getting really into the French Montana song that had been playing, but Guillermo hadn't gotten any ideas to take advantage. Troy would've been unbearable.

"I'm choosing me," I stated, standing as strong on the topic as I could. "I just hope you can support me in this."

My mother released me, her gaze on the tile floor as the gears seemed to turn in her head. "I have a few phone calls to make."

"Mom." Horrified, I hoped she wasn't getting involved with Troy, or worse, Guillermo.

"I can't be Guillermo's supervisor and your mother. It's complicated."

My emotions rose. A light at the end of the tunnel. "What?"

My mother pursed her lips and met my gaze, seeming to hold back a smile. "Daren isn't exactly a hard-ass like your mother, but I trust him to get the job done. I'm stepping back from overseeing Guillermo's involvement in the program. I'm trusting you and your choice, because you're a good kid and I don't give you enough credit. Guillermo's a good kid, *now*, and maybe I should be open-minded, so long as you're comfortable and happy."

"And Dad?"

"Dad is going to have to get over it. The same way he's gotta accept that Avery would rather watch *Nato* before ESPN."

Tears lined my eyes as I smiled. "That's *Naruto*, Mom."

She waved me off. "Whatever. Just understand that I want you to know that you have a voice, in this house and out of it, and it matters. When someone, especially a man, does something you don't like, you speak up and fight for your right, no matter what. Do you hear me?"

I hadn't before, but now I would fight with all that I had. "Yes."

She relaxed. "Well then, I guess it's time to get you to school. You're going to want to speak to Mrs. Greer about dropping accounting, huh?"

Guillermo

My family was seated around the kitchen table eating breakfast as I came into the room with a little pep in my step. I could finally rest easy now that I knew my father was proud of me and trusted me.

"Oye, José, look at this one," my mother said, staring at me with wonderment. "He's not so grumpy anymore."

My father observed me and smiled knowingly. "My boy must have finally gotten himself in order. But I'd say that little skip he was doing in here has to do with a girl."

My mother regarded me carefully. "Oh, is that true, Memo?"

Yesenia stopped eating her pancakes to look at me, giving me all of her attention like the rest of my nosy family.

I rolled my eyes and grabbed the heaping plate of eggs my mother had made, giving myself a helping. "No sé."

My family wasn't giving up that easily.

"Must be someone special if you won't share." My mother reached out and ran her fingers through my hair. At least she never complained about the length. That morning, I'd decided not to hide it; it was just hair, and for that, I left it down.

"Her name better be Regan," Yesenia warned.

"And if it's not?" I dared to ask.

She narrowed her eyes as she leaned down and sneaked Smokey the last of her sausage. "You don't want to know."

Yesenia had just turned fourteen. She was still scrawny, not intimidating in the least. "Whatever, you just stick to your books and TV shows."

She scoffed. "Oh, so dating is okay for you but not for me?"

At the same time my father and I said, "Pretty much."

Yesenia stood from the table and walked her plate to the kitchen sink before leaving the room, mumbling in Spanish.

My father and I shrugged, obviously on the same page.

My mother wasn't moved. "You Lozano men are all the same." She wagged a finger at me. "Don't be the guy you don't want your sister to end up with, Memo. Set the example."

I looked to my father, seeing everything Yesenia could ever need in a future partner. He was honest, loyal, and faithful to my mother. And he was incredibly patient when it came to Yesenia and me. My father was humble, something I was learning to be.

Facing my mother, I asked, "How did you fall for Dad?"

"Tu madre no pudo resistir," my father said proudly, leaning back in his chair.

My mother tried to hide her smile as she glared at him. "I was trying to change you."

In seconds, a distant look fell over my father's face. A smirk, a hint of arrogance, a vague peek at an older version of me. "Please, Elodia, you stood no chance."

My mother was a goner and soon they were making googly eyes at each other. I took it as my cue to go.

After shoveling down a few forkfuls of eggs and chasing

them with orange juice, I was quick to leave the kitchen. The heat was getting too stifling.

I got in my car and made my way to pick up Jenaya. As usual she was already outside her house waiting for me. She got in my car nibbling on a Pop-Tart.

"Hey," she said as she buckled in.

I tipped my head toward her. "Sup?"

She squinted at me but stayed quiet as I drove to school. Today felt like a good day.

I was bobbing my head to a song on the radio when Jenaya finally spoke up. "You must've had a pretty good weekend with someone."

I fought a smile and focused on the road. "I'm just in a good mood."

"Uh-huh. Want a bite?" Jenaya asked, waving her silver-wrapped pastry.

I leaned over, keeping my eyes on the road while Jenaya offered up the Pop-Tart so I could take a bite. From the corner of my eye I caught sight of brown icing. It was already in my mouth before I could pull away.

Frowning, I chewed it down. "Geez, Naya, chocolate?"

"What's wrong with the chocolate kind? Judging from your little crush, I thought you liked chocolate."

A smirk washed across my face. "I'd rather have the brown sugar kind in this case."

"So it is Sofia that has you being all happy," Jenaya observed.

I stayed quiet as I pulled into the student parking lot and spotted Raviv and the others standing by the back entrance to the school. I wanted to wait until we were alone again before I told Jenaya about Regan and me, or at least until Regan and me were *Regan and me.*

Jenaya made no effort to join the guys after we climbed out of my car. She waited by my trunk, arms folded, her hazel eyes boldly measuring me up. "When we grabbed lunch, you said it didn't work out with Sofia, but now you're glowing like something happened."

There was no lying to Jenaya. "You mad nosy, you know that?"

She hummed, not at all offended. "Mmm-hmm, spill. Troy cheats on your dream girl, leaving her free, and it didn't work out with Sofia, so what's good?"

"Regan—"

"Ay, Convict!"

His charged voice shot through the air, demanding my complete attention and pulling in onlookers.

Troy was crossing the parking lot toward me, the angry expression on his dark brown face letting me know to hop on guard.

I stood in front of Jenaya as he approached, his chest rising and falling with blatant anger.

"Morning, Troy," I said, trying to be casual.

His face twisted in a sneer. By now some of his usual entourage had come for backup. The sight of their light-green-and-purple varsity jackets made me question whether this would be a fair confrontation or if I was about to be jumped. One thing since my move to Arlington High, I hadn't outright aligned myself with guys who fought often, or who would be willing to jump in for me. I was probably the toughest of all the guys I knew, and that was okay during a one-on-one, but with a five-on-one or ten-on-one, it sucked.

"You know you gotta shoot the fade real quick with all this sneaking around you been doing with my girl," Troy said as he sized me up.

"Sneaking around?" I asked.

"A few of my people seen you at the club last night."

So we'd had an audience. "So what of it?"

"Give me one good reason why I shouldn't swing on you." He crossed his arms, his pissed-off expression doing nothing to scare me.

"Because I would swing back and then we'd be fighting. Can you afford a fight right now, Troy? Do you wanna lose potential interest from scouts?"

"In case you haven't heard, I'm MVP, nothing I do will send scouts away. Besides, you've had an ass beating coming, Con."

"And why is that?"

"You tried to steal my girlfriend."

I sighed, shaking my head. "No. No. No. 'Try' implies that I put in effort while you two were together. Instead, I took the wait-till-he-fucks-up route, which of course worked."

Troy's nostrils flared, giving away his irritation.

I kept calm as best as I could. Whether he wanted spectators or not, we had them. The last thing I needed was for this to blow up or become viral. Harvey wouldn't give a shit about how it started; he'd rip me a new one for involving myself with Regan in the first place against better judgment. "You're a dog, Troy, but Regan isn't a chew toy in a game of tug-of-war."

Troy wasn't amused. "Oh you got jokes. Don't tell me you're a punk."

I was runnin' out of patience I didn't even have. "Believe me, I'm not."

"Let's run it then."

"Can't do that," I declined. "I'm not going to fight you."

He stood back, incredulous. "You're willing to get your ass kicked over Regan?"

A small part of me was willing to break my new persona and give him a piece of my mind. But I knew the results wouldn't be worth it. "No, I'm willin' to get my ass kicked because self-defense, although provoked, isn't in my best interest right now. I'm not with Regan, this isn't even over Regan, it's your ego. She was never a Trophy. She was a girl who loved you and you betrayed her. You're fighting your ego, not me."

Some of the crowd enjoyed my response while a few egged Troy on to kick my ass. I was sure I could take him, but I was really hoping he'd listen. Fighting me wouldn't get Regan back or prove anything.

Troy took a step forward, and I braced myself to figure out what I would do if he took a swing.

"Hey!"

In a blur, Avery wedged himself between us. Small in his patterned T-shirt, he wasn't the least bit threatening. However, whatever look he was shooting Troy must've been serious. Troy took a step back.

"This doesn't concern you, Avery," Troy said.

In a bold move, Avery reached out and shoved him, drawing an "ooh" from the growing crowd around us. "You cheated on my sister and humiliated her. You want to bully someone, fuck with me." Avery stepped toe-to-toe with him, confidently calling him out.

The effort was admirable, but Troy had a good eighty to ninety pounds on Avery. I was not letting this happen. It was time to intervene.

"Avery." I tried to step between them.

"Shut up, Mo." Without taking an eye off of Troy, Avery

pushed me back. "You hurt my family, Troy. I don't give a damn about your football status, you're dead to me."

Troy looked around, noticing how large our following had become. His anger lessened a degree. Avery was smaller, it would be too easy to tear him apart. Even Troy was decent enough to see that as he took another step back.

I pinched the bridge of my nose. Damn. Those classes in juvie, the lectures from Harvey, and even Mrs. London's reprimanding had rubbed off on me.

Once more, I stepped between Avery and Troy. "Avery, listen to me, Troy is a piece of shit for what he did, but you don't want to do this. He's not worth it." Reluctantly, I looked at Troy. "Do yourself a favor and get goin', you've done enough here."

Troy narrowed his eyes.

He couldn't be this stupid. He couldn't be willing to let his ego win and play out a one-sided beef with me over a girl he'd lost all on his own.

Could he?

Tommy J came forward and planted a hand on Troy's chest, pushing him back. "Come on, bro. Coach don't care if the season's over, I'm not tryna run laps for you."

Begrudgingly, Troy loosened up, shrugging out of Tommy's touch before backing away. "See you around, Con."

Slowly the crowd dissolved, but Avery's tension remained as he turned on me, clearly agitated.

"Why'd you do that?" he demanded.

I placed my hand on his shoulder, leaning down to meet his angry eyes. "He's not worth you gettin' out of character, Ave. There's nothing wrong with defending your sister's honor, but Troy isn't worth it. He fucked up messin' up with a girl like Regan and he's going to learn that real soon. He just lost a real one, and he's never going to forget that. You, you're too good to be fighting and gettin' in trouble over his ego."

"I could've handled him!" Avery snapped. His pride was on the line, echoes of his father's disappointment in his desire to prove himself.

"Violence doesn't solve the issue. It causes more problems than not. Look at me, I'm on probation, trust me, my life hasn't been the same since. I don't want that for you." Trying to ease his mind and anger, I went for a joke. "Besides, if Troy touched you, Naya was jumpin' in, and we all know all hell would've broke loose if she messed up her nails."

Jenaya instantly observed her long acrylic nails. "Damn right."

Avery managed to smile, revealing dimples in his cheeks that reminded me of his sister. "No one messes with my sister and lives." He was serious again as he looked me in the eye. "That stands for you, too, Mo. I know you like her, and she likes you, but if you hurt her, I won't hesitate to kick your ass, got it?"

Avery wasn't aware just how much his sister loved and cared for him, and Regan didn't know just how much her brother loved and cared for her.

Holding my fist out, I smiled. "Understood."

He bumped his fist against mine and all was settled.

Who knew, maybe this mentoring thing was my calling.

Regan

For the first time in forever I felt free. I felt alive, as if electricity was running through my veins, keeping the spark of my mother's approval thriving.

I was free to do what I wanted and it was exhilarating.

My mother had dropped me off at the front entrance, and I buzzed in early to speak with Mrs. Greer before school. There was no going back, I wanted out of accounting and into a class more fitting for me.

Mrs. Greer wasn't my favorite member of the staff; she had a way of forcing what she wanted out of you and your schedule. Hence my taking chemistry instead of waiting until my senior year to satisfy the three science credits I needed. She'd advised taking four sciences, to impress the colleges I would apply to. That was another thing about Mrs. Greer: the topic of college wasn't a what-if, but a definite yes in her eyes. If you didn't go to college, you weren't going to make it far.

Personally, I hated this pushy mentality. It wasn't encouraging in the least. Some kids didn't have the answers, and rushing into a four-year commitment seemed pretty costly.

I didn't have all my cards laid out either, but I had an idea of where to start.

"Regan, what brings you by this morning?" Mrs. Greer was sipping coffee and reading her emails when I stepped into her office.

"I wanted to talk to you about changing my schedule," I said, taking a seat before her. "I don't want to take accounting anymore."

Her brows knitted together in a frown. "I'm sure accounting is challenging at first, but to just drop the class isn't a very good idea."

Of course she wouldn't make this easy. "I *hate* accounting. It's never been my thing. It just isn't for me."

She came away from her computer and gave me her full attention. "What's going on here? Why take accounting if it's not your 'thing'?"

It was time to speak up, time to be honest. "It's always been my dad's dream, and for the longest time I went along with it because I didn't know what *I* wanted for myself. Now I've got an idea."

Mrs. Greer appeared thoughtful as she grabbed a sticky note and a pen. "And what idea is that?"

"Maybe a veterinarian. I know we've got the Animal Care & Management course here."

"That's a two-year program for juniors and seniors, and we're already two months into the school year, Regan."

I was very aware of the risk I was taking, but I was ready. "I'll work really hard to catch up. I'll stay after school to do extra work. I don't care what it takes. This is what I'm interested in."

She seemed to sympathize with me. "And you don't enjoy accounting?"

I shook my head. "I hate it. I'd rather drop out and get an F for the grading period than continue to struggle. Sometimes you have to fail to succeed, and I'm prepared to do that to secure my future."

My parents would kill me if I got an F on my report card, but it would be worth it in the end. I'd done my research; the Animal Care & Management program provided internships, job placements, and scholarships. I would walk away with a lot of opportunities by the end of my high school career, leaving me better equipped for college or a trade school.

Slowly, Mrs. Greer began to smile, and she jotted something down. "I'm not making any promises that they'll take you into the program so late in the grading period, but come back after school and I'll have word for you."

It was a start. There was hope. Fireworks went off inside of me. I so needed to speak up more often. "Thank you so much, just for trying for me."

She reached out and placed her hand on mine. "It's not a problem. In the meantime, I want parent signatures confirming that they acknowledge and are okay with you dropping accounting. Understand? This is a big step you're taking, Regan."

Because I was confident in my decision, I offered Mrs. Greer a big cheesy smile. "Yes, ma'am, I know. This is what *I* want."

Guillermo

Word spread around school about my run-in with Troy. Because some people thrived off of high school drama, I was approached in a few classes. Some guys were impressed by how calm and collected I'd been, and some teammates of Troy's were itching to show their loyalty by attempting to intimidate me. None of it got to me as I kept my head down and said nothing.

As much as I didn't want to, I distanced myself from Regan for the day. If only to avoid appearing as though I was antagonizing Troy or staking claim. She wasn't a pawn either.

Regan seemed to understand, keeping space between us in our shared classes, and eating lunch with Malika.

I buried my discomfort and kept a watchful eye on her all throughout lunch, making sure no one bothered her. People were idiots to still champion Troy. To think, all because the guy could catch and run with a damn football.

Pathetic.

I cruised into the community center later that day, hoping

Mrs. London wasn't on our trail just yet. There was only so much confrontation I could take for the day.

"There you are." Mrs. London was leaning against the front desk as I stepped into the building.

If she was pissed, I couldn't tell. Mrs. London was the type to keep you on your toes.

"Yes?" I said as I came to a stop before her.

She didn't shy away from the fact that she was sizing me up. She must've liked what she saw, as a corner of her mouth quirked up. "Let's talk."

I didn't want to go in blind. "Am I in trouble?"

She tilted her head to the side. "Why would you be in trouble? It's not like you went back on your word and took my daughter out and kissed her. No, a smart boy like yourself would never do that."

Her sarcasm made me smile. I was caught, but I wasn't afraid. Not when her taunting tone was making light of the situation.

"I'm sorry," I came out and said. "I like Regan."

"Clearly. I gathered that from your little date last night."

A nervous chill ran down my spine. "You know about that?"

Mrs. London ate up my fear with joy. "We literally live across the street from each other. It wasn't that hard to look out the window and watch her race right up to you." Her attention was drawn past me. "Ah, just the perfect person to complete our trio."

I glanced behind me to see Daren entering the facility. He was a young White guy, bald, sported glasses, and dressed like a hipster. He was a few inches shorter than me, but never seemed intimidated, not even by the body builders who frequented the center's gym. Daren always came off as easygoing and laid-back. I guess going through the Respect program really had changed his life.

Still, I wondered what was up as he came and stood beside Mrs. London and me.

"Afternoon, Guillermo." Daren reached out to shake my hand.

"You two already know each other," Mrs. London went on without skipping a beat. "I've decided from now on Daren will be overseeing your service here at the center, Guillermo. You and I are crossing a personal boundary outside of work, and I feel that would potentially set an unfair bias toward you. The Respect program is very important to me, to Daren, and for your growth. I think we all agree we don't want to compromise it."

A lot had been said, leaving me in general confusion. All I could grasp was that Daren was taking over for Mrs. London as far as I was concerned, but I couldn't pinpoint why.

He stepped in to explain further. "You've shown phenomenal growth over your two months here, Guillermo. Gloria and I want to see it through in a way most beneficial to everyone. From now on, you'll report to me should you have any questions or concerns. You know me, I welcome fun, but we're here to serve the community and do a job."

"Understood." But really, what was going on?

Mrs. London must've sensed my confusion as she placed a hand on my shoulder. "Before you guide Guillermo for the day, I'd like to have a word with him."

"Absolutely." Daren stepped to the side, allowing us to leave.

Mrs. London led the way outside of the facility and I was quick to walk in stride with her.

For a while we walked in silence, taking in the back of the

center and all the outdoor activities it offered. The general vibe coming from both Daren and Mrs. London felt bright and positive, so I at least knew I wasn't in trouble.

"You knew about Troy and Regan," Mrs. London said, more as a statement than a question.

I didn't know what she knew, about Troy or about me. It wasn't my place to expose Regan, so I answered carefully. "I knew there was trouble, yes."

We neared the playground, and Mrs. London watched as the little boys and girls in their fall jackets ran free in innocence and glee.

"She didn't tell me everything, but I got the gist of it. You let me sit there and judge you, tell you how happy my daughter was with Troy, and you knew I was wrong."

"It wasn't and isn't my place to overstep and tell Regan's truth. You know Troy better than I do, I could only hope there was more I wasn't seeing."

Mrs. London shook her head. "My daughter wants to make her own choices and I have to accept that she's a young woman with her own mind and opinion. She has to live her own experiences. Should she choose to be with you, I won't fight it."

I blew out a heavy breath, my shoulders relaxing. She didn't want to *fight* us.

"I don't want to be tolerated, Mrs. London. I really tried to avoid Regan, but it felt inevitable and I grew a soft spot for her. She's amazing, ma'am." Most of all, I liked how different we were, and how the change of pace with her was more than easy and welcome.

"Relax, Guillermo. These things happen, and I'm okay with you seeing her. When she felt like she couldn't confide in anyone, she chose you, and you didn't take advantage. My daughter seems to be happy and comfortable with you, and that's all I could want for her in a partner." Mrs. London stuck her hand out. "Thank you, for keeping her safe and being there."

I could've never seen this coming from the beginning. Mrs. London didn't seem the type to back down and accept another way rather than her own. To have her approval and respect was humbling.

We shook hands and I felt myself begin to breathe at a normal pace. "Thank you, not just for being okay with whatever develops with Regan, but for teaching me that I'm not a monster. I was lost when I got here, confused, angry, and I didn't see a light at the end of the tunnel. You didn't give up on me and you weren't easy on me either."

Mrs. London appeared thoughtful. "Do you have any regrets?"

Did I regret my past? In some ways, I did, and in others all my screwups made me who I was and led me here. I'd learned from my mistakes and seen the error in them. Tynesha had hurt me, betrayed me, and had I nursed that wound in Rowling Heights, I probably would've been on a destructive path to cope—I *had* been on a destructive path prior to our little affair, all on my own. Beyond that, I never should've fought my best friend. I'd taken it too far. My downfall was my own doing, and it took me a while to learn and accept that.

Here, through my probation and discipline, I could see that there were other ways through the dark.

And in time I'd guide my friends, especially Raviv.

"Had I not messed up, I don't think I would've survived Rowling Heights. Regretting it puts me back out there in the street and making poor choices. I'm ashamed of what I did, but the bigger picture is it led me here, to a better environment," I told her honestly.

"Violence isn't the answer, as cliché as it sounds, and it's important that you learn that," Mrs. London said. "One of my biggest concerns was stopping a situation where you and Troy got into it over Regan. If that had happened, I wouldn't have hesitated to call Harvey and let him know. I'm happy that it didn't and you were smart enough to step back the right way this time."

It *had* been tempting to give Troy what he wanted, but in the grand scheme of things, it was a lose-lose situation. To some, I'd look like a punk for backing down, but honestly, who cared? I was capable of defending myself, and that was all that mattered.

Not all fights had to be fought.

"This isn't last time. I really want an honest start," I said.

Mrs. London nodded with understanding. "Because of your involvement with my daughter, I decided to assign Daren to be in charge of you. I'll attend to other incoming probationers. Daren may talk a big game of being strict, but everyone knows he's a softy. But I trust you to do right and listen to him."

The smile she was giving me made me feel special, as if she were doing something she wouldn't normally do, just for me.

"Thank you, Mrs. London," I said.

In the next moment she was all business once more. "Now, let's get back in there, you've got rooms to clean."

She may have been a tough one, but I wouldn't have had it any other way.

I couldn't say I wouldn't ever put my hands on someone again. Had Troy hit Avery, there was a great chance I would've stepped in. When it came to defending the people I loved and was close with, I would stick my neck out every time.

But I was learning there were more ways to fight than one. There were other ways to win the battle and the war.

A black Envoy pulled up and parked near the front entrance. A familiar face soon climbed out of the truck, gaze landing straight on me.

Harvey.

Mrs. London patted my shoulder and entered the facility without me.

I stood by the front bench and waited for Harvey to come over.

"Gloria and Daren told me you'll be switching supervisors," he said. "It seems you're a conflict of interest?"

"I didn't mean to be," I swore.

He snorted, shaking his head. "Her daughter must be *really* pretty for you to go and get tangled up—again."

"It's different this time," I told him. "She's just a girl that I like, and she likes me back, there's no games or bullshit involved."

Harvey lifted his chin, eyes serious. "That's what Gloria said. She said she wasn't too thrilled, but judging by your behavior and how you've rubbed off on her son, she doesn't feel bad about it." Even with her blessing, he appeared skeptical. "This is risky business, Lozano, you understand that, right?"

Potentially going out of my way to date my supervisor's daughter? Probably one of the stupidest things I'd done yet—but it was worth it, I could tell. "I understand, but I also know what's on the line, and I'm not going to let anything set me back."

Harvey's heavy hand fell on my shoulder, stinging just a bit. He'd done it on purpose, we both knew. "That's what I like to hear. Makes me remember why I love this job."

His honest desire to see me and other troubled kids excel was inspiring. "Thank you, Harvey, for believing in me."

For just a moment, he smiled, a proud smile. And then it was gone, and straitlaced Harvey was back. "Yeah, well, don't thank me yet, we've still got two whole years together."

I snorted, and we entered the facility side by side. Two years together or not, my reckless days were long behind me. That I knew for certain.

Regan

The park was deserted. It probably had everything to do with the late October chill that had set in. Regardless, it served as a perfect meeting place to finally set things straight with Troy this Wednesday afternoon.

I was sitting on a swing, waiting for him and dwelling on the drama of the past few days. While I'd been sorting out my life Monday morning with Mrs. Greer, Troy had been attempting to bully Guillermo. What horrified me most was news that Avery had stepped in. *Avery.* My younger brother wasn't the type, and yet he'd done that for me. It tugged at my heart, even though we hadn't spoken about it. At home, Avery kept in his room and out of the way.

The crunch of wood chips told me Troy had arrived.

I turned to find him wearing a gray hoodie, his hands buried deep in his pockets.

"Regan," he said dryly.

I offered a small smile. "Hey, Troy."

He looked around before turning back to me. "You wanted to talk?"

I gestured to the swing beside me. "Sit, please."

He tentatively approached and took the swing farthest from me.

We hadn't spoken since Sunday, and after the mess Monday morning, I'd sent him a very clear cease and desist text message, one that obviously had him feeling a way.

"Monday was interesting," I spoke up.

Troy ran a hand over his head. "What's up, Rey? You here to throw the fact that you're with Con in my face or something?"

He still didn't get it, and I was quickly losing my patience.

"Are you insane? I heard you tried to fight Guillermo and Avery!" I snapped.

"Avery was steppin' up for you. You know I don't want no smoke with him. That's family."

I was so disgusted with Troy and the new low he'd sunk to. "Guillermo has too much to lose to be fighting you over the fact that you can't handle what you did."

"You really care for this jailbird, huh?" Troy rubbed his chin, staring across the street. "Damn shame."

What was it with these people?

"You don't see *any*thing wrong with what you did to me?" I stood up, prepared to walk away. To hell with him—he didn't even deserve my time and effort to give us both closure. "There was one moment where I almost kissed Guillermo, but I stopped myself and thought of you. And to find out you'd already cheated on me? That hurt. I respected you, and you couldn't extend me the same. You never could!"

Troy recoiled, his gaze falling to the ground. "I'm an ass for cheating, and I'm really sorry."

"This goes beyond that, Troy. Consent. Permission. Do you know what those terms mean?" I challenged.

Troy looked up at me. "Yeah?"

"Do you? All you ever did was grope me and make me feel like a child because I wasn't spreading my legs for you. I'm a person, not a piece of meat. My body belongs to me. My choices belong to me. My consent matters, and I choose to be with someone who respects that. I deserve to be treated nicely and appreciated. Not cheated on because I'm not ready to give up a part of myself that's dear to me," I said.

For once, Troy sat and listened to what I was saying. "I…I didn't mean to pressure you, Regan."

"But you did, Troy. You did, and it hurt. I can't even completely blame you for all of it because some of this is my fault." If only for prolonging the situation instead of walking away. In my gut, deep down, the truth had always been there.

Troy shook his head. "Don't say that. I fucked up. Not you."

It was time to be honest.

"I shouldn't have been so close to Guillermo, especially when I knew I felt something for him. I should've come to you about that night we almost kissed. I felt horrible about it, but I should've told you. I am sorry about that."

"So you didn't do anything with him while we were together?"

I shook my head. "No. You shouldn't have tried to fight Guillermo. This is our relationship, or it was. To be honest, I take blame because I knew for a while that this wasn't working. Before you I wasn't allowed to date, and then you pursued me and my dad instantly let me go out with you because you're 'Troy Jordan.'

"I admit I thought you were cute and sweet, but it was like I was finally free to try something everyone else was doing. I liked you and eventually I loved you, but our being together had everything to do with my father. I was doing things to make him happy. Accounting. You." I shook my head as I thought of that old No Doubt song that played at the center, "Just a Girl." My life wasn't about me until I decided to not only stand up, but to speak up as well. "I can't do that anymore. I need to do things for me."

"And that's with *Con*—Guillermo?" Troy asked.

"With him or anyone else I see fit. My point is I should study things because I want to, date people and see how things can go on *my* terms. Isn't that what growing up is all about?"

Troy sighed, brushing his hair and kicking at the wood chips. "Sure, Rey."

I frowned. "Troy, I don't wanna be enemies. You're an important part of my life."

He looked at me, a brow raised and a smirk on his face. "You just said you only were with me because your dad liked me."

"I did fall for you."

"Until *I* ruined it," he concluded. He hung his head, shame resting on his shoulders. "It don't feel good, you leaving and going to someone else, but it feels worse hearing that I made you uncomfortable. You make me sound like a predator, shit, that's probably how I've been actin' these past few months. There's no excuse for that, but I really am sorry. It was never just about your body, I loved *you*, Regan, too. I was actin' like a dog in heat, and I'm sorry for trying to pressure you."

Because I could tell that he meant it, I softened up and sat down next to him. "Thank you."

"I'm going to learn from this," Troy went on as he stared up at the sky. Sadness tugged his mouth into a frown. "I should've treated you better, I really should've."

I reached out and held his hand. "I don't hate you, and

I do forgive you because I can see that you're sorry. I want good things for you, Troy, and I hope you want good things for me."

For a long time, he simply looked at me, and I could see all the hurt and shame in his eyes. "I do. Do what makes *you* happy. I can tell your pops really had an influence on us being together. You never was feeling me in the beginning, it was one of the reasons I liked you. You were different. I messed up, Rey. I really did."

It was too late now, but we'd both move on and learn from this. In this failure and pain, I'd found my voice.

A gust of wind blew by and sent both Troy and me to our feet.

"Damn, I'm not ready for another winter." He tugged his hoodie on closer. He surveyed the deserted park. "You need a ride home?"

Briar Park wasn't that far from the subdivision where I lived. A walk would do me some good even if it was a little chilly.

"No, I'm okay. I need to clear my head."

Troy scanned at me, starting at my head and ending at my feet. "I guess this is goodbye, Regan."

The idea of saying the words took my breath away. I fought the urge to frown. "No, more like, see you later."

The walk home wasn't long enough. Talking Troy down had been the easy part. Facing my father was a whole other story.

We still hadn't discussed accounting. With the mess of Monday and his busy work schedule Tuesday, I hadn't gotten a chance to tell him I was dropping the class. My mother had signed the form for Mrs. Greer, and through pulling a few strings, I was going to begin Animal Care & Management at the start of the next grading period. I would more than likely finish this grading period with a C− in accounting due to dropping out, but it was better than an F.

My father wouldn't see it that way, and that was something I'd have to get used to.

He was in the family room watching a movie on TV. Simba was by his side, chewing on a squeaky newspaper toy. Noticing me, my father muted the TV and gave me his full attention. The expression on his face, incredulous and shocked, alerted me.

"You got something to tell me?" he asked.

"Yes?" I wasn't sure which news I should break to him first, given his tone.

"First you break up with Troy," he pointed out. "And now what's this I hear about you dropping out of accounting?"

"Things just weren't working anymore, Dad. Troy wasn't working out for me," I said. "Neither was accounting."

He rose to his feet. "Not working out? Rey, what about the plan?"

The plan had been for me to marry Troy and become a successful accountant while Troy played pro football. Cliché. Almost like a fairy tale. Life wasn't a fairy tale, and if it was, I wanted to choose my own prince and my own journey.

Across the street I envisioned Guillermo lying back in bed listening to hip-hop and dissecting the lyrics. It made me wonder if my father could ever see an embattled boy on the path to redemption as a part of "the plan."

I focused on my father, becoming strong enough to have it out. "Some plans change."

My father blinked a few times, shaking his head. "That's all you can say, 'some plans change'? You're screwing up your future over what? Because a class got hard? Because you and Troy got into a fight or something?"

It wasn't my father's business why I broke up with Troy. I shouldn't have to explain it beyond stating that it was over. One thing I was learning and loving was that "no" was a whole statement of its own.

"I'm not screwing up my future anymore. Following your path was doing that, not this one I'm choosing."

My father narrowed his eyes. "This is about that boy, isn't it? Troy said he suspected something was going on. Well, I forbid it, you're not seeing him."

He couldn't be serious. He couldn't think he could just step in and control who I wanted to see like that.

"No!" I snapped. "I like Guillermo. I let you have so much, and the one thing I want for me, I can't have? That's not fair!"

He stood back. "Excuse me? What do you mean you *let* me have so much?"

"I let you have accounting and I let you push me to be with Troy even when I wanted out. You're standing here mad that I'm not doing what you want, but you haven't even asked me what *I* want. What about me, Dad? When do I get to do something for me? And not even just me, what about Avery? When are you going to let us choose our own way?"

For a moment he appeared to sympathize with me, but then he shook his head. "You can do things to make you happy, Regan. You don't want to try accounting, something I thought we both agreed was a good career path for you, fine. You don't want to be with Troy, I can accept that, even if I really like him, but no, you will not be with a boy like Guillermo. Troy's a good boy, hell, we finally got Avery into football. He's up there right now watching a few reels. Guillermo, the boy is on probation for God's sake. That should tell you something. You deserve better."

He had it all wrong.

"I want to be with Guillermo, whether you approve or not. He treats me with respect and cares about my goals, about *me*," I said with finality. "Come the new grading period at school, I'll start Animal Care & Management because I really love and care about animals. I think this is what I'll enjoy doing." Squaring my shoulders and putting on a brave front, I prepared to walk out of the room, but not without one last word. "Oh, but thanks for asking. And that good boy you love so much? He cheated on me. Guess *I* wasn't good enough for him or you."

I didn't wait for his response before heading upstairs. Simba abandoned his toy to follow me.

Our talk hadn't gone over well, but I couldn't beat myself up over it. My mother was supportive, and if my father really saw any lick of potential in me, in time, he'd come around, too.

The door to Avery's room was open and suddenly my father's words rammed right into me.

Avery? Football?

I crept over to his room and indeed, he was inside with a YouTube video running on his large TV.

Across his desk was an array of discarded manga and a few dusty action figures. This was who Avery was, not some jock.

"Hey," I spoke up.

Avery pulled his attention away from his TV. He paused the game and came over to the doorway, blocking my view of the TV, appearing guarded. "What's up?"

I took in my younger brother, slightly taller than me, same medium brown complexion, same dimples, but his handsome face was a mixture of tired and empty. His stoic eyes bored into mine, sending a chill through me.

"Dad said you were studying football?" I gestured to the TV and released a dry chuckle.

He lifted and dropped his shoulder. "Maybe, so what?"

For most of his life he'd been the quiet boy with his nose in a graphic novel or comic book, or obsessing over the latest superhero movie. Now he wanted to trade that all in for sports reels and Friday night lights?

All because what? Our father would be more proud? Making our father proud should've come from our own interests and accomplishments. Not his pushy way.

"Avery, you don't have to do this," I let him know.

He studied me, like he was reading my soul. He seemed to go from a boy to a man right before me. "I know, but for the time being, he'll be too busy with me to hover over you and Mo. Consider it a gift."

My heart clenched as tears sprouted in my eyes.

I opened my mouth to say more, only Avery was quick to take a step back. In one fluid motion he shut the door in my face.

Where I thought he was extending an invitation for us to bond and grow closer, he was shoving me out in a harshly clear goodbye.

In that moment, it felt like there was more than just a door between us.

I guess I couldn't fix everything in my life all at once. Go figure.

Guillermo

When I had the fortune of being off from my volunteering duties at the center on a Friday night, I made it a habit to chill with my friends.

They didn't say it, but I could tell my parents were especially happy whenever I opted to hang out under our roof as opposed to going out and finding an adventure. They would probably still be wary over my steps, but for the most part, they trusted me again. And I wasn't going to break that trust for anything.

"We are not letting Raviv pick another movie," Jenaya was complaining.

She, Raviv, and I were in my family's rec room. It had been two weeks since he and Cami split, and Rav was still nursing some wounds. In the morning, before I was due at the community center, he and I were going to link up and play a quick game of soccer at the park. For tonight, it was movies, pizza, and chill.

Raviv tossed a pillow at Jenaya. "Who invited you anyway?"

"Hey, be nice," I stepped in. These nights were for all of us.

Jenaya was better off hanging with people who cared about her rather than the toxic environment that was her home life. Raviv was better off sober. And as for me, I welcomed the distraction and comfort.

But Raviv really had been picking a stream of bad movies for us to watch.

"Let Naya pick," I said. "You're on time-out."

Raviv rolled his eyes and sat back against the recliner to stare at the TV and wait.

Happy with this victory, Jenaya started searching through Netflix.

Footsteps sounded on the basement staircase and I angled my head back to see my father poking his head downstairs. "Pizza's here."

Raviv shot up. "Awesome! I'm starvin'."

I could tell he'd smoked before he came over, but I didn't say anything.

Jenaya continued to browse the menu while I went upstairs with Raviv.

A hand came down on my shoulder, my father stopping me in my tracks before I could go to the front door.

"You're a good kid," he told me. "Estoy orgulloso de ti."

My chest tightened, and I had to clear my throat to gather myself. I blinked, trying to see straight. "Gracias."

I was still getting used to hearing my father telling me he was proud of me. I was used to the lectures, the disappointment, the shame, but this…this was something bigger.

He patted my shoulder, tilting his head toward the kitchen. "Let Rav take care of the food. You get the paper plates together. No dishes on weekends."

It was a tradition my mother started, as she preferred for her and my father to take Fridays and Saturdays off from cooking.

I went for the kitchen pantry. At least, that was my intent before I spotted the one person I'd been missin' for weeks, it felt like.

Regan was standing there, dressed casually in a T-shirt and jeans.

She was here, finally, after so much time.

Mrs. London had given me a green light, but Regan and I hadn't really spoken beyond a hi and bye, or even texted each other for almost two weeks. I figured she was sorting things out and I didn't want to intrude or rush her. It had taken some time, but my life was falling into place, and I knew how tricky these things were.

But still, I missed her. Each glimpse in the hall, in class, at the center, across the street, was killin' me.

"Hi," she said, waving awkwardly.

My heartbeat sped up just from the sound of her voice and the sight of her dimpled smile. "Hey."

"So, it's been a minute," Regan said. She took me in, seeming to admire my hair as her gaze ran over me.

I could faintly hear Raviv somewhere in the background shutting the front door. My mission resumed as I went to our pantry.

"Feels like forever."

"We should talk." Regan hung back and watched me retrieve the paper plates and Solo cups. "Can I ask you something completely random?"

It felt like we were stalling the inevitable, but hell, I'd take any second with her. Kissing her had been a mistake— all I could think about was doing it again, playing pool with her again, dancing with her again, being with her for real. Thoughts of Regan London had consumed me, and here she was, in my kitchen.

I was the prince of nothing charming, but hey, life wasn't a fairy tale anyway. Maybe the redeemed bad guy could get the girl in the end.

"Shoot," I said as I turned and gave her my attention.

She smiled coyly. "What's your favorite song?"

Pausing, I took a moment to rack my brain. "Right now? Definitely, 'Self Care' by Mac Miller. What's yours?"

I watched as she bit her lip thoughtfully. "Guess."

"'Crazy in Love,'" I threw out.

She snorted. "Not even close."

"So tell me."

"David Bowie, 'Heroes,'" she said. "I was listening to it the other day, and my mom was shocked I knew such an old song. It gives me strength and I could use that a lot these days."

She and Troy had split officially. During lunch he still reigned over his fan base, and Regan happily sat with Malika and a few other girls here and there. Her father was probably devastated he was losing Akron's hero as his future son-in-law.

"Where are we, Regan?" I wanted to know.

She wrung her hands, frowning. "I've got good news and bad news."

I could already guess where this was going. Yeah, she was here, but she sounded sad, not happy to be around me.

I focused on counting plates. "Yeah?"

"Which do you want first?"

I put up a brave front. "Good news first, I like a realistic ending."

Regan softened up. "The good news is I told my parents about accounting and Troy and me being done."

"Good for you, I know it took a lot," I said.

She didn't disagree. "I'll be seventeen next week, and after a not-so-sweet sixteen years of control, I'm looking forward to doing things my way."

My hands itched to take her into my arms, but I held back. Her words were giving me hope. "What's the bad news?"

"My dad knows I'm into you, and he doesn't approve. So, while my mom likes you, don't look forward to my dad inviting you over anytime soon to watch Sunday night football." She winked at me, letting me know that there wasn't really any bad news.

I blew out a sigh of relief. *¡Órale!*

Her father didn't like me? I saw that coming, but it didn't sound like he was going to get in the way.

"If we pursue something...?" I had to know.

Regan heaved a sigh and tucked some of her hair behind her ear. "He doesn't like the idea of you, but he knows I'm going to do what I want regardless. Having my mom on my side makes me feel weightless in this. I like you. I like you because you listen and you care, you ask me what I want and if things are okay, and I need that. You're the first boy I've wanted to date, and I want that in my life above anything else right now. My dad will just have to deal with it."

Some battles wouldn't be won, but that was okay. We'd wage this war together, if time should let us.

It was a Friday night, and Fridays were for hanging out with friends and having a good time. Not grieving over things that didn't matter.

"Will you stay, for pizza?" I asked. "There's plenty, and Jenaya's picking the movie, so it's sure to be good."

Regan brightened, like her father was the last thing on her mind. "Yes, I'd like that."

Feeling bold, I went over to her, sizing her up. I liked her.

She liked me. The future was looking good from that starting point.

"How do you feel about being with me as more than friends?" I took in her face, gauging her reaction.

Regan bit into her lip, playing shy. "Are you asking me to go out with you?"

"I'm *needing* you to go out with me," I clarified. "I've never had a serious girlfriend before, but with you, I'd really like to try."

She grinned. "That's something I'd love to try, too."

"There's something I've wanted to ask you for a very long time now," I began, inching closer. "Can I take you out, to a *real* Mexican restaurant?" As she burst into giggles, I went on, holding back my own laugh, "I don't think I can leave this earth with you thinking Taco House is the best."

Regan threw her head back and laughed, and it was almost like she was glowing. Her happiness—her genuine happiness—was infectious. She reached out, playfully swatting at my chest. "Yes, I'd love to go out with you and try some *real* Mexican food."

Things weren't squared away neatly and perfectly, but that was okay. This was a fresh start, for the both of us, and the possibilities were endless.

Regan

"Annnnnd Regan is done!" Jenaya announced for the camera as it recorded us. "As you can see, I got my girl lookin' like yasss, and if you like it, you know the vibes. Hit that subscribe button, let's run up them likes, and I'll see you next time. This has been Jenaya's World."

At the last second, Malika stuck her head into view for the camera. "And don't forget her handy assistant Malika. Follow your girl on all socials at Malika-underscore-Roy, that's M-A-L-I—you know what, I wrote it down in case it's easier." She held up a slip of paper with her handle for her social media accounts written large in all caps. Only Malika. "Let's get your girl up to a thousand followers."

"Happy with yourself?" Jenaya teased as she ended her recording.

Jenaya had started a YouTube channel for her makeup looks and hairstyles. When she asked if she could record my makeover, I was shy about it, but I couldn't say no. She *always* looked good, and it was good content for her subscribers to see her work her magic on me.

I checked myself out in the mirror, primping my hair and adjusting my sweater.

My look was minimal, as my parents weren't ready for me to walk around with a full beat. Small victories were still very much appreciated.

Together, Malika and Jenaya had tag teamed me in my effort to get myself ready for my first official date with Guillermo. Before Guillermo, I had never really spoken to Jenaya, but there was no missing her sense of style and her presence. I wasted no time crossing that bridge and properly introducing myself before asking her to help with my look. Malika had been all too ready to join in and style my outfit.

Jenaya left my hair straight, pinning some of it back on one side with a rhinestone hairpin. She'd given me natural makeup, with a nude matte lipstick that I really loved on me. Malika had picked out an off-the-shoulder chunky gray sweater with black skinny jeans and matching suede booties.

"I look so pretty," I gushed as I examined myself in the mirror.

Jenaya hovered over my shoulder, peering in the mirror as well. "You *are* pretty, Regan."

Coming from her, the compliment meant a lot. "Thanks."

"We're going to let you go," Malika announced as she gathered her bag from my bed. "But I will be up for *all* the details, which I expect to be glowing since Mo is amazing."

"Wait." I grabbed my cell phone, quickly holding it out as I stood to my feet. "Let's take a photo first."

Jenaya and Malika squeezed in on either side of me and I snapped a quick selfie. Outside of Guillermo, I definitely wanted to get to know Jenaya better.

"What's your handle?" I asked her as I prepared to post the image with the caption Date Night.

Jenaya recited her info before offering me a hug. I walked both girls down to the front door, watching them climb into Malika's car before taking off.

Back up in my room, I put on some perfume, my favorite by Ariana Grande, wanting to totally entice Guillermo on our first date.

"Ahem."

Behind me, I caught my father in the doorway. His eyes took their time to study my booties and then move on up to my hair and makeup.

"That boy is down there waiting," he told me.

"Guillermo," I corrected as I turned and faced him. "His name is Guillermo."

My father grimaced, still not over Troy. "Not a fan." He folded his arms, getting comfortable as he rested against the doorjamb. "Before you go, I just wanted to say something." He eyed me. "I'm sorry about Tanner. It's nice to have Simba here and he's cute, but I know deep down it's not easy going on without Tanner."

While we hadn't stopped looking, it was becoming more and more clear that this time, chances were we wouldn't get him back. I liked to think that a nice family had him, that they were giving him all the love that he was worth. Refusing to cry, I focused on my hands and how they were shaking in my lap. "I know."

"Your mom and I plan on getting Simba chipped, just in case…" Just in case he lost this one, too. "But I intend to be more watchful, less careless. And outside of Tanner, I *am* sorry about pushing accounting on you so heavy. I just wanted you to have a shot at a guaranteed career and a future. It's a big part of our family, and I assumed you were interested. I never stopped to see what you wanted, and if it's animal care, I'm behind you one hundred percent."

My mother was already in support of me; to have my father not hold a grudge and be with me as well caused hope to blossom in my belly. Maybe, in time, he'd like Guillermo, too. "Thank you, Dad. I think this is the right path for me."

"Well, I'm with you," he assured me. "And, I really appreciate Guillermo going out of his way to look for Tanner, and coming across Simba. Your mother told me about how you two rescued him. I guess it's been clear all along where your strength and heart was. What you did was brave, Rey."

I'd never felt brave or strong before, but now I did, and I was beyond happy my father could see it too. That he saw something in my new path. Everything was finally in place, and that was amazing.

"And," he began, "I'm sorry Troy cheated on you and I wasn't making it any better by pressing you so much to be with him. I'm disappointed in him, but more importantly, I'm just glad you're happy and doing what's right for you first."

Unable to contain myself, I held my arms out and my father crossed over to give me a tight hug. To have him completely on my side? Nothing beat that.

"Dad," Avery said, poking his head into my room. "I'm heading to the park to shoot some ball with Nathan and Kevin."

My father's brows rose toward his hairline as he stood up. "Basketball?"

Avery shrugged. "I missed football, so why not?"

Our father looked impressed, a proud smile washing across his face. "Don't be out too late, and call me when you get there and when you're on your way home."

He walked out of the room, passing my brother and patting him on the back.

Avery sneaked me a look, nodding his head in an unspoken agreement. He was taking one for the team. While he had become distant from me ever since his campaign to wow our father with his new interest in sports started, I knew deep down we'd be okay.

I turned off my lights and made my way downstairs, a wave of nervousness taking over. *Here we go.*

It all blew away at the sight of Guillermo squatting down, grinning as he gently played with Simba. Gone was the weight of his past, replaced with the light airy sense of a great future. His hair was down, he was wearing a denim jacket over what looked like a long-sleeved black thermal shirt and jeans and sneakers.

"Whoa, we match," I said to announce myself.

Guillermo lifted his attention to me, his eyes going wide and his mouth falling open slightly. The look made me bite my lip.

He collected the large bouquet of red roses I suddenly realized was beside him and came and stood in front of me, towering but not intimidating. I could feel him radiating a magnetic energy that made me want to wrap my arms around him and not let go.

Instead, I settled on a cheesy smile as I held my hand out. "Hi."

His gaze fell to my extended hand, a thick brow arching. He smirked as he leaned close, giving me a delicious whiff of his cologne as he paused by my ear. "You. Look. Incredible. Dimples."

There was no containing the huge blush that spread across my face.

Guillermo handed over the roses. "Happy birthday, Regan."

Spending Friday night off from the center, the day after our Halloween party for the kids—where I left with a hearty stash of candy of my own—with the boy who made me feel comfortable was perfect.

Best birthday ever. "Thank you."

"You two have a good evening." My mother was peeking around the corner down the hall. I had no idea how long she'd been watching.

Guillermo's warm, strong hand took mine, his fingers tangling with my own. "We will, and thank you, for being okay with this."

My mother nodded as she came and took the roses to place in water. "It's what Regan wants and deserves."

With her blessing, Guillermo opened our front door and led me outside, where his car was parked in our driveway. Keeping up with the chivalry, he opened my door for me, and just as he shut it, I leaned over and opened his for him. A gesture that made him grin as he got in the driver seat.

"So, Mexican food?" I asked.

He turned toward me, his eyes drinking me in once more. "Yup, I wouldn't be a very good boyfriend if I didn't get you cultured."

I leaned back against my door. "Boyfriend?"

The grin that sneaked onto his mouth was inviting me to kiss it. "Well, yeah, at least I'm hopin', assuming this date goes well."

In reality, we were pretty much an item already. Texting had commenced nonstop, as well as hand-holding and stolen kisses for days. This date, our first date, was just a ceremonial thing to solidify our relationship.

I loved the sound of that. *Guillermo Lozano is my boyfriend.*

"I kind of have this rule about not kissing until the third date," I said, feigning seriousness. "For you, I may reconsider, if tonight goes well."

"Haven't you heard?" He came close, stopping at my lips, gazing up at me for permission. "I break all the rules."

Raw need consumed me, setting my heart and soul ablaze. Throwing caution to the wind, I leaned over and kissed the boy I wanted most.

★ ★ ★ ★ ★

PLAYLIST

Down Bad
Dreamville ft. J. Cole + EARTHGANG + JID + Young Nudy + Bas

Yes
Beyoncé

Regrets
Jay-Z

Medicine
Queen Naija

Voices in My Head / Stick to the Plan
Big Sean

Pretend
Tinashe ft. A$AP Rocky

a lot
21 Savage ft. J. Cole

Sorry (Original Demo)
Beyoncé

Hair Down
SiR ft. Kendrick Lamar

Drew Barrymore
SZA

Hold On, We're Going Home
Drake ft. Majid Jordan

Are You That Somebody?
Aaliyah

Way Back Home
Cordae ft. Ty Dolla $ign

Forgive Me
Chloe x Halle

Don't
Bryson Tiller

Butterflies
Queen Naija

Crying Out for Me
Mario

Good Girl
Kiana Ledé ft. Col3trane

Changes
Justin Bieber

Hitchhiker
Demi Lovato

Trip
Jacquees

A Sweeter Place
Selena Gomez ft. Kid Cudi

R.A.N.
Miguel

Wild Thoughts
DJ Khaled ft. Rihanna + Bryson Tiller

Second Chances
Kiana Ledé ft. 6LACK

Dilemma
Nelly ft. Kelly Rowland

Un-Thinkable (I'm Ready)
Alicia Keys

Permission
Ro James

ACKNOWLEDGMENTS

First, I gotta thank my city, Akron, Ohio, for not only being the setting, but a large part of my inspiration for this book (and the books that follow). Someone tell LeBron I'm coming for the king of Akron title LOL.

From my elementary school to my middle school and finally to my high school, one thing was certain: I lived in a world of color. I looked around at my peers and always had a sense of the world around me. They tell you to write what you know, and because of where I come from, having a secondary character, or even a main character, who's a non-Black POC or even White is just natural to me.

I grew up a reader, and I'm big into films and TV, so another inspiration for me are those early 2000s teen dramas and not to mention the films from the '90s/00s. And okay, also John Hughes because I find his work timeless and he's probably my fave writer ever. I loved the edginess of those old shows and movies, hence why I never want to write too clean of a teen, because even today that rings true for some youth. But one thing I noticed from my fave reads to films to shows was the mass Whiteness, and if there was a character of color, they were that one little dot among the overall White cast. Oftentimes, characters of color are attached to a White character as a friend or love interest, but we deserve our own stories.

I really wanted to write a world that looked like the world I grew up in, with people who looked like the people I went to school with, with people like the people I see shopping at the local grocery store. I wanted a YA world where POCs are thriving and living and dealing with things like the normal people they are.

With these Arlington High books, I wanted to break that cycle. I wanted a whole book series featuring couples of color, friendships of color, families of color, teens of color just dealing with the everyday struggle of growing up and life in general—à la John Hughes. So I think about all these kids in this book, and the others, and I'm so proud of their potential and what they can do and show. I can only hope that teen readers of color can find someone they see themselves in and feel a sense of home and a connection. That's all I ever wanted as a reader.

Being that this is based from the atmosphere of my old high school, Garfield (Go Rams!), I had to put a sense of home in this book. My junior year, I took chemistry and my teacher Mrs. Rummell HATED the color orange and we legit used to torture her by bringing in orange things or wearing orange. Not to mention she really had a recycling bin that either she made or a student made for her named Earl. I couldn't have this book without that little light. I wasn't too amazing at chemistry, but I did love that class because of her.

The brothers Troy and Tommy Jordan were inspired by the fact that my school had two sets of brothers who were big into football, one duo making huge waves in the newspaper. I just loved that and always wanted to embody that.

Now I HAVE to thank my dear, sweet Anaisja Henry. When we first met, you were a reader on Wattpad under the username @onelessproblem_ but you were never a problem for me (cue sappy music y'all). Over the years, you've been one of my FAVORITE readers on Wattpad and you were a big, BIG fan of the Arlington High books when they were first on Wattpad, and when I wanted to rewrite Guillermo and Regan's story, you were the first person who came to mind. You're always a treat to talk to, as I totally am not shy to admit I value and admire your thoughts and opinions greatly. Through my highs and lows of my eternal overthinking and fears, you're always there to listen and offer feedback. I can't thank you enough for beta reading this for me when I rewrote it!

I also have to admit that it's hard to explain where my exact inspiration for *The Right Side of Reckless* comes from as it's actually a rewrite from another idea I had for Guillermo and Regan I wrote in 2012–2013. Before Guillermo was a troubled bad boy and new student, he was also a careless, cocky flirt, and not to mention his past was anticlimactic when it's all revealed. A part of me knew I wanted to redo the story and make it stronger for both arcs, and the idea of probation came to me, but I had no grounding. Which brings me to my next BIG THANK-YOU, one of my managers at my job, Gary Cymbor! I don't even remember how it started, but you were grabbing lunch one day and you started to say how much things had changed for you, and then you told me how your wife saved your life when you were young. You told me how you were arrested on three separate occasions and the overall life-threatening, reckless path you were on before you met your wife and she helped you change. I was in awe and intrigued (insert that GIF of B. J. Novak writing in his notepad LOL). From that very moment, I had my story for Guillermo's past, and I can't thank you enough, Gary, for telling me your story and allowing me to base Guillermo's struggles on it.

I want to thank my lovely, lovely sensitivity readers for helping me bring Guillermo and his family some authenticity. Stephanie Vega, ugh, girl, I ADORE you. You're also one of my fave readers from Wattpad, not to mention writers. After reading your work in your WIP and just enjoying your comments as a reader, I knew I wanted your personal take on how Guillermo read. Thank you so much for giving me raw, honest feedback and suggestions to bring him to life!

Alessandra Magaña, thank you so much for taking the time to read and give me your personal take on Guillermo as well, especially the suggestions on language and film! It was a pleasure working with you and gaining an own voice opinion on how Guillermo read. You were such a big help, and I can't thank you enough for telling me some of YOUR story to help me visualize better and get a greater sense of how things were reading. Thank you forever!

Gaby Cabezut, thank you so much for helping me with my translations and making the phrases ring true!

I'm grateful to these ladies for helping me with Guillermo's journey and story, and I take full responsibility for any error with his story otherwise.

To my loyal Wattpad readers who championed this book in its early days and were day one fans of the potential, a forever humble thanks. #ArlingtonHighHive.

To my agent, Uwe Stender, thank you, thank you for always being in my corner and championing me and my work!

To my editor, Natashya Wilson, forever thanks for taking another chance on me and helping my dream come true with bringing Arlington High to life. I love these kids and I'm so happy you were able to, as well.

To the team at Inkyard Press for helping make this book possible and shine. To Gigi Lau's amazing art direction and Noa Denmon's awesome illustration that captures Guillermo and Regan, many thanks!